# VANESSA

GARY MILSOM

LITTLE BEAR PUBLICATIONS

*For Malissa, who held me in the darkness until the sun shed light on the ocean like she shed light on true love.*

ISBN 978-1-9161281-3-2
Little Bear Publications
Sudbury, Suffolk, England.
www.littlebearpublications.co.uk

Cover illustration by Cara Thurlbourn

# PROLOGUE

*O*ffices of the Cornish Times, May 1990

Vanessa had scant respect for most men, and if she used her charms to get what she wanted it hardly bothered her. It had taken her some time, and several late-night visits to bars she'd rather not frequent, to find the person who could confirm her suspicions. What she had learned in Söller had led her here, and to the library's records which verified what she already believed to be true.

She unfolded the newspaper cutting she'd carried around with her for the last three years and studied the photograph of the beautiful woman playing the violin. She read, for the last time, the words that accompanied the photograph before gently tearing the cutting in two and dropping it into the wastepaper basket.

Her train back to London left in an hour. She loved Malissa and Henry, appreciated how happy they were, and realised she had already decided that sharing her secret could bring nothing but harm. She would see them, and their new baby daughter, tomorrow as planned. New day, new beginning.

# PART I

*Her Mother*

*Born into then nurtured in love*
*In love you're more likely to live*
*But if love is stolen*
*You'll feel undeserving*
*And love will be harder to give*

# MAY 1990 RETURNING FROM CORNWALL

*I*t had been a long day and, as she settled into her seat for the journey to London, Vanessa realised how tired she was. She had the confirmation she sought, and though she would love to ask Henry more, how could she without destabilising the lives of two people she had grown to love?

When she spoke to him in Majorca last summer, she felt sure he glimpsed the secret she harboured; the secret that she was Emma's half-sister. They could so easily have discussed her. Surely in Henry's eyes she saw the seeds of a question developing in his mind, a question perhaps he was too afraid to ask. He had hesitated, but then was clearly reluctant to pursue the conversation in the direction she tried to lead; a direction which may have led to discovering the real reason he first came to Söller, and something instinctively told her not to push it further. Now, almost a year later, she was perhaps beginning to understand why. Maybe one day Henry would tell her the truth; maybe one day she would tell him. But until then she would, as she had done for the last three years, continue to live with her secret.

Not telling Malissa had never sat easily with Vanessa; but Malissa didn't even know about Emma's existence so telling her had never seemed right. Telling her now certainly wouldn't be. She rested her head on her hand against the window, hoping the soporific motion of the train would afford her the sleep she craved. She smiled to herself, wondering if Malissa had agreed to name their baby as Henry had suggested. She doubted it.

Then she closed her eyes and thought about the story her mother had told her. It was a story of a journey; a journey to England her mother had taken as a child with *her* mother Edith, which had ended so tragically with the abandonment of Vanessa's older half-sister.

## MAY 1946, LONDON

### EDITH BROUDIER, VANESSA'S GRANDMOTHER

**Three months after she arrives**

*E*dith gently pulled back the curtain which screened off the other end of the room which served as their bedroom. Was Anna really asleep? She hoped so. She hoped that image of her daughter's face peaking at her ten minutes ago was just one from her imagination. There were things she would have hated her to see.

She despised the bastard who'd visited her, but paying her rent any other way would mean them not eating. She could still taste him and his sickening scent lingered in her nostrils. She touched her daughter's forehead, softly sweeping away the auburn hair that had fallen onto her brow. She was a beautiful girl, but what lay ahead for her? What could Edith do to ensure Anna would not be consigned to the life she herself had fallen into?

Should she leave this house they could ill afford and take refuge in the workhouse? It would, in its way, take care of them both, but where would that lead? Surely, there was another way. Maybe she should do as Betty suggested; use her dancing skills and good looks in the pubs and earn a little extra in the back rooms. She had resigned herself to paying much of her rent in a similar way so would it be any more shameful?

Kenneth was not going to turn up, so why did she still hold on to the possibility? And if he did, and found her here, what would he think of her and what she had done to survive these last few months? She wondered and she hoped, but in her heart she knew she had been abandoned and she could only guess the reasons. She curled up beside her daughter and cradled her in her arms. Surely something good would come along soon.

## MARCH 1985, VANESSA'S MOTHER
## ST. FRANCIS XAVIER HOSPITAL, PARIS

$\mathcal{V}$ anessa sat by the vending machine in the waiting area drinking her coffee. What the doctor had told her this morning was no surprise. Even on admission ten days ago, they held out little hope, and Vanessa had been with her mother every day and witnessed her decline. As far as she could remember, it was the longest consecutive period they had ever spent together and, for the first time, she felt the connection she always imagined belonged to a mother and her daughter. She could make little sense of her feelings, which swung from great sadness and regret to relief that at last her mother would be leaving a world which she said she never really understood. Vanessa was grown up and independent, she had to be, but at 19 she was about to lose her mother. Unexpectedly, she realised she was going to miss her.

"She's awake and asking for you." It was the nurse. "She's weak and..."

"I know. It's okay." Vanessa smiled, getting up out of her chair.

"Finish your coffee. We're just going to give her something to ease the pain... And a little make up."

Vanessa smiled. Her mother insisted she looked presentable whenever visitors came.

She looked at her watch. Philippe said he would bring Gabrielle after work. She wondered if they'd get there in time. Her own father visited last week. Should she try and contact him now? Her parents had never married and though Vanessa had no doubt that, in his way, her father had always loved her mother, she had always known that her mother had never really loved him. She wondered who, if anybody, her mother had loved.

Her father's name was Marcel Cozzette. Vanessa had taken his surname but feared everything else she had inherited came from her mother, Anna – Anna Broudier. The woman who had given birth to her. The woman who she had loved and loathed, had admired and been ashamed of. Hers was a sad story. One which, only now, on her death bed, had Vanessa begun to understand. How much of her mother lived in her? How much of Edith, her grandmother, lived in Anna?

The day Vanessa first came here to the hospital, when her mother knew she was dying, they talked. Her mother shared her innermost secrets and Vanessa had appreciated how things could have been so different. If only...

Vanessa had long since brushed aside any resentment towards her mother. She had, up until ten days ago, replaced it with some kind of indifference, but now she felt something else. She wasn't exactly sure what she felt, but had no doubt it was born of out of an appreciation that life could inflict a set of circumstances that could wipe out any chance of a decent existence, and leave a wound that was impossible to heal.

Her mother had confirmed a story; a story that was so often the subject of her father's more inebriated and resentful ramblings. She told Vanessa about the girl she had given birth to in England, more than 30 years ago. A girl who was Vanessa's half-sister and who was so cruelly stolen from her mother.

Her mother could still picture her, could remember the minute after her birth when she held her child. But she had no idea what had happened to her after, only that she was taken to an orphanage and subsequently adopted. She didn't know if her daughter was alive or dead. She remembered little detail and her illness was taking its toll as she recounted the events, but Vanessa felt a great empathy with her and, for the first time, understood why her mother had been who she was.

Anna Broudier harboured a sadness few could imagine. When she was seven years old, her own mother took her to England in pursuit of a wonderful new life. Anna had relayed the story of their struggle; how the man her mother had met during the war, and who had promised them a new life, had simply disappeared one day, leaving them alone in London.

They got by, but when her mother died, Anna was raped, when she was barely fifteen, by the people who were meant to care for her. She gave birth to Vanessa's unknown half-sister but save that precious moment after she was born, Anna never saw her daughter. The torment of what had become of her had plagued Anna ever since.

By the time she returned to France and met Vanessa's father, Anna was already damaged beyond repair; full of hate and with a trust for nobody. She left her father when Vanessa was two years and had another child, Gabrielle, with Philippe, before they too parted when Gabrielle wasn't much more than a baby. It was a sad but perhaps inevitable series of events, and Vanessa was beginning to understand why her mother had lived the life she had – a life designed to quash those memories. Even if there was a chance she could survive her illness now, Vanessa knew her mother had little desire to do so.

Along the corridor, the nurse came out of her mother's room. Vanessa nodded to her. Something told her she was about to see her mother for the last time and great sadness came over her. She opened the door. Her mother was sitting up and Vanessa was surprised how well she looked. She smiled as Vanessa entered.

"You're very beautiful, Mum," Vanessa said softly, taking her mother's hand. She felt her squeeze it.

"I'm sorry I haven't been the mother you needed," she said. Her mother's voice was clearer than it had been that morning. "But never doubt I have loved you."

Vanessa smiled. This wasn't the first time this week her mother had told her she loved her. Anna's hand shook a little as she raised the beaker to her lips to take a sip of water. Vanessa helped her and gently took the beaker from her when she had finished, the red outline of her lips on the rim reminding her of her childhood.

"You are your own person, Vanessa," she continued, "and a strong woman. Strong because you have survived. I have watched you grow from a distance and I am so proud of you." Her voice was losing clarity and Vanessa leant closer. Her mother slowly raised her hand to touch her daughter's face and Vanessa nestled into it, feeling her mother's touch on her lips. Before it could fall Vanessa cradled her mother's hand gently, keeping hold as she laid it back down on the bed. Her mother smiled and closed her eyes as she breathed in. Vanessa wondered how many more times she would hear that intake of air. She watched as she breathed those slow, shallow breaths. Many people had remarked on her mother's allure over the years, but Vanessa had never seen her look so serenely beautiful. Surely, she wasn't in pain.

The nurse appeared at the door and peered in. Vanessa indicated all was okay. She looked at her mother waiting, wondering if she'd open her eyes but reluctant to wake her. She tried to picture her as a child, hoping her early years with her own mother at least provided some innocence and laughter, and then she pictured her as a 15-year-old sitting in a doorway agonising over the whereabouts of her lost daughter.

Vanessa checked her watch. Did she really wish that Gabrielle, her sister; her mother's youngest daughter was there to see their mother die? Would their mother want that?

Her mother suddenly stirred, resuming her conversation as if oblivious to the recent silence.

"I was not as strong as you." Her voice was barely a whisper. "I didn't fight and didn't want to. But you, you have built a strength, Vanessa, a strength I never could. My mother was a dancer and she was happy. And if things were different..." She managed to smile, but Vanessa could see she was struggling against an overwhelming desire to sleep.

"I'm sorry for so many things too, Mum ..." Vanessa whispered, squeezing her hand and feeling the swell of tears behind her eyes.

"Shhh," her mother interrupted, seemingly finding a burst of energy from somewhere deep within. "You've no need to be sorry for anything, Vanessa. Your life has been hard, and I have been responsible for much of that. You know men. Maybe like I did. But embrace that knowledge, my angel, and put it where it belongs. You're safe now and the world is different. Live that life, Vanessa. You have earned it. Dance in that life like you dance on the stage and..."

Her eyes closed as she searched for another breath. She found one and opened her eyes wide, adamant they wouldn't shut, determined her daughter hear her last words.

"Use what you've learned my darling," she whispered. "Live. Don't waste your life. Dance on that stage. Dance like you danced when I saw you, when you didn't know I was there... Dance, Vanessa. Dance my darling..."

Vanessa tightened the grip on her mother's hand as she slowly closed her eyes. This time she knew they wouldn't reopen.

～

Vanessa remained with her mother for almost an hour. Her hand was still warm when she let go. Maybe she would have sat there longer had she not decided to phone Philippe to tell him that his estranged wife had passed away. With regards to her own father, she'd tell him tomorrow, if he was sober. She thanked the nurses, signed some papers, discussed the hospital procedures for collecting her mother's body, and left.

She hadn't cried and wondered why. In truth, she felt numb. This time at her mother's bedside had represented a reparation, mutual forgiveness and a deeper understanding. It was as though all the love Vanessa had ever sought from her mother had been rolled into these last ten days.

She had learned so much more about her mother's past and surely now appreciated why her mother had done so many of the unfathomable things she had. Perhaps Vanessa too had learned more about herself. She saw the parallels in the lives of her mother and grandmother; how they seemed destined to suffer the same kind of misfortune because of who they inherently were. Had her mother always been afraid that a similar fate would inevitably meet her daughter? Was that why she left her and remained so detached? Did she think that would sever the connection?

Her mother this week had repeated how proud she was of her, how she loved her, and these were words Vanessa had never heard before. "You have built a strength, Vanessa..." Was that her aim? To make her as independent as she could possibly be? She smiled to herself. She didn't feel strong. She'd never felt strong. Or had she? Was she? Is that why she wasn't crying now?

She left the hospital and found a bar. She needed an hour to herself before heading home. Time to remind herself who she was. She had agreed with Philippe that he should break the news to Gabrielle. Like her, their mother had abandoned Gabrielle long ago. Unlike her, however, Gabrielle had been brought up in a kind environment and Vanessa doubted she regarded their mother as anything other than the woman who gave birth to her. Vanessa was not particularly close to Philippe, but they were amicable with one another and he was a good father to Gabrielle.

Gabrielle. Her younger sister. Also abandoned by their mother. Was that so she could protect her youngest daughter too? But what about Vanessa's older sister, the one who she'd only just discovered? Their mother didn't leave her, but they too were torn apart. What had become of her? Where was she now? Vanessa tried to piece together the story she'd been told, desperately trying to comprehend the events that had conspired to make her mother the woman she became.

# JULY 1946, LONDON
## EDITH BROUDIER

**Five months after she arrives**

*E*dith's preconception that England had avoided the scars of war that were inflicted on her own country was far from the truth. Food in London was as scarce as in Paris, as were decent paying jobs. Everywhere lives and buildings needed to be rebuilt and, apart from a privileged few, everyone was united in a common struggle.

She was a French citizen, but also possessed documentation confirming her father was English. She was, she assumed, therefore entitled to dual nationality. Her papers though had been barely inspected. Maybe because so many people had lost their identity papers the authorities attached less importance to them than before.

She was, however, grateful for her parentage. She had always spoken fluent English and her daughter had, to some extent, also been exposed to the language from a tender age. Within three months of their arrival here they found themselves talking English almost exclusively.

It took a month to find Anna a place at a school. Up until then they had lived off the money Edith had brought with her from France. The job she had taken at the button factory, even when supplemented by the ad hoc shifts she could get in the local café, barely covered the rent let alone put a decent meal on the table. She needed to earn more.

Before the war Edith had been a dancer. She had gone to the West End on several occasions looking for work, but the dancers they required in London were different from those they sought in Paris. There were, however, several pubs and one or two more convivial gentlemen's clubs a bus ride away where men would pay to see her take off her clothes in the afternoon. If she was propositioned and the price was right, she wouldn't say no. It wasn't anything to be proud of, but she brought home much more than she did when she worked at the factory and it was far enough away for it to remain her secret.

Last week, she was sure she saw Staff Sergeant Adams in the audience. She could tell that he had recognised her too, but as soon as their eyes met he finished his pint and left. Maybe he was uncomfortable to see her on the stage, or maybe he was embarrassed because he knew why she came to London.

John Adams was good friends with Kenneth, and in the two months following the liberation of France the three of them often enjoyed a drink together. He was aware of their intention to marry and surely could shed light on why Kenneth effectively jilted her at the altar. But when she approached the table after her act to ask about him, the men he was with were vague, more interested in a private performance than telling her where she could find him. She indulged one of the men and, after assuring him she had no ulterior motive, handed him a note and asked him to pass it on to John Adams. Although her heart said otherwise, there was a chance that Kenneth's disappearance was more justifiable than she believed.

# MARCH 1985, PARIS

## HER MOTHER'S FUNERAL

*V*anessa was pleased that her father had refrained from drinking and that his conversations about her mother following the funeral were reasonably coherent and devoid of the bitterness he so often exuded. Quite the opposite; he painted her as the beautiful woman she was, saying she lived for the day and would deal with anything life threw at her. Vanessa doubted much of what he said but had little doubt that he had, in his own way, loved her. Their relationship, however, was always destined to fail.

He was 40 when Vanessa's mother called upon him after returning to France; 20 years her senior. Anna Broudier had remembered him as someone who had shown her own mother kindness and he was the only person she could turn to. He took her in, but like so many men he soon succumbed to her apparent zest for life and disregard for rules. Almost inevitably, they became lovers.

Theirs could not, however, be described as a stable relationship. They both drank too much and Vanessa's mother had a string of affairs. Before Vanessa was three, her mother left and moved to the South of France.

She was gone for over a year, returning one summer evening when Vanessa and her father were having tea. She should have been a stranger, but Vanessa ran to her and they hugged for most of the evening. Her father went out. Vanessa could remember going to bed that night feeling everything was going to be fine, only to hear her parents fighting when her father eventually came home. She hid beneath her blanket and sobbed until morning. She hoped against hope her mother would still be there when she got up, but she had left again.

Her mother's funeral was not a grand affair. Few tears were shed, which made Vanessa feel sad; her mother had certainly made a good job of alienating all those who once loved her.

Vanessa had stood at the graveside with her arm around Gabrielle. She was ten years old and their mother had been in and out of her life since she was born. Perhaps that was why Gabrielle showed little emotion. Perhaps Gabrielle was the greatest evidence of her mother's apparent desire to ensure love never darkened her doorstep.

A dozen or so people came back to the bar where Vanessa had arranged a small buffet. When Philippe and Gabrielle left, Vanessa and her father adjourned to his local. Vanessa didn't have fond memories of the bar her father had always favoured, but she wanted to talk to him.

"Mum told me your story," she said, bringing their drinks to the table and sitting down.

"Story?"

"The child she had in London."

He brought the glass to his lips and looked at her quizzically. The days when she would have felt the need to tread carefully with him had long gone. She held his gaze, waiting his response.

"I told you. Didn't I tell you it was true?" He nodded enthusiastically, trying to make himself more important to her than he was.

"So, what do you know?"

He picked up his beer again and Vanessa wondered what was going through his mind. "Well, what I've always told you." He avoided her eyes.

"Tell me again."

"She had a baby when she was young. It was taken from her and she never saw her. You know your mother."

"Mum said she was adopted."

He shrugged his shoulders.

"Surely she told you that?" Vanessa said.

"Yeah, I think she mentioned that."

"Mum always wondered what became of her."

He shrugged his shoulders again and finished his pint.

Vanessa wondered if he could actually enlighten her more. How much would her mother have confided in him and why would he know any more than she'd already learned from her mother anyway? She changed tack.

"Tell me about Edith," Vanessa said firmly.

"Your grandmother?"

Vanessa nodded. "Your first love."

"Your mother told you that, did she? What would she know?"

Vanessa glimpsed that bitterness resurfacing in him but wanted to hear him out so suppressed her desire to leave. She asked if he wanted another drink. He did, so she went to the bar. "Mum told me some, Dad, but I'd like to hear your story," she said when she'd sat back down.

"You'd like the truth you mean," he said defensively.

Vanessa doubted her father had ever strung two truthful sentences together in his life, but she had waited all day to hear his version of the story her mother had told her. She smiled and nodded. "And no holds barred."

He looked to both sides and leant forward as if what he was about to say was important and somehow privileged information. Vanessa moved closer, bowing to his misplaced ego.

"Edith Broudier," he said slowly. "We were never lovers, despite what your mother may have said. Not my choice, I would have married her the day I met her. Or when she was old enough. She was still at school, you see. Not that you'd think so when she was dressed up. Yep, Saturday 14th July 1934, a glorious, sunny day. She was a looker alright. But... Well, she was just like your mother really. Turned by a pretty face or the promise of something unreal..."

He continued to tell her his story, echoing much of which she had learned from her mother.

Her father, Marcel, had been best friends with Jean Broudier when they were at school. Jean was popular with the girls and had always been ambitious. At 15, he was employed as a stagehand at one of Paris's most respected theatres and within five years became stage manager.

Edith had never been to the theatre and the lure of attending had prompted her to finally accept one of Marcel's persistent invitations to go out with him. As a favour, Jean had set aside the best seats for his old school friend and the girl he was desperate to impress.

Edith enjoyed the evening immensely, but when they met up with

Jean after the performance Marcel quickly realised his plan had backfired. Within a week, Edith and Jean were dating and a year later, two days after Edith's 18th birthday, they were married.

Until they found their own place, Edith often stayed with her mother. Jean worked most evenings and slept at his parents' more palatial home in the middle of the city. When she did move out, Edith felt guilty leaving her mother, who was not in the best of health, to fend for herself. Her father had died some years before – a result of wounds received during the war – and with his demise Edith's parents' once comfortable existence perished too. Her mother died within a year of Edith leaving, aged only 44 and it took Edith some time to come to terms with her passing.

Life, however, was good to Edith. She learned to dance and proved a perfectly adequate stand-in when one of the regular performers at the theatre was ill. This meant that she and Jean saw one another more than they may have done had she worked elsewhere. It was only when their daughter, Anna, was born in 1937 that she took up a more traditional role as housewife and mother.

The outbreak of war meant the closure of the theatre. Within six months they had to move out of their rented house and into a bedsit in the city. Jean found work wherever he could but Edith worried that he would be called upon to join the army. She believed the first war with Germany was responsible for the death of both of her parents and did not want the same fate to befall her new husband. As it turned out, fate dealt an even crueller blow when Jean, his parents, and most of his family were killed in a bombing raid in 1940.

"Of course, I was sad for her," her father said. "I'd always kept in touch. With both of them. I asked her to marry me and maybe she would have said yes if it wasn't for that British soldier and his false promises. Maybe she'd always wanted to go to England, who knows? I know her father always went on about it when she was young. Anyway, she went. With your mother too – she wouldn't have been much more than six or seven then. Told you. Both of them turned by a pretty boy and the promise of something better."

Vanessa was surprised by her father's sudden and more reflective tone. He downed his pint. "Well, the rest is history. Edith died in England and Anna, your mother, came back when she was a woman. Strange, eh? But, like I said, me and Edith were never more than friends." He let out a sarcastic laugh. "Well, one of us was a friend... the other? I don't know the answer to that question, Vanessa."

Her father had obviously had enough of her questions and was now slurring his words. The bar was filling up, the clientele more akin to the type her father would enjoy spending the rest of the night with. Vanessa smiled at him, gave him some money for another drink and left. It was a cool night, but she decided to walk home. It'd take 30 minutes. She wondered if her father, now nearing 70, was a good-looking man when he was young. Her mother had assured her he was her biological father and Vanessa had no real reason to doubt it. Yet they seemed so different. It was strange. Her mother had just died, but she had never felt closer to her in her life.

# 6

# APRIL 1985, MADAME PELLETIER'S CAFÉ, PARIS

They may have had different fathers, but Vanessa had always regarded Gabrielle as her full and legitimate sister. Although she was only eight years old when Gabrielle was born, Vanessa instinctively adopted the role of protector, shielding her from the worst excesses of their mother. By the time Gabrielle was two, their mother had already started to repeat the pattern of the mother Vanessa had known as a young child; disappearing without notice, often for weeks on end, and no doubt procuring a string of lovers.

There had, however, been a time when Vanessa saw her mother in a different light. When she met Philippe D'anvers, she seemed happy. When they married, Vanessa moved in with them, living in their big house in the suburbs. Her mother found a job, cooked dinner and sat in watching TV or playing games in the evenings. She even cut down on her drinking and enrolled Vanessa into a dance school. Vanessa could recall how her mother enthused about her daughter's natural talent for dancing and had fond memories of those precious years.

They still argued, of course – they'd always argued – but shortly after Gabrielle was born those arguments became more spiteful and when her mother started drinking again it was easier for Vanessa to stay at her father's, visiting her sister when she knew her mother was in a good mood or, better still, absent. As Gabrielle turned from baby to toddler, those absences became more frequent and when their daughter was three years old Philippe sought a divorce and a restraining order against his wife.

To help care for Gabrielle, Philippe's mother came to live with him. She was only in her forties then, divorced and relatively wealthy. Vanessa liked her and could tell she was fond of Gabrielle. Her sister would always call her Mémé, but in truth Madame D'anvers became the mother Gabrielle's own could never have been.

Later, Philippe met Marguerite, a woman his own age who had two children of her own. They all moved into an even larger house in the same street, and while Vanessa had been concerned this would have an adverse effect on Gabrielle, it was quite the opposite. Marguerite assumed the role of Gabrielle's mother and Madame D'anvers that of a more traditional grandmother and the three children got on well. Vanessa understood why Gabrielle had never regarded Anna Broudier as her mother and hadn't been surprised that she didn't cry at her funeral.

The coffee shop they were meeting in today was Gabrielle's favourite. Halfway between her school and home, they often met there. Vanessa would have a coffee, her sister a banana milkshake and a cream cake, and then Vanessa would walk her home.

Vanessa was still thinking about her mother. She had mixed feelings regarding Gabrielle's apparent indifference to their mother's passing; pleased because she would not want Gabrielle to be unhappy, but sad for her mother because her death hadn't impacted on her sister as the loss of a parent should.

Their mother's death had not impacted on Vanessa the way it maybe should have either. She couldn't describe herself as grieving, but she was certainly reflective. Somehow Vanessa had always loved her mother, had seen beyond the callousness she often displayed, and knew those last days together at the hospital were precious to them both.

"So, how is it?" asked Gabrielle. "Can I come and see you?"

Six months ago, Vanessa, much to her sister's delight, had secured a position in the chorus line at the Moulin Rouge. Gabrielle always asked her about her dancing.

"Well, I'm not sure you're quite old enough yet, Brie. But I'll see what I can do."

"You're going to be a famous dancer. I know it. And your name will be up in lights."

23

"It's the chorus line. Not the classical ballet."

"But they'll see you dancing and offer you the part in Swan Lake you've always wanted."

Vanessa smiled. Truth was, she was a little too full in the figure for the ballet now. Perhaps the Moulin Rouge suited her best. It was well paid and, though she had recently been considering moving to London where she was sure she could find work, she wasn't convinced it was the right time to leave Gabrielle. She also wondered how much of that recent deliberation was influenced by her growing desire to track down her older half-sister. "We'll see," she said.

The waitress came over and Vanessa ordered another coffee but refused to buy Gabrielle another cake. It would spoil her tea and Marguerite would not appreciate that.

"Shouldn't I be sad, Ness?" Gabrielle suddenly said with a degree of concern.

"Sad?"

"About Mum."

It was a difficult question to answer. Vanessa took her hand across the table. "She wasn't as bad as people think. It was just difficult for her to be a mother."

"But you cried. I saw you."

"Yes, I was sad. But that was because our relationship was different. I'd only ever had one mum. You, on the other hand, have been blessed with two, no, three really." She squeezed Gabrielle's hand before letting go and smiled.

"Well, I would have been sad if it was *Mémé* or *Mamam*."

"Exactly," Vanessa reassured her, hiding the sudden sadness she felt for their mother. "Now, tell me about school. How many of those boys have asked you out?"

"I don't like boys. They're grubby," Gabrielle protested, and they spent the next ten minutes talking about her activities at school.

"Sorbonne be warned," trumpeted Vanessa when Gabrielle told her she'd got top marks in her recent history exam. "Make way for Gabrielle D'anvers. Philosopher extraordinaire and connoisseur of banana shakes. Don't be fooled by her incredible beauty, this is a woman of our times."

"You're embarrassing me," laughed Gabrielle.

"And her embarrassing sister who once got a bronze medal at tap."

There were only a few people in the café but they turned to Vanessa and Gabrielle, wondering about the sudden outburst.

"Hey. I don't work Mondays and Tuesdays," Vanessa said when they'd stopped laughing. "How about I ask your dad if you can have a sleepover this Sunday? I can take you to school and we could have some fun."

"Could I watch you dance?"

"We'll see. Now, let's get you home. I'm sure Miss Clever Clogs has homework to do and I need to be at work at 7pm."

On the walk home, Gabrielle told Vanessa that Philippe and Marguerite had talked about getting married. Their mother had never signed the divorce papers but that didn't matter now. She wondered if Philippe knew about the child his wife gave birth to in London. Perhaps she'd talk to him.

Vanessa considered telling Gabrielle about the other sister they had and about the general misfortune that had plagued their mother's early life. Surely it would give Gabrielle a greater understanding. But she didn't tell her what she had learned. Gabrielle needn't know - not yet anyway. She was eleven years old, safe and happy, and deserved to enjoy her childhood.

# 7

# AUGUST 1946, LONDON

## EDITH AND ANNA

It was difficult for Edith to make friends locally and keep her daytime activities secret, but she was delighted her daughter had. It was Friday, and on Friday nights Anna and a few school friends attended a sewing class organised by the local Girl Guides unit.

Despite the upheaval in their lives, Anna seemed content; maybe being brought up during a time of shortage and danger had already instilled low expectations in her. Their home was the upstairs floor of a Victorian terraced house; one room, divided by a curtain which screened off the bedroom from the sitting area and kitchen. Although the lavatory was in the back yard, they did have access to an indoor bathroom which all residents shared. It was far from perfect, sparsely furnished, but at least they had gas and electricity.

Edith had seen other lodgings, but the rent for those was double what she was paying. Her life was in limbo and she was unsure what to do for the best. She had written a letter to Marcel in Paris. Dear Marcel. He had always been there for her. Should she have accepted his invitation to marry him? He was a good man and had pleaded with her not to leave France, but as much as she loved him as a friend she could never imagine them being together like that. Funny, there was a man who would undoubtedly look after her - look after her and Anna - but he offered no excitement. Was it excitement she was experiencing now? Was it really excitement she craved? She hadn't posted the letter but kept it in the drawer.

She hung up the dress she had bought Anna today. She'd look lovely in it and perhaps they could take the bus into town tomorrow and have lunch in one of the nice cafés there. She retrieved the pack of cigarettes and the half-full bottle of gin from the cupboard. Her Friday night treat. She noticed her wedding ring and the necklace that once belonged to her mother-in-law. Should she sell them? Together they would fetch enough for six months' rent.

She wouldn't drink all the gin but knew she would welcome the slight numbness a couple of glasses offered. Anna would be home in an hour. She sat on the chair and unfolded the letter she'd received last week from John Adams. It made no mention of Kenneth, but she would meet up with John in the Spread Eagle on Tuesday as he suggested.

When Paris was liberated, joy had rained down on the city. And that was when Edith had met Kenneth, a British soldier. They started an affair and soon fell in love, and Edith wondered if this could be a new beginning. She was worried about telling him she was pregnant, but he seemed overjoyed at the prospect of being a father and suggested that they should move to England and marry. It wasn't the reaction she was expecting, and it triggered a childhood memory of her father's dream who, up until the day he died, had always talked about them returning to England where he was born. Perhaps meeting Kenneth was fate; perhaps she'd find happiness again.

When Kenneth's unit was called home, she followed him, leaving Anna in the care of Marcel's sister for a week. The house they found in South London would only be temporary and by the time the baby was born Kenneth was sure he would have been discharged from the army and they could move to the Cotswolds, a beautiful part of England where he had an engineering job waiting for him.

Edith returned to France and they kept in touch as best they could. When she lost the baby, Kenneth was concerned for her welfare, but she told him to stay in London and that she'd be there as soon as she could. She sent him another telegram the day before she and Anna boarded the boat, but when they arrived at the house, he and all his belongings had gone.

The landlord who lived in the next street was unaware he had disappeared. As far as he was concerned, the rent had been paid until the end of the month. There was no note from Kenneth and no neighbours could shed any light. The barracks in Woolwich, to which she believed he was attached, would not inspect their records, even when she told them he was her fiancé and she was worried for his welfare. If his clothes had still been there, she would have thought something untoward had happened; but they weren't, and everything she discovered suggested he'd simply had a change of heart.

The obvious thing to do was to go back to France, but there seemed nothing to return to. For the next few days, she and Anna explored the neighbourhood or sat in their house. She was amazed at her daughter's resilience. Anna was two when her father, Jean, was killed, and they'd rarely talked about him since. She had only met Kenneth a handful of times yet readily shared Edith's excitement about the new life they planned in England. But she also seemed to easily accept the situation in which they now found themselves and even sought to reassure her mother. Anna was special; she was Edith's strength.

That was six months ago and there had been little time to dwell on any heartbreak. Like so many women, Edith was alone with a child at a time where day-to-day survival exceeded all other concerns. She heard voices outside. It was good of Mrs Warren to walk the children home. She put away the gin and forced a smile. She was sure her daughter would be thrilled when she saw the dress.

# 8

# NOVEMBER 1986, LONDON

## MALISSA OVMEISTER

*V*anessa first met Dawn when Dawn travelled to Paris looking for work the summer after Vanessa's mother died. She didn't get the job at the Moulin Rouge where Vanessa was working, but Vanessa introduced her to a dance company which toured Paris and who'd employed her for the best part of a year. Dawn was a lesbian who made no secret of her feelings for Vanessa and for a couple of months they lived together, whilst Monique, Vanessa's lover and flat mate, was away.

Vanessa had told Dawn at the outset that she was not looking for a relationship that was anything other than casual, but Dawn was still upset when Vanessa ended their affair. Dawn knew about Monique, but Vanessa convinced her that the woman she regarded as her rival had absolutely nothing to do with her decision. Monique and Vanessa had a relationship that had no rules, they always had and always would have, and neither were the type who would settle down. Eventually, Dawn accepted the situation and when she moved back to London Vanessa was pleased their friendship seemed intact.

She and Dawn had often talked about the opportunities for a dancer in London, but when Vanessa decided to look for a job there, she was a little apprehensive about accepting Dawn's offer of a bed at the flat she shared with a few others. However, Dawn told her that she had met someone else and Vanessa accepted that friendship was all she sought. It therefore came as a surprise to Vanessa when, on meeting Dawn's new girlfriend, she realised she felt a tinge of jealousy.

Vanessa had some savings but had decided if she needed to earn more money during her stay, she could always take up a hostess job at one of the so-called gentlemen's clubs. Dawn, however, suggested she tried the Cabaret Club in Piccadilly - in essence a smaller version of the Moulin Rouge - and for the last three weeks Vanessa had been dancing there three or four nights a week. Still playing on her mind was the older sister she never knew, and as much as Vanessa tried to convince herself she had come to London to further her career, she realised it was impossible for her to ignore her desire to discover what happened to her.

St Mary's, the orphanage her mother had mentioned, had been demolished 20 years ago and was now the site for a block of offices. Vanessa had spoken to several people who could remember the establishment, but nobody who could give her any information about her older half-sister who her mother had told her had inherited the name Ovmeister when she was adopted.

Ovmeister was not a common name in England and the only reference in the phone book was to a business in Kensington named Ovmeister-Carmichael. It was an impressive building, but the receptionist was hardly co-operative when Vanessa called in expressing her curiosity regarding the firm's name. If nothing more turned up, perhaps she'd go back another day. Maybe she'd write a letter.

Although they were all employed in the same industry, it wasn't often that Vanessa, Dawn and their other flatmate, Jenny, found themselves socialising together. The pub was busy. They were standing at the bar and, once or twice, Vanessa had felt the brush of Dawn's hand against her thigh. Nothing else she did or said, however, suggested she wanted to resurrect their affair. Dawn's real ambition was to find a position in one of the top ballet's, but she was considering joining Jenny as one of the dancers in Itchy Feet, a musical which had just opened for a second run. Apparently, the producers of the show were always on the lookout for talent and Jenny suggested Vanessa call on them too. Maybe she would after Christmas.

"But what about Madame B?" Vanessa said to Dawn. "I thought that sounded promising?"

"You know, Vanessa, I think I'm beginning to give up on the ballet thing. It's too much and I'd probably have to lose a stone anyway."

Vanessa laughed. "I know that feeling."

A man pushed by them to get to the bar, apologising then asking if he could buy them a drink. They said no, but Jenny who had recently split up from her boyfriend and had been telling them that getting a quick replacement was the best way to soften the blow, was clearly more interested. "Well, I wouldn't mind taking advantage of you," she said, turning to him.

"You're so subtle," laughed Dawn.

The man was clearly taken by Jenny's approach and started talking to her as he ordered his drinks. A friend of his joined him.

"And an Hofmeister please, luv," the man shouted, adding to his original order.

Vanessa was surprised to hear a word so similar to the one that had lived in her mind these past 18 months. She looked along the bar as the barmaid placed a glass beneath the yellow beer tap that displayed the name. Dawn followed her gaze. "Always reminds me of Malissa. I'll have to ask someone if she owns a brewery too. Wouldn't surprise me."

"Sorry?"

"Malissa Ovmeister. Whenever anyone orders a Hofmeister it reminds me of her."

"Malissa?"

"Yes, Malissa at Fenner's."

Vanessa looked at her questioningly, wondering what she was talking about.

"Oh, I forgot. You don't know her. Malissa Ovmeister, though it's spelt with a vee not an eff. Fenner's is the agency I told you about before you got the club job, remember?"

Vanessa could recall Dawn telling her about a dance agency that would find her a job if she had no luck herself. She couldn't, however, remember her mentioning the name of any of its employees. Her heart skipped a beat. "Ovmeister?"

"Yeah, with a vee."

The man at the bar asked them if they were sure they didn't want a drink before paying for his round. They declined again, but another friend

31

had joined him now and Vanessa knew they'd think it okay to try to chat them up. She wanted to know more about Malissa Ovmeister. She clasped Dawn's hand and squeezed it. Dawn smiled and they moved away from the bar.

"Sorry, Dawn," Vanessa said when they'd found a bit of space, "blokes still give me the creeps."

"Well, I guess Jenny will have the choice of all three now," Dawn giggled. "A noisy night back home."

"You wanna go somewhere else?" Vanessa asked.

If Dawn was thinking Vanessa was seeking to resurrect their relationship, she couldn't blame her for misreading her intentions. She could simply tell Dawn the story, the reason for her interest in the name she had so innocently mentioned, and that would be that. But she knew she wouldn't; Vanessa had learned to be careful with whom she shared secrets.

Neither, however, did she want to rock their new-found friendship. Most of all though, Vanessa wanted to know more about the woman who could be her sister, or at least be related to her. It would be some coincidence to discover she ended up in the same industry. Vanessa could feel her heart pumping and fought to keep her excitement in check. She needed to know, and if she had to use the lure of sex to get what she needed, it would hardly be the first time she'd done so.

"We could get a coffee next door," Dawn said.

They made sure Jenny was okay and left the pub. Two minutes later, they were sitting in the Wimpy Bar. They ordered coffee.

"Do you remember the Wimpy near the Rouge?" Dawn said, stretching her hand across the table.

"Dawn," said Vanessa, softly. "You know how fond I am of you, but my situation hasn't changed. And you have Sally, remember. She's a nice woman and you're good together and I'd hate you to do anything you'd regret."

The waitress brought them their drinks.

"Vanessa," Dawn said in a serious manner. "As much as I've missed some of those things you do, I think I've grown up a bit now. She does happen to be away for the week though," she added with a mischievous smile. "By the way she thinks you're dishy too, but I told her you only like men. I've never told her about us."

"You haven't?"

"I think I know you well enough to know you value your privacy. You seeing anyone? In France maybe? Is Monique back?"

"Monique? Last time I heard she was sailing around the Med with the man she intends to marry."

"A man, perhaps she's seen the light," Dawn said mockingly.

"I think she's seen his yacht. She said she's coming back to Paris for Christmas but what she says and what she does are two entirely different things."

. "And you're back to Paris for Christmas?"

"Yes. I miss my sister and have always spent Christmas with her. But to answer your question, I'm not seeing anyone. I haven't since you."

Dawn smiled. "You fancy a burger?"

"Rather share a plate of chips."

They talked a little about the times they shared in Paris, but Vanessa was confident, as far as their relationship was concerned, that Dawn had moved on. What she wanted to discover was just what Dawn knew about Malissa Ovmeister.

"Will you stay in Paris?" Dawn asked when they'd finished eating.

"I don't think so. I like London. I think I'd look for another job after Christmas. Here I mean. Perhaps Itchy Feet or maybe I'll call on that Malissa Ovmeister, you mentioned. Do you know her?"

"Some... I've met a few times. Drop dead gorgeous but as straight as an arrow. One of those self-made businesswomen. Having said that, all I hear is that she does a good job. Rose and Martin – you remember Martin?"

Vanessa nodded.

"They swear by her. Me and Jen have talked about signing up too."

"So, she's alright then?"

"As far as I know. Married to some bigwig businessman, though I do think she got where she is on her own merits."

Vanessa's heart sank a little. Ovmeister must be her married name which negated the possibility Malissa was her sister. She hid her disappointment at the revelation but the name, of course, still intrigued her. "She runs it?"

"As far as I know. Well, the dancing side anyway. Fenner's is an agency for all sorts. You should look in the magazines, they're always advertising."

"Yeah, perhaps I'll give her a call after Christmas. So, Ovmeister is her husband's name?"

Dawn looked across the table, possibly wondering why Vanessa would seem so interested in a name.

"Yes, I guess it is."

"Perhaps he owns the brewery then..." Vanessa smiled, placing her hand momentarily on Dawn's and trying to make light of her questioning.

"Yeah. Unusual name, but like I said spelt differently. I like your hair like that, by the way."

Vanessa had discovered as much as she needed for now. So, she thanked Dawn for the compliment and suggested they get back home before Jenny and God knows who else turned up.

"For old times'?" Dawn smiled. "And no strings."

"You learn quickly."

"Well, I had a great teacher. And when the cat's away..."

# 9

# AUGUST 1946, LONDON

## LORD FELIX

*W*hether it was guilt or concern that compelled John Adams to respond to Edith's note, she was surprised by his invitation to meet. Out of uniform, he was already sitting at a table when she walked in the pub just before 2pm. He stood up, greeted her, and bought her a drink. They sat back down.

A few people had stared when she walked in. Men were getting more used to women in pubs these days but it was still unusual for a woman to walk into one alone. She doubted John Adams lived locally and this was the first time Edith had been in a pub she wasn't working in. If the locals wondered what they were doing there Edith did too, but she was sure she was about to find out.

"I didn't know, Edith," John said. "I was told you stayed in France. Ken said he told you."

"Told me what?"

"That he... That he had changed his mind."

The fact Kenneth had changed his mind didn't surprise her. The fact John Adams was telling her did.

"Obviously not," she said.

"Obviously. Bastard. Excuse my language."

Edith smiled across the table. "I appreciate you telling me, John. I know you didn't have to."

John had not seen or heard from Kenneth since he left the house Edith now lived in, but presumed he had gone back to the Cotswolds. He was one of many men under John's wartime care who had returned to civilian life. John did have an address which she might want to have but, knowing Edith as he did, he doubted she would want it. She didn't.

John leaned across the table and whispered. "I think when you told him about losing the baby..."

He didn't seem to want to finish the sentence. Edith briefly touched his hand and finished it for him. "He no longer felt duty bound and all that," she smiled.

"I guess," he said.

"These things happen, John. We all get by."

He took a sip of his beer. Edith sensed there was more to his visit than telling her what she probably already knew. "You still...?" Again, he didn't finish, but raised his eyebrows and nodded slightly. His coyness made Edith smile.

"Still...?" she replied. "Still entertaining the troops? Well, needs must, John."

Her reply wasn't quite as quiet as John may have expected and he quickly glanced about the pub probably wondering if anyone was listening. They sat quietly for a minute.

"I have a friend," John said after a moment's reflection. "A gentleman and I think he might be able to help."

"Help?"

"He's looking for someone. Someone special to look after him. Him and his house."

This time, Edith raised *her* eyebrows. "Look after him?"

"Yes," he said. "Oh, and he's French. That's important. Lives up West."

Edith had an idea of what John was proposing but was still uncertain why he thought she'd fit the bill.

"I've known him many years," John continued, "a war hero. You know, the first time round. Could have been a General but he moved to London on French Government business in the twenties. He's still attached to the role, attending meetings and that kind of thing, and is looking for someone to look after his affairs at home. When he's away and things."

"Go on."

"Well, with you speaking both languages and your understanding of men and things... things they like, and your experience and discretion... I think he could be your ticket out of here."

Edith sensed John was being diplomatic. She remembered their friendship back in France and the esteem in which he was held by his men. She knew his intentions were good, but she needed to help him air them.

"This... gentleman," she said. "This French gentleman. Would his interest in me be because he has seen me perform by any chance?"

John smiled, seemingly a little relieved that she had obviously made the connection that saved him from explaining the job vacancy further. "Not Lord Felix. I doubt he would approve of such establishments... Not that there's anything wrong with them, you understand."

"I understand, John," she smiled. "A Lord, no less. I thought Lords were the preserve of the English, I'm impressed. So, I look after some papers, speak a bit of French, perhaps a bit of cleaning and keep him entertained."

"It's a live-in job."

"In a big house in the West End? So cooking, fetching and discretion. I assume he's married. Does he not have a housemaid?"

"He has someone who comes in once a week, but he's looking for something more permanent. Looking to pay well for the right person."

"And his wife?"

"Yes, he has a wife. Of course, he does. She's not been well for many years. Mostly bedridden and unable to..."

"And this job involves looking after her too?"

"In a way, but from what I understand, the doctor comes by regularly."

"So, he must be quite an old man?"

"Only 50 something."

"So, still active?"

John smiled.

"And you think because times are hard and because of my 'experience' I'd obviously jump at the opportunity?"

"Edith. Please, I didn't mean anything..."

"John," she interrupted him again and smiled. "I think we both know I may well be very suitable for the role. He knows I have a daughter?"

He nodded and seemingly relieved finished his pint and relaxed a little.

"I told him, if you're interested, you'd call on him tomorrow afternoon. At 3pm. I have his address." He reached inside the pocket of his blazer and retrieved a piece of folded paper. "Oh, and he's got two children too. About your daughter's age. Anna isn't it?"

She took the piece of paper and studied the address. She placed it in her pocket.

"I thank you, John, and I'd be pleased to meet Lord Felix. So, your boys are all deserting you. What's for you now there's no Germans to fight? Do you get to return to civilian life any time soon?"

John Adams was a good man. He'd make a great husband one day she thought, but Edith doubted, once they left the pub, that their paths would cross again.

The street in Pimlico where she was to meet the man Adams referred to as Lord Felix, reminded Edith of the Avenue de l'Opera, a place where she had spent many glorious afternoons with her friends when she was a teenager. For a moment she was taken back to life before the war and the existence she may have enjoyed with her husband. That life, however, was far removed from the one she found herself in today.

The house, four stories high, was one of a dozen or so in a curving terrace. Each had a front garden, separated from the road by ornate white railings, and on the other side of the road lay a park which backed onto an area of woodland.

The neighbourhood was clean and quiet, and its comparison with the area where she currently lived was stark. Half a mile away, like in so much of the city, there remained evidence of the German bombing, but unlike many other places, work had already commenced on clearing away the rubble.

In contrast to an hour ago, when she commenced her journey, she didn't feel overdressed and she knew moving to this place with Anna was in both of their interests. She smoothed her dress over her hips, adjusted her jacket and rang the bell. She was confident Lord Felix would find her suitable for the role.

# 10

## DECEMBER 1986, THE FENNER AGENCY, LONDON

*A*s soon as Vanessa walked through the door she felt the buzz. Busy people carrying files and papers crisscrossed the foyer, hardly aware of her entrance. A few people waiting to see someone, were seated on the chairs and sofa that lined the left-hand side of the reception area. She smiled at them, and made her way to the reception desk and to the woman wearing a headset.

"Hi," she said. "I'm Vanessa Cozzette. I have an appointment with Malissa Ovmeister."

The receptionist smiled, pushed a button and sang, "Fenner Agency, good morning." Then added "I'll put you through," and pressed another couple of buttons before thumbing through some pages in front of her. She found what she was looking for. "I'll let her know you're here, Miss Cozzette. Please take a seat." Another button flashed on the switchboard. She pushed it and took the call.

Vanessa sat a little anxiously waiting for her interview. On the face of it, she was just another dancer keen to sign up to the agency, but she might also be about to meet a woman who knew the whereabouts of her older half-sister. She didn't need to wait long.

"Vanessa?" enquired the young woman who approached her. Vanessa stood up, shook hands and followed the woman through the swing doors which opened into an open plan office where everybody seemed to be on the phone. She was ushered past a bank of desks to the office at the far end. Through its window Vanessa saw a woman look up, smile and close the folder she was reading as she entered.

Malissa was a naturally beautiful woman. Older than Vanessa, three or four years she guessed, with lively hazel eyes and golden hair that tumbled softly onto her shoulders. Her lipstick was pale, and her make-up subtle which contrasted so wonderfully with the vibrancy of the deeper blue sweater she wore. She smiled kindly and welcomed her but despite her warmth Vanessa sensed she was a woman who could get things done. She liked her immediately.

Malissa took the folder Vanessa handed her, asking if she wanted a tea or coffee. Vanessa said she was fine. They chatted easily while she thumbed through Vanessa's portfolio. She said she loved Vanessa's accent and they exchanged a few simple sentences in Vanessa's native language.

Vanessa told her that English had always been in her family - on her mother's side - and she had spoken both languages for as long as she could remember. Malissa admitted she spoke only a little French. "My husband speaks a little more," she'd added casually.

Malissa closed the file and looked at her. "Well, Vanessa, everything looks fine. Fantastic even. But it seems you're fixed at least 'til Christmas anyway."

"Yes," replied Vanessa. "I'll go home for Christmas, but when I return in January, I'd be looking for something, so it made sense to sign up now."

"Well, we'd love you on our books."

Malissa outlined the role of the agency and the work they were sure they could offer her. An agency that supplied freelance dancers was a new concept in London but not in Paris, but Vanessa was impressed by the scope that Fenner's offered.

Formalities seemingly over, Malissa asked her more about her work in Paris. Vanessa had performed with some of the most prestigious dance companies in France companies Malissa would probably have heard of, and though most of her assignments were relatively short term - emergency cover - they clearly demonstrated Vanessa's all-round ability. Her most recent engagement back home was at the Moulin Rouge, and whilst her performances there hardly demanded that she reached into the upper limits of her technical prowess, the theatre enjoyed worldwide fame and she had a glowing reference from them.

"I've never been, I'd love to though," Malissa said after listening to Vanessa's account of her experience there.

Vanessa smiled, but was a little disconcerted by how they had so quickly fallen into such an easy-going discussion. It was as if they were already friends and she had to remind herself of the main purpose of her meeting. "Well, next time you're in Paris, I'll take you."

"I'll hold you to that. It's unbelievable you speak English so well."

"My grandfather was English." Technically, it was her great-grandfather on her mother's side who was born in England, but Vanessa was not meticulous about family. She had, after all, never known grandparents of any description. Malissa's comment did, however, afford her an opportunity to ask a more relevant question. "And you, Mrs Ovmeister? You speak French, but I can't imagine that's a French surname."

"Vanessa, we're all on first names here. It's Malissa," she smiled.

Vanessa smiled back. "I was just thinking it sounded German."

"I do believe it is. My maiden name is Keats. Now that is English. Somewhat easier to say too. But perhaps not as memorable. Funny, I can't remember the last time I was called Malissa Ovmeister. Even my husband calls me Miss Keats."

"So, your husband is German?" Vanessa was mindful that this was supposed to be an interview and that they had only just met, but Malissa didn't object. Quite the opposite, Vanessa was sure she was happy to talk as if they were friends.

"Henry?" she laughed. "No, he's almost the typical Englishman. Mind you, there's nothing typical about Henry. Ovmeister is just a family name."

Malissa's phone rang. She answered and held a short conversation with the woman at the desk just outside the office.

"Sorry about that," Malissa said when she replaced the receiver. Then with a broad smile added, "Do you have plans for lunch?"

The phone call she had taken was from her secretary telling her that her lunch appointment had been cancelled. Malissa showed her around the office, introducing her to several people and elaborating on the role of the agency. Vanessa hadn't signed any papers and as far as she could tell Malissa hadn't confirmed her employment, but she introduced her as though the deal was already done.

"Nice to meet you, Vanessa. When are you starting?" one of the men, Malcolm, asked her.

Malissa answered for her. "She'll start when she wants to, after Christmas. But she's assigned to Sophie, so don't get your hopes up. You have to watch this one, Ness," she said as they headed for the door, "delusions of grandeur."

Vanessa laughed, surprised to hear Malissa call her 'Ness'. Only Gabrielle had ever called her that.

The staff at the bistro greeted them warmly as they were shown to their table, further enhancing Vanessa's opinion that Malissa was a woman who was liked and well respected. Malissa asked her more about her dancing career in Paris. Vanessa answered but the details of her so-called dancing career in her mid-teens had no place on a CV. She could do nothing but warm to Malissa who showed genuine interest in her.

Vanessa told her about some of the clubs she sang in and more about the Moulin Rouge which Malissa continued to enthuse about. Vanessa couldn't believe how easily they talked, it was somewhat disarming, but she was unable to dispel the instant connection they'd made. Malissa had a grace, an inner contentment, a belief that all was right with the world, and an outlook Vanessa could not comprehend. How different they were, but how strange those differences seemed to so naturally unite them.

Malissa was also possibly the most naturally-beautiful woman Vanessa had ever seen, yet strangely she felt no physical attraction to her. She had little doubt that Malissa was purely heterosexual, but it wasn't that, it was something else, something that made Vanessa look beyond her physical appearance. Was it that she sensed a fragility, an innocence that should never be challenged? But Vanessa had also witnessed Malissa's self-assuredness. Perhaps she intrigued her.

They had been in the restaurant for more than an hour. They'd talked as though they'd known each other since childhood and Vanessa had to keep reminding herself she was there, in part at least, to discover if this woman could shed any light on the whereabouts of her half-sister – a woman who, for some reason, shared her sister's adopted surname.

It was gone 3pm when Malissa excused herself to phone her office to check for messages.

"All okay?" asked Vanessa when Malissa sat back down.

"Usual call from my mum. She thinks I should be home with Lewis. She does like to put me on a guilt trip."

"Lewis?"

"Our son. I do feel guilty, but I'd go nuts if I was home *every* day."

Vanessa hadn't for one moment thought Malissa had a child. As it turned out, Lewis wasn't even three months old, but Vanessa would never have guessed she had recently given birth. Malissa's mother looked after Lewis on Mondays and Tuesdays and, as far as she was concerned, these were the only two days her daughter worked.

"Yes, if my mum knew I was leaving him with the child minder so much I'm sure she'd report me to the welfare. I told her something urgent cropped up."

"She's caring about you."

Malissa smiled and went on to explain that she had intended to work just two days a week, then it became three, then four. Last week was the first time, in several months she had worked a full week. She and Henry had, however, taken a whole month off together when Lewis was born. Vanessa wondered if Malissa felt she was judging her.

"Anyway," Malissa said summing up, "Henry's home next week and things here should quieten down, so we should have a good few weeks at home over Christmas."

She had mentioned Henry. A chance for Vanessa to ask more.

"Does he work away a lot?"

"Henry? Well, he travels a lot and for the past year or so has probably spent more time in New York than here, but that particular job should be finished soon. We're looking forward to Christmas."

"How did you meet?"

Malissa laughed. "Now, that is a story."

Malissa outlined how they met at the races, how they married secretly in Dubai and then again in England. It was a beautifully romantic story and, as Malissa recounted it, Vanessa could tell she truly loved her husband. She didn't doubt Henry loved her too; Vanessa liked their relationship and could tell they were happy.

"So, does she know now? About Dubai? That's some secret." Vanessa asked.

Their wedding in Dubai was an impromptu affair, with no family present. Malissa hadn't told her mother and that's why they did it all over again when they returned home.

"Yes, but it took me nearly two years to tell her."

"What did she say?"

"She said she knew all along."

"Do you think she did?"

"Do you know, I don't know, Ness. Sometimes I think she's the most naïve woman I've ever known and sometimes I think she's the wisest woman in the world who just makes out she's naïve. She's never mentioned it again."

"What about Henry's parents? Are they local? So that they can look after Lewis?"

Malissa hadn't yet mentioned Henry's family in her story and maybe Vanessa would have naturally asked such a question. She did, however, momentarily hate the thought that she may have deliberately manipulated the conversation back to Henry and any possible connection with her sister.

Malissa paused, but only momentarily. She certainly seemed to regard the question as a completely innocent one. "I'm afraid my husband has no parents."

"Oh, I'm so sorry to hear that."

"He was an orphan. Or still is, technically, I guess," she said slowly.

The word orphan startled Vanessa and she wondered if she hid her alarm. It was a connection to her sister but not one she was expecting. Would an orphan have a sister? An adopted sister? Or was the surname just a coincidence?

"Oh," Vanessa said, wondering if she should have added 'she was sorry to hear that' too.

The restaurant which had been practically empty for the last hour was starting to fill up for the evening session. Malissa looked at her watch. "Hey, I'd better be going. I'll have Mummy *and* Veronica on to me if I'm not careful."

Veronica was the child minder. Malissa reached across the table and touched Vanessa's hand. "It's been lovely to meet you, and do you know? I feel I've known you for ages not just a few hours. First time I've had a girlie chat for a long time. And you only came for an interview."

Malissa was smiling softly at her and Vanessa didn't feel comfortable probing anymore. She smiled back, realising she felt the same way. "Thank you for lunch. It's been wonderful."

"Anyway, let's catch up again soon. Before you go back to France. Come in and sign the papers or something." Malissa retrieved a business card and handed it to her. It displayed her home number too.

"I'd like that very much, Malissa."

Vanessa found it difficult to sleep that night. She had wanted to know more about Henry, about any possible connection to the half-sister she had never met. She was surprised she hadn't asked Malissa outright. Vanessa had learned to be secretive, to be careful of the information she volunteered. Even those she had been close to didn't know everything about her. But this wasn't about her. It wasn't even about some hidden secret, not really. She was simply trying to ascertain what become of the sister she never knew and, surely, telling Malissa the story and explaining her interest in her name, would have been the most natural thing to do? Yet, she hadn't... and she wondered why.

The following Tuesday, Vanessa popped into The Fenner Agency as Malissa had suggested. She had been surprised how much she looked forward to seeing her again, and when they met they greeted one another like good friends. They went for a coffee and Malissa told her about a few jobs she was lining up for her when she returned in the new year.

Henry was home, looking after Lewis, and Malissa was just tidying up a few things in the office before the Christmas holiday. Malissa loved Christmas, loved being with her family and was clearly excited. She was telling Vanessa of their plans when she must have thought about Vanessa and the Christmas she'd be spending in Paris.

"I'm sorry, Ness, I've been going on about Christmas and I didn't think." She squeezed her hand across the table. The first day they met

Vanessa had told Malissa her mother had passed away last year and Vanessa guessed that Malissa felt all her talk about family and Christmas was a little insensitive.

Vanessa smiled. "It's okay."

"So, you'll be spending it with your dad and Gabrielle?"

Malissa had naturally assumed she and Gabrielle had the same father. Vanessa hesitated, thinking how to reply. She didn't want to lie but Malissa saved her the trouble of answering.

"Well, Christmas can also be a reflective time," she said, "I used to wonder if Henry ever thought about his parents. You know, at those times when people talk about family?"

"And did he?" Vanessa asked, aware of the fact that the question may have been more for her own benefit.

"He never knew his parents. He was brought up by an aunt, or someone he called his aunt. She was German, hence the name. He always said she was his family, well, him and Alice I guess, but he doesn't really talk about it. I guess to him that was normal..." Malissa paused, then changed the subject. "Hey, the office is having a bit of a do on Friday night. Why don't you come? You'll meet Brian Fenner. You'll like him."

Vanessa quickly tried to make sense of what Malissa had just told her. Alice, who was Alice? "Well, I'm supposed to be working, but yes if I can I'd like that."

Malissa smiled. "I never asked. Do you have a boyfriend?"

An innocent and natural question. Vanessa had never discussed her sexuality outside any relationship she had been in. It wasn't that she was worried about being judged it was more she regarded it as irrelevant, a subject that would inevitably add another dynamic to a relationship. She considered how she should answer before responding. "Nope. Not interested in that at the moment. Too much trouble and I've got a blossoming dance career to consider."

"Well, I won't tell those boys in the office you're single, they'll be over you like a rash. Hey, you'll have to meet Brad..."

The conversation continued in much the same vein. Light-hearted revelations which allowed people to get to know one another more. Malissa was a lot more forthcoming than Vanessa, but she had little to hide; certainly nothing that a relative stranger would cast judgement upon.

They kissed goodbye this time and hoped they'd see each other again Friday. Henry wouldn't be able to make it.

~

That evening whilst dancing at the Cabaret Club, Vanessa aggravated an old ankle injury and pulled out of the last few routines. If she rested, it should be completely okay in 24 hours.

Although she had still not signed any papers, or given her notice, she knew she would join The Fenner Agency after Christmas. It wasn't what she had planned. Her original meeting with Malissa was intended to be a fact-finding one where she'd ask about any possible connection Malissa had with her sister. Yet when they met earlier today, Vanessa didn't try to steer the conversation in the direction she thought she might have.

She had already gathered Henry was about ten years older than Malissa. That would have made him the same age as Vanessa's missing sister. His company's office was in Kensington and Vanessa had no doubt this was the same office she had already visited. She had also learned he, like her sister, was an orphan. She wanted to ask the name of the orphanage he was adopted from but didn't. She wanted to ask who Alice was, but didn't.

Next time they met, perhaps she would ask Malissa outright. She had to. Or did she? The desire to discover her lost sister niggled at her, but there was something else that troubled her more which she couldn't quite identify. Vanessa was naturally secretive and played her cards close to her chest, whereas Malissa was genuinely open. Telling Malissa about her sister seemed the most obvious thing to do, and it was something other than Vanessa's inherent defensiveness and distrust that told her not to. Something else. Her instant fondness for Malissa perhaps? She trusted her, was drawn to her in a way she'd never been drawn to anyone. And she didn't know why.

# 11

# CHRISTMAS 1986, PARIS

*M*onique was at the apartment when Vanessa returned to Paris on the 22nd December. Although Monique had suggested she would be home for Christmas, Vanessa was still surprised to see her. It had been ten months since they'd last met up and the only conversation they'd had since was in the summer before Vanessa went to London. However, they quickly slipped into the unconditional, no rules friendship they'd always enjoyed. Monique had been telling her about Julien, a man she had met in Monte Carlo and who'd ask her to marry him.

"But even you always said money isn't everything," Vanessa remarked when Monique had finished telling her about the last six months she had spent with her new boyfriend.

"Well, he's fun too. And great in bed."

"Great?"

"For a man, I mean. But not as great as you, of course." Monique kissed Vanessa on the cheek then paraded round the kitchen, opening the cupboard doors whilst she continued her account of her jaunt around the Med with the man she intended to marry.

"They're in the bread bin."

Monique found the packet of chocolate biscuits. Vanessa didn't want one.

"Well it sounds as if you've made up your mind. I'm happy for you." Vanessa smiled.

"You won't miss me?"

Vanessa frowned.

"You always miss me, My Little Kitten," Monique purred. "Now tell me about London..."

~

The Parisian apartment Vanessa and Monique shared belonged to Monique's estranged parents who had agreed she could live there, rent free, for five years. At first, Vanessa and Monique lived together as a couple, but Monique had never been one to stay in one place for long, and during the last two years especially, had only returned to Paris on a handful of occasions.

When she first moved out Vanessa missed her, but as time progressed Vanessa began to enjoy living on her own. She was always aware that living there as she did couldn't last forever, and when Monique told her that her parents wanted to sell the property it didn't surprise her.

Vanessa had spent Christmas Day with Gabrielle and her family, and took the opportunity to tell her younger sister that she had been offered a good job in London and planned to return there early in the new year. Gabrielle was a little upset; she had missed their weekly meetings at the café and feared they would become strangers. Vanessa assured her that would never be the case.

In truth, Vanessa too was apprehensive about leaving Paris and her sister, but Gabrielle was happy, in safe hands and no longer needed her big sister to make sure everything was okay. They saw in the New Year together and spent the next two days shopping and taking in the delights of the city.

Vanessa had also called in on her father before Christmas. He hadn't been well for several months, but she was surprised to see how much he had deteriorated. She'd promised to visit again before she went back to London. She opened the door to his flat announcing her arrival as she walked in. He was sitting in one of the two armchairs that had been there forever. He looked old and frail and Vanessa tried to summon up some sympathy for him, but the return to the place which harboured so many bad memories only served to harden her.

When she saw him last week he talked about the good days with her mother and the two years after Vanessa was born. His memories didn't resonate with hers. Today, at 11am, he was already drunk.

She confirmed she had paid his phone bill, gave him the number of The Fenner Agency and left.

# JANUARY 1987, PARK HOTEL, MANCHESTER

*V*anessa's ankle injury hadn't quite healed as she'd expected and, while she was quite prepared to take on the job Malissa had lined up for her, Malissa thought it wiser to give it a few more weeks. "We look after our assets, Ness," she'd joked.

Instead, Vanessa took on an office role. If she wasn't already impressed by Malissa, what she had witnessed in the last two weeks left her in no doubt as to her employer's ability to run a busy office. She seemed unflappable, taking everything in her stride, and her ability to motivate people was quite remarkable.

Her partner, Brian Fenner, had been off work with a recurrence of gout since Christmas so Malissa busied herself overseeing the publishing side of the business too. Usually, Brian would attend any book launches but, in his absence, Malissa was only too happy to step in and travel up to Manchester in his place. She had asked Vanessa to go with her.

A man called Jack, owner of a string of bookshops in the area, was the last to leave the event. With the hotel bar now empty Vanessa sat down at one of the tables while Malissa phoned Henry.

"I thought he'd never go," Malissa said as she joined Vanessa. "Thank God they didn't have another room available."

"I think he was rather hoping you'd offer him to share yours," Vanessa smiled.

Malissa laughed. "I don't think he buys enough books for that. Anyway, I do believe *Miss* Cozzette, you'll find any romantic overtures were intended for you. Thanks for coming."

Vanessa knew nothing about the publishing industry. In fact, she told Malissa she couldn't remember the last time she'd read a book. It seemed, though, her presence there was to help things runs smoothly and 'use that accent to its best effect'. It had been a long and tiring day.

"Have you heard from your dad?"

"Yesterday. Just the same really."

"You're sure you shouldn't be with him?"

"I'll be there when it matters."

Vanessa had told Malissa that her relationship with her father was far removed from Malissa's relationship with hers. Nonetheless, she thought her comment sounded a little harsh and wished to soften it. "I'm in touch with the doctor. My father refuses to go into hospital, but if it's okay I think I should return soon."

"Anytime Ness, you don't have to worry about that. What about Gabrielle? Does she see him?"

Malissa knew that Vanessa and her sister had different parentage, but she probably thought that Gabrielle enjoyed some kind of relationship, at least, with Vanessa's father.

"Well, Gabrielle's only young and their relationship isn't close. He has friends who call on him." Gabrielle had never met Vanessa's father and Vanessa had nothing but contempt for some of her father's so-called friends but Malissa didn't need to know that. She brought the subject back to the book launch.

"Well, I think it went well," she told Malissa. "I'd never have thought Peter would have written books like that." Peter Arnold was a slight, shy man with a stutter, completely at odds with the brash, macho hero in his novels.

"I think a lot of writers write about who they'd like to be, rather than who they really are. But yes, it went very well."

"Did you speak to Henry? All okay with Lewis?"

Malissa laughed. "Well, he's in my Mum's bad books and I think Veronica gave him a piece of her mind. Apparently, he called her the babysitter."

Henry had been home since Christmas and his idea of looking after

Lewis was often at odds with that of the woman they employed as their childminder.

Malissa recounted the story of her phone call. Her mum and sister-in-law had called by this morning, 'just to check everything was okay'. Henry, who was flying back to New York at the weekend, had spent last evening with his business partner, making sure everything was in order before he left, and was in bed nursing a hangover when his Mother-in-law arrived. "Don't know what all the fuss was about, Miss Keats," he'd said to Malissa on the phone. "Me and Brad were there last night, and Ronny seemed perfectly happy to come round at six."

Whenever Malissa talked about Henry, Vanessa was reminded of the wonderful love they shared. Malissa had hoped that they would spend a lot of time together after Christmas but with Brian away it had proved difficult. Malissa had suggested Vanessa spend a weekend with them soon. She'd like that.

"Do you see your brother often?" Vanessa asked.

"We try and get together at least once a month, usually at my mum's. Carol's really nice, you'd like her. Simon's ok too. For a brother, I mean."

"And Henry, does he see his sister often?"

For a moment, she thought Malissa looked at her a little quizzically.

"I mean, I know he's an orphan," Vanessa continued, "but I just thought...You know, Alice."

"Well, she's not strictly his sister, but Alice, yeah Alice is like a sister to him. Though he says she thinks she's his mother."

Vanessa took a sip of her wine and smiled. Had she just discovered her own half-sister?

"They grew up together," Malissa continued. "She was his aunt's sister's child. She was probably ten when Henry was adopted. You'd love her, daft as a brush at times but so gentle. She's married to Charlie who runs the stud farm in Cornwall where Henry has some of his horses. We'll go there in the summer. It's beautiful."

Vanessa quickly digested Malissa's words. The age gap scuppered the possibility that Alice was her sister. Was she disappointed? She tried not to react.

"So, she's an Ovmeister too?"

"No, she's a Taylor now. I think her maiden name was Grosman or something. Her mother's name. Henry's the only Ovmeister I've ever known. And Lewis of course. Oh, and me."

Vanessa realised she may have been staring at her friend, eager to hear her response, and broke the gaze. She hated the thought that she may have been deceiving Malissa by asking these questions.

"I'd love that. To meet Alice. And go to Cornwall," she said.

"You should meet Henry first. Hey, I've got something to show you." She reached into her handbag and retrieved a photograph. She passed it to Vanessa. It was an aerial view of a piece of coastline.

"My Christmas present from Henry."

Vanessa frowned. "A photograph?"

Malissa smiled and placed a finger on the image. "That, my dear friend, is Söller." She moved her finger a little. "And that is where we're going to build a villa."

# 13

# FEBRUARY 1987, NORTH EAST PARIS

*I*t was almost two years since her mother died, and any resentment Vanessa may have once held for her had gone. Maybe something similar could happen in respect of her feelings towards her father.

He had refused to go into hospital and Vanessa hadn't pushed the point. Neither had she discouraged him from drinking the whisky which eased his pain. He was approaching 70, not terribly old, but he'd had enough of life and yesterday Vanessa had seriously considered his request that she help hasten his departure.

She had talked to Malissa several times since she'd returned to Paris. It was amazing how close they'd become in such a short time and Malissa had even offered to come out to Paris to be with her. Whilst Vanessa could imagine Malissa would like the area where she herself lived, she was sure Malissa would not feel so comfortable in the place Vanessa had spent so much of her childhood.

Malissa's upbringing was so different from hers. Vanessa could feel the bond Malissa shared with her family whenever she mentioned them. She tried to imagine how Malissa would cope if she knew her own father was dying. Perhaps Vanessa should be grateful for having never felt that bond?

The doctor had finally agreed that her father should be transferred to hospital. An ambulance would come that afternoon. The grey dank day was the epitome of so much of her life here, and as she entered his miserable apartment she knew it would be for the last time.

He was sitting in the chair covered by a tartan blanket. For a minute she thought he was dead, but he opened his eyes as she approached him. His whisky bottle was empty, but he hadn't touched the soup she'd left for him yesterday. He raised a smile and tried to make himself more comfortable. Vanessa helped him. She could smell he'd soiled himself. She emptied the ashtray on the table beside him and lit him a cigarette. He offered her one, she refused.

"You're going to hospital this afternoon. They'll make things easier," she said.

He didn't protest. "I'm sorry I've not been the father you deserved. I wish things could have been different." He coughed into his blood-spattered handkerchief.

"So you keep saying," she said. He had been apologising in a similar vein for the last two weeks. "You should go to the bathroom and get changed. Come on, I'll help you."

She helped him into the bathroom and undressed him. She placed his dirty clothes into a bin bag and laid out the ones she had washed on his bed. On the way back to the front room she knocked on the bathroom door to ensure he was okay and then swapped the cushions of the two armchairs. She put the kettle on and washed the soup bowl. She picked up the old photograph on the mantelpiece, as far as she knew the only one in existence of her and her parents together.

It had been many years since he'd revelled in telling her she wasn't his daughter. She could remember him coming home at night and stumbling round the room, spouting off the names of all the men who could have been her father. She had confronted her mother many times over his remarks, but her mother had always maintained he was her father. On her birth certificate, he was. Lawfully, he was. Perhaps it didn't matter what Vanessa felt in her heart. She placed the photograph in her handbag. There was nothing else she needed to take out of the flat.

She felt sorry for him but wondered why she didn't feel sorry *about* him. Had she ever loved him? Did she love him when that photo was taken? Her mother had never loved him, and he seemed completely aware of that. Theirs was a story of little expectation or structure, and their relationship could never have worked. Yet at one time he must have been a good man; there were after all, some things her mother had said that painted him in a much better light. His apparent love for *her* mother, Edith, for example, and the fact that he took *her* daughter in when she was desperate. Vanessa got the distinct impression, however, that his reward for doing so was her mother allowing him to share her bed.

He came out of bathroom.

"There are some clean clothes on the bed," Vanessa said. "You've got pyjamas and a toothbrush in that bag. If there's anything else you want to take, you should put it in. Let me know if you need a hand."

She took off her coat, poured the water into the cup and pulled out the stool from underneath the table. He re-entered the sitting room and, appreciating she'd changed the cushion, sat down.

"Here," she said. "You won't be taking this," and she handed him the whisky she'd brought with her. "And try not to wet yourself before they get here."

"You're a good girl, Vanessa. Despite... Despite... everything."

It had just gone midday. She'd been told he would be collected by 2pm. She sat at the table and watched him pour his whisky. He lit another cigarette.

"So, you want to find Emma?" he suddenly asked, his voice less raspy having been soothed by the alcohol.

"Emma?"

"Emma Ovmeister," he said seriously

Vanessa looked at him. Was he talking about her older sister?

"In the drawer." He pointed to the sideboard.

Vanessa got up and crossed the room, her mind a little confused and her stomach tightening.

"The second drawer."

She opened it. Amongst the junk and papers was a red biscuit tin that wasn't there before. She lifted it from the drawer and handed it to him. He sifted through the contents and handed her an envelope. She sat back down and opened it.

She unfolded the newspaper clipping. It was from an English newspaper and beneath the headline *Miss Ovmeister delights the audience on the last night of the concert* was a photograph of a woman playing the violin.

She began reading the text.

"It was sent to your mother ten years ago", he said.

She stopped reading and looked at him wondering what he saw in her eyes. Something was building inside her, but she wasn't sure what.

"She wasn't here of course," he added. "Read the letter."

Vanessa unfolded the other piece of paper and read;

*Dear Anna,*

*I don't know if you'll get this letter or if you remember me but I hope you are well and have found a good life. It took me some time to get over you and I was angry, but I'm married now with two children. I've thought about you a lot and what may have become of you. I found this in the newspaper. The girl playing the violin is named Emma Ovmeister and she is 22 years old. I don't know if you're still there or whether you ever managed to find her and, if so, this is not news but, just in case, I thought I'd send it. I loved you and couldn't have it on my conscience.*

*Tom*

There was no address or any further clue to the sender's identity, but Vanessa was sure she remembered her mother mentioning a 'Tommy' in the story she had told her. The envelope was stamped London E16 and dated 24th August 1974.

Vanessa raised her eyes and stared at her father. His face was expressionless.

"You never gave it to her," she said amazed at how calm she sounded. It wasn't a question.

He reached for the bottle and poured another glass. "We weren't together then." He downed the whisky and interpreting her expression added, "and, yes, Vanessa I regret it."

"And you give it to me now to ease your conscience." Any empathy that may have been building earlier had dissipated.

"Vanessa, you are a strong woman. I no more deserve your love than I did your mother's. But that's how it is. I hope you find your sister and in doing so find some happiness out of such a sad story."

It was a statement bordering on humility and so far removed from anything she could recall hearing from him before.

She laughed out loud, stood up and walked to the window. She looked out over the road she used to play in as a child. It hadn't changed, except there were more cars parked there now. The houses were shabby, just like this one. A dog barked and she wondered if it had been abandoned. What a shit place to live.

She turned to him. His face had taken on a look of concern. His weak, sorry eyes looked at her, trying to gauge a reaction. She put the newspaper clipping in her pocket and held his stare for a second before retrieving the blanket that hung over the back of the other chair. She placed it over him and kissed him lightly on the forehead.

He found her hand and squeezed it, and for a moment she wanted to hug him. For a moment she desperately wished he was a decent father. He let go of her hand before she could pull it away.

She put on her coat and picked up her bag, feeling his eyes on her back. She paused and breathed in before turning to him. "They'll be here in an hour," she said. "Take care, Dad."

She closed the door behind her and rested against it. Her mother should have seen that letter. Her father should not have kept it from her. Was she angry? Surely she should be, but she just felt sad. Sad for him and sad for her mother. Sad for their sorry lives.

Two girls who should have been in school came through the doors chatting excitedly as they started up the stairs. They looked at Vanessa, wondering what she was doing there, and giggled as they passed her on their way to the next flight up. Would they escape here? Did they have a chance of something better? If so, they'd have to harden up.

Vanessa descended the steps, the *click* of her boots echoing up into the stairwell that was once so familiar to her.

# 14

# PARIS MARCH 1987, PHILIPPE'S HOUSE

*V*anessa was pleased Gabrielle had more readily accepted the idea of her sister moving to London than she thought she may have done. She was 13, had decent parents and a wide circle of friends. She'd be fine. Gabrielle still enthused about them living together one day, holding on to the many conversations they'd had over the years when things weren't so settled for her. They would keep in regular contact and perhaps during the school holidays Gabrielle could even come to England.

Vanessa had walked Gabrielle home, kissed her goodnight, and was now sitting in the kitchen with Philippe. She did not expect to see Gabrielle anywhere near as often as she had these last thirteen years and she just wanted to ensure she would be looked after as she imagined.

Vanessa still had most of the 'hush money' from her affair with Etienne and had deposited a significant sum in trust for her sister, to be accessed when she was old enough. She had also opened a post office account for her into which she would transfer monthly pocket money. Philippe was not poor and had always provided adequately for his daughter, but Vanessa had told her sister that the pocket money would come in handy. There was no need for Gabrielle to tell her father about the arrangement.

Philippe was 18 years older than Vanessa. She liked him because he had looked after Gabrielle. She also empathised with the unenviable task he once had in trying to control her mother. It made her laugh, the way she'd catch him looking at her sometimes, and she would usually dress more modestly when she visited, but her unbuttoned blouse this evening was to ensure he paid her sufficient attention. She was leaving for England tomorrow and wanted him left in no doubt that she would always be enquiring in respect of her sister's welfare.

"So, you're giving up your flat entirely?" Philippe asked.

She had told Monique she was moving to London and wouldn't be needing the flat they had shared for the last five years. Monique didn't need it permanently either, but she didn't have to give it up until the end of the year, so maybe they'd keep it for the time being; after all, her parents were still paying the bills. Vanessa would leave some belongings there and would still, for the time being, keep hold of a key.

"Seems pointless paying rent when I won't be there. I can always check into a hotel when I visit."

"Well, there'll always be a spare bedroom for you here."

"I didn't think of that," she lied. "That's very kind of you." She smiled and touched his hand. "I'll miss her," she added.

"And she'll miss you. We all will."

She held his gaze until he looked away.

"Your mother would be very proud of you, Vanessa."

She wanted to laugh but didn't and returned the subject to Gabrielle. "Philippe, you have been a good influence on Brie. I know my mother wasn't the most reliable person in the world and I'm so grateful knowing she's well looked after." He smiled, seemingly delighted at the flattery. "You have my address and the number of the agency I will be working at," she added.

He nodded. He was still holding the piece of paper she had written on.

Vanessa continued. "If there's anything she needs that you can't provide please let me know. Now, I must be going."

"Do you need a lift?"

"You know, Philippe? It's such a nice evening, I'll think I'll walk up to the terminus and catch the bus. But thank you. Say 'bye' to Maggie and your mother for me."

She stood up. He followed her into the hallway and helped her on with her jacket. She kissed him on the cheek, bid him *au revoir* and left. He didn't shut the door until she was out of sight.

Her father's death had delayed her move to England. It hadn't surprised her that he had left a myriad of unpaid bills and unresolved matters, but he did have a small life insurance policy amongst his papers that paid for his burial. Other than a sister her mother once mentioned, she had never known whether he had family and only she attended the simple funeral service she had arranged. Once again she was reminded that the word 'family' was alien to her.

She had kept in touch with Malissa, warmed by the support she so naturally gave. She had even sent Vanessa flowers.

Malissa had enquired about her ankle and, satisfied she was okay, had secured her six weeks' work with the London Contemporary Dance Company. Since she hadn't danced professionally for more than three months, Malissa had also arranged for her to attend a dance school to get her to an appropriate fitness level beforehand. No wonder she was successful and admired.

Vanessa had not asked Malissa about the woman she now knew as Emma Ovmeister; perhaps that was a question for Henry. She missed Malissa and that still bothered her. She couldn't remember having ever missed anybody, really. There was surely no sexual attraction? She hadn't detected that from Malissa at all, and she was sure Malissa had little idea of her new friend's sexuality, but there was something that drew them together. Perhaps it was a subconscious curiosity about their differences. Whatever it was, she looked forward to seeing her, to getting back to work and embarking on something new. Something softer and kinder.

She lit a cigarette and, beneath the light of the bus shelter, studied the picture of Emma. She looked forward to meeting her one day. She was leaving behind a life in France, a life full of turbulence and events that had left their mark. Other than Gabrielle, all that had bound her to Paris had gone. She was alone but, in reality, she always had been. She stamped out her cigarette, folded the newspaper clipping into her bag and boarded the bus.

## 15

JUNE 1987, DELAHAY HOUSE, SURREY

*V*anessa had been in London for two months. Immediately after her arrival, she had reported to The Fenner Agency and was pleased to discover everything had been set out as Malissa had told her. She attended a dance school for the first two weeks to get her into shape, and last month was assigned to the London Contemporary Dance Company who supplied backup dancers to several West End shows.

The chief choreographer there was impressed by Vanessa. In truth, all the routines she was required to learn were well within her capabilities, and when she wasn't required on stage, she assisted him in teaching some of the less experienced dancers. Fenner's didn't have a dance school, but Malissa had hinted at the feasibility of establishing one.

She had considered looking for new accommodation, but since she had been away the landlord had refurbished the building Dawn and Jenny lived in and she now occupied one of the two bedrooms on the top floor. The other was reserved for a businessman who spent only one week in four in London, so she effectively also had exclusive access to the newly refurbished bathroom.

The shared kitchen and living room were on the ground floor and this suited her too; it wasn't unusual for her flatmates to entertain visitors and her room was far enough away for her not to be disturbed by any late-night revelry. Dawn had made no mention of the night they spent together before Christmas and they remained good friends.

The newspaper clipping her father had given her yielded few clues to the fate of the woman, Emma, who Vanessa didn't doubt was her older half-sister. She had scoured the article many times looking for a lead, forming her own image of the woman from the profile of her face that rested on the violin. She was, Vanessa felt, truly beautiful, angelic even, and her blindness, that perceived vulnerability, stirred great emotion in Vanessa. Finally being able to put a name to her probable sister hadn't, however, yielded any more information about her.

There was no specific date on the cutting or indeed in the letter from Tom, which made searching for related articles regarding the concert difficult. She still hadn't mentioned anything to Malissa and was certain that her friend knew nothing of an Emma Ovmeister. It was, of course, totally feasible that Malissa and Henry simply shared a surname with her and nothing else, but Vanessa had still not discovered any other Ovmeisters in England. Vanessa wondered if her sister had, as her mother had seemingly thought quite possible, ended up in Germany.

On one occasion, when she dipped into her bag, Vanessa considered presenting the newspaper cutting to Malissa, but something powerful stirred inside her telling her to hold back. She wasn't sure what had made her suddenly feel that way, but realised she had decided it was Henry, who she still hadn't met, who was the person who could answer her questions.

Vanessa hadn't yet been able to return to Paris. She missed Gabrielle but usually managed to phone her twice a week and was pleased she seemed to be doing fine. The people Vanessa met in London were new people, people who had no knowledge of her past. She had no desire to get into an intimate relationship and had even bought a cheap 'engagement' ring to excuse unwanted advances. Malissa raised an eyebrow when Vanessa explained its intention but didn't ask anything more. Unusual, perhaps, for such close friends, Vanessa and Malissa rarely talked about sex, and Vanessa wondered if Malissa had been told about or had guessed, her sexuality. It didn't seem to matter and their relationship continued to flourish, as did her enjoyment of her new life in London.

~

She had met Malissa in Knightsbridge this morning to do some shopping before spending the weekend at her and Henry's house. Henry wouldn't be there, but Vanessa looked forward to meeting Lewis who she had learned so much about.

Whilst Henry and Malissa's house was large and beautifully-situated in the countryside, it was by no means pretentious. It was warm, homely and welcoming; an obvious reflection of their success in business yet it yielded a humility that suggested neither took anything for granted. It was a family home and Vanessa immediately felt comfortable.

"Delahay?" Malissa repeated in response to Vanessa's question of how the house was named. "Delores Delahay. Remember I told you how me and Henry met at Goodwood? Well, Delores was the horse he was running there and later, when she won the Oaks, Henry suggested we use the prize money to buy this place. Seemed appropriate to name it after her."

"Must have been an important race?"

"I think he also won a fair bit from the bookies. Anyway, I suggested the name and I think he liked the idea."

Malissa picked up the phone and called Veronica, who was looking after Lewis. She would be bringing him home in ten minutes.

"I can't wait for you to meet him. Now, let's have a cup of tea and then I'll show you where you're sleeping, and while I'm putting these clothes away you can choose which movie we watch tonight."

Vanessa went into the sitting room. Malissa often mentioned family to her. Perhaps she thought she had missed out all these years and was only too happy to share hers.

Malissa and Henry had a lot of videos.

Vanessa had never regarded herself as even remotely maternal and was surprised by how much she enjoyed the time she and Malissa spent with Lewis. She was also surprised by how natural a mother Malissa was and understood why she struggled to balance her work commitments with those of being a parent. "I wish I could spend more time with him, Ness," she repeated on several occasions

Veronica, their child minder, was 45 years old with three grown-up children and a seven-year-old who came along as a bit of surprise. She had been the Ovmeister's housekeeper before Lewis was born and Malissa had clearly built up sufficient trust in her to allow her to look after Lewis. Vanessa had no doubt Malissa valued the woman highly and, whilst she thought they might not necessarily socialise, she received the distinct impression that Malissa took a keen interest in Veronica and her family's welfare.

Malissa joked that Lewis was hypnotised by Vanessa's accent. "Like most men, no doubt," she said as she put Lewis to bed.

When Malissa had finished reading to Lewis, Vanessa found herself singing *Frère Jacques* to him. Malissa looked in from the doorway of the bedroom, smiling for some moments before she went downstairs. As Vanessa left the sleeping Lewis to join her friend in the living room, she again felt that urge to question her own more jaundiced view of friends and family life.

"I think he likes you," smiled Malissa as Vanessa sat down on the sofa.

"He's very lovely, Malissa. You should feel truly proud."

Malissa looked at her for a second before saying she was delighted with her choice of video, but before they watched it she wanted to know more about her time at the Moulin Rouge. "You said you sang a bit, Ness, but I'm sure it wasn't *Frère Jacques*, as lovely as that was."

Vanessa smiled. "No, it wasn't. I think it was a different bedtime serenade *that* audience wanted."

Vanessa was genuinely pleased Malissa wanted to know about her work in France but spent several minutes convincing her that although she sang as part of the chorus line, she was not the star attraction. Her solo singing career to date was limited to late-night appearances in clubs in order to supplement her income from her daytime job, and those clubs were far removed from the venue Malissa so enthused about.

Vanessa was purposely vague, as she had been on several previous occasions in responding to some of Malissa's more searching questions. She managed not to lie, but always tried to steer the subject back to her experience and knowledge of the theatre and mentioning the Moulin Rouge always did the trick. Sometimes, however, Malissa would ask a question which Vanessa wanted to answer more truthfully, to share a feeling or a story, but she felt unable to. She sensed Malissa wanted to believe that her life in France, although more difficult than her own, was a reasonably happy one. So, the tale of a young girl who had a love and talent for dancing, and who had managed to find a job doing what she loved, was the story she stuck to.

When Malissa got up to fetch a second bottle of wine, Vanessa followed her, stood at the kitchen door and gave her a few bars of *La Vie en Rose*. Not at full volume, but with sufficient zest to satisfy her friend's curiosity and hopefully move the subject on from her singing career.

"That's so sexy. You can really sing, Ness. I'll put that on your port. I'd love to know what you wore when you sang that one."

"Not a lot!" Vanessa laughed.

Malissa put the video into the player. Vanessa looked at the photos on the mantlepiece, most of which were of Malissa and her husband and Lewis. "So, who's Delores Delahay? That definitely sounds a French name?" she said.

"Sorry, Ness?" Malissa said, making herself comfortable on the sofa.

"Delores Delahay. Henry's horse, and your house is named after her, so I was just wondering if she was a French woman I should have heard of."

Malissa smiled. "You know, Ness. When I first met Henry, that day at the races, I thought she was his wife. 'So, Delores Delahay is your wife?' I asked him. 'Two too many legs for me,' he said. Then I thought she must have been a past girlfriend. But no, apparently she was someone who his aunt knew during the war and he obviously named the horse in honour of her."

"A French woman who was his German aunt's friend during the war. That's intriguing."

"Yeah, I guess it is, but if there's one thing I've learned about horses, they do have some peculiar names. So Nature, another one of Henry's horses, was Delores's mother and named after his aunt. It's an anagram of Aunt Rose."

"I think he was very fond of Aunt Rose."

Malissa paused the video. "I've no doubt he was, Ness. She would have been quite old when she adopted him, more like a grandmother but I guess that's the nearest thing to a mother he ever knew... It's a funny thing about Henry – he rarely talks about his past and I never push him. He says it's the here and now that's important. I have asked him whether he ever thinks about his real parents, but I guess... I don't know. It's hard for me to

understand a life without my parents, they mean the world and if I lost..."
She interrupted herself and reached across the sofa, grimacing the way she
did when she thought she'd said something insensitive. "Sorry Ness, I
didn't think."

Vanessa smiled and squeezed her hand. "Although mine are gone, I
think you know I was never really that close to them. I miss knowing
they're there, but maybe because they were absent so much I'd already got
used to being without them."

She had told Malissa her parents had separated when she was young
and that they shared custody. In truth, she would often go months without
seeing either, but Malissa had probably formed her own, kinder opinion, of
how Vanessa was brought up.

Malissa poured the wine and handed her a glass. "Yeah, I guess we all
have different childhoods. I dread to think how I'd cope when, you know,
that time comes."

Vanessa touched Malissa's arm and they both smiled. Unlike herself,
Malissa would prefer to think of childhood and parenting as a wonderful
part of life. Such different upbringings. "Well, *c'est la vie*. Past is past and
now is now," Malissa added and raised her glass. "And cheers to Delores
Delahay, whoever she was."

"Delores Delahay!" Vanessa responded

"You'll have to meet her."

Vanessa raised her eyebrows.

"The horse. She's retired now and lives in Cornwall. With Alice.
You'll meet her when we go." Malissa pushed 'play' on the video. "And as
for Henry's past girlfriends," she continued, "I don't think there was
anyone serious at all. Unbelievable really. In fact, he told me he'd only ever
been in love once before we met and that was when he was 14!"

"And no horse with her name?" joked Vanessa.

Malissa smiled. "Broke his heart at such a tender age he vowed never
to love again. Her name was Emma... I like that name. No, I imagine he
was a bit of a lad, but I'm glad he doesn't talk about it really."

Vanessa was sure her eyes had suddenly widened and that she was
staring at Malissa. She let out a nervous laugh and reached for the crisps,
desperately trying to suppress any reaction to Malissa's casual mention of
the name that had been haunting her for the last few months.

A myriad of ludicrous thoughts invaded her mind and she pushed them away. Malissa was looking at the television. "Typical men," Vanessa said eventually, not sure the words were either audible or apt.

Malissa smiled and turned up the volume. "I love this film," she said drawing up her legs and sitting sideways. "Good choice."

Vanessa looked at the TV, slowly gathering herself together, grateful that the opening sequence warranted Malissa's full attention. They were fully three minutes into the film before Malissa turned to her, her face happy, innocent and beautiful, "Lay down, Ness. Make yourself comfortable. And be a doll and pass me the crisps."

Vanessa smiled and handed her the bowl. On the TV, the hero was running for his life in an ancient underground temple after disturbing some sacred secret, but all Vanessa could see was a beautiful blind woman holding a violin and smiling as she acknowledged the rapturous applause of the audience. And as those visions became clearer, she realised the man in the black tie and applauding so enthusiastically was Henry... Malissa's husband Henry.

Malissa took a handful of crisps, thanked her and smiled, and Vanessa realised how much she truly loved being in her company. That strange feeling, that sixth sense that had always nagged her, that her sister was not a subject she should discuss with Malissa, now shouted loudly and she thought she was beginning to understand why.

Vanessa put the bowl back on the table, grateful the shock to her system was subsiding. She stretched out on the sofa and took another look at Malissa who was already engrossed in the film and smiling softly. Vanessa hoped nothing would ever threaten to extinguish the spark in those beautiful, innocent eyes.

She rolled onto her side to watch the video and laughed with Malissa when Harrison Ford fell into the lake. She wondered if Malissa saw anything of Indiana Jones in her husband. Perhaps she'd ask her later.

# PART II

*Monique*

*I danced on the stage as a child*
*The dancer the mirror of me*
*But as I studied the dancer's reflection*
*I doubted the dancer was me*

# 16

# SEPTEMBER 1987, PARIS

## MONIQUE'S APARTMENT

*R*eturning to Paris and meeting up with Monique was like taking a step back into a previous existence. The streets, the buildings, the clubs, even her friend were just the same, yet something was so vastly different.

Vanessa had loved the last six months of her life. She had made new friends in London, gained recognition as a dancer there, and had forged such a special bond with Malissa. Monique was her great friend in a different time; her mentor, someone who had helped her survive. Malissa, so different from her, was unwittingly showing her how to live.

Vanessa had known Monique for six years. It was she who showed her a road to independence, she who had encouraged her to seduce Etienne when he was barely 17 and later extort money from his father. "Believe me, Vanessa," she'd said, "he's rich, knows a good deal when he sees one, and would be happy to pay you to stay away from his son." Monique was right, of course, like she had been right about many things, and Vanessa, who felt this would be the last time the two of them would share a bed, would always be grateful to have known her.

She came into the bedroom, handed Vanessa a coffee and opened the curtains slightly before sitting on the bed beside her. The light from outside filtered into the room. Monique was already dressed and kissed her gently. "I'll miss you," she said.

Vanessa sat up and pulled the duvet up over her breasts. "And I'll miss you too. Do you think we'll see each other again?"

Monique smiled. "I think, Vanessa, you always ask that, and we always seem to bump into one another at some time. I'll write when I'm settled."

"But you don't know where I live."

"I'll just write to that agency again. Or fax them, 'for the attention of *My Little Kitten*'. Unless that Malissa of yours would get jealous."

"She's straight. I told you that," Vanessa smiled.

"But you said she was lovely, so I'm assuming you'll work your magic."

How different they were, Monique and Malissa. As physically attractive as Malissa was, Vanessa had never entertained a desire to sleep with her. Monique wouldn't understand that.

"She's just a friend."

"Just?"

"You know what I mean."

"Have you got your stuff together?"

Part of the reason Vanessa had come back to Paris was to collect the belongings she had accumulated over the years. There wasn't much and she nodded to the single suitcase in the corner. "I'll collect it tomorrow on the way to the airport. And keep a key for good luck."

"So little baggage to take to London. That's good," Monique said slowly, and Vanessa understood the double meaning of her statement. "The van comes Thursday," she added with a snap. "Then Mummy and Daddy can have their house back."

"Won't you miss it?"

"Compared to the one in Monty? What do you think?" She kissed her again. "I'll miss us."

"But won't forget?"

Monique studied her for a few seconds then smiled and reached behind Vanessa's neck. "Here," she said when she had fastened the pendant.

Vanessa looked down and clasped her hand around the ruby. "Won't Julien ask where it is?"

"I'll tell him I lost it. I'm sure it's insured."

The two women looked at each other for a moment before Vanessa threw her arms around Monique. "Are you sure it's what you want?" she whispered.

She felt Monique's arms tighten before she kissed her on her forehead and broke the embrace.

"Yes, I think it is. He's fun and maybe it's time to settle down. But if I ever need real passion. I'll call you."

Vanessa smiled. "Be happy," she said as Monique stood up.

"You too, My Little Kitten. And be safe." She headed out of the bedroom but paused at the door and looked back. "My address is on the table. *Au revoir Mon Petit Chaton.*" She blew her a kiss and ten seconds later Vanessa heard the front door close. *Au revoir?* She knew it was goodbye.

Vanessa had slept with many men and several women. She'd loved none. Only with Monique had sex felt something other than a physical act. Perhaps they were not so dissimilar. Neither outwardly exuded affection and neither had ever said 'I love you'. There was no jealousy between them nor any judgement, and Vanessa was certain Monique's wish that each of them found happiness was sincere.

Monique had been the only person Vanessa had ever confided in, yet she hadn't told her that Malissa mentioned the name Emma. She wondered why? Had she grown so fond of her friend from England that she would never divulge anything that could possibly cause her harm? She recalled Monique's comments last night as they lay there, talking about their futures: "Perhaps it's her purity you're attracted to," she'd said.

It was nearly 8am. Vanessa had arranged to take Gabrielle shopping later, and afterwards have dinner with Philippe and his family before returning to London tomorrow.

She got up, went into the kitchen and poured more coffee. She noticed the piece of paper Monique had written an address on and wondered if she would take it with her; would Monique expect her to? Would she want her to?

She entered the bathroom and turned on the bath taps. Tipping the remainder of the lavender bubble bath into the running water she smiled to herself, remembering the time they had shared a bath in Monique's parents' more sumptuous bathroom in their house in Dinard.

She checked herself in the mirror. The necklace was truly beautiful. A drape of deep red stones set in silver, supporting a larger ruby in the centre. She didn't doubt it was genuine and would have cost as much as Vanessa could earn in six months. She unfastened it and walked back into the bedroom, placing it on the bed. She looked at her suitcase and smiled, mentally comparing the ruby coloured jewellery set she had put in there last night; the one Monique had bought her on her 15th birthday; the one Mademoiselle Lauren had forbidden her to wear.

# 17

## APRIL 1981, PARIS

### MADEMOISELLE LAUREN'S RESIDENCE

"*I*t's very pretty, Vanessa and I'm sure we'll be able to find someone to mend it," Mademoiselle Lauren said replacing the necklace on the dresser. "Or maybe we could buy you another one. You'll be earning good money for a girl of your age."

Mademoiselle Lauren smiled as she looked down on her, switched off the lamp and moved towards the window. She peered out. Usually so authoritative when she was teaching, her voice was now soft and a little quivery. Her shadow was dark against the grey of the evening, but intermittently illuminated whenever the neon sign of the Eiffel Tower on the building opposite went through its cycle.

"Ah, a Paris night in springtime," she added, and, with a look over her shoulder and in an even softer voice, whispered, "I heard about those nasty boys."

Vanessa didn't react and after several seconds Mademoiselle Lauren returned her gaze to the street below. She continued her murmurings, enthusing about Paris and reminding Vanessa how lucky she was to have been chosen to dance at one of the city's most prestigious venues and in a ballet which was sure to be a great success.

Then she reminisced about her own childhood and how she wished she'd had a teacher who would have looked after her; had the opportunities that existed today. But her childhood ambitions were scuppered by the effects of the war and a time when artistic talent was so easily overlooked.

Vanessa guessed her mother had told her dance teacher about her being raped. Two boys, just before Christmas. Maybe she told her when Mademoiselle Lauren asked her to sign the letter requesting that Vanessa be excused from school. Funny, Vanessa didn't think anyone cared if she went to school or not. She certainly didn't.

She wondered how many francs Mademoiselle Lauren had to give her mother to get her to sign.

Mademoiselle had also called on her father, suggesting that Vanessa live with her for the duration of the assignment. "It would be so much more convenient," she'd told him.

Vanessa doubted her father gave a shit where she lived, but when she was packing some clothes he did ask her a little about the ballet she'd been chosen to star in. As it turned out, she needn't have packed anything. Mademoiselle had bought her a couple of entirely new outfits. The opera company must have been paying the dance school well.

Vanessa wondered if her teacher's empathy about 'those nasty boys' was genuine. Maybe, but it didn't matter. Strangely, apart from a few cuts and bruises that took a while to heal, Vanessa had been able to shut out the memory of the ordeal more effectively than she thought. Since then she'd also had sex with Etienne, but he was gentle and it took place at the house he shared with his friends.

Monique had told her it was wrong and she should value herself more; but Monique had expectations and came from a completely different part of the city, and as much as Vanessa liked her, Monique would never understand some things. She was secretly pleased, however, that Monique had confronted one of the boys who raped her and even got the police involved. It was the first time Vanessa could remember anybody sticking up for her.

Three weeks ago, though, Monique had moved with her family to Brittany. Vanessa missed her and hoped she would see her again. The necklace she bought her before she left was precious to Vanessa, but Mademoiselle was right to say she shouldn't wear it whilst she was dancing.

Mademoiselle Lauren was still speaking. Vanessa lay on her side, half listening, but knew the words were just a prelude to another act. She was summing up. "How lucky it was, Vanessa, that your mother brought you to me all those years ago. This is surely just the beginning."

Mademoiselle drew the curtains and fell silent for a moment before circling around to the other side of the bed. She had recently showered and was wearing a dressing gown. The aroma of her perfume strengthened slightly as she slipped out of the gown and sat on the edge of the bed. Vanessa laid still on her side, focusing her attention on the faint light that filtered through the gap in the curtains, guessing when the sign would light up.

"Those nasty boys," she repeated. "So rough. No idea of the tenderness of a woman." She placed a hand gently on Vanessa's head, trailing her fingers through her hair, before laying down behind her.

Mademoiselle Lauren breathed in deeply as she slipped a hand under the duvet, gently stroking Vanessa's thighs before manoeuvring it so it rested on top of her pubic hair. Vanessa parted her legs a little, but lay still, allowing Mademoiselle to explore her. She wondered if this time she'd actually dare to put a finger inside her. Her dance teacher rolled slightly so she could comfortably touch her own sex too. And then the heat of her dance teacher's quickening breath on the back of her neck, and her pathetic attempts to suppress that grunting noise she always made as she brought herself to orgasm.

Before she got up to go to her own bedroom, Mademoiselle Lauren reminded Vanessa they had a busy day tomorrow and that she should now be able to concentrate fully. She also repeated that she knew Vanessa could keep secrets and that she was safe here. Vanessa said nothing. The sign had lit up 23 times, two less than she'd guessed.

Mademoiselle Lauren had been good to Vanessa over the years. Dancing was the one thing that was stable in Vanessa's life and the one thing she loved. Her teacher had always encouraged her, keeping her on despite the back log of tuition fees. The bedroom that Vanessa would be sleeping in for the next six months was warm and cosy and the house so much nicer than any other place she could live. If Mademoiselle felt it necessary to visit her from time to time to remind her just how safe she was, she'd tolerate that.

# 18

# AUGUST 1981, PARIS

## THE OFFICES OF THE PARISIAN OPERA AND BALLET COMPANY

"Of course, dear, you will have to be careful what you eat. Certainly, none of those hamburgers you children seem to lust after."

Vanessa wondered whether Madam Lagrange had ever actually danced before. She also imagined she ran a tab at the Wimpy Bar down the road. Perhaps they should have met there!

"She's a good girl," Mademoiselle Lauren replied, answering for Vanessa as she had done for the last half hour, "and dancing is her life. She keeps strictly to our diet, a model pupil. Dancing is her life," she repeated and took Vanessa's hand.

The two women continued to discuss Vanessa's future. As far as Mademoiselle Lauren was concerned accepting a place at the Academy was a foregone conclusion, a no-brainer; it was just the details that needed ironing out. Vanessa wasn't quite old enough to look after her own money, but if her earnings continued to be deposited into the dance school Mademoiselle Lauren would personally ensure that her bills were paid and that she had a little pocket money. By the time she was eighteen she may well have accumulated a sum that many young adults would envy.

*"Things weren't good at home..."* Both women had discussed that at length, empathising profusely, and Madame Lagrange, who it seemed had known her dance teacher for ever, thought how kind it was of Mademoiselle Lauren to allow Vanessa to stay 'as long as she needed to' at her

wonderful house; less than ten minutes' walk away. "She's no trouble at all Madame Lagrange. I hardly know she's there."

Sometimes Vanessa just wanted to laugh.

In truth, Vanessa had enjoyed the last few months. Four days a week she had been one of the principal dancers in a Pierre Demetro adaption of the 'The Ballerina' – a ballet predominantly comprised of children. In the ballet she played a thirteen-year-old orphan who escaped poverty through her ability to dance. The irony was not lost on her.

It was a successful show and they had extended its run for another six months but, at 15, Vanessa – who now more resembled a young woman than a child – would have to make way for another dancer. Despite Mademoiselle's overtures, neither Izzy or Nadine, younger students at her dance school, were considered suitable for the role and Vanessa's replacement had been chosen from elsewhere.

Vanessa's performances hadn't gone unnoticed and several establishments had offered her a placement at their colleges. She had also been approached independently by Dominic Chard, an agent, offering her an audition for the part of Giselle in one of Paris's longest running ballets. Dominic didn't realise she was only 15 but told her to keep in touch. Vanessa also gleaned, from her discussions with him, that by the time she was 18, unless she starved herself, she would probably be a little too 'full in the figure' for some of those leading ballerina roles. According to Mademoiselle Lauren the world was Vanessa's oyster, but her dance teacher was adamant that the Parisian Opera and Ballet Company offered 'her star pupil' the greatest opportunity.

Vanessa was not surprised, nor did she care, that neither of her parents came to see her. She was pleased, however, that Philippe had brought Gabrielle on more than one occasion. Monique, during a week's stay in Paris, saw her photo in the paper and Vanessa was delighted when she came. They met up afterwards and Monique suggested she come and holiday with her in Brittany when the show finished it run. Vanessa had saved much of the allowance that Mademoiselle Lauren had given her and had more than enough for the train fare.

Vanessa knew she was her dance teacher's greatest asset and suggesting to her that she needed more rest in order to give her best performance on stage had seemed to stir her conscience. The frequency of her visits to her bedroom had lessened over the last two months. She held little malice towards the woman for touching her. She never felt threatened, understanding the encounters simply involved her laying with her while she touched herself. Somehow, Vanessa always felt that she herself had the control. She let it happen because it suited her; because it gave her a decent place to live and days doing something she enjoyed. Or was she rewarding Mademoiselle Lauren for placing so much faith in her dancing ability? Or was it simply that she was offering herself as payment for the fees her mother never paid?

Tonight, whilst Mademoiselle Lauren enthused about Vanessa's dancing career, she would ask her for more money, money that was rightly hers. If what she offered did not meet Vanessa's expectations, she would steal it from the tin she kept in the cupboard. Vanessa would be dancing for nobody in the near future and tomorrow she would travel to Brittany.

She continued to listen to the two women nonchalantly discussing her future. The little she said was designed only to massage their over-inflated egos. Were all middle-aged, middle class women this stupid?

# 19

# LATE AUGUST 1987, DELAHAY HOUSE

*J*uly had been a busy month for Vanessa. She had often worked seven days a week on the two productions the London Dance School had assigned to her. She had booked a week off in September to return to Paris to sort out the flat she and Monique shared, but Malissa insisted she spend the weekend with her before she went.

They had planned to go to Cornwall earlier in the month, but work commitments scuppered those plans. Henry would have been there too. Vanessa had still not met Malissa's husband and had to hide her disappointment they weren't able to go. Ever since Malissa had mentioned the name Emma, she was adamant there was a connection to Henry and was desperate to discover just what it was.

Surely the Emma that Malissa referred to as Henry's teenage crush was Vanessa's older half-sister. It was too much of a coincidence for her to be anything else. Last month Vanessa had subtly steered a conversation with Malissa around to the name of the orphanage from which Henry was adopted. Malissa couldn't recall but remembered it was in the East End of London and that it had long since been demolished. Vanessa felt sure if she prompted 'St Mary's?' Malissa would have confirmed it.

The only thing that had changed in Vanessa's mind was the relationship Henry and Emma shared. If they were adopted at the same time would they would have grown up as brother and sister? Or did that relationship change? A teenage crush Malissa had intimated or had she misunderstood? That photo at the Royal Albert Hall. Emma was 22 and though the image of the man in the black tie was not face-on she could easily imagine it to be a younger version of Henry. But what happened to Emma, and what was her relationship with Henry today?

Keeping her secret from Malissa pricked her conscience and whenever Vanessa was with her great friend, which was quite frequently, she had to push any thoughts of Emma aside. Something told her that whatever she believed about Emma and Henry would need confirmation from Henry and not Malissa. And there was, of course, the chance that she was completely wrong.

Vanessa had grown fond of Delahay House and had visited Malissa and Lewis several times. Business commitments meant Henry spent more time in the States than he did in England, so whenever he did come home, the time he shared with his wife and child was precious. Perhaps that was why Vanessa hadn't met him yet.

The garden of Delahay House faced southwest and Malissa and Vanessa often spent evenings sitting outside on the patio, drinking wine and talking as the sun went down. It was peaceful, far removed from the bustle of London's West End and a completely different world from the Parisian slum where Vanessa spent so much of her youth. It had been a perfect summer's day and the sun was an hour away from setting.

"Just imagine the sea down there, beyond the hedge, really blue, and imagine that side of the hedge is the orange grove, and where the cherry trees are is a little beach. More stones than sand, but you can't have everything," Malissa said as she uncorked the bottle.

They had been talking about the home in Majorca that Malissa and Henry planned to build.

"It does sound perfect," Vanessa smiled.

Malissa had shown Vanessa the plans and she could easily share Malissa's vision.

"In fact, Ness, I've decided Henry must have a thing for south-facing gardens. Not that he'd probably know it."

Vanessa loved Malissa when she was tipsy; she became philosophical in her own special way.

"Take Feelview, for example," she continued.

"Feelview?"

"That's the Cornwall estate. That faces south too, 200 miles down there." She raised her left arm, then the right, then suggested it might be straight ahead.

"And a thousand more in the same direction, Söller?" Vanessa asked.

"Exactly, Ness. You get my point."

"So, have they started?"

"Ness!" Malissa exclaimed. "Their idea of starting is having meetings, the local council I mean. As far as I can make out, they've had ten so far. So yes, they have started, but if you mean has anyone turned up with a shovel yet, then the answer is an emphatic no."

Vanessa laughed. "Well, I guess these big projects take time."

"Hmm," Malissa said cynically. "Anyway, when Henry's finished in New York I shall get myself out there and give them a piece of my mind." She drained her glass and reached for the bottle she'd just opened. "Hey, you could come too."

"I'd love to."

Malissa refilled their glasses. "Henry's dying to meet you," she said.

"And I look forward to meeting Henry."

"Yeah. I'll be glad when that States business is over. That's the trouble with these big businessmen, Ness, always trying to make sure they're ready for the next big thing. I mean, money doesn't buy everything."

"Villas on islands?"

"Okay, you got me there. Anyway, I told him what a great dancer you are and he can't wait to see you dance."

"He likes the theatre?"

"He doesn't exactly enthuse about it, but I'm sure he does. I mean, everyone loves the theatre, don't they?"

That prompted a discussion about Vanessa's next assignment. She had the option to stay with LDC, but if she fancied a change there were several options. After checking on Lewis and deciding against another bottle of wine, Malissa suggested they move into the living room. It had gone 9pm and the temperature was dropping.

Vanessa made some coffee and brought it into the lounge. Malissa was sitting on the sofa, smiling. She was dangling something in her hand. "I've been checking up on you," she said.

For a moment, Vanessa couldn't see Malissa's smiling face and considered a myriad of unsavoury things Malissa could have discovered.

"Really?" she said, putting the cups on the coffee table and taking the photograph Malissa was presenting to her.

Vanessa was relieved but still somewhat surprised when she recognised the photo. It was of the cast of a children's production she had been involved in when she was eight years old.

"How did you get that?" Vanessa asked, trying to shake off her feeling of discomfort.

"Well on your resumé you mentioned the Paris National and The Nutcracker, but you never said you were Clara. That's some achievement, Ness. You're too modest."

Vanessa smiled and examined the photo. Surely Malissa's interest in her past was just innocent curiosity.

"There was a production on again this year," Malissa continued, "at the same theatre and Angie was there. When she told me, I mentioned you were in it when you were young and she saw the photo in the foyer, took a picture of it and faxed it over. I could tell it was you even if the names weren't there. But the part of Clara? Miss Cozzette, you're far too modest. I've updated your CV accordingly, of course."

Vanessa smiled. It wasn't unusual for theatres to display information of previous productions on their hoardings. She was just relieved that the clubs she later danced in didn't exercise the same policy. She handed back the photo.

"I was Olga in The Ballerina too," she said casually.

"You were Olga?" Malissa looked astonished.

"When I was 15. POAB."

"Parisian Opera!"

"Yep." Vanessa smiled.

"Ness, you are a genuine star. That's a serious part. Why's that not on your port?"

Vanessa smiled. "Well, those sorts of parts don't seem so relevant these days I guess." Vanessa's CV made scant reference to her younger days at the dance school.

"But, Ness you could have been a great ballerina."

Vanessa tilted her head, smiled and ran her hands down her body. "You don't think I'd need to be slimmer?"

"Ness, you've got the greatest body I've ever seen. Why do those ballerinas have to be so dainty?"

Malissa would have understood why ballet could never have been Vanessa's forte, but she continued to enthuse about her early dancing achievements. To Vanessa, it seemed a lifetime ago, but she still remembered that day her mother first took her to Mademoiselle Lauren's and the joy she felt when winning her first competition at the age of six.

Malissa seemed to take a keen interest in Vanessa's dancing career as a child, but Vanessa allowed her to form her own opinions of how wonderful it must have been. Vanessa had often wondered what would have happened had she accepted a place at the Academy when she left school, but talking with Malissa now, enjoying the new life she'd been given, made her smile. She was happy.

# 20

# AUGUST 1981, DINARD, BRITTANY

*M*onique's father was the chief executive of a chemical company based in Rennes. Her mother was a teacher. To them their only daughter was a bitter disappointment. She had twice been asked to leave the private schools she had been sent to and there was little respect between child and parents. Despite their wealth, Monique's upbringing in some ways was as dysfunctional as Vanessa's.

Monique's parents had purchased their house here last summer. They'd always holidayed in Dinard and when they retired planned to live there full time. They also had a smaller house in Rennes but had recently sold their apartment in Paris.

Monique was reluctant to move out of the city but at 17, with no independent income or prospect of further education or suitable employment, she had little choice but to move with her parents. They had found a job for her, a reception position at a car rental company owned by her father's friend. Monique said they regarded it as her last chance to prove to them that she could actually turn out to be a valuable member of society.

The job lasted two weeks. She was asked to leave after making advances to her boss, who was mortified that his friend's daughter could be so forward. As far as Monique was concerned it was a plan well executed; she'd much rather work at the casino and had been promised a job there as soon as she turned 18.

Her parents were embarrassed and ashamed, surprised that even she could stoop to such levels. Yes, Monique was a disappointment to her parents, but to Vanessa she was a fascinating and valuable friend.

Dinard was amongst the best of Brittany's seaside towns and once a favourite holiday destination of the British aristocracy. Over recent years its popularity as a tourist resort had grown and the number of discerning tourists visiting these days would effectively treble its normal population come holiday season.

Monique's parents' house was a mile or so inland. It was a large four-bedroomed detached property set in half an acre of land, with an annexe in which Monique spent most of her time; especially when her parents, who lived much of the week in their town house in Rennes, were there.

Vanessa had no intention of leaving Mademoiselle Lauren a note, but as she prepared to leave her house she decided to do so. It said simply that she had no interest in joining any dance company and that she was leaving Paris. She didn't tell her dance teacher where she was going, but after a moment's thoughtful hesitation Vanessa did add a PS, thanking her for all she had taught her over the years and saying she was sorry but felt she had to leave.

Maybe she left the note because of the talk they had last night. Mademoiselle Lauren seemed to listen to her and agreed she deserved a greater proportion of the money the POAB had paid to the dance school for her services and would have been happy to go to the bank with her today, open an account in Vanessa's name and deposit 5000 francs. Vanessa was pleased Mademoiselle's tin in the cupboard held nearly that amount.

Monique didn't have a driving licence but picked up Vanessa from Dinard train station in her parents' car. They had a coffee in town before driving to the house.

Her parents wouldn't be back until next weekend, but even if Vanessa stayed longer than that Monique assured her they wouldn't mind her being there. Vanessa wasn't convinced by that statement but believed her when she said her parents never came into the annexe where she'd be sleeping.

They had been drinking wine and eating sandwiches in the garden. Monique wasn't sure that Vanessa should give up dancing but agreed discontinuing her association with Mademoiselle Lauren was a good thing. They had several days to figure out what they'd do next.

Vanessa wasn't totally surprised by the events leading to Monique's dismissal from the car hire company but was a little shocked when she heard about her new way of earning money at the harbour.

"You can be such a prude at times Vanessa," she joked. "It's money for nothing and keeps me occupied in this boring place. Anyway, maybe I'll stop all that when I get the job at the casino."

"Don't you have to be qualified for that?"

"Well, the croupiers do but they're all blokes. No, you just smile and show a bit a cleavage."

"Bar work then? That doesn't sound that exciting."

"No, not bar work. It's easy. You latch on to some rich man and offer yourself as their good luck charm. Smile a bit, flirt, make them spend more and the casino pays you a bonus."

"What, so you encourage them to lose?"

"Well, that's one point, but Claudia, she lives in town, told me she's met loads of wealthy people doing it. Sometimes they win, think you're the greatest thing to have ever crossed their path and take you to Mauritius for a week. She's even had proposals of marriage."

Vanessa loved the simplicity of her friend's way of thinking, but she did recall Monique's anger about the rape and her subsequent concern regarding Vanessa's relationship with Etienne which seemed to contradict what she was saying now.

"But you said I should value myself more, about Etienne for example. Are you not devaluing yourself by what you do?"

Monique reached for Vanessa's hand. "Oh, My Little Kitten. I was just worried you were letting Etienne take advantage of you. With these men, I'm taking advantage of them."

"So, valuing yourself literally?"

"And having some fun," Monique smiled. "Now tell me what that bitch of a dance teacher said when you said you were leaving."

Vanessa had hardly slept last night, sneaked out of Mademoiselles Lauren's house before sunrise and boarded the train at 7am. It was now 7pm and the journey, the wine and the sunshine were beginning to take their toll. They were laying on a blanket and Vanessa would have been quite happy to fall asleep.

"You get more beautiful each time I see you," Monique said softly running her hand through Vanessa's hair when she'd finished relaying the conversation she'd had with Mademoiselle Lauren. "Such flaming locks."

"And you," Vanessa replied touching her cheek, "have the face of an angel."

"And the heart of a lion?"

"Possibly a devil."

Both girls laughed and hugged each other.

"Let's have another bottle," suggested Monique. "Let's get drunk and have a bath and tomorrow we can go shopping."

They folded up the blanket they'd been laying on and headed indoors.

The inside of the house was palatial. The furniture seemed brand new and everything was so neatly organised Vanessa wondered whether she dared sit down.

"I think they really love me being here when they're away. To keep an eye on things, make sure everything's shipshape," Monique joked. "But don't worry, the cleaner comes Friday."

Monique fetched some cheese out of the fridge and, after studying a few bottles, chose one from the wine rack. Vanessa wasn't sure she could drink much more. The evening was warm, and they opened several windows in an attempt to discharge the heat of the day. They sat down and talked some more about the casino and Vanessa's dancing before Monique went upstairs to run a bath.

Vanessa was almost asleep when she heard Monique calling her. She made her way upstairs. The bathroom was as big as most people's lounges. Marbled tiles adorned the walls and on the shelves Monique had placed several candles, their fragrance competing with the sweet scent of the bath water.

Monique was at one end of the bath, cushioned by bubbles, which like soft warm snow lay gently upon her perfect breasts. In the flickering light her skin almost shone and with her dark hair tied back, exposing the delicateness of her neck, she looked truly beautiful. Vanessa's heart beat quickened; she felt, for the first time, a longing to be intimate with another human being.

Monique put down her wine glass and smiled at Vanessa. Neither said anything as Vanessa slowly undressed and stepped into the water. She knelt in front of her friend, who put her arms around Vanessa's neck, drawing her closer. They kissed. Delicately at first, but when Vanessa felt the touch of Monique's fingers between her legs, she kissed her hungrily. It wasn't how she had been touched before and her body responded, that feathery feeling in her belly gathering intensiveness until she could no longer hold on to it. She caught her breath and held tight to Monique as she came.

She drew away slowly. She looked into Monique's eyes, saw her feelings reflected and knew this was a precious moment. Monique smiled. "You're very beautiful," she said.

When they returned to the annexe, their love making continued. Vanessa had witnessed a side of Monique she didn't know existed, a softness, a vulnerability and a delicateness she was sure she much preferred to hide. How similar they were in that regard, she thought.

Before they slept, however, the angel that had possessed Monique for the last couple of hours, exhausted and content, floated away and the more devilish, confident young woman who Venessa knew well reappeared. "I know some men who'll pay a lot of money to see us do that on their yacht... Even more when I tell them how you can shake that beautiful arse of yours. Goodnight, My Little Kitten."

Vanessa smiled to herself. She felt safe with Monique but did wonder just what, exactly, her friend had in mind.

# 21

# CHRISTMAS 1981, PARIS

*V*anessa and Gabrielle had always loved the way Madame Pelletier decorated her café at Christmas. She also made the most delicious bûche de Noël which they both adored. As in previous years, Vanessa would spend Christmas with her sister at Philippe's house. Sometime over the holiday she'd also try and see her mother. She believed she was living with a friend in the Chinese Quarter but, failing that, Vanessa knew the bars she'd probably hang out in.

She had just told Gabrielle that last week her father swapped her best pair of shoes for a bottle of vodka. She meant it light-heartedly, suggesting he could have got at least three or four bottles for what they cost, but her sister seemed a little concerned.

"Why don't you come and live with us?" Gabrielle asked. "Dad would never steal your shoes." It wasn't the first time her sister had posed such a question.

Although Vanessa got on well with Gabrielle's father Philippe and thought the world of his mother, who cared so much for Gabrielle, Vanessa couldn't live there. Their house and the neighbourhood they lived in were infinitely more desirable than where she lived with her father, but Vanessa was not the 15 year-old child she had led the members of that household to believe.

"Because, Brie, I'm happy where I am and it's near my school and the academy."

Maintaining the charade that she was still attending school and had been offered a place at the Parisian Opera and Ballet Company, stopped Gabrielle asking too many questions; or worrying too much.

"I think it's because if you did, you'd have to do what you were told."

Vanessa was impressed by her sister's intuition and laughed. "Anyway, pretty soon I might get a place of my own, or at least share a flat with Monique. Remember her?"

"Well, I could come and live with you then."

"Don't you think you're a bit too young to leave home? And anyway, what would Mémé say?"

Vanessa steered the conversation back to Christmas and the riverboat trip she'd booked as part of Gabrielle's present. She'd stay with Gabrielle until the day after Christmas.

Although the Metro was quicker, Vanessa loved the view and the noise provided by a stop-start journey through the city. She was charged adult fare, but she didn't protest. She had grown up these last few months. She still had most of the money from Mademoiselle Lauren but, since returning from Dinard, had taken a cash-in-hand job at a greengrocers and more recently had yielded to Monique's suggestion that she could earn 'easy money' simply by 'strutting her stuff' on a Friday in a club they knew in Rue Burq. Two five-minute sessions there could net her the equivalent of her daily rate in her day time job. Despite knowing she'd still have to live with her father for a few more weeks, she was happy.

The three weeks Vanessa spent with Monique were the best three weeks of her life, and by the time she returned to Paris she realised she had discovered an inner strength and confidence she hadn't known existed.

Monique was right. Those men who held parties on their yachts were very appreciative of their company. It was a game to Monique, possibly a dangerous one, but Vanessa watched how she changed from girl to woman, from cute to masterful, and how she could manipulate men to her advantage. There were one or two scary moments as far as Vanessa was concerned, but her friend could seemingly diffuse any situation. Three years older than her, Monique was adept at her craft, but Vanessa learned quickly.

The nights she spent with Monique in the annexe, when the angel replaced the devil, were precious and Vanessa wondered if what she felt for her was love. She hated leaving, she would have stayed there forever, but after Monique had a big row with her parents Vanessa thought it best to return to Paris.

Her father seemed indifferent when she turned up and assumed, since her assignment at the theatre had finished, that Mademoiselle Lauren had thrown her out. "Typical of the bitch," he said, "uses you to promote her dance school then chucks you out." He did, however, seem impressed by what she told him she had earned. She was welcome to stay there for 100 francs a week, despite the fact he could get more if he let the bedroom to someone else. She would soon leave him for good.

Within two weeks of Vanessa's return to Paris, Monique got in contact. She had turned 18 and it seemed her parents had finally given up on her. They hated the idea of her working in the casino, but said that if she wanted to find an apartment in Paris they would buy it and she could live there rent free until her 24th birthday; or if she seriously mended her ways, she could return to Dinard. It was an arrangement that suited both parties, her only obligation to endorse, if asked, her parents' story that she was continuing her education in the city. She soon found an apartment, a two-bedroom flat on the 3rd floor of a block in the heart of the city in Saint Germain, a nice area, and both her and Vanessa would move in there as soon as the formalities were completed, sometime in January they hoped.

Monique, in the meantime, had been living in a bedsit owned by an elderly couple. It was strictly against the rules for Monique to entertain visitors in her bedroom, but the old man agreed that as long as they were quiet Vanessa could stay there occasionally, especially on a Wednesday when his wife was out and when Vanessa and Monique, in appreciation for his understanding, were happy to treat him to a little girl-on-girl voyeurism.

Monique couldn't get tickets for the New Year's Eve Moulin Rouge performance, so this evening, December 28th, was their own celebration. Vanessa was a little apprehensive and as they walked in was asked to verify her age. Monique smiled at the doorman and whispered in his ear. Vanessa didn't even have to show her driving licence, which even under the half light of the hallway would surely be recognised as fake. They were shown to their table.

"What did you say to him?" Vanessa whispered when they were seated.

"I told him you were older than me, that you were the daughter of Andrea Dumas, and that I was in charge of showing you the delights of Paris on this special night."

"What did he say?"

"He didn't say anything, just sort of grunted as if to say oh and thank you, and let us in."

"Who's Andrea Dumas?"

"Fuck knows, but I think the doorman thought he should. Anyway, most of the time children are allowed in here so I don't know what all the fuss was about. What do you think?"

Every dancer had heard of the Moulin Rouge, but Vanessa had never stepped foot inside. "It's magical. Even more impressive than I imagined."

They talked a little about dancing, Monique seeming certain that one day, Vanessa could be starring here.

"Instead of Rue Burq?" Vanessa asked.

"Well, you must admit that was a step in the right direction. Anyway that's temporary. Now tell me about Etienne."

Vanessa first met Etienne back in January at the same place she met Monique two years ago. He was 17, came from a wealthy family and was studying for a business degree. He lived with several other students in a house not far from the Eiffel Tower. He was kind to Vanessa, always told her she was beautiful, and she had spent several nights with him before moving to Mademoiselle Lauren's last April.

She didn't see him at all during the summer, but when she came back from Dinard she bumped into him and they had seen each other several times since. He insisted on telling Vanessa he loved her, but Vanessa's feeling towards men had changed and their relationship, much to Etienne's disappointment, had faded into one of a platonic nature.

"So, you don't fancy men at all now?" asked Monique.

The question surprised Vanessa. She would have thought Monique knew that *she* was the only person she'd consider having sex with, but she didn't react.

"Well, not at the moment."

"It's a phase, My Little Kitten, you'll get over it."

The curtain went up and they joined in the applause. It was the first time Vanessa had considered that Monique's feelings towards her did not match her own.

# 22

# LATE JANUARY 1982, PARIS

## VANESSA'S FATHER'S APARTMENT

$\mathcal{T}$he thought of spending another night in this shit hole when she didn't need to, did not please Vanessa. She had told Monique she'd be back at their flat by 9pm. She could leave her father a note, or she could just leave. He wouldn't notice she'd gone for several days anyway. If he was in the bar she could catch the bus by the flea market instead and call in en route, but she'd be carrying a heavy suitcase, and at any rate didn't fancy confronting him there. Or she could order a cab.

She picked up the phone. Her father still hadn't paid the phone bill and the line was dead. Fuck it! She'd leave and to hell with him. She looked around one last time. How did he ever get into this state? What did her mother see in him, for fuck's sake?

She saw the photograph on the mantlepiece and picked it up. Her father used to tell her the dress she was wearing was pink, exactly the same colour as the ribbons in her hair. He looked so different then. Clean shaven, respectable – even handsome. You could tell he was older than her mother, but they looked happy. Maybe once upon a time they were, but Vanessa couldn't remember. She placed it back, gently sliding her thumb over her mother's face and thinking how pretty she was. She heard the street door open and then the heavy thud of her father's footsteps. It had just gone 830pm.

She heard him trying to unlock the door and cursing when he dropped the keys. He was drunk. He came in and saw Vanessa. "You okay?" he said, brushing past. He stank of whisky and cigarettes. He didn't notice the suitcase on the floor beside her.

"I'm moving out," she said.

He took off his coat and slumped himself on the armchair. "Eh?"

"I'm leaving. Moving out."

He scratched his head and screwed up his eyes before seeking clarification. "Out? Where are you going?"

"I'm going for good, moving out. Leaving you."

"When will you be back?"

"For fuck's sake, Dad, don't you ever listen?" She wished he wasn't drunk. "I'm moving into the city and won't be coming back. You've got the place to yourself now. I just wanted to let you know so you didn't worry." Did one part of her actually consider he might worry?

"What about school?"

"Dad, do you even know how old I am?"

"Have we got any drink in the cupboard?"

She had seen a bottle in the kitchen cupboard. She fetched it and a glass and placed it on the table beside him. She didn't want the day she finally left home to be scarred by an argument.

He poured himself a drink and she waited a response. The bus she wanted to catch left in 20 minutes.

"Like your mother?"

"What?"

"You're fuckin' leaving me just like your mother did?"

"You're drunk, Dad, and I don't want a fight. I just wanted to tell you. I'll be in touch." She picked up the suitcase and headed for the door.

"You're a fuckin' whore. Just like her."

She stopped, the blood beginning to boil in her veins.

"Leave it all to me," he continued, "just like your mother did. Leave me to sort things out. Yes Anna, I'll bring your fuckin' daughter up. Looked after you when you couldn't find anybody else to fuck yer, didn't I? Fuckin' women. All the same."

She turned to him. He hadn't spouted off about her mother like this for some time. "You're a sad old man," she said.

"Sad old man maybe. You ever thought why your father's a sad old man, Vanessa?"

She bit her lip. She didn't want to fight. "Goodbye, Dad." She turned to go.

"Cos not only did he have to look after some fuckin' whore that just turned up, he had to look after her bastard child too," he shouted after her.

Vanessa was at the doorway. She put the suitcase down again, resting it against the door so it wouldn't close. She turned and walked slowly toward him, her eyes fixed on his, full of hate, the acid in her stomach feeling it was about to explode. He had hit her before but if he tried to this time, she'd kill him, and the look in his eyes told her he understood. Her instinct was to shout, but she supressed it.

"You are pathetic. That's why you live alone. The company you keep, like you, are scum. Every now and then you deny you're my father. But every day, every single minute of every day, I hope something turns up to confirm you are not."

She stared at him hard, almost afraid of what she might do next. Then she turned and left. He said nothing more.

# 23

## JANUARY 1982, MONIQUE'S APARTMENT, PARIS

### THE DAY AFTER THEY MOVED IN

*T*he joy Vanessa had been feeling the last couple of months had deserted her. The exchange with her father last night had rekindled too many memories, and she was unable to share Monique's enthusiasm as she talked about all the things they needed to buy for the flat and how they would make it their home.

They had slept on the floor on a blow-up mattress under a thick duck down duvet that Monique had bought. Their bed wasn't being delivered until Friday. Monique sprang up, remarking what a beautiful morning it was and made some coffee. She talked about them going shopping, continuing from where she left off last night.

"First thing we need to do Kitten, is work out this heating," Monique said slipping back under the duvet.

"Thanks." Vanessa smiled, taking the coffee.

"Hey, what's wrong?"

Vanessa smiled softly. "It was just some of the things my dad said. Things he's always said, but it'll pass."

"Bastard. You know my dad – we say things too - but I deserve them. I mean, you couldn't have seen a worse spoilt little brat than me, but you? You deserve better."

Vanessa smiled, but she couldn't laugh.

"Tell me," said Monique, "tell me what really bothers you when he spouts off like that? We're married now, I'm supposed to look after you. I'm the man by the way," she grinned.

Vanessa appreciated her friend's attempts to make light of things and rested her head on Monique's shoulder. The only *man* she knew who looked out for his family was Philippe, and even he had enlisted the help of his mother when it came to the day-to-day care of his daughter.

"I had a friend called Kat when I was about seven," Vanessa said softly. "She was older than me and went to the dance school." Vanessa wasn't quite sure why the memory of Katriane had encroached upon her thoughts.

"Was she as good as you?"

"Her house was just around the corner and it was convenient to stay there. Certainly, better than at my dad's." She sat up and wrapped her hands around her coffee cup. "Well, one morning I was in the shower and her stepdad walked in and looked at me." Vanessa half expected Monique to quip something like 'Typical man' or 'Was his name Cedric?' who was her landlord from the bedsit she'd just vacated, but she said nothing.

"It carried on for all the time I stayed there," Vanessa continued. "Sometimes he'd come in and talk to me and sometimes I'd just see him touching himself at the door. Me and Kat joked about it, I mean, it didn't seem to bother me at the time and I didn't even think it was wrong."

Monique put her arm around her and pulled her close. "You were seven, Vanessa, how were you to know what was right and wrong?"

"My dad didn't want to know, said I was imagining it."

"Did this guy touch you?"

Vanessa took a deep breath, the memories in one respect so distant and in another so fresh in her mind. She wondered why being raped when she was 14 hadn't seemed to have left such an impact. Was that because she was older when that happened? More resilient? Or was it because she was just thinking about Katriane, a child? The only pervert who had physically touched Vanessa was Monsieur Paige, her father's rent collector who said it was okay because it kept the rent affordable. She'd told nobody about that.

"No, he just watched me," she said. "It was Kat who he touched, but I didn't know."

They said nothing for a minute and just sipped their coffee. Vanessa didn't want sympathy and didn't want to talk about it anymore. She didn't really know why she had mentioned it.

"And those things your father says," Monique said tenderly, "about your mother. Do they make you think about that? Somehow make you feel guilty, like it was your fault?"

Vanessa considered her friend's words carefully, understanding there was probably some twisted truth in them. "Sad, I think. Not guilty."

"But that's all behind you now. We've got a wonderful new life ahead of us."

Vanessa smiled. She did feel a little better for sharing her thoughts and as she looked around the room tried to imagine how it would look when they had furnished it. "Yes, we have, Monnie," she said determined to shake off her sadness, "we'll take Paris by storm. Now let's get up and go shopping. I've got nearly 5000 francs to spend."

Monique kissed her on the forehead and 20 minutes later they were dressed. They'd get breakfast in the café down the road and then head into town.

"Do you still see Kat?" Monique asked as they were putting on their coats.

Vanessa smiled, but the memory of that sad day would always be with her. "No, she left the dance school and I never saw her again."

Monique looked at her as if awaiting further information.

"And, no. She was not as good a dancer as me."

# 24

## MAY 1982, PARIS

*V*anessa and Monique loved sitting and talking in the park opposite their apartment. During the week, the main road could be busy, but on a Sunday there was very little traffic. It was like a little oasis in the city, and on a warm, sunny day many people enjoyed picnicking on the grass.

They had furnished their flat the way they'd wanted. They had painted the walls in light pastel shades which gave the impression of space and cleanliness, and nearly everything in there was modern and new.

The apartment belonged to Monique's parents but to Vanessa it represented her first permanent home. She was 16, Monique 19, but compared to so many others their own age, they were grown up and in control of their own lives.

Monique received an allowance from her parents but to supplement her income had, shortly after they moved in, taken a job in a hardware store. She stuck it for three weeks, which was two weeks longer than either of them had anticipated. Monique quickly realised that there were easier and far more lucrative ways of making money and for the last two months had been earning a living in the strip clubs in the north of the city.

For two weeks in March, Monique went to the South of France to catch up with a school friend. Vanessa missed her and wondered if she was sleeping with her friend. She did ask her, but Monique simply reminded her that they should never ask such questions because it could mean they'd be tempted to lie. She then softened her statement and probably gave Vanessa her answer by saying, "There's sex... and then there's the sex we have."

Whether it was jealousy or something else, Vanessa invited Etienne back to their apartment whilst Monique was away. They had sex, and although Vanessa was perfectly capable of performing with a man it didn't provide the intimacy she always experienced with Monique. When she told Monique that she had slept with Etienne again, Vanessa wondered if she would show any signs of jealousy. She didn't. She just said, "I told you not liking men was just a phase."

Tomorrow, Vanessa was going to a club with Monique. This time, however, she too would be taking off her clothes. She had been to a couple of venues with Monique over the last few weeks, watching from the wings and talking to the other girls. The clubs Monique performed in were far more sophisticated than the decadent joints in Vanessa's old neighbourhood - safer too - but she still felt nervous.

"You'll be fine, Little Kitten. Just think of it as training, like at Mademoiselle Lauren's. You'll be on the big cabaret stage in no time. You were great in Dinard."

Vanessa did enjoy those nights on the yacht in Dinard, but she regarded the time there almost like a holiday; like peering into another world full of champagne and wealth. There she and Monique danced, watched by four of five men they sort of knew. One or two of them weren't bad looking, but the audiences here would be old and ugly and complete strangers.

"I'd be more comfortable there," she smiled.

"But I don't think my parents would be. I've a 100 kilometre exclusion zone."

Vanessa laughed. "I talked to someone I used to know on Friday. A guy at the Klaus. I was asking about dancing jobs."

"With clothes *on?*"

"Yeah, the Klaus is a good theatre."

"What did he say?"

"Well, first you have to be 18, *and* prove it just to get an audition. But at least they don't have the 1.75m height minimum the Moulin has."

"You've got two years to grow 3cm. No sweat. Shall we get an ice cream?"

## 25

# SEPTEMBER 1987, CHAMPS-ÉLYSÉES, PARIS

*V*anessa loved taking Gabrielle shopping, and since she didn't expect to see her again until Christmas when she returned from London wanted to treat her to a new dress. She was a little early and sat drinking coffee while she waited for her. She had been thinking about Monique all morning. They'd been through so much together and Vanessa couldn't help but think that this morning may well turn out to be the last time they saw each other. Monique was pursuing a new life and, in theory, finally settling down. And so was Vanessa.

Vanessa had been to the bank earlier to transfer the money in her current account to her bank in London. She didn't however, close the investment account in which, as soon as she was 18, she'd deposited more than 25,000 francs; the proceeds of her liaison with Etienne. She smiled to herself; the hotel where Monique and Vanessa had met Etienne's father was less than five minutes' walk away. Poor Etienne. She wondered what he was doing now.

# 26

# JULY 1982, PARIS

## RESTAURANT LE PAVILLION BLANC

*C*laude Capron started his own investment company in the 1960s. He sold it 20 years later to France's biggest banking group, in order to concentrate on his political ambitions. Monique had suggested he would pay handsomely to ensure his son didn't pursue the ludicrous idea of marrying Vanessa, and after asking her all that she knew about Etienne and what he had said about his father, Monique concocted a plan to extort money from him.

Vanessa always listened to Etienne and about the difficult relationship he had with his father. She listened and said little. Compared to her own experience of fathers she couldn't really see the problem. To Monique, however he was another child who could turn out to be a disappointment to his self-indulgent, rich parents - and she should know! Etienne's relationship with Vanessa, she said, was one of escape.

Vanessa didn't love Etienne, and even if she did was aware that their relationship could never work. But that didn't stop her feeling cruel. She could imagine the conversation he would have had with his father last week and pictured him cowing in the corner after he announced he had made a girl pregnant and thought it only right to leave university and marry her.

Monique had phoned Claude Capron three times. Vanessa couldn't believe how she could speak so authoritatively to a seemingly powerful man. Each time she came off the phone to him she'd change back to herself and they'd find themselves giggling about the conversation. She would have made a great actress. After the third call, however, Monique confirmed that he had agreed to meet them.

They arrived at the restaurant an hour before and had already eaten lunch when Monsieur Capron arrived as agreed at 3pm. There were few diners there. Monique adopted the same manner she had during those telephone calls and for the most part Capron just sat and listened, sipping water.

When they ordered sweet he excused himself, saying he needed to make a phone call. Vanessa could feel his anger but, like the diplomat and businessman he was, believed he left the table to calm down and calculate his options.

"I told you he wouldn't believe I was pregnant," Vanessa whispered.

"I'd imagine if he believed you were, he'd even doubt it was his son's baby anyway. We may have to suggest one of those DNA tests if he brings that up. Don't worry, I've read about them."

"It makes me nervous, Monnie. We could just go?"

"No. It's going to plan. Trust me."

"What if he's phoning one of those gangster types, you know, to solve his problem?"

"Vanessa, that would not solve his problem. Remember, it's scandal he doesn't want, and anyway I'm sure the going rate for knocking off two women in public is a great deal more than we're asking."

"Well, who's he phoning?"

"I don't know. He might be at the bank getting the money or counting it out of sight. Look, he knew why he was coming here."

"I know, but it just makes me nervous."

Monique gave her a stern look. "Look. You just sit there looking cute. Looking wronged. I'll do the talking. He knows the score. Thing is, My Little Kitten, Etienne had sex with you when you were 14, fourteen! That's illegal, baby or no baby. No, he knows his son, and he won't want any trouble. Shh... he's coming."

Capron come back into the restaurant, his face expressionless and sat back down. He looked around. The restaurant was empty apart from the couple at the far end who probably accepted Monique's earlier intimations that the man they were talking to was her uncle.

He spoke in a soft controlled voice. "Okay, I agree. And I'm trusting you." He pushed the envelope across the table. "When I'm satisfied you are keeping your word then I shall pay the remainder. As we agreed."

"And Uncle... " replied Monique. She paused, leant across the table and lowered her voice. "At that time we will forget everything about the baby and everything we ever learned. Who knows, we may even vote for you?"

Vanessa wanted to laugh, or hide, she didn't know which, but she certainly had to give her friend the credit she deserved.

Monsieur Capron looked at each of them for several seconds. Vanessa found herself looking away, but Monique held his gaze. Vanessa sensed his grudging admiration for her friend. He got up and took a furtive look around. Possibly satisfied he hadn't been recognised and had concluded his business, he smiled wryly. "Well, I shall bid you goodbye."

Monique stood up. "Thank you, Uncle Jacques," she said and moved around the table to hug him.

For a moment, he looked mortified and Vanessa wanted to laugh again, but Monique quickly broke the embrace. "And thank you for lunch. We could never have afforded to eat here."

Monsieur Capron grinned at her before he took out his wallet, counted out some notes and placed them on the table. "I trust you ladies shall not be ordering a bottle of Dom Pérignon," he said.

He had placed more than enough to cover the cost of their meal. "That wouldn't be right in Vanessa's condition, Uncle." Monique smiled.

Vanessa sensed Monsieur Capron actually wanted to laugh. He took a last look around and leaned forward. "Have you ever considered a career in politics, Miss Maigret?" he asked.

Vanessa still felt uneasy as they counted out the 25,000 francs that evening and wasn't quite able to rejoice as Monique had done. To ease Vanessa's trepidation Monique assured her that while the payoff represented a lot of money for her, she expected that Monsieur Capon would be feeling he'd got off lightly and that it was money well spent. She even said she imagined he actually enjoyed the experience. Monique would pay the money into her own account and transfer it to Vanessa when she reached

18 and could open her own. When Vanessa asked if Monique would really have gone to the papers had he not paid she just smiled and said, "What do you think?" Vanessa didn't know.

Vanessa had to tell Etienne that the baby was not his, that she didn't love him, never had, and that she was moving out of Paris. Monique and her had to be careful for a while, but when he called round for the third time he told Monique he was transferring to the university in Marseille, that he would always love Vanessa and if Monique ever saw her again would she please give her his letter.

Claude Capron never paid the balance of the money, nor did they ever consider asking him to. When Monique transferred the money to Vanessa's account, she refused to take any commission for her trouble. "It was you who was wronged My Little Kitten," she said. Vanessa would always be in awe of what Monique considered a fun thing to do.

# PART III

*Emma*

*New script that seems so inviting*
*The chance to dance on a new stage*
*But a prologue that needs understanding*
*So hinders the turn of a page*

# EARLY DECEMBER 1987, PIMLICO LONDON

*L*ike most Wednesdays, since she had returned to London, Vanessa had met Malissa for lunch. They talked as they usually did, close friends discussing much more than dancing and the theatre. However, despite her certainty that the blind girl playing the violin was connected to Malissa's husband, Vanessa still felt unable to ask Malissa specifically about Emma Ovmeister.

She already knew that Henry, like Emma, was an orphan and that other than Alice, Malissa said Henry had no family. Emma and Henry were adopted from an orphanage as babies, and although Malissa didn't seem to know the name of the orphanage she had said it was in East London so surely it was St Mary's.

Vanessa had also learned that Henry was raised by a woman he called Aunt Rose, but whose real name was Gertrude Ovmeister. Emma's name was Ovmeister, she was the same age as Henry and adopted from the same place around the same time. Surely she too was adopted by Aunt Rose?

If she hadn't seen the newspaper cutting, maybe Vanessa could have assumed that Emma had died as a baby and that Henry had little recollection of her. But that article suggested she was alive and well. Of course, there was a chance that this Emma Ovmeister may be no relation to Vanessa at all.

The truth was one of several scenarios. The first was that Henry and

Emma were adopted by the same person, grew up together, and that Emma was the teenage crush Malissa had mentioned. The second was that Henry and Emma were adopted by the same person but then led separate lives. And the third was that the whole thing was some remarkable coincidence. One thing Vanessa was absolutely certain of however, was that the name Emma Ovmeister didn't resonate with Malissa, and if it did with Henry, Vanessa couldn't imagine why that should be the case.

She hadn't heard from Monique since they said goodbye in Paris; she hadn't expected to. Monique was the same age as Malissa and both were so confident in their outlook on life, yet their ambitions and beliefs were totally different. Malissa reminded her of the angelic side of Monique, the side Vanessa so loved in the early days of their love affair. On the other hand, although Malissa was one of the most attractive women Vanessa had ever known, and she felt such a deep connection to her, Vanessa never imagined Malissa being anything other than her great friend..

It was dark by the time Vanessa arrived at the street where her mother had told her she once lived. It was a wealthy part of London, with big Georgian Houses, almost Parisian, but Vanessa was unsure if anybody her mother would have known still lived there.

Many of the properties, including number 22, which was amongst the most prestigious of the buildings, had been turned into apartments. Just had she had done for the three previous Wednesday evenings, Vanessa sat in the local pub hoping she would meet someone or discover something that would shed light on her mother's life here and maybe help her to unravel the mystery of Emma.

"I'd give a pound for those thoughts, let alone a penny."

Vanessa smiled.

"I've been watching you," the man continued. "Not in that sort of way. You were here last week, weren't you? I'm Jon by the way, J-O-N, no aitch." He held out his hand.

Vanessa shook it. "Monique," she said.

"Ah, you're French. So, what brings a beautiful French lady down to this neck of the woods? I hope I'm not interrupting."

He was only interrupting her thoughts. He was mid 30's and didn't look like anybody who could give her any information, but she knew that sitting alone in a pub always attracted attention from men. He was the fifth or sixth one to make an advance to her over the last few weeks.

"Can I buy you a drink?" he asked.

"I've only just got one. But thank you anyway," she smiled.

"Well, I'm on my own too. Until my friends arrive."

"So, I'm a reasonable stand in until they come?"

Jon laughed. "I didn't mean that. I'm sorry. I just thought..."

"You Englishmen are all the same," she interrupted. "And I was told it's the French or the Italians who I should be wary of."

He continued chatting her up and Vanessa feigned enthusiasm for what he was saying. It wasn't until he told her that he was born in the area that her interest heightened.

"When was that? she asked.

"You're asking my age?"

"Making conversation."

"Fifty-four, 1954, that's when I was born here," he said, possibly wondering if she believed he was too old for her.

Her mother would have been back in France by then. "You look good for your age."

"Thank you. I won't ask your age of course – being an *Englishman* - but I'd guess 20. Maybe 21."

Vanessa raised her eyebrows and tilted her head slightly.

"Or you could be younger, or older. I mean, you're a very attractive woman."

Perhaps she was very practised at a making a man feel slightly uncomfortable, but he wasn't disturbing her and the fact that this was probably going to be a brief encounter suited her. "Your parents must have been very wealthy," she smiled.

"Well, to live here now you'd certainly have to be."

"Nice area to grow up in."

"Yes, it was. My parents moved here from Rhodesia, well, it's Zimbabwe now, just after the war."

"They're still here?"

"No, unfortunately not. My father retired in 1970, moved to the country and died a year later. My mother's still alive. Lives up north."

"I'm sorry to hear that."

"Yeah, so much for early retirement."

"So, were your parents English?"

"Yeah, you couldn't get more English really. Dad earned his stripes out there and came back for a job in the High Commission, the Rhodesian one obviously."

"High Commission?"

"Yeah, I don't know what you call it in France, it's like the Embassy, but for all the Commonwealth Countries, you know, the British Empire and all that."

"So, he was an Ambassador?"

Vanessa contemplated whether Jon, through his parents, could provide any tentative link to the man who employed her grandmother. Jon leaned forward and smiled. He obviously thought her interest was in him.

"Of sorts, I guess. Here, can I get you that drink?"

"What about your friends?"

Jon smiled. "White wine spritzer? Lemonade or soda?"

He went to the bar, no doubt thinking that guessing what Vanessa was drinking had nudge him up a notch or two in her estimations. She smiled at him as he ordered. He was back in two minutes.

"Yeah, I meet a couple of friends down here every so often. I'm in insurance, in the City, so the pubs there are my usual haunt. You speak great English, by the way. What do you do for a living? No, don't tell me." He rolled his head around slowly as if he was accumulating everything he had learned about her in order to come up with the answer. Evens he'll say secretary she thought.

"Got it. Personal secretary," he said with a smile.

Vanessa raised her eyebrows ever so slightly and took a sip of her wine.

"Not in finance," Jon continued. He was on a roll. "No, with your command of the English language..." he paused, he was so predictable. "And your other assets..." he grinned, "I'd say for a French company with a branch office here, or even for the French Government. We're in Embassy land after all, Monique. Great name by the way - really suits you."

This time *Jon* raised his eyebrows. Twice. And nodded. Vanessa wanted to laugh and had to take another sip of her drink. "I'm impressed," she said and then, steering the subject back to something more interesting, added, "I heard a French Ambassador lived here after the war. Probably whilst you still lived here too – Felix somebody or other. Perhaps your parents knew him. Number 22 I think?"

"We lived at 56."

"Neighbours then. Did you know him?"

Jon was possibly disappointed that she had interrupted his flow, but surely he thought trying to enlighten her on a subject she was interested in would be equally impressive.

"French you say? Felix?" He took a couple of mouthfuls of beer and was either genuinely searching his mind or feigning to do so. She thought he might need a little more encouragement.

"Yes, my cousin is desperate to know what became of him. He was her great-uncle. I've always thought how wonderful it would be if I could give her some information." She smiled, took another sip of wine and licked her lips.

"I wish I could I remember, Monique. There were a lot of government type people round here, many foreign. My mother might know. I could always ask her and report back to you next week. Or you give me your number and I could call?"

Vanessa smiled. It had been a long shot, but perhaps it was time to go. Jon's friends appeared. He saw them and one came over, the other one made his way to the bar. Jon introduced her.

"Well, lovely to meet you, Monique," Jon's friend said pulling up a chair. "Now, I'm intrigued why such a gorgeous woman would be having a drink with my dickhead friend here?"

Vanessa laughed, but it was time to go. Jon, a little coyer now, relayed the details of the conversation they'd been having. Vanessa finished her wine and picked up the coat she'd draped over a vacant chair.

"Well, if you want to know anything about what's gone on around here in the last fifty years ask Fred," Jon's friend spouted as he accepted the drink from the other friend who'd just joined them.

"Fred?" Jon asked.

"Fred Nugent. You know him. Barman here since he could pull a pint. You could take some lessons from him." He turned to Vanessa. "He'd be better pulling pints than beautiful Parisian ladies. You are from Paris, I assume?"

"Yes. Arrived a couple of days ago..."

His comment precipitated a conversation about Paris, and Paul, Jon's friend, who had twice visited there, took the opportunity to try to impress Vanessa of his familiarity with the city he assumed she admired. Vanessa listened, smiling and feigning interest in his great knowledge.

"So, Fred Nugent," Vanessa asked casually when Paul seemed to have come to the end of the list of places he'd visited in France. "Has he lived here a long time?"

"Yeah, years. Ran this place before the war. Retired in the seventies."

"Didn't he move into those new flats in Duke Street," Jon said, "after his wife died?"

Vanessa wondered if Jon felt a little disheartened by Paul's mention of Fred Nugent. Surely he could have suggested the old barman may have been somebody who could have assisted her in her enquiries. She wondered if Fred Nugent was still alive.

"Yeah, still does as far as I know, ground floor, number two..." Paul had answered the question she hadn't needed to ask and Jon, looking a little eclipsed, conceded it was his round.

Malissa stayed another 30 minutes gathering as much background as she could on Fred and the area. She did consider giving Jon a false phone number or simply not turning up on a re-arranged date, but in London she had discovered she needn't be as defensive as she had become back home. Instead, she compromised and told him and his friends her trip to London was to find a wedding dress. Some were as good as those in Paris but so much cheaper.

When she said goodbye, she smiled at Jon. "By the way, the man I work for in Paris is Monsieur Legrand. I've been his personal secretary for two years. His company does a lot of business in the UK and he needed someone who spoke English fluently. As well as other assets." Jon at least deserved that.

It seemed Fred Nugent was alive and well. "*Ground floor, number two, block of flats right on the corner. Left hand door, first one you come to. Can't miss it.*" She would call on him shortly.

# WEDNESDAY 16TH DECEMBER 1987

## LUNCH WITH MALISSA

*O*fficially, Vanessa had two days off each week, but she'd invariably spend them at The Fenner Agency assisting Malissa. Wednesday afternoons they'd have lunch or a coffee together after a morning's work, and on Thursdays, Malissa's day off with Lewis, Vanessa would sit in Malissa's office addressing her paperwork backlog.

The role Fenner's undertook on behalf of the performers on their books was a new idea in London, but in Paris there had always been several companies offering similar services and Vanessa was quite au fait with the way such an agency worked. Vanessa didn't know what Malissa had told her staff about her presence there, but she had seemingly been immediately accepted as an integral part of the team. In fact, she believed many of the staff even regraded her as their stand in boss.

In truth, she didn't have to make any difficult decisions. People who specifically wanted to speak to Malissa were usually happy to wait until the morning, and if Vanessa needed to speak to her, she could always ring Malissa at home. Vanessa had learned much about the operations of The Fenner Agency and enjoyed mulling over ideas with Malissa who was also always keen to discover how things worked in France.

Their Wednesday afternoons in Antonio's would usually last an hour or so, but they often found themselves chatting well into the early evening.

Vanessa's current assignment was coming to an end and they had been discussing her new placement in the musical 'Cats'.

"Sound good to me," Vanessa said – she would start in January.

"So, it's Gabrielle for Christmas. When are you going?" Malissa asked.

"Yes. I'm looking forward to it. Seems ages since I last saw her. Christmas Eve."

Malissa smiled. "I think it's been quite a year for you, Ness." It had, and Vanessa was happy. "Simon's only staying for the day, they're off to Portugal for New Year, so if you and Gabrielle fancied a change we've plenty of room."

Vanessa thanked her for the invitation, but Gabrielle loved Christmas at home.

"I look forward to meeting her one day."

"And me. I look forward to meeting your brother too," Vanessa smiled. "So, when do you go to Majorca?" Malissa had told her that the plans for their villa had, subject to one or two further clarifications, finally been approved.

"As soon as possible after Christmas, but Henry seems really tied up in January."

"New York's taking up a lot of his time."

"Yes, it is. He's really hoping to get things completed by the summer though and spend every day thereafter in England. He comes home on the 23$^{rd}$ and goes back on the 2$^{nd}$. Sometimes I think he's actually getting a bit fed up with it. He actually talked about us retiring and living in the villa when it's built. Yeah, I can imagine him retiring ... not. Listen, I have to go," Malissa said, collecting up the papers and putting them into her bag, "but we'll catch up next week, or Sunday if you aren't dancing. Lewis misses you."

They kissed goodbye and Vanessa ordered another coffee.

The assignment to 'Cats' was a three-month contract. After that, many dancers from The Fenner Agency would be drafted into the Sadler's Wells Theatre and a new production based upon a stage play written by one of the Fenner's authors. It wasn't common knowledge yet, a few t's needed crossing, but it was an exciting development for Malissa and her team.

Vanessa wondered if she'd enjoy being a cat. She smiled to herself. She hadn't heard from Monique, but she would have been pleased to tell her that her little kitten had now, officially, grown up. She finished her drink and realised she didn't need to refer to the note she had scribbled down in the pub last week. *Ground floor, number two, block of flats right on the corner. Left hand door, first one you come to. Can't miss it.* She hoped Fred Nugent would be home.

.

# 29

# JANUARY 1988, LONDON

*V*anessa had spent Christmas in Paris with Gabrielle. She promised her sister she could come and stay with her in London in the summer holidays, and that she would try and visit her at least once every couple of months. Gabrielle was nearly 14 now and, as far as Vanessa could tell, very happy.

Vanessa had seriously considered accepting Malissa's invitation for her and Gabrielle to spend Christmas with them, especially as it would have given her the opportunity to meet Henry. Although Gabrielle wasn't aware of *everything* Vanessa had got up to when she lived with Monique, Vanessa still worried if her sister might unwittingly say something to Malissa that could cause embarrassment. In truth, Vanessa believed Malissa had guessed that much of her 'burlesque' dancing career in Paris had not always mirrored the sophistication of the Moulin Rouge, but Vanessa, with her new life in London, would much prefer to keep those episodes of her life to herself.

She lay in bed thinking about the parallels in people's existences; how daughters inherit something from their mothers which can unwittingly govern the course of their lives. She felt lucky to be in London, lucky to have found a new life, and to have broken a cycle that could have so easily led her in a different direction. She thought how fortunate she was to have met Malissa and she thought about Emma and what had become of her;

what did Emma inherit from their mother and had she, after her disastrous start to life, managed to break that cycle?

When Vanessa had called on Fred Nugent before Christmas, he wasn't home. He was, according to his neighbour, spending Christmas with his family. Vanessa had sat in a café thinking long and hard about whether she should write to him but that would mean using her real name and giving him the office telephone number. Instead, she wrote a note and, after briefly explaining to his neighbour the reason she wanted to see Mr Nugent, slipped it through his letter box saying she would be passing by today. She had left no contact details so wasn't sure he'd actually be in when she rang the bell. But he was.

Mr Nugent was a small, kindly-looking man in his eighties. Vanessa wouldn't have thought he would have spent all his working life behind a bar - he didn't look the type. He was expecting her and, to Vanessa's delight, seemed genuinely pleased to have a visitor. His house was clean and tidy, a credit to him, and she mentally compared how different it was to her father's flat in Paris.

As he made tea, he gave Vanessa a little history about the area and about his life. He had been married once, but his wife died while he still ran the pub in Pimlico. It wasn't the same without her and he moved out of London to live with his daughter. Within a year, however, he moved back to the area and into the flat he now occupied.

Every now and then, he'd catch the bus and go for a beer in his old pub, but his social life seemed to centre around the club at the end of the street where he could play cribbage and dominos every day and bingo at night. He was a contented man and Vanessa had warmed to him immediately.

He had two armchairs in his front room, but there was no sign of a whisky bottle.

"Enough about me, young lady," he said when they'd finished their tea and were seated in the sitting room, "I believe you came here to find out more about Lord Felix?"

Vanessa was surprised how he'd suddenly switched the subject to the one she had written to him about.

"Yes, Mr Nugent. Lord Felix is related to a cousin of mine and she is curious to discover what become of him. I think she'd like to track him down. Or his sons."

His smile was kind and he looked at her for a moment. She wondered if he believed the reason for her interest in Lord Felix.

"Well, Monique," he said, "I believe your intentions are nothing but good, so I shall tell you what I know."

They talked for more than an hour. Fred didn't know Lord Felix personally, he never came into the pub, but like every good publican Fred listened and talked to his regulars. He had heard rumours of a scandal, but he'd always heard those. "Those so-called diplomats didn't believe that normal rules applied to them," he'd said, and suggested a rumour surrounding an illegitimate child would not have been unusual.

Much of what Fred told Vanessa about the neighbourhood reflected what she had heard from her mother and, whilst this was welcome, nothing he said suggested he knew the whereabouts of Lord Felix or his sons. Just when she thought it was time to go, he smiled, crossed the room and handed her a bundle of letters.

Lord Felix's housekeeper, who quite possibly assumed the duties after her grandmother Edith passed away, came into the pub regularly. Her name was Betty, and she and Fred's wife became good friends. In 1963, when Lord Felix moved to Hertfordshire, Betty moved with him and kept in touch with Fred's wife for a while. Fred's wife loved to write letters and he told Vanessa that she was quite welcome to look at those she had received from Betty. He'd found them amongst so many of the memories he had kept of her. Vanessa wondered if Betty was the Mrs Daniels her mother had mentioned.

Vanessa wondered if Felix Lasserre was still alive and whether he still lived at the address emblazoned on the letters. If he was, and if he did still live there, should she try and contact him? Would he be able to tell her anymore about Emma? Would he have information to help Vanessa track her down? Or did she want to meet him in order to extract some kind of revenge on behalf of her mother?

# 30

## OCTOBER 1952, EAST LONDON
### ANNA BROUDIER

"*I*t's lovely, Tommy, thank you."

Tommy smiled. "I'll paint it pink tomorrow."

Anna trailed her fingers around the cot. "We're going to be so happy." She kissed him on the cheek and tended to their supper while he got changed.

It was a cool night and they had no heating so after they'd eaten Tommy slipped into the bed while Anna mended a tear in one his shirts. He smiled at her and when she'd finished sewing suggested she came to bed. She knew he wouldn't want to sleep just yet and after she kissed him gently he drew her close, his desire for her obvious. The thought of anybody entering her repulsed her but the excuse that she was still sore from giving birth was wearing thin and she could feel his frustration.

"Come on, Anna, it'll prove you love me," he said.

Anna didn't love Tommy, but he represented the best chance she had of getting back her daughter.

"Tommy, you know I love you, I just need a little more time. Now, I know you like this," she smiled, gently stroking his penis, "and I can show you love in other ways, the way you like." She kissed him again before putting her head beneath the blanket.

Tommy sighed and whispered, "I do love you Anna."

Mrs Daniels had risked everything in telling her where they had taken her daughter and in aiding Anna's escape. Since a month had passed, and Anna hadn't seen or heard anything of them, she assumed Lord Felix had believed his housekeeper's story and hoped no harm had come to her.

Mrs Daniels had given her an address in Aldgate, and the name of a woman she could trust and who would give her a place to sleep. It took half an hour to walk to the orphanage from there and for the first few days she had sat in the park keeping an eye on the gates. It was impossible to get in and when, in desperation, and against the advice of Mrs Daniels, she went to the police, she quickly realised they had no interest in helping her.

Only Tommy, the orphanage's porter who she had befriended, could help. He was 19 and lived in a room within 15 minutes' walk of the orphanage. She told him her story one night and had not been back to Aldgate since.

It had taken Tommy a few days to locate her daughter. He didn't have access to the dormitories the babies slept in but knew someone who did. After two weeks he had come up with a plan, and next Wednesday afternoon Anna would have her daughter back. She'd be sleeping next to her in that pink cot. The thought of marrying Tommy did not enthral her, but she could deal with that later. She needed to be patient.

# FEBRUARY 1988, MAJORCA

## VANESSA AND MALISSA

*V*anessa's enjoyed the role as one of the dancers in 'Cats'. Physically it was quite demanding, but technically it wasn't difficult and Fenner's had several dancers who had learned the routines and who could cover in case of injury. This meant it was easy for Vanessa to have a few days off and accompany Malissa to Majorca.

Malissa and Henry loved Söller, a resort nestled behind the Tramuntana Mountains on the north-east coast of the island. It was the place they had honeymooned and the place they planned to build a second home. Initial groundwork had already started, but the plans had been drawn up by an English architect and Malissa was meeting with various people over the next couple of days to discuss them. Earlier Malissa had driven Vanessa up to the peninsula to show her just where the villa would be built.

They were having dinner at The Söller Grand, the hotel where they were staying, which was located in Söller Port and part owned by Malissa's husband's company. It had been a sunny afternoon, warm for the time of year, but the evening had cooled somewhat, and having shared a bottle of wine at one of the outside tables, they decided to move inside to eat. There were only six other people in the restaurant and Lewis was asleep in his pushchair.

The Grand was located on the seafront at Söller Port which was more touristy than the old town. It sat midpoint on the bay which curved from the harbour overlooked by the mountains on the left, for 2 kilometres to the rocky headland that formed the peninsula where they planned to build the villa, on the right. Either side of The Grand, shops and bars and smaller hotels fringed the bay, and behind them, white houses with red tiled roofs and a scattering of commercial buildings stood amongst the pines and orange groves which crept up to the town, dissected by the inter-connecting road and the tram track.

"You'll love the old town, Ness," Malissa said.

Vanessa had already thought how quaint the old town was when they drove through it earlier. "It's very pretty," Vanessa agreed. "Perhaps I'll take Lewis up there tomorrow."

"Take the tram, Ness. You'll love that."

Lewis stirred and Malissa lifted him out of his pushchair and sat him in the highchair between them. "You ever thought about children, Ness?"

She had, and the thought of a child going through what she had did not enthral her. "If I do think of children, I dismiss the idea," she said. "Lewis has been introduced to a wonderful world, has wonderful parents and a wonderful life in front of him."

"And you weren't, so you think your children won't be either? Sorry, I didn't mean that to sound so abrasive."

Vanessa smiled. Even if she discounted the obstacle of her sexuality there was a lot of truth in Malissa's statement about why the thought of a child had never appealed. "I guess my father thought more of his whisky than me. But, eh, that's how it goes."

"And your mother?"

Although they had discussed their respective upbringings on many occasions, Vanessa had never gone into detail. Malissa surely appreciated, however, their childhood experiences were quite different. "My mother? She liked whisky too, but probably preferred gin."

Malissa laughed. "My mum had two snowballs once. At Christmas."

"Snowballs?"

"Advocaat."

"Oh."

"But you turned out okay."

"I guess it leaves its mark. Now, where else can I take Lewis?" Vanessa asked, attempting to change the subject.

Malissa suggested a few places, but strongly recommended she take the old train that carved its way from the old town, through the mountains and into Palma. It was bigger version of the Soller trams really. She was also adamant that the day after tomorrow they should go to the peninsula again.

"You must see the farmhouse me and Henry stayed in, Ness. It needs a bit of work but it's truly charming. Built right into the mountain and the view's fantastic."

"Sounds wonderful."

"I just thought," Malissa said with a broad grin. "Once they start building, it'll mean staying here quite a bit, you know, to keep an eye on things. It'd be a great place to stay. I'll talk to the builders tomorrow and see what they say. It'd make a great holiday home."

The hotel manager appeared, carrying a telephone, and informed Malissa that Mr Ovmeister would be calling in a minute. He placed the telephone on the table and plugged it in. Malissa thanked him and introduced him to Vanessa. Thirty seconds later, the telephone rang and Malissa lifted the receiver.

Vanessa listened, sensing the love Malissa shared with her husband. After five minutes Malissa held the receiver so Lewis could talk to his father. Lewis recognised his dad and while he was a little too young to hold a meaningful conversation, he smiled broadly.

"Say 'bye bye' to Daddy, Lewis," Malissa said before putting the phone back to her ear. They talked some more and then Malissa smiled across the table. "And, yes, my love, Vanessa is fine. And such great company. Why don't you talk to her yourself?"

Vanessa had never talked to Henry and, momentarily recalling the pressing reason she'd like to, felt a little uneasy as she accepted the receiver.

"Mademoiselle Cozzette. So nice to speak to you. I hope Malissa is looking after you and has shown you the delights of that wonderful town." Henry's voice was soothing and confident, his words delivered with an underlying humility that inspired immediate trust. His French was passable too.

She replied in French. "Mr Ovmeister. Nice to speak to you too, and yes, Malissa is telling me all about Söller. It's a charming place."

He reverted to English. "Well, I certainly look forward to meeting you.

Malissa has told me much and believe me she is a shrewd judge of character. Oh, and congratulations on 'Cats'. Perhaps we can come and see you next time I'm back?"

Malissa was smiling at Vanessa as she exchanged a few more pleasantries with her husband before handing back the phone.

"No, Henry, she's even *more* pretty than she sounds," Malissa said with a smile, surprising Vanessa as she reached across the table and touched her hand. "Talk soon. Love you." She replaced the handset.

"Well, that's Henry," she said.

Vanessa had already formed a deep affection for Malissa and the brief conversation with Henry left her in no doubt that same fondness would be extended to the relationship she shared with her husband. Such love was alien to her. Malissa carried on talking, and Vanessa had to mentally shake herself back into the conversation when she found her mind wandering to the relationship Henry may have shared with Emma. She realised she had pictured them as lovers.

Vanessa had already fallen in love with Lewis. Exploring Söller with him reminded her of how she used to look after Gabrielle when her sister was of similar age. Remembering too how she naturally learned English as well as her native language when she herself was a baby, Vanessa found herself speaking to Lewis in both languages. *"Ice cream Lewis. In French, la glace."*

She had also fallen in love with Söller. The main square in the old town, with its plethora of little shops and cafés, was overlooked by St Bartholomew's, an impressive 16th-century church as beautiful as any she had seen. The streets that ran off the square in all directions gave way to cobbled terraces lined by sand-coloured stone houses with wooden doors and shuttered windows, where all the residents seemed to delight in decking their frontages with a colourful abundance of potted flowers. Of particular interest to Lewis were the trams that ran down to the port, their tooting making him laugh each time they cut across the square and the streets they shared with the pedestrians.

To Vanessa, Söller was more French than Spanish, especially in the old part, and she had immediately felt at home. She had spent two days exploring with Lewis and knew this would not be her last visit here. Before leaving for home, Malissa wanted to show Vanessa the old farm-house that sat at the top of the peninsula where they were building their villa.

Malissa had been a little disappointed to learn that the preliminary groundwork for the villa would take longer than she had hoped but was delighted that the same firm of builders could start work on the old farm-house within a couple of weeks. As they walked up the hill towards the farmhouse, Vanessa could see why Malissa had enthused about the building's potential as a holiday home.

Built into the hillside, its front garden commanded a view that was truly stunning. To the left, heather-clad scrubland stepped its way down to the access road that led up here, and beyond the road the cliff edge plunged down to form this sides boundary of Söller Bay. You'd have to move further down the peninsula and look back to see the whole of the town, but from where they stood you could see the western half of the semi-circular shoreline and the mountainous backdrop that looked down on the harbour like some giant guardian.

To the right the stretch of coastline was rugged and precipitous with sheer drops to the sea, but immediately in front, the land undulated more softly downhill, through an ancient orange grove before stepping down onto a little pebble beach. Vanessa could understand why Malissa and Henry had chosen this place to build their dream.

"I said the view was good, Ness," Malissa smiled

"It's truly beautiful, Malissa."

"Come on, let's check out the farmhouse."

Casa de la Colina, the house on the hill, was built of flint and stone and oozed the charm of its 16th century origins. The hillside itself, which towered behind it, effectively formed its rear walls. The floors were made of stone. Downstairs was a kitchen and a large sitting room, and upstairs three bedrooms. Power came from an old generator housed in a shed on the right-hand side of the garden, but there was no mains water. It was sparsely furnished, and although Malissa and Henry had slept there on several occasions Vanessa appreciated there was much to do to make it a comfortable place to live.

"I was thinking a shower room here, and a small bathroom upstairs. Perhaps they could divide the big bedroom." Malissa had been telling her about the conversations she'd had with the builders yesterday. "It would need a new kitchen, of course, but in the great scheme of things not a lot of work really."

"And electricity and running water?" Vanessa loved the house as much as Malissa did but didn't share her, 'not a lot of work' belief.

"They said they could install a large water tank at the side, and the generator, although it's a bit temperamental, has never let us down... well not much. Anyway, I'm sure they'll eventually agree to run water and electricity up here. I mean, how difficult can that be?"

Vanessa smiled. She had witnessed how Malissa could instil belief in the most sceptical of people and had no doubt she would get the builders and the authorities to think her way.

"Think of the holidays we could share here, Ness. And you haven't even seen the beach yet. Remember its February, much warmer here in the summer."

The peninsula was as enchanting as the rest of Söller, and as they drove back to the hotel Vanessa wondered if she would ever take a holiday here. So much in her life had changed in the last year and she with it. Tonight, they were having dinner at the harbour with, as Vanessa had come to understand, the people who ran this town. Tomorrow they'd return to London. She was glad Malissa had asked her to accompany her to Majorca.

## 32

## MARCH 1988, LONDON

*V*anessa had telephoned Gabrielle. She was well. She was also excited that Vanessa had landed a job in one of London's top musicals. However, Gabrielle didn't realise that today was the anniversary of their mother's death. Vanessa didn't remind her, but it made her sad that their mother could be forgotten so easily.

According to directory enquiries, Felix Lasserre was still listed at the address Fred Nugent had shown her. She had, up until now, resisted any urge to contact him, failing to see exactly what it would achieve. As she thought about her mother, however, and imagined the impact losing her daughter had upon her, she knew it was something she would have to do sooner or later.

# 33

# NOVEMBER 1952, EAST LONDON
## ANNA BROUDIER

"Any news, Tommy? What did Warren say?"

"He knows nothing, Anna. I'm sorry."

"Oh, Tommy, why can't we find her?"

She burst into tears as she had done every night since discovering her daughter had been removed from the orphanage two days before they had planned to rescue her.

Tommy put his arm around her, aware nothing he could do or say would offer any comfort. He took her hand and unfolded her fingers. The scrap of paper fell to the floor and Anna buried her head into his chest, her soft sobs echoing around the room.

"Someone must know. Surely someone must know, Tommy."

"We've tried everything, Anna."

"We can't give up, Tommy."

"We won't, I promise. Hey, I got us some fish. From Jack's."

Anna tried to smile as Tommy gently let go of her and fetched the food he'd brought in with him.

He sat back on the bed and unwrapped their fish and chip supper. "Hey, maybe we could write something in the paper," he said. "You know, in one of those lost and found columns? Or in the ads. It's worth a try."

"Or go to the police again. It'd be the same result." Anna picked up the piece of paper.

Tommy watched as she unfolded it. "Well, we have a name. That we *can* thank Warren for. He'd get the sack if they found out," he said.

"Tommy, are we sure that's the name?"

"As sure as we can be. There was nothing in the register. Warren says that's unusual but does happen. But it's the same name written above her cot and the same name the matron wrote down. He saw her do it."

"Ovmeister." Anna said softly. She had said the name a thousand times.

"You see, Anna, it's not like her name's Smith. I mean, how many Ovmeisters can there be?"

"Then why can't we find her?"

Tommy said nothing.

"I'm beginning to think you're right, Tommy," Anna whispered.

Tommy put his arm around her and pulled her close.

She felt her stomach tighten and that burn in her throat. She wondered if her sore eyes could shed anymore tears. "I think you're right," she repeated. "I think she's been taken to Germany."

"That's not definite, Anna. It was just something I said when we couldn't find out anything."

"But it's a German name and you said Warren heard her talking with a German accent. She's in Germany. I know it."

Tommy said nothing, but Anna knew he believed it too.

"What can we do, Tommy?"

"We can hope, and we can keep looking. We can still get married and have children of our own and one day, when we least expect it, we could find her." He paused, before saying what he had said several times during the last few weeks. Words he thought would offer comfort, but to Anna they just reinforced her belief that her child was gone forever. "And Warren said she's gone to a good home. He had never known Mrs Whitley to talk about a baby as she did. Absolutely insistent she went somewhere suitable."

Anna scrunched the paper slowly in her hand. She knew her heart would never mend.

# 34

# JULY 1988, CORNWALL

## FEELVIEW BAY

*W*hen she was nine years old, Vanessa sprained her ankle. The doctor had told Mademoiselle Lauren that she should not dance for at least six weeks, but her dance teacher was adamant that minor injuries were merely part and parcel of being a dancer and should not interfere with training. Since then, Vanessa had relied on strapping to support the inherent weakness.

Two months ago, Vanessa felt that familiar twang and had to hold on to a colleague to avoid tumbling. The audience didn't notice. She should have left the stage but carried on and by the time she finished the set she was in excruciating pain. She was examined by the physio and a doctor was called. The following day she was in hospital and x-rays revealed that the ligaments had torn and there was a slight fracture. The doctor was amazed that she had been able to carry on dancing and ordered complete rest. He also told her only surgery could bring about a significant improvement and she might want to consider the option. She was discharged after two days, her ankle lightly plastered. She would be off work for at least eight weeks.

Vanessa was far from convinced that the Fenner Agency insured their dancers in the way Malissa had told her, but Malissa was adamant she heed the doctors advice and take time of work. She did, but when she could at least walk unaided, Vanessa insisted she assist Malissa in the office as she had done before. It also provided the perfect opportunity for Gabrielle to come and stay with her and they spent a week or so exploring London together.

They also stayed a weekend at Malissa's. Malissa, as Vanessa anticipated, quizzed Gabrielle about Vanessa's upbringing. "She never tells me anything," she'd joked, and while Gabrielle did intimate that her sister's younger days were far from perfect, she didn't say anything too different to what Vanessa had already told Malissa. On the odd occasion where Malissa would seek to delve a little deeper, Vanessa could always step in, alternating between French and English to steer any conversation away from something she'd rather not discuss. She was glad she still hadn't told Gabrielle about Emma.

Vanessa remained surprised by the esteem in which she was held at the office. Once a week, usually on a Friday, the staff would spend a lunchtime in the local pub; 'Brian's Orders' they called it. At one of these lunchtime gatherings, a colleague, Malcolm, asked Vanessa for a date. He was persistent and the old Vanessa would have left him in no doubt that she wasn't interested, but in this new environment she thought it best to simply tell him that she had a boyfriend in France. This still didn't deter Malcolm, but Sharon, one of the office workers who was party to the conversation, came to her assistance. When Malcolm had gone, Sharon said if she needed someone to mix with in the evenings, she was single; she was also a good friend of Dawn's.

Vanessa had no desire for a girlfriend but didn't know whether Dawn, who she saw only in passing these days, had told Sharon about the relationship they once enjoyed. Perhaps she would go out with Sharon one night to tell her that she was no longer the woman Dawn may have described and convince her, if it was on her mind, that her friendship with Malissa was just that - friendship. Again, Vanessa realised how much she had come to value the relationship she shared with Malissa and hated the thought that any of Malissa's employees regarded their office relationship as anything other than professional.

Although she felt fit enough to dance again, Malissa had taken it upon herself to assign another dancer to 'Cats'. Another few weeks' rest would do no harm and next month she could join the rest of the team when they started rehearsals for 'Love in Idleness', the Fenner's own production which Malissa seemed so excited about. In the meantime, the enforced period of recuperation also presented a great opportunity to go to Cornwall with Malissa to meet Alice and Delores Delahay, the racehorse Malissa had told her about.

Feelview Bay was a stud farm and convalescence centre for racehorses. The establishment was owned by Henry and run by Alice's husband, Charlie Taylor. Alice, to all intents and purpose, was Malissa's sister-in-law and Malissa had told her much about her. "Ness, she can seem as daft as a brush, but she's really lovely. You'll love her."

On the drive down, Malissa told her many stories about Alice; about the first time she met her with Henry, and how she imagined Alice must have struggled with Henry's flamboyant nature when they were young. The stories made Vanessa laugh, but those references to the time when Alice and Henry lived together made Vanessa think of Emma and the relationship she must have shared with Henry. This reminded her she had still to discover the truth and ignited that familiar pang of guilt for having never shared the story of her older sister with Malissa. Sometimes Vanessa tried to convince herself that Emma and Henry had never known each other - that everything she had discovered was just coincidence - but the evidence was overwhelming. Alice had known Henry since he was a baby. If Vanessa was right, then surely Alice would have known Emma too. Vanessa didn't wonder why the prospect of meeting Alice made her a little nervous.

They pulled up outside the house. Alice rushed out, throwing her arms around Malissa immediately she got out of the car and greeting her and Lewis as enthusiastically as Malissa had predicted. When she saw Vanessa she seemed momentarily lost for words and looked quickly at Malissa who smiled and said, "This is Vanessa."

"Of course, it is," Alice said slowly and extended her hand. Malissa had told Vanessa to expect a less conventional greeting. "You're not what I expected," Alice said, quickly looking at Malissa again who stood there smiling. "I mean, you are, but you shocked me a bit. I mean, you don't look like a ballerina."

Vanessa smiled. Malissa laughed.

"I mean, ballerinas are thin," Alice continued. "You're...Well, you're normal. I don't mean fat. God no, you've got a lovely figure, it's just Malissa said you were in the ballet."

She wasn't quite the animated Alice that Vanessa had been led to expect, but Vanessa immediately sensed her gentleness and thought Alice may have considered she'd said the wrong thing. "That was a long time ago, Alice," Vanessa said smiling, "I'm more your contemporary dancer these days."

"Yes, that's what I meant. Ah funny. Sorry, just one of those things you say without thinking." And as they walked into the house Alice's tempo picked up, more akin to the woman Malissa had told her to expect as she explained the difference between thin, stick thin and something she called 'ballerina thin'.

They sat down as soon as they entered the kitchen, but then Alice sprang up and, like Malissa had predicted, told them about the cakes she had made. She gave Lewis one first, before fumbling around for plates and putting the kettle on. "How he's grown, Malissa," Alice enthused. "Looks just like Henry. Well, better looking of course, because of you."

With tea made and seated back at the table Alice calmed down, asked about their journey and talked to Malissa about some horses, Henry's horses Vanessa guessed. Malissa had told Vanessa that Alice was shy, but after a while the furtive little glances she directed Vanessa's way turned into the more conventional eye contact you'd expect when three friends were engaged in light conversation. When she asked Vanessa about dancing she seemed most impressed she had starred in 'Cats'.

"Well, I wasn't actually the star, Alice, just one of 20 something back-ground singer-dancers, though I did have the occasional line, well, purr really."

"Ness is too modest, Alice," interrupted Malissa. "She could star in any London musical. In fact, when she was young, she danced in the most famous theatre in Paris..."

Malissa proceeded to tell Alice about Vanessa's dancing career in Paris. On several occasions Vanessa felt compelled to deny that her achievements were of the magnitude Malissa suggested. Like Malissa, however, Alice was intrigued that Vanessa had danced at the Moulin Rouge and, like Malissa, she too would love to go there one day.

When they talked about Vanessa's injury Alice thought it rather apt that she had come to Feelview. It was after all, a place for convalescing, and most of the guests also had leg injuries. They were still in the kitchen when Charlie arrived at about 5pm. "This is Vanessa," Alice said to him when he came in. He seemed a little surprised and looked back at his wife as is if seeking clarification. "She's Malissa's friend, you know, the dancer I told you about."

Charlie smiled broadly. "It's good to meet you, Vanessa," he said, and kissed her lightly on the cheek before saying hello to Malissa.

When Lewis had gone to bed, they played Scrabble. It was hard to believe Alice was in her forties and Vanessa imagined her outlook on life was still the same today as it was 30 years ago. Alice seemed impressed by Vanessa's ability at Scrabble, "seeing as you are French, I mean," and Vanessa had to explain that her mother spoke English fluently and that she herself was brought up naturally speaking both languages. Plus, she had added with a smile, many words that scored highly in Scrabble were derived from the French language.

Vanessa found it difficult to sleep that night, and at one point retrieved the newspaper cutting she always carried around with her and went into the bathroom. She mentally compared the image of Emma with her reflection in the mirror. They were not dissimilar, and recalling Alice and Charlie's reactions when they first met her she wondered what they saw. Did they know Emma, and if they did had Vanessa momentarily stirred a memory?

Apart from the odd occasion, Vanessa had managed to dismiss any thoughts of Emma when she was with Malissa – disassociate any connection – but meeting Alice and Charlie had brought the thought of her older sister to the front of her mind. The same scenario played over in her mind. If Henry knew Emma, Alice knew Emma. But when? Vanessa hated feeling she was some kind of amateur detective trying to unravel a mystery that somehow implicated her new friends in England. She forced her thoughts aside; she'd get her answers when she finally met Henry. But before she did, she realised she had decided to call upon Felix Lasserre as soon as she possibly could.

Eventually she drifted off to sleep, thinking nice things, thinking about how kind it was of Malissa to introduce her to her friends and family, and bring her to Cornwall. She looked forward to tomorrow and the plans they'd made. But just as she felt sleep would come she startled herself, suddenly sitting up in bed and realising she had the overwhelming impression that Emma had been here.

The following day she met Delores Delahay, who was stabled near the house, and visited the riding stables that were located on another part of the estate. Vanessa had never ridden a horse but Alice was a good teacher and they spent three hours trekking around the countryside. In the evening they all visited the model village in the nearby seaside town of Polperro where they also had dinner. Vanessa warmed to Alice; they quickly became friends and much of the shyness she had displayed when they first met disappeared. She could, as Malissa had said, seem as daft as a brush, but this surely came from her natural belief in the goodness of people and Vanessa thought she was probably the gentlest human being she had ever met.

Wednesday dawned bright and warm. Part of Malissa's reason for coming to Cornwall was to call on one of The Fenner Agency's writers who lived about 30 miles away and Vanessa was only too happy to look after Lewis while she was gone. She suggested to Alice she might take him to the beach. "Malissa said there was a little cove by the cottage," she said.

Alice seemed surprised at Vanessa's suggestion and suggested Polperro might be more suitable; the beach by the cottage was very rocky.

"Oh, Malissa said it was lovely down there."

"It is," Alice said. "I just thought if Lewis wanted an ice cream or something, there's more things there. I just have to check on some of the horses and we can drive down."

Vanessa looked at the clock. By the time they'd driven to Polperro and found somewhere to park, they'd have little time before they'd have to head back. "Perhaps I'll just take Lewis for a walk. The doctors told me to exercise this ankle, anyway. Does the lane outside lead to the cottage?"

Alice seemed a little uneasy. "Yes... it does. To the cottage."

"Is it far?"

"No, 15 minutes at the most."

"Pushchair friendly?"

"Well, as far as the cottage it is. There are steep steps to get onto the beach."

"Sounds lovely. Is there anybody there this week?" Malissa had told her the cottage was a holiday let.

"Usually there is, but no, they don't turn up 'til Friday."

"Or we can go to Polperro. I don't mind. It was just that Malissa said she'll be back just after lunch."

Alice smiled. "No, it's fine. We can go to the cottage beach. It is nice and I'll come with you and show you around."

"Perhaps we could take a picnic? It's such a lovely morning and I think Lewis would like that."

Alice made a few sandwiches and put them in the basket with an assortment of cakes. They put Lewis in his pushchair and headed down the gravelly lane. It was about a kilometre to the cottage, but within 100 metres the lane began run parallel to the sea, about 50 metres from the cliff top. Alice was by nature a fidgety person, but Vanessa detected an uneasiness as the cottage came in sight.

"Usually it's occupied," Alice repeated. "I mean, it will be Friday, but generally it's booked out all summer. A lot of winter too. And always Christmas."

"It's truly beautiful, Alice. You are very fortunate to live in such a wonderful place. And a 15 minute walk to your own private beach."

Alice smiled. "Well, it used to be longer. I mean, you couldn't walk here. Not down this road. You'd have to take the main road. We still tell people to drive in from the main road. We just use this as access really. Years ago it was only a little path, we built it..." she paused. "It's much easier to go this way, not that we come here that often. To the cottage, I mean. Except to greet the visitors sometimes, of course. Cheryl does the cleaning."

Last night when they were all having dinner Alice seemed completely relaxed but she seemed a little edgy this morning. Vanessa hated the thought that being alone with her made Alice feel uncomfortable.

"Alice, your cakes are the most wonderful I have ever tasted. Perhaps you could teach me how to make those lemon drizzles before I go."

Alice smiled and linked Vanessa's arm which surprised her. She told her lemon drizzle had always been Henry's favourite and she would be delighted to cook with her tomorrow. She also suggested several other varieties they could bake.

They reached a gate. The cottage stood 50 metres in front of them, set in its own garden, beyond a small stream that tumbled seaward, chan-nelling water down from the surrounding hills. They lent on the gate for a minute, before walking through. Vanessa lifted Lewis out of his pushchair - they could walk the rest of the way.

They crossed the garden, exiting through another gate, and onto a pathway just wide enough for them to walk side by side. Raised kerbstones bordered the path, just as they had along the lane that led here and also the walkway that seemed to go all the way around the cottage. Vanessa wondered why the pathways had been constructed that way but didn't ask.

They reached the edge of the cliff and another gate which opened onto the steps that led down to the beach. The tide was in. The gentle whoosh of breaking waves and 'clack' of rolling pebbles merged with the crackling splash of the water from the stream which fell to the beach a little way to their right. Alice lifted Lewis onto the wooden fence, holding him carefully as the three of them looked out to sea.

"Truly beautiful," Vanessa said.

"Feelview Bay," Alice said softly

Vanessa looked at her. Alice seemed pensive.

"Feelview," Alice repeated with a smile. Maybe the sting of the breeze had brought the moisture to her eyes. "Henry called this place Feelview. He said you can *feel* the view." She turned to Vanessa, looking at her more seriously for a moment. "If you close your eyes, I mean."

# 35

# DECEMBER 1988

## FELIX LASSERRE

*A*lthough rehearsals started as planned, the opening of 'Love in Idleness', a comical ballet written by one of the Fenner writers and based loosely around Shakespeare's A Midsummer Night's Dream, had been postponed until the new year. This suited Vanessa, as although she had attended all rehearsals she was not convinced her ankle had totally heeled and the six-week delay would give it more time.

Vanessa told Malissa of her concerns and they decided that Fenner's would sponsor her to further her knowledge of choreography. So, for the last few weeks, instead of accepting ad hoc assignments Vanessa had been assisting the production's choreographer, Paul Mason - one of the best in London - at his studio in Soho. "Fenner's Dance School, I like that," Malissa had said, contemplating the establishment of their own facility.

Vanessa was also surprised to hear from Monique who had written to her saying she was spending Christmas in Paris and hoped they might me up. Other than her brief returns to see Gabrielle, Vanessa had lived in London for almost two years and had changed. She still wasn't the most open person in the world, but was pleased she had largely overcome her acquired distrust of people and certainly no longer considered it necessary to use her sexuality to get what she wanted. She had friends here, friends who knew little about her past, friends who did not judge and, of course, the most precious of those was Malissa.

She often thought about her time in Paris; about Mademoiselle Lauren, the boys who raped her and the drunken men old enough to be her grandfather who would throw money at her to remove her clothing. Yes, they had used her, but she had used them too. She'd think about Etienne who she seduced and feigned pregnancy in order to extort money from his father and those hapless men who had given her hush money fearing she would tell their wives what they got up to. She had shed so much of her old life and now enjoyed a period of contentment longer than any she had ever known and wondered how she would react to Monique if she did see her when she returned to Paris for Christmas.

The last few months had been busy, helping Vanessa push aside any thoughts of Emma. She tried to convince herself that discovering the truth about her older sister, someone she never knew existed for most of her life, was somehow irrelevant. The more she considered her time with Alice though, the more convinced she became that Feelview Bay, Alice and Emma were connected. The Emma Ovmeister who played the violin was blind and Vanessa couldn't help but surmise that the little raised edgings that surrounded the cottage had been laid to define borders for someone who couldn't see. And she remembered Alice's remarks; "You can feel the bay... if you close your eyes, I mean." Perhaps it was her mind working overtime but Vanessa knew she would find it difficult to rest until she knew the truth.

She had thought long and hard about contacting Felix Lasserre but eventually telephoned him using the name Monica Smith. Only when she spoke French and hinted that she was abandoned to an orphanage in 1952 did he agree to see her. How much of her desire to meet Lord Felix was because of Emma and how much because of her mother she didn't know, but somehow both were intrinsically intertwined. She hoped meeting with him would provide some kind of closure.

The journey to Baldock was about 45 minutes. There were few people on the train and Vanessa used the time to write down all that she had learned from her mother, ordering the sequence of events that eventually led to the birth of Emma. She was dressed in a smart grey trouser suit and mock Burberry trench coat she had borrowed from Paul Mason's costume department and with her assumed name, wasn't surprised that by the time the train stopped at the station, she felt like an amateur detective.

During the 15 minutes it took for the taxi to reach Morden Hall Lodge she realised that whilst she may well discover a little more about Emma, the main purpose of her visit was to confront Lord Felix on behalf of her mother. She understood the nervousness she felt but by the time she knocked on the front door she could also feel an anger building.

She was led into the drawing room, and with each step she took Vanessa could feel herself reverting to the woman she had been in France. By the time Felix Lasserre entered the room, she had changed; her new-found contentment had been brushed aside and replaced by thoughts of her grandmother who the bastard used, her mother he didn't protect and *her* daughter who he simply cast aside.

Felix Lasserre was an old man with a wave of white, wiry hair, bushy white eyebrows and a white beard. He was dressed in a smart navy suit and tie, and was wheeled into the room by his 40 year-old housekeeper, no doubt the woman who had dressed him that morning and who obviously harboured her own agenda. Felix Lasserre was definitely not fucking *her* though.

Her eyes snarled at Vanessa as she wheeled her employer up to the table. Vanessa met her gaze and smiled spitefully before turning her attention to the man she had thought about meeting for the last 12 months. To his housekeeper's disgust Lord Felix dismissed her, asking her to close the door when she left the room.

He offered Vanessa a drink as he wheeled himself to the sideboard. She declined. He poured a glass and wheeled himself back to the table. She studied him for a full minute. He did not divert his eyes. Vanessa sensed he had been expecting this moment for many years. He spoke first. "So, Miss Smith. How can I help you?"

She let his question hang in the air, breathing deeply so she could control the surge of resentment that had been building inside her. "My mother's name was Anna," she eventually said. She spoke in French; it seemed more fitting.

The statement didn't surprise him. He took a sip of his brandy and kept his eyes on hers.

"And her mother's name?" he asked.

Vanessa said nothing. Her eyes told him he knew that answer.

"Edith," he whispered after a while. "A wonderful woman. I'm pleased things have worked out for you."

It suddenly dawned on Vanessa that if he believed she was the grown-up version of the infant he sent to an orphanage 36 years ago, he would believe he was talking to his granddaughter. Of course, Vanessa was 14 years younger than Emma would have been but the thought both amused and sickened her.

"You have her eyes," he added. "You have Edith's eyes."

Vanessa laughed and stood up. He swivelled in his wheelchair so his eyes could follow her as she circled the room. There was a light knock on the door and a voice from outside, the housekeeper asking if he was alright. "Joan, I would appreciate some privacy. I'm sure you have better things to do than stand at the door."

Vanessa lit a cigarette and fetched the decanter of brandy over to the table. She topped up his glass and lent over him so she could whisper in his ear. "I am my mother's daughter. And, yes, I may have her mother's eyes. But thankfully I am no relation of yours."

For a moment, Vanessa regretted what she had just said. It may have been more convenient for him to continue to believe she was Emma. She felt the spite of her childhood rise inside her but could still cover it in blanket of cold indifference.

"Then who are you?" His voice could not hide his concern.

"I am a woman who seeks justice."

"Money?"

"You think money would be justice, Monsieur Lasserre?"

"It was a long time ago, Miss Smith."

"Tell me about Edith." Vanessa heard the spite in her voice. "Tell me why you felt it okay that your sons could fuck my mother when she was just thirteen years old? And tell me what happened to my sister."

He said nothing for a few seconds while he calculated who Vanessa might be. "It was a long time ago and my memory fades."

"Perhaps your sons have better memories?"

Vanessa had no idea where either of his sons were, but the mention of the bastards who had thought it their right to repeatedly abuse her mother seemed to jog his memory. His expression softened as he searched for a suitable response.

"My sons," he said quietly. "Miss Smith, I have both dreaded and yearned for this day for more years than I care to remember. Perhaps I hoped it would be someone else sitting there, someone older than yourself, but for my own selfish reasons I am happy to tell you everything I know. Please, sit down and please let me offer you some tea."

He summoned Joan.

"Everything all right, Mr Lasserre?"

"Everything is fine, Joan. Perhaps you'd be so kind as to bring us some tea. I've much to tell Miss Smith and I would appreciate not being disturbed. Perhaps you'd like to pop into town and see your mother?"

She didn't look at Vanessa. "Certainly, Sir," she said, and left the room.

"She's waiting for me to die," he smiled. "Don't judge her too harshly. I can tell you value loyalty highly."

He reached across the table and touched Vanessa's hand. It surprised her but she didn't recoil. "You have every right to hate me," he said, "and I seek no forgiveness. You are Edith's granddaughter, that I can tell, and I can only but guess the journey that brought you here."

He released Vanessa's hand. "Edith came to me in the summer after the war. It had been a cool grey summer, but that day it was warm and sunny, and in her blue floral dress and pale pink hat her smile was the epitome of a sunny day. She was 25, I dare say not so much older than you, and so beautiful – so real, so aware of life, yet with an air that could grace any circles she cared to walk in."

Vanessa watched as he wheeled himself to the other side of the room. He rummaged through a drawer, and returning to the table handed her a photograph. "Regrettably, this is the only photograph I have. She's the one to the left of me."

It was the first time Vanessa had seen an image of her grandmother, but she could have easily pointed her out amongst the half dozen people in the photo. Joan appeared and placed a tray on the table before announcing she was off to town and would be back by mid-afternoon. This time she did shoot a darting look at Vanessa before leaving.

Felix Lasserre and Vanessa talked for two hours. She left with a strange comfort inside her; not just because she had exacted some sort of recompense for what had happened to her mother, but because she had learned so much more. Felix Lasserre was not as terrible as she'd imagined, and she believed he had been truly fond of her grandmother. She didn't doubt they had been lovers, nor did she believe it was merely duty that compelled Edith to share his bed.

He talked about her early years in France and her dream of being a dancer. He seemed to know more about her life than her own mother did, telling Vanessa how she lost her parents when she was relatively young and how her first husband, the father of Vanessa's own mother, was killed along with his family in a German bombing raid early in the war.

Edith died of tuberculosis at the age of 31. She was buried in a cemetery in London managed by the Royal Parks Commission. Her headstone simply read 'Edith Broudier 1919-1950...', but her grave was kept tidy by the authorities. His obvious affection for Edith did not, however, excuse the treatment of her daughter and the subsequent abandonment of Emma. His regret and guilt were obvious and in a moment of deeper reflection Vanessa saw a swell of tears in his eyes as he recalled the events. "I will carry that burden until the day I die, and I fear God will judge me," he'd said. Vanessa tried hard to dismiss any sympathy she felt for his remorse.

His own wife and, as far as Vanessa could determine his ticket to the privileged lifestyle he enjoyed, was ten years older than him and suffered from what would now be called chronic fatigue syndrome. "She had no interest in love, even before her illness, just stature and her place in the community..." Poorly she may have been, bedridden mostly, but she still outlived Edith. At one point, Felix told Vanessa that he would have married Edith and taken care of Anna if things were different. "But you didn't," Vanessa had snapped.

Emma was abandoned to St Mary's Orphanage. Lord Felix assured Vanessa that the institution was paid handsomely to ensure Emma was looked after. He paid a worker there the equivalent of half of his weekly wage to act as a go-between and keep him informed of her wellbeing. Felix didn't know and didn't want to know the identity of the people who took her but was assured she had been adopted into decency. He never made any attempt to track her down, nor had he tried to find Anna when she ran away a month or so after Emma was born. They were an obstacle in his life, a source of potential embarrassment and despite his apparent affection for Edith it seemingly did not extend to her daughter or the baby so cruelly taken away from her.

"How convenient for you," Vanessa had interjected.

"Yes, Miss Smith. It was convenient."

She had appreciated his honesty.

When he had finished recounting his story, Lord Felix asked Vanessa what became of Anna and her daughter. Although she thought she detected his genuine concern regarding their fate, Vanessa wondered if he deserved to know. She could tell him about her mother, of course, but with regards to Emma, other than her name, the fact she was blind, and had once played the violin at the Royal Albert Hall, everything else she may have considered was speculation.

"To ease your conscience?" she'd asked

"I have no doubt what you think of me, Miss Smith, and I know I could not buy my way out of what I allowed to happen to your mother."

Lord Felix told her he was ill and expected this coming Christmas to be his last but didn't seek her sympathy. He told her that if he could make some sort of amends he would. He had little contact with his sons, few friends, was still relatively wealthy and if she needed any financial assistance he would regard it as paying an overdue debt.

He knew she was not Monica Smith, but Vanessa was hesitant to reveal her true identity. She did, however, towards the end of their discussion soften her position. He had, in some way, given her grandmother a good home in her time of need and she detected his affection for her was genuine. She saw too, that there was little love lost between him and his own sons, and she wondered how much of that was because of what they had done to her mother. Without going into detail, she told him her mother had died. "And her daughter, your older sister?" he'd asked.

Vanessa looked at him. A myriad of scenarios flashed through her mind, scenarios she had considered for the last three years but none seemed more plausible than the other. Was she in England? Germany? Somewhere else. Was she really connected to Henry as she believed? Was she happy?

"She's no longer here either," she eventually said softly, and immediately wondered why she had said that.

"My granddaughter," Lord Felix had whispered, a genuine sadness in his old eyes.

Vanessa didn't respond.

∽

Before she left, Felix gave her a card with his solicitors details. She should talk to them next week and they would verify that they had indeed donated the money to the charities they'd discussed. As she boarded the train for the return journey to London she thought about meeting Monique during her forthcoming trip to Paris. Yes, Vanessa had a new life, but the meeting with Felix Lasserre left her in no doubt that she could always revert to the woman from Paris who had learned to survive on her own wits and sexuality.

# 36

## APRIL 1989, SADLER'S WELLS THEATRE

### THE DAY BEFORE VANESSA MEETS HENRY

'*L*ove in Idleness' had opened as rescheduled in the second week of January. It was an immediate success, and since the middle of February had been running at two performances a day, six days a week. Vanessa managed 20 of them before her ankle gave way. This time she was hospitalised for three days and wore a cast for a month. When it was removed it was obvious that the injury would need longer to heal this time, and Vanessa doubted she would be able to resume her role before the show closed in May.

She did, however, put the training she'd received from Paul Mason to good use and for the last six weeks had assumed the role of assistant choreographer for the show. Though the production had a cast of only 15 dancers, two shows a day presented Fenner's with a logistical challenge. They needed to use almost all of the 60 or so dancers on the Fenner's books, and Vanessa's first-hand knowledge of the show and the differing abilities of her colleagues meant she could quickly bring the new dancers up to speed. She also helped with the ticketing and often tended bar in the evenings. It was a Fenner Agency production, so if she couldn't take part on stage she could at least do something constructive to justify her wages.

It was good to see Monique over Christmas but, as she expected, the dynamic between them had changed. She and Julien had married in Monte Carlo and they were trying for a baby. Monique needn't work but had found part-time employment in a shop selling very expensive shoes. Vanessa laughed out loud when Monique told her how much people with money would spend on footwear that looked truly hideous on them. When they said goodbye, they didn't arrange to meet again.

Jonathon Mitchell, one third of Mitchell Morgan and Hills, Felix Lasserre's solicitors, had telephoned Vanessa last month, informing her that Lord Felix had died and insisted she visited their offices. Vanessa had never disclosed her identity to Felix Lasserre but had, at his suggestion, done so to his solicitors as Felix had promised that if anything came to light regarding Emma he would have them contact her.

Her visit, though, had nothing to do with Emma. They'd called her in to confirm that Lord Felix had bequeathed her the sum of £50,000. When she suggested it should be given to the RNIB, like the £100,000 he donated following Vanessa's visit before Christmas, they regretted they were unable to comply as it was categorically against their client's wishes. There was also a covenant that she'd need to sign on the money's release that she neither would pass on the money to a charity. "Though I am not quite sure how we would monitor that," Mitchell had said.

She left their office with £20 to cover her expenses and a letter from Felix Lasserre. Mr Mitchell also gave her a 'Letter of Authority' and his firm's address in London. Should she ever change her mind about the money she need only present the letter to them to access it. She needed to do this within 25 years otherwise the money would go elsewhere.

The letter written by Lord Felix expressed his regret, and committed to paper much of the story he had told her when they met.

*Dear Miss Smith. I shall die not knowing your name but shall be content that something of Edith lives on. You are the image of your grand-mother and I have thought of little else since your visit...*

He guessed she may refuse the money but urged her to accept it. It did, after all, take something from those who had been so cruel to her mother. Surprisingly, he also provided details of his sons; their names and whereabouts... *and you must do what you think best with this information...* He obviously wasn't convinced, as she had intimated, that she already had those details. If Felix Lasserre was a God-fearing man, he was certainly trying to make amends.

Vanessa half wished she had been more forthcoming with Lord Felix. Maybe if she had he could have used his resources to instigate a more meaningful investigation into the fate of her older half-sister. And then she thought about why she often hesitated in her endeavour to discover the truth about Emma. No matter how many times she considered her fate, Vanessa could not convince herself that Henry and Emma were strangers. Quite to the contrary, her instinct told her they had known each other well, and Vanessa wondered how much of her hesitation in making public her interest in Emma was the feeling it may harm Malissa.

## APRIL 1989, SADLER'S WELLS THEATRE

### VANESSA MEETS HENRY

*T*onight was the 100th performance of 'Love in Idleness', and Fenner's had invited many of their business associates to help them celebrate the occasion. Vanessa had seen the show several times so would be helping out in the bar instead, but she was confident that, this evening, she would finally meet Henry.

The applause from the auditorium told her it was time for the interval. She looked at her watch; 8:34pm, they were running to schedule. Within a couple of minutes people began filing through the door to collect their pre-ordered drinks. Malissa looked over and waved before sitting down at one of the tables in the far corner. Vanessa finished serving a customer before excusing herself to go over and see her. They kissed hello before Malissa took her arm and they headed over to a group of people standing around another table.

"Excuse me, Richard," Malissa said pulling Henry away from the conversation, "but I need to borrow my husband. Henry, this is Vanessa."

Henry turned and as he did his smile dropped and his deep brown eyes widened as he focused his attention on her. "Miss Cozzette," he said, it was almost a question, "how wonderful to meet you at last." He extended his hand to greet her and looked back at his wife fleetingly before returning his attention to Vanessa and smiling again. "Malissa mentioned you were a picture of radiance, and if she has similarly undersold your ability as a dancer then I very much look forward to seeing you on the stage."

Malissa laughed, said something sarcastic to Henry and then told Vanessa she'd get used to his excesses. Then she excused herself to return to her guests, saying she would see them both later.

"I'm pleased to meet you too at last, Henry," she said shaking the hand that still held hers.

"Yes," he said with a wrinkled brow, and Vanessa was reminded of that moment she first met Alice. She felt him searching for something else to say. Perhaps, "haven't we met before?"

"You don't like ballet, Henry?" Vanessa said before he spoke again: Malissa had just told him "not to rubbish the ballet...".

She saw him mentally shake himself. "I love ballet. Well, I certainly appreciate it. I'll admit I'm not quite the enthusiast my wife is and that can provoke discussion. But it's okay. Now, tap dancing..." He paused, he looked at her questioningly. "Now, that I certainly would rubbish."

Vanessa smiled. "Tap dancing and ballet are, of course, compulsory elements of a dancer's portfolio but I agree they are not quite as exciting as the more contemporary facets of our trade." She surprised herself with the tone of her reply. She was almost humouring him. She detected he had been caught off guard something she imagined was quite alien to him.

"Quite," he said simply. "Malissa tells me you have an injury that's keeping you from dancing. I'm sorry to hear that. Hey, you don't have a drink, would you like one?"

"I'm afraid I'm on duty. Maybe later?" Malissa had invited her to join them and the Fenner's guests for dinner after the show.

"Miss Cozzette, Malissa has talked much about you and it's difficult to believe we haven't met before."

It was true. Vanessa and Malissa had been close friends for two years or more. She wanted to ask him if he was sure they hadn't met, to test her belief that she had triggered a memory of Emma. Perhaps that was the real intention of his statement – to make her ask.

"It is, Henry, I agree. But I've heard much about you too and of course we've spoken several times on the phone. So, while this is the first time we have met in person, perhaps by association with those who are close to us, we feel that we are already quite well acquainted."

He took a sip of his champagne but kept his eyes on hers and for those few seconds, while he was possibly considering her remark, she wondered what he was thinking.

Suddenly he smiled broadly, placed his glass on a nearby table and changed the subject. "So, this injury of yours. I believe it has prevented you from dancing for some time, but Malissa tells me you have choreographed many of the routines in tonight's show."

By the time the end-of-interval bell rang, they were talking like the good friends Vanessa knew they'd become. Perhaps she'd be able to talk more at the aftershow dinner.

~

Before she went to bed that night Vanessa sat and studied the photograph of Emma. With her hair now cut shorter it fell so similarly to her sister's and she could easily understand why Henry may have seen the resemblance.

Before they sat down for dinner Vanessa had managed to ask Henry about his surname, suggesting it was most unusual. He told her it was of German origin but didn't elaborate. She mentioned Cornwall, her visit there, the cottage and Alice's remarks about feeling the view. And then she asked if he had always lived in London. The question hung in the air for a moment and induced a longer version of that inquisitive gaze he gave her earlier that evening, but Malissa's interruption saved him from having to answer.

Malissa had said that other than Alice, Henry had no family, certainly no one he regarded as an adopted sister. What she saw in Henry's eyes, however, confirmed what she knew in her heart. Henry and Emma were in some way very close. If they regarded themselves as brother and sister why wouldn't Malissa know about her? If Alice knew about another sister, why hadn't she told Malissa?

Henry and Emma knew each other, of that Vanessa was certain. Whether the man in the black tie in the photograph was Henry she couldn't be a hundred percent sure, but tonight had delivered the certainty she sought and she was adamant they knew one another beyond being small children. The Emma who Malissa mentioned was 14 years old; the Emma in the photograph, 22.

Did something happen that meant neither Henry nor Alice could speak about Emma; like a murder in some Agatha Christie crime novel? Did she run away? Did she disgrace herself in some way? Vanessa paused at this point and considered whether foul play could be the case. Surely neither of Alice or Henry could have been capable of that and surely that was definitely Vanessa's imagination running completely wild. But if they didn't regard themselves as brother and sister then they must have been lovers, and that love was probably beyond the teenage crush Malissa had intimated.

But what happened to Emma? Where was she now? Why did her memory seem so secret? As Vanessa mulled over all that she knew a sadness came over her, as she found herself fighting against the overwhelming feeling that Emma was no longer alive.

Vanessa had sat next to Malissa at dinner. Malissa was her friend, a good, trusting, close friend who believed everything in the world was good. When she again asked Vanessa if she would go with her to Majorca, she realised she had already made up her mind to do so. She didn't get the opportunity to talk to Henry further that evening and in two days' time he would be returning to New York. Now they had met she felt sure they would see a lot more of each other. But when she would have another opportunity to ask him about Emma, she didn't know.

# PART IV

Majorca

*Green lee 'neath purple-bronze mountain*
*Flush sunrise kissing silver-blue sea*
*Shimmering morn a new day is born*
*Colouring a grey memory*

## 38

## JULY 1989, MAJORCA

*V*anessa came back out into the garden and sat down. She'd let Lewis sleep some more. A few clouds had gathered during the afternoon, bringing welcome relief from the hot sunshine. She heard the builders say 'goodbye', then as expected saw Juan making his way up the hill. When he was 25 metres away he swung his heavy tool bag from one shoulder to the other, a ritual he'd always undertake when he felt compelled to display his muscles. He did have an impressive physique, but his display was wasted on Vanessa. It always made her chuckle though.

He nodded as he opened the gate and sat down at the patio table opposite her.

"It's hot day, Miz Vanessa," he said, wiping his brow and tugging at his vest.

Vanessa agreed and offered him a drink. He continued to talk about the weather in his broken English while Vanessa fetched him a beer. In truth it may have been easier for them to communicate in Spanish. Vanessa was not exactly fluent, but because she hadn't needed to study English at school she was given the opportunity to learn Spanish and could hold a simple conversation.

"We finish roof tomorrow. I think Miz Ovmeister be very happy," he said when Vanessa had sat back down.

She looked down at the villa. Apart from during the very hottest part of the day the builders had been working hard since Malissa left last Friday, and if the roof was indeed in place by the time she returned she would, as Juan said, be very happy. And very surprised.

"Yes, I think she will." Vanessa smiled.

"Hey, I have you something."

He reached into his bag and retrieved two oranges and handed one to her. She thanked him and suppressed a giggle as he lifted his bag over the table, ensuring she noticed his bulging bicep before placing the bag on his other side. It wouldn't be unusual if he repeated the bag swap a couple more times; it seemed to depend on the amount of fruit he'd collected. He bit into the orange, not worrying to peel it.

"Louis sleeps?" he asked.

"Lewis. Yes, Juan. I shall wake him up soon."

He corrected himself with a stern nod of the head. "Lewisss!"

She liked Juan. Despite his muscles he was gentle and unassuming. She imagined many women would quickly let him know they were attracted to him, and Vanessa's indifference obviously gave him a little cause for concern.

"You not like?" he asked.

Vanessa was still holding the orange, peel intact. She was sure it would be as nice as all the others he had brought up here during the last two months.

"I'm sure it will be lovely, Juan. I shall eat it later."

"Very juiceful."

"Juicy," she smiled.

"Juiceee," he repeated.

He finished eating and looked around. Vanessa extended her palm. What was left of his orange he placed gently in her hand with a smile. He sat up straight and slapped his thighs loudly. Then, probably thinking the last ten minutes represented yet another unsuccessful attempt to chat her up, stood up and said he should be going.

Vanessa smiled. He picked up his bag, repeated he should be going, and headed off back down the slope. At his 25-metre bag swap spot he turned and waved. She waved back, smiled to herself and went inside to wake Lewis.

~

Vanessa loved putting on loud music and dancing around the living room with Lewis. Her ankle had heeled but as a precaution she'd still wrap it during exercise. It didn't, however, compromise her normal day-to-day activities. She hadn't danced professionally since January but had enjoyed making up the routines for 'Love in Idleness' and when the rights for the show were sold, the company who bought them offered her the job of choreographer. It would have changed her association with Malissa, and she declined.

As the sun began to sink into the sea she put Lewis to bed. He was exhausted and fell asleep immediately. She poured herself a glass of wine and sat out in the garden. The villa below her was taking shape. She had seen the architect's drawings many times and didn't doubt how beautiful a dwelling it would be when it was finished.

She had been here with Malissa for two months. The farmhouse had power from the generator and a water supply from a large external tank that was filled weekly. A bathroom had been installed upstairs and the kitchen and living room refurbished. It took a little time to make it cosy, but now it was the loveliest place Vanessa had lived.

Malissa was currently in London; her third trip back since they'd arrived here in May. Spending so much time together had deepened their friendship. A month ago, they had slept outside. They had drunk and laughed and before they slept had embraced one another. Vanessa could still see the questioning look in Malissa's eyes as she wondered whether to kiss her again and their bodies pushed together. Vanessa was pleased their intimacy that evening didn't develop into sex. In the morning little was mentioned by either of them, but in a subsequent light-hearted conversation Vanessa replied to Malissa's hypothetical question with; "Well, if it was me and I was pushed to choose, and could only have one, then the gentleness of a woman would be preferable." Malissa laughed and called her an old slut and said she had always known, then jokingly asked Vanessa why she had never found her attractive.

They both agreed it was strange they had rarely talked about sex. It was because their friendship was "too special" Malissa said, but whenever Malissa discussed how close they were Vanessa felt that familiar pang of guilt. Not only about the secret of Emma but about some of the more sordid details of her formative years she'd kept herself. She'd tell her one day.

Henry had been in New York since they had been out here, but his secondment was coming to an end. Next month he too would be joining them. She looked forward to talking to him again.

Vanessa's love affair with Söller and the farmhouse continued. She smiled to herself as she looked out over the villa with its half-finished roof, and beyond to the little beach which nestled behind the orange grove. How things change. Here Malissa was the tough one. Here Vanessa was regarded as the sweet, carefree, unassuming woman who would always stop for a chat and even take the trouble to learn their language. If only they knew.

The sudden whoosh as the old generator kicked in brought her back to the present. She had finished the wine and it was gone 9pm. Lewis would be jumping on her bed at 6am, insisting it was time to get up. Perhaps they'd go into town tomorrow. Maybe he could buy his mum a welcome home present.

# 39

## AUGUST 1989, MAJORCA

### VANESSA AND HENRY

*H*enry had arrived as promised in July and shortly afterwards his great friend and business partner Brad Carmichael joined them. Although Brad stayed only a few days, the four of them and Lewis had a wonderful time touring the island and relaxing on the small beach at the villa.

Malissa, like Vanessa, enjoyed swimming and they had devised a challenge involving swimming around the two rocks that lay just off their beach. Henry and Brad quickly became embroiled in the challenge too and it had sparked many magical moments. The chemistry between them all was special, and Vanessa felt part of an extended family. Gabrielle was coming out next week and Vanessa looked forward to sharing with her, so much of the new life and new, valued friendships she had made.

The love Malissa and Henry shared was beginning to dispel Vanessa's inherent belief that all marriages were doomed to failure. Sometimes as she watched them she tried to picture Henry and Emma; how *they* would have been in their younger days. At other times, because of their closeness, she questioned her belief, considering – possibly even hoping – that her ideas about her sister and Henry were purely products of her imagination.

Several times Henry had looked at her, and Vanessa had wondered just what was going through his mind. She had never trusted men - she'd never trusted many people really - but with Henry she found herself drawn to him, and once or twice whilst laying in her bed imagined him there with her. These were new thoughts and Vanessa hated their encroachment. One evening, whilst they were out, the subject of relationships cropped up. It was a light-hearted conversation, initiated by Malissa who thought how wonderful it would be if Vanessa and Brad 'got together'. Brad, who was a kind, caring and intelligent man had blushed a little, but Henry's smile told her he knew she wasn't interested in men, no matter how handsome and wealthy they were.

Vanessa also loved the dynamic between Henry and Brad. She had never seen such love and mutual respect between two men. She loved too how Malissa interacted with them, and she loved how she, herself, had been so readily accepted into this wonderful circle of affection.

Brad had already returned home and Vanessa had given Malissa, who needed to be in London, a lift to the airport that morning. She'd be away for a couple of days. Lewis and Henry had stayed and the three of them had spent the day together. Henry was giving her a tour of the old town and Vanessa had been wondering how she could approach the subject of Emma. They stopped at the old schoolhouse that Malissa and her had thought suitable to turn into a dance school. Henry unlocked the door, picked up Lewis and they walked in.

Last month Malissa had learned the building was probably coming up for sale and casually remarked to Vanessa what a wonderful dance studio it would make. This instigated a conversation about her dancing career and whether opening a dance school here would be a viable proposition. As they talked, Vanessa realised just how much she had fallen in love with the town and what started as a casual remark, soon took on a degree of seriousness and they were both now very keen on the idea.

Vanessa showed Henry around, outlining the development plans she and Malissa had discussed.

"Well, if you ask me Vanessa, I think it would be perfect. Not that I've actually been in many dance schools, of course. So, you'd give up the stage altogether? And before I've seen you dance?"

"Well, a dancer's career doesn't go much beyond 30 anyway, and I fear this ankle of mine is always going to be a bit delicate."

Henry looked at her, quizzically.

"I know," she said. "I'm only 23."

Lewis was running about, talking excitedly and spinning around in the large empty room.

"And they've said it's definitely for sale?" Henry asked.

"Well, not in so many words, but talk is they will keep the museum where it is."

"Hmm," said Henry.

Malissa had told her that a 'hmm' from Henry meant he was thinking. Sometimes trying to decipher exactly what it was he was thinking about was the challenge she'd said.

"Yes, Miss Cozzette. I do believe this would be a most suitable venue and Söller surely needs a dance school. Have you talked to Don Antonio and his merry men yet?"

Antonio Garcia had been Chief Councillor of Söller for the last 20 years. Henry, who had ploughed a significant amount of money into the development of tourism here, had enjoyed many colourful meetings with him. Malissa often said her husband's love for Söller was a serious hindrance to his usual negotiating prowess, and Señor Garcia and his associates (The Söller Mafia Henry called them) were not averse to taking advantage.

"Not yet. It was Señor Perez – you know him?"

Henry nodded

"He told us. It's a bit hush hush, but he also gave us the key."

"Hmm," he said again at the mention of the name, but Vanessa did not believe Henry regarded Señor Perez, curator of the museum, part of the mafia. "In that case, I believe you'll be kept suitably informed. Come on, Lewis, let's go and try that orange ice cream Vanessa's been raving about."

Henry seemed to delight in showing Vanessa the old town, a part of Söller he obviously knew well. He told her he first stumbled across the place several years ago when taking some time off work and touring the island. "Why Majorca?" she'd asked. He didn't know for sure, but somewhere in his memory he recalled being told his mother lived there once.

Whatever the reason, it wasn't important. The main thing was he had found a place he felt a connection to, and when they came out here on honeymoon he was delighted Malissa felt the same. "The harbour's lovely of course. But this part just remains... well, almost as it's always been."

Tour over, they sat outside a little café, drinking coffee. Henry had been asking her about her dancing career and her ambitions.

"It seems to me, Miss Cozzette, that you are indeed ready for a new challenge. I do believe Söller has got to you too."

"Well, maybe it's a pipe dream, but Malissa seems so enthusiastic too. We had talked about opening a dance school in London."

"Well, that would certainly be a more obvious option to those who have never been to Söller. But obvious options, those formulated in your head, don't always offer the rewards of those that float around in your heart, and I think if London was for you, you would have accepted the job with the LDC."

The London Dance Company were the people who had bought the rights to 'Love in Idleness' and offered Vanessa the choreography job. She had never told Malissa about the offer and was surprised Henry had mentioned it. Henry saw her furrowed expression.

"I think Malissa was really pleased you turned it down," he said. "Although she did say it was a fantastic opportunity and wanted to tell you to seriously consider it."

"I had little to consider. How did she know?"

"I'm not sure there's much she doesn't know about the London dance scene and all that goes on there. It's her job I guess."

"You don't think that's why she's so enthusiastic about the dance school here, do you? I mean, she has even talked about investing in it."

"And you'd be afraid she was doing something nice for a friend?"

"Something like that."

"No, if Malissa believes something is a good idea she will fight tooth and nail to realise it. I do concede, however, that she would hate the thought of not seeing you so often."

"She's a wonderful woman, Henry."

"She is," he smiled. "By the way, there'd be no need to mention I told you she knew about your job offer. I mentioned it because I see how you've reacted to this place and seriously believe you could make a great success of a dance school here. And believe me, having someone at your side who believes in it too, is priceless."

"Brad?"

He smiled. "Malissa is my inspiration, but a great friend who you trust implicitly and who knows the weaknesses you cannot share with those even closer to you, possesses another strength altogether."

Vanessa wondered whether there was any double meaning in his statement. Was Emma a weakness he could not share with Malissa? "I shall not mention our conversation to Malissa. As you say. There's no need."

She smiled and looked into his eyes. He held her gaze for a few seconds before returning the smile.

"Sometimes, Miss Cozzette, we burden our friends with information we should bear alone. Information, maybe of a business nature for example that would be unwise to share elsewhere. Sometimes withholding information requires a greater strength; is a greater responsibility, for its revelation may only cause pain to those you'd least like to hurt."

"That's very profound."

"Sometimes we need to keep thoughts to ourselves, even questions we have. For airing them may give rise to many more that have no definitive answer, and the search for that answer can cause conflict between what we perceive to be wrong and feel to be right."

"And if Malissa knew you told me she knew about the job offer you think that would have undesirable consequences?"

He smiled. "There would be little consequence to that. But I sense, like me, you have fallen in love with her openness and more innocent sense of what's right and wrong."

Lewis stirred in his pushchair. He didn't wake up but Henry removed the cap that had fallen over his eyes.

"I think I'll have a beer, Miss Cozzette. Would you like one?" Henry got up from the table and went inside. Vanessa reflected on the conversation they'd just had, certain there was so much more weight to his statement.

"So, how long did you stay? In Söller... taking time out?" she asked when he returned with the beers.

"I was probably here for six weeks or more in all. Not all in Söller. The island has some wonderful places."

"But this is your favourite?"

He smiled, and she thought he was about to return the conversation to the more cryptic one they'd previously been engaged in. He didn't and instead reiterated his belief it was the historical connection to France that added to her love for Söller. When she asked him where he stayed when he first came out here he hesitated, but using his arms told her if she turned left at the end of the street, walked up the hill and took the little dusty track passed the petrol station, she'd find an old stone cottage with a leaking roof awaiting demolition. She sensed he would not want to take her there.

"Not at The Grand then?"

He laughed. "No, the first time I stayed there was our honeymoon. Taste's change I guess."

"And now you own it."

He laughed again. "Well, the company does. Most of it anyway. There was talk of it closing a few years ago, but it only needed a bit of TLC, and despite what Brad says he loves owning hotels. Cuts down on travel expenses."

Vanessa smiled. She had witnessed Henry and Brad's discussions about the merits of their company's investment in the touring industry, and Malissa had told her Henry's enthusiasm for investing in Söller was certainly not the anticipation of a monetary return.

"So, did it work?" she asked.

"Work?"

"Coming out here, to take some time out. Did it give you your answers?"

Again, she felt his gaze. Was he wondering if there was some deeper meaning behind her question? She expected him to 'hmm', but he didn't.

"Miss Cozzette," he said, "I believe you too know that answers to some questions do not always materialise because of the places you visit."

A moment's silence.

"Unless the place you visit is your heart," she said.

He smiled, but she wanted to ask about Emma. For a fleeting moment she considered just asking him, asking him outright. Why shouldn't she? Then she could tell him she was her sister. Or would she need to withhold that information? What would be the consequences if she told him? Something told her she couldn't ask. "So, you found what you were looking for in Söller?"

Again that look. That gaze of a wise man who always considered whether there was anything deeper behind a simple question. She wondered how strong her resemblance to Emma was at that moment.

"Find?" he pondered. "I guess if you are looking to find something, you must have previously lost it."

"I guess so."

"Something precious no doubt if you travel a long way to look."

Vanessa said nothing but was suddenly aware of the presence of the man opposite her, and imagined he would not be too dissimilar to this in an important business meeting. She suddenly felt she was challenging something she knew little about, like an apprentice who was questioning their master and she felt strangely inadequate.

"And after looking, and realising that the something so precious you lost it is not there," Henry continued, his voice soft but full of authority, "you accept that it has gone forever and you have to tell yourself it never existed, it was just a dream, otherwise you will spend your whole life searching to replace that which is irreplaceable."

She felt shackled under his gaze for a few seconds as his earlier words about information that shouldn't be shared ran through her brain. Then he smiled and his smile released her, and she knew this particular conversation was over. He looked at his watch. Lewis had woken up and Henry turned his attention to his son who was hungry. He switched the subject to where they should eat and they decided to feed Lewis now then return to the farmhouse where Vanessa would make a spaghetti bolognese. His favourite.

Vanessa lay in bed. She was sure Henry, who had remained downstairs, would find it equally difficult to sleep tonight. She had no doubt she had stirred his memory.

They had eaten dinner on the patio and shared a couple of bottles of wine. In a moment that was akin to a game of truth or dare, she had let him look into her heart, to tell her his version of her story, one he surmised involved an inherent distrust of people and a scepticism of love. He too had let her in, and picking up on his remarks that afternoon about losing something precious, she suggested love was the most precious thing of all; and if the loss of that love was thought irreplaceable understood that by denying it ever existed, would save futile comparison, and allow you to love again.

She had no doubt she had lit a a memory but didn't asked Henry to share it. His grip had tightened on her hand as he looked across the table, and amidst the pain in his eyes she saw the reflection of her sister. Several times that day, she had expected him to say something more, to shout the name 'Emma', but he didn't and she was not going to press him. Like her, he surely had reasons to keep part of his past a secret.

Malissa should be back tomorrow and they'd resume their holiday. In three days Henry would return to work, leaving his wife and Vanessa to keep an eye on the progress of the villa. Maybe when Gabrielle arrived they'd introduce her to the Blackpool-Brighton challenge. Vanessa knew the three of them, and Lewis would enjoy a wonderful week together.

Vanessa would not tell Malissa she had discovered that she was concerned about her accepting the choreography job with the London Dance Company and neither did she feel she would ever be able to speak so intimately with Henry again

# 40

# OCTOBER 1989, MAJORCA

*A*lthough tourism in Söller was growing, it was nowhere near as popular as the more fashionable holiday resorts in Majorca. Perhaps its seclusion behind the Tramontana Mountains afforded it that relative privacy. It was noticeable, however, that the town and the harbour were considerably less busy once the summer season was over. Vanessa had loved her time here, and the magical week she spent with Gabrielle when she came over in the summer left her with the distinct feeling she was showing her sister her new home, her new life.

Three months ago, Henry had agreed with the authorities to finance the rejuvenation of the harbour area of Söller Port, but Brad, his business partner, hadn't immediately shared Henry's enthusiasm for the new hotel their company had promised to build. When the time came for Malissa to return to England she and Brad suggested Vanessa stayed to oversee the completion of the villa and, on behalf of Brad, sit in on the meetings between the town councillors and the other bodies as they discussed what Brad liked to describe as Ovmeister-Carmichael's worst ever investment. Vanessa had needed little persuasion to stay.

She had made several friends but remained reticent about getting too close to anyone. Truth was, although she spent much time alone she enjoyed the freedom it provided. Juan seemed to believe that Brad

Carmichael was her boyfriend; she didn't deny it and felt it gave him a tangible reason why she was immune to his advances.

Her association with Malissa and Henry afforded her a great deal of respect in Söller. Sergio, the manager at the Söller Grand, and his staff clearly believed her visits there were to keep an eye on things. She often helped out on reception and occasionally behind the bar where her command of English, French and her improving Spanish proved a valuable asset.

Her ankle had heeled completely, but she had no intention to return to dancing. The old schoolhouse that she and Malissa thought would make a good dance studio still hadn't been put up for auction, but she was certain it would be before too long. She had conducted some tentative research regarding the viability of a dance school in Söller and was quite encouraged. Malissa had told her that either Fenner's or her husband's company, or she herself would be happy to purchase the building. However, Vanessa had some savings, and if she also took the money bequeathed to her by Felix Lasserre, she believed she could actually buy it herself.

Last week Malissa had told her she and Henry were expecting their second child, and Vanessa was delighted for them. In hushed tones, Malissa told her she was certain conception took place in July on the farmhouse lawn.

The villa would be finished on schedule next month and Malissa seemed keen to spend Christmas there. Henry, who had spent much of the last year in the States, now spent most of his time in England. He often answered the phone when she called Malissa, and while they would exchange pleasantries, they never talked in the same depth they had earlier in the year.

The dilapidated property where Henry said he stayed when he first came to Söller was now derelict, but used to be owned by two brothers who were fisherman. It wasn't far from the library which Vanessa often visited and where she met Lorena, the shy librarian who couldn't disguise her feelings for Vanessa. Lorena had come out to the farmhouse for dinner on a couple of occasions, and whilst they got on well, and Vanessa was attracted to her, she believed Lorena sought the kind of relationship Vanessa was not prepared to commit to. Lorena was, however, the closest friend she had made since arriving in Majorca.

Vanessa had visited a couple of bars in the old town where the local fisherman drank. She could feel uncomfortable spending an evening in them, but if she was ever going to meet someone who remembered Henry when he first found Söller, someone who could confirm what she believed, chances are they would be in one of those establishments. Henry had already suggested that back then he'd frequent the less salubrious watering holes.

Vanessa had little doubt Emma and Henry had been lovers. She had little idea why Malissa didn't know, nor did she understand why Henry kept it secret. However, she often considered the consequences if Henry actually confirmed her suspicions. Would he then ask her to keep it secret too? Would he tell her why? Would they then share a secret that they'd have to keep from Malissa? Would Henry burden her with that?

And what about her own relationship to Emma? She had kept that secret from Malissa *and* from Henry. How would the revelation of *that* fact be received? How would that impact on their friendship and her new life? Vanessa often felt as though she was snooping, often thought that someone would say 'you must be Emma's sister'," but of course no one knew, no one but her. If she wanted to find out what had become of Emma she no longer believed that Henry could be the source.

She had never met Emma and had no idea what she was like. Emma was her older sister but in essence just another human being Vanessa had never known. Discovering what happened to her was unimportant in the grand scheme of things, but the need to find out, still niggled her. Vanessa's discussions with Henry left her with the strong impression that his first visit to Söller and Emma were, somehow connected.

# 41

# NOVEMBER 1989

## THE COMPLETION OF THE VILLA

*V*anessa had spent all of yesterday adding the final touches to the inside of the villa. She had witnessed its construction but still marvelled at the home the builders had created. More remarkable than the villa itself was its landscaped garden, somehow carved out of the rock upon which the villa sat. Tonnes of soil had been delivered over recent weeks, and though the trees and shrubs that had been planted were still young, and only a few had flowered so far, you could imagine the abundance of colour come springtime. The watering system wasn't quite complete and they wouldn't fill the swimming pool for several months, but Vanessa knew that when Malissa saw what had been created it would exceed even her elevated expectations. She was excited to show her.

Vanessa had picked up Malissa, Henry and Lewis from the airport. Throughout the journey Malissa had constantly asked her for details, for her opinion, but Vanessa's stock answer remained 'wait and see'.

Turning on to the new driveway which led up to the dwelling, she stopped the car. "Now, if I said don't peek, I know you would so..."

She retrieved a scarf from the glove compartment and tied it around Malissa's head.

"Is that necessary, Vanessa?" Henry called from the back seat. She turned to him, her smile disappearing as she witnessed a look of horror on his face.

"Oh, let her play her games, Henry," said Malissa, confirming the scarf was in place and she couldn't see a thing. Vanessa swallowed hard, suddenly realising the impact her action could have had on Henry. She had just taken away somebody's ability to see, for God's sake. How could she have been so thoughtless?

She put the car into gear and pulled forward, Malissa's words of excitement and anticipation lost in the vision she held of the look on Henry's face. When she stopped and helped Malissa out of the car, Vanessa was relieved to see Henry had regained some composure, but she was pleased when he eventually removed the blindfold. Malissa, as expected, was overwhelmed by what she saw.

Vanessa was more relaxed by the time they'd finished enthusing about their new home, and Henry was back to his usual self. Henry wouldn't have known that Vanessa understood the reason for his apparent discomfort regarding the blindfold. Perhaps she had over reacted, read too much into it.

# CHRISTMAS 1989, PARIS

*P*hilippe and Marguerite had moved into a larger house just on the outskirts of Paris, and as well as her own bedroom Vanessa also had use of the guest bathroom. Gabrielle enjoyed a solid family life and Vanessa was particularly pleased to see how well she got on with her stepbrothers. She stayed to see in the New Year but before returning to Majorca needed to go to London to keep the appointment she'd made with Mitchel Morgan and Hills.

Malissa had suggested that Vanessa and Gabrielle spend Christmas at the villa with them. Vanessa loved the idea, but Gabrielle's grandmother was seriously ill and Malissa understood why Vanessa wanted to spend Christmas in Paris with her sister. However, Vanessa would be travelling to London in January to sort out her financial affairs, and if Malissa was available they could talk about the old schoolhouse in Söller that was now officially up for sale.

# JANUARY 1990, DELAHAY HOUSE

## VANESSA, MALISSA, BRAD AND HENRY

*H*enry and Brad had gone to the races for the afternoon. Malissa told Vanessa that in all the years they had known each other, it was the first time the two of them had ever gone racing together. "Brad is completely baffled why Henry would buy racehorses. Doesn't understand the attraction at all," she'd said.

Vanessa was spending the weekend at Malissa's before flying back to Majorca to conclude matters on the old schoolhouse. She had considered using the £50,000 from Felix Lasserre to buy the building outright but explaining away such a sum would surely mean lying to Malissa. However, that wasn't the only reason she had agreed to buy the building jointly with Malissa: she also loved the idea of them sharing the adventure.

Henry was prepared to buy the building and lease it to them, and Malissa had already talked to Brian Fenner who loved the idea of The Fenner Agency Dance School in Majorca. But this was Vanessa's project - Vanessa and Malissa's - and Vanessa was adamant it should be independent of any outside influence, no matter how good their intentions.

It would be an expensive venture and Vanessa could, and wanted to, pay her fair share. She had already told Malissa she had some savings, but as they prepared dinner, Vanessa mentioned it was also quite possible she'd soon receive the benefits of an inheritance from long ago. "That's why the solicitors wanted to see me," she said, "to give me an update. They're pretty sure it'll be sorted soon."

"Well, Ness, if anyone deserves a bit of good fortune, it's you. What a great legacy from your great-grandfather – a million pounds *and* your natural inheritance of the Queen's English – and with that accent!"

Vanessa had told her the inheritance really should have been given to her grandmother, which she didn't regard as lying. "Malissa, it will not be a million."

"Well, you never know with these things." Malissa uncorked the wine and placed it on the dining table. "It's a bit unfair this pregnancy lark, Ness, but a small glass tonight won't do any harm."

Vanessa suddenly wondered if her own mother ever considered limiting her alcohol intake when she was carrying her. She doubted it.

Henry's car pulled up on the driveway and within a minute or two he and Brad appeared. Henry picked up Lewis and swung him around before tucking him under his arm, kissing his wife whilst rubbing her belly and then telling Vanessa she looked absolutely stunning in a pinafore. He was a little tipsy. Brad announced his arrival in a more conventional manner.

"I trust you were driving, Brad?" smiled Malissa.

"Yes, Henry said it was an important part of the etiquette to share a bottle of champagne when a horse makes his debut."

"Looks like he shared most of it with himself. He won then?" she asked a little excitedly.

"No, Malissa," said Brad slipping off his jacket. "This wonder horse, one leg of which just happens to belong to a good friend of mine with inside information, came - despite being primed for this race, which was merely a steppingstone for the big one at Cheltenham - last. And I am £50 poorer for the experience."

"He came eighth," Henry protested.

"Henry, there were only eight runners."

"Nine. One pulled up. Anyway, you can't win them all and I did say it was a tough race to win first time out."

"That was after the race Henry."

"Hmm," muttered Henry, feeling they had talked enough about horses. "Dinner smells good. I can't wait to hear about the dance school plans, Vanessa. A new year and a wonderful new adventure." Henry lifted

Lewis over his head, blowing raspberries onto his tummy, and when he put him down reminded him never to be as cynical as his Uncle Brad.

At dinner, they chatted like the good friends they were, and after Henry put Lewis to bed they talked about Majorca and the new hotel. Henry had met with the Söller council just before Christmas.

"Did I hear a rumour that a digger actually turned up?" Brad asked sarcastically.

Henry looked at him. Brad was still to be convinced that building such a prestigious hotel on the harbour was a good idea.

"The locals are getting really excited about it now," Vanessa interjected thinking she was coming to Henry's rescue.

Henry smiled. "Enough about hotels, what about the dance school? When do you think you'll get that up and running?"

Vanessa and Malissa explained their plans for purchasing the building and the refurbishment they thought it would need. Neither Brad nor Henry could understand why they were borrowing the money from the bank, but Malissa left them in no doubt this was not a project that needed their intervention.

"Since Söller will be your official home, Vanessa, will you move into town?" Brad asked.

Malissa answered for her. "And leave that lovely old farmhouse, Brad? I wouldn't have thought so. You wouldn't want to move into town, Ness, would you?"

Vanessa loved the farmhouse. She had talked to Malissa about paying rent, but as far as Malissa was concerned she was there ensuring no harm came to the villa. Once the dance school was up and running, they could discuss such things.

"No, Brad. I love the farmhouse. Did I tell you we have electricity installed now? And quite soon telephones too."

Brad always worried about keeping in touch with the office whenever he was away.

"A telephone, Brad!" smiled Malissa. "Imagine that. Looks like regular holidays for you now too. And no excuses. And when this baby's born, Ness, I'm going to take six months off and join you there."

"Hmm," said Henry. "I'd be very jealous of that."

# 44

# MARCH 1990, PARIS

## MADEMOISELLE LAUREN

*M*adame D'anvers, Philippe's mother and Gabrielle's grandmother, passed away on the 15th of March – one day after the fifth anniversary of Vanessa's own mother's death. It was the second funeral Vanessa had attended with Gabrielle, but this time Vanessa had to help console her sister.

On the evening of the funeral, when everybody else was in bed, Vanessa and Philippe sat up talking about their respective mothers. Vanessa was surprised he was still reflective about his first wife and talked about the good times they enjoyed when they were first married. "I remember that day she first took you to the dance school, Vanessa. True we argued, and you know that, but we shared some wonderful times."

That evening, too, was the first time she'd asked Philippe whether her mother had ever told him about a child she gave birth to in London when she was young. She had, but seemingly only during an argument. She had provided no details and he didn't know whether to believe her drunken, convoluted story or not.

Without going into detail, and certainly not mentioning any connection with Henry, Vanessa told him that her mother had told her the same story and that she believed it to be true. He confirmed he had never told Gabrielle and they agreed she needn't know.

Malissa had phoned the following morning to ensure Vanessa was okay and to tell her she'd received a fax. The old schoolhouse was now officially the property of 'The Söller Dance School' and they should get together as soon as possible to celebrate.

Before she returned to Söller, Vanessa had one more visit to make. The bus dropped her off at the stop that was once so familiar, and as she walked the 200 metres to Mademoiselle Lauren's Academy she thought how little had changed. For several years she had felt the need to call upon her old dance teacher, but she couldn't really figure out why. She hadn't spoken to Mademoiselle Lauren since the night before fleeing to Dinard to stay with Monique. It was incredible to think that was nearly ten years ago. She wondered if Mademoiselle Lauren would recognise her.

The school bus was parked where it had always been so Vanessa assumed Mademoiselle still ran her Wednesday afternoon sessions for pupils from the local junior schools. If so, those classes would usually be run by one of her junior staff and she would be in her office. At any rate, those sessions finished at 4pm, so even if she was teaching Vanessa wouldn't have to wait long.

She pushed through the swing door. The singular rhythmic notes from the piano greeted her as she went in and then she heard the tape instructing the pupils what to do next. She remembered the tape and knew it had five more minutes to run. There were seats in the corridor but no other visitors today. She peered through the glass in the door, the scene exactly the same as she remembered it. Mademoiselle Lauren, a little heavier than she remembered, circled the group of dancers, chanting "1-2-3" and "now we turn" and maintaining that rhythm as she sang out the names of any pupils whose feet or arms weren't quite in the correct position.

Mademoiselle Lauren looked Vanessa's way but Vanessa made no attempt to hide. She stopped her chanting and stood holding one of the girl's arms for many more seconds than needed. The pianist carried on thumping out the notes and the cassette deck continued to spout instructions. Her old dance teacher had obviously recognised her and Vanessa looked away and took a seat directly opposite the door to the smaller studio where she had once spent so many hours.

The piano and cassette tape stopped in unison and were replaced by the chatter of the children as they changed their footwear and the voice of their dance teacher telling them what they should practice at home. A few of the pupils looked at Vanessa as they passed her but soon she could only hear two adult voices in the room and then the pianist appeared. "I'm here to see Mademoiselle Lauren," Vanessa answered when she asked if she could help her.

The pianist was just about to reply when Mademoiselle Lauren came out of the studio. "Vanessa," she said with an exaggerated smile, "how wonderful to see you. It's okay, Nadia, Miss Cozzette is a past pupil. I'll see you tomorrow."

"This is a surprise, Vanessa," she said when Nadia had gone through the door.

Vanessa said nothing. A strange sensation came over her as she wondered why she was there. She wasn't the child who attended the academy, wasn't the rebellious teenager who lived with Monique, nor did she feel she was the contented woman who lived in the farmhouse in Söller. She could remember the ten years she had spent here as a pupil like it was yesterday, but couldn't recall how she felt back then, and she certainly couldn't fathom her feelings towards Mademoiselle Lauren. Perhaps coming here had impacted on Vanessa more than she thought it would?

"Come into my office, Vanessa. I'll make some tea."

Vanessa followed her into her office and sat down. Her eyes followed Lauren as she shuffled awkwardly about her office trying not to look at her as she collected two cups and filled the kettle.

"You look good, Vanessa. I think life has been kind." Mademoiselle Lauren said.

She had her back to Vanessa but was probably waiting for an answer. When it didn't come, she turned around. "I've worried about you. I did hear you were dancing..." She interrupted herself. "I heard you had found some work at Le Moulin Rouge. That's very good."

Vanessa's thoughts had been gathering gradually. Had she intended to come here to make her old dance teacher feel so awkward? She didn't think so.

"Kind?" Vanessa said quietly.

"You look well, Vanessa. I know life wasn't always very kind to you."

When Vanessa was her pupil, Mademoiselle Lauren would often tell her 'life hadn't been kind to her'. It was a true enough statement, but Vanessa had quickly appreciated its intent was to suggest that she should be grateful to Mademoiselle Lauren and her dance school as they represented the nearest thing to kindness she knew. Vanessa wondered if her old dance teacher was considering whether her 'kindness' actually justified some of her actions.

"Mademoiselle, you taught me to dance and for that I am grateful. You took me in and gave me a home when I could have been so vulnerable, and maybe I should be grateful for that too. Grateful for *that* kindness. But as you say, Mademoiselle, what would I have really known about kindness then?"

"Vanessa," Mademoiselle said softly, then paused as if she didn't know what to say.

Vanessa studied her eyes, wondering whether they exuded sorrow or shame. Perhaps they showed both, perhaps she was recalling those nights she had laid on Vanessa's bed whilst she touched herself.

"Vanessa," she continued, "I don't know what to say. I never meant to...I certainly didn't mean to hurt you. You were so... perfect. And I am sorry." A tear leaked from her eye and she turned away. She poured the water into the cups.

When she sat down and handed her the tea, Mademoiselle's eyes were moist, her expression sad and for a moment Vanessa felt sorry for her. What she had done was wrong. Vanessa was 15 and at the age of consent, but her dance teacher was in a position of power and surely she felt she had taken advantage of her. Ironically, after the shock of the first time, her touch had hardly bothered Vanessa, and even now she could dismiss it as just something that happened. If there was a prize for an adult's malign intentions towards her, Vanessa could list several more contenders more worthy of that dubious award. But she shouldn't have done it and she should expect Vanessa to be outraged. Perhaps Vanessa was concerned she may have touched someone more fragile? Maybe that's why she was here. Not so much revenge but concern, and of course to set the record straight.

"Sorry for laying on my bed?" Vanessa asked.

This time Mademoiselle Lauren could not stop herself from crying. She apologised while she wiped her eyes and tried to bring her sobbing under control. Yes, she was sorry for *that* of course she was, and she was sorry for crying now. Maybe she had been sorry ever since the day she got up that morning and realised Vanessa had gone.

"I never intended to touch you, Vanessa, and you must believe I have never touched another girl. I know it was wrong I just fell in... God how can I say that, you were a girl, it was never my intention, never did I want anything other than to admire you. You were a special..."

"Special and so had special treatment?" Vanessa interrupted, her voice calm and calculated.

"No, Vanessa, I admired you and, as mad as that sounds now, when you left... When you left, my dreams left with you. They were broken. Of course, I thought those dreams were for you, for us, for our future, but they were for me. You were the dancer I always dreamed I could be..."

It was as though Lauren was at confession, spouting words she had rehearsed over many years. How different to the authoritative figure so many people knew. She allowed her to ramble on and Vanessa half listened. Much of what she said, she had already told Vanessa years ago; about her own dreams, her own ambitions, her own love of dance, but this time she did so with sadness and remorse, and without blaming other events or people.

"And now?" Vanessa said, interrupting her.

"Now?"

"And now, Lauren. Now you are older. Now I am older. I trust you no longer regard me as special in quite the same way?"

It was the first time Vanessa had addressed her so informally, and Mademoiselle's reaction suddenly made Vanessa realise that her own manner had slipped back into the one she'd have typically displayed during the time she was a dancer in the Parisian nightclubs, or when she confronted Lord Felix. She wasn't entirely comfortable with the realisation and wished the woman opposite her would take on the persona of the Mademoiselle Lauren that exercised such control. Vanessa looked into her eyes and felt pity.

"Vanessa, I remember the day your mother first brought you to me. You were four years old. Your mother never paid your fees, I didn't expect her to..." She paused and Vanessa wondered if she was considering suggesting her actions were justified in lieu of those unpaid bills. If she was, she obviously changed her mind. She carried on.

"You had talent, talent that I saw. Talent that many witnessed. You were eight years old when you played Clara and you played her so beautifully. The Paris National wanted you and I should have let you go. I didn't let you go and that was selfish. I exploited you, I know that now and I wanted to keep you. Other girls joined because they thought I could make them as good as you. Parents brought children to me almost as soon as they could walk, thinking that like you they'd be a star when they were eight years old..."

She carried on, eulogising over Vanessa's ability as a young dancer. Vanessa had never heard her speak this way and at times it made Vanessa wonder just what she could have become. She shook those thoughts out of her head. That was then - this is now. By the time Mademoiselle Lauren had finished, her tears had dried and she was calmer. It was as though she had relieved herself of some great guilt she had harboured for many years, and not just the guilt she must have felt for all those nights she had laid behind her in her bedroom.

"An angel with passion and poise," Mademoiselle whispered as if summing up. "So vulnerable in life yet so strong and so formidable on the stage. The dancer I so wish I could have been, and I couldn't help but want to hold you, and protect you, and keep you for myself. And for that, Vanessa, I am sorrier than you will ever know."

If the purpose of her visit had been to extract this apparent confession it hadn't been Vanessa's conscious intention. Was she still considering what possible motives lay behind Mademoiselle's words? Was her remorse as genuine as it appeared? Or was Lauren afraid that Vanessa might report her to the authorities?

"And your way of handling special people, Mademoiselle, are you comfortable with that?"

"Vanessa, you were the only one," she said slowly, her expression pained as she looked directly into Vanessa's eyes.

Vanessa held her gaze for several seconds before Lauren looked away. They sat in silence. Did her dance teacher exploit her? Did she take advantage of her those nights in her bedroom? She could remember sniggering to herself, guessing how many times that neon sign would flash before Mademoiselle would reach her orgasm. She couldn't remember ever being scared and when Vanessa decided it was time to stop, it did.

Did Mademoiselle Lauren ruin her life by blocking a possible move to the most renowned dancing academy in France? No, she didn't - Vanessa couldn't imagine anything more fulfilling than the life she had found in Majorca. Mademoiselle Lauren was the only person who didn't believe Vanessa's destiny was to remain chained to the circumstances of her birth, and if she hadn't been taught to dance, Vanessa had no idea what she would be doing now. But none of these things changed the fact that Lauren was an adult who had taken advantage of a teenager in her care and although Vanessa was beyond the age of consent her actions had been inappropriate at best.

"Please try not to hate me Vanessa. I know what I did was wrong." She reached across the desk and clasped Vanessa's hand for a moment. "I had never done anything remotely like that before or since, you must believe me."

Mademoiselle's life had been her dance academy and Vanessa represented its greatest success. What would have happened to Vanessa if her mother had not taken there? Vanessa's young life was one of sporadic attendance at school, a father who couldn't care less and a mother who came and went. The dance school and Lauren's insistence Vanessa developed her talent for dance, was perversely the only stability she experienced as a child. No, she did not hate Mademoiselle Lauren – hate was the wrong word.

"I have no children, Vanessa and I am not getting any younger. I owe you, that much I do know. I have thought about...."

"Katriane," Vanessa suddenly spouted, interrupting her.

"Katriane?"

The memory of her poor abused friend, she used to dance with, exploded into Vanessa's mind and a sudden and unexpected anger rose inside her.

"Katriane?" Mademoiselle repeated, "your friend? I don't understand. It was sad. Terrible, but I don't know why you mention her."

Perhaps the talk of abuse and exploitation had triggered Vanessa's memory. She thought briefly about the rape she endured too and realised the surge of anger she felt was not because of anything her dance teacher had done.

Lauren was still talking, saying how the tragic death of Katriane had saddened the community. Her death, however, had nothing to do with Mademoiselle Lauren.

"Mademoiselle Lauren," Vanessa said, "I don't hate you."

The two women looked at one other across the table. Mademoiselle Lauren reached for Vanessa's hand and for a moment Vanessa wanted to say more but had little idea what about. She shook off whatever thoughts had invaded, pulled away her hand and started putting her coat on.

Mademoiselle Lauren stood up and went over to one of the filing cabinets. "Here," she said, "you should have this." It was Vanessa's dance file.

Vanessa took the file. "Goodbye, Lauren," she said and headed for the door.

"Please come again, Vanessa, I've much I would like to tell you."

Vanessa stopped momentarily.

"When you're next in the area. Please pop in any time. I'll be here," Mademoiselle Lauren added.

"Goodbye, Lauren," Vanessa repeated and left.

Vanessa had hoped to sleep on the journey back home but the meeting with Mademoiselle Lauren had woken dormant thoughts she had buried. Just what compelled her to meet up she wasn't sure. Maybe the death of Madame D'anvers and witnessing the sadness of Gabrielle had prompted the impromptu visit. On the flight home she thought about her childhood.

Apart from her early schooling career, when she lived with her mother and Philippe, her attendance at school had been patchy. The school near her father's house was rough, with high truancy levels and parents who little cared where their offspring spent their time. Those early days had taught Vanessa to fend for herself; scrapping to ward off potential bullies and erecting an emotional wall that was equally hard.

She probably attended Lauren's academy, which was some distance from her father's house, as often as she attended school and she couldn't recall ever playing truant from there. She had several friends at the dance school all of whom came from more affluent and functional families. She'd often eat at their houses and sometimes stay overnight. Her father didn't care whether she was home or not.

Vanessa didn't doubt her childhood experience had hardened her. She always felt older than her peers and often found herself in the role of protector. She had, however, always been polite and showed respect to those who showed her kindness and several of the 'more affluent' parents of her friends would often give her small jobs to do. She now realised these jobs were probably a pretext for them giving her money – they saw how neglected she was, but also how defiant and independent and wished to encouraged her.

Her father rarely gave her pocket money. Sometimes she would do the grocery shopping and at particularly pressing times she had resorted to shoplifting the odd item in order to pocket a few of the francs her father had given her to pay for it. Her mother would also invariably give her a little money whenever she saw her and somehow Vanessa always managed to get by.

Vanessa had to grow up quicker than many of the children she knew, especially those who attended the dance school. She wondered how much she had been hardened by the events of those years. Her early teens had been plagued by traumatic events but looking back she had seemingly shrugged off those incidents. She wondered if she could be so resilient now.

Her love and ability for dancing had probably saved her from falling into the shambolic life of so many of those from her neighbourhood, and for that she should perhaps always be grateful to Mademoiselle Lauren. Dancing had also led her to Malissa and the wonderful life she now enjoyed, and as she looked out of the window as the plane prepared to land at Palma, she found the smile returning to her face as she thought about the farmhouse, the people of Söller and the new dance school she would soon be opening.

She had the taxi drop her off at The Grand. There were no messages, but Malissa had faxed through the details from the solicitors confirming they were the rightful owners of the old schoolhouse. Sergio congratulated her and insisted it called for champagne. It was nearly midnight by the time he gave her a lift back to the farmhouse. She was tired but knew she wouldn't sleep.

She sat down, poured herself a glass of wine and flicked through the faxes. Malissa had also sent her a handwritten note saying she was pulling her hair out, couldn't wait for the baby to arrive, had been told she couldn't fly in her condition, but could really do with some company while Henry was away next week. Vanessa could fly to London first class, Malissa's treat. She smiled, she hadn't seen Malissa for two months and missed her company. Of course, she'd go, though there was no option to travel first class.

She thought again about Mademoiselle Lauren. Vanessa had never heard of, or witnessed any child experiencing anything inappropriate. Neither, up until she stayed at her house when she was 15, had Mademoiselle Lauren made anything remotely resembling an approach to her. Vanessa believed she was the only one her dance teacher had ever found 'special'.

She opened the dance file she'd been given. She was surprised to see a copy of a reference that had been sent to Fenner's. References were, of course, confidential but she was surprised Malissa had never mentioned it. She felt a little betrayed but realised she had no right to; after all, Vanessa had met Malissa on false pretences and, of course, still held onto the secret of Emma. The feeling passed immediately. She refilled her glass and read:

*Dear Miss Keats*

*I enclose copies of Vanessa's qualifications, newspaper clippings and childhood résumés as requested. As a fellow professional I have no doubt you will agree that her achievements are remarkable. In 30 years of teaching, Vanessa remains the most talented and creative dancer I have ever coached.*

*On a personal note, I can tell you that she is reliable, hardworking and loyal, and that her achievements are even more remarkable considering the childhood challenges she faced. She came from a humble background, to say the least, and received no parental or other outside adult support, either in her dancing or her daily life. In France, those who attend dance schools, generally come from a more privileged background, and it is a credit to Vanessa that she dealt with and overcame so many obstacles that would have hampered so many. She is a special person.*

Special? Perhaps seeing the word written in this context justified Mademoiselle's use of it earlier.

She read the letter several times, wondering why Malissa never told her she had asked for a reference. She cast her mind back to that time Malissa asked her about her role in the Nutcracker, when she said Angie found the old photograph. The letter Mademoiselle Lauren wrote was dated July 1987, surely about the same time. Perhaps Malissa requested the reference after she told Vanessa she was too modest and should be proud of her achievements as a child?

Did it matter Malissa didn't tell her she had received the reference? It said nothing untoward. No, she needn't feel betrayed. God, she herself was withholding much more sensitive information. She cast any negative thoughts aside.

She sat back in the chair. It was 2am. Now, back in the farmhouse, Vanessa was happy and content; how different to the mix of emotions she had felt earlier. She continued to flick through the file, looking at the merit certificates, photographs and reports that possibly depicted the happiest moments of her childhood. There were several items that referred to her performances in 'The Ballerina'. She was 14 when she was first auditioned for the part, a couple of weeks before Christmas. But that Christmas was not a pleasant one; surely it had left a scar?

# 45

# 21ST DECEMBER 1980, CHEZ JEAN, PARIS

*I*f Vanessa wanted to see her mother, Chez Jean was as good a place as any she might find her. She hadn't, however, seen her here for several weeks. Although only two streets away from the salubrious establishments of Montmartre, Chez Jean was a place for the less discerning locals. Men played cards and drank in the upstairs bar, whilst the members' bar downstairs was a regular haunt for women looking for business.

Drinks were cheap but the landlord augmented his income from the commission paid by the strippers and prostitutes. Men in their eighties drank alongside children even younger than Vanessa, but all had something in common; they had little expectation of life. It was here Vanessa met her friend Monique. There was a games room at the back that served non-alcoholic drinks and parodied as a youth club. "His investment in the future," Monique had told her when they first met a couple of months ago.

It was usually Wednesdays and Sundays when Vanessa would come here; two days she didn't need to attend the dance school and two days when she knew her father would be drunk when she got home. She had learned it was best to avoid him on these days if she could, and she had often stayed the night at the flat her mother shared with a friend. She'd been told, however, that her mother had moved out a few weeks ago and Nina, her flat mate, didn't know, nor did she care, where she had gone.

If she had the money, she could take the bus back to her father's apartment, but it was near enough to walk home if she needed to. Monique lived in a posher part of town and had promised Vanessa she could stay there some nights if she wanted. It was 8pm and Vanessa had hoped Monique would have been here by now.

"Hey, Vanessa, how's it going?"

It was Stephan, a boy she had known at school but who had recently left. He had bought her the occasional drink. He was okay. She smiled.

"This is Bridget," he said. "Bridget, meet Vanessa. Sit here and I'll get us some drinks." He walked through the door which was meant to separate the 'youth club' from the adults only bar.

Vanessa said 'hello' to Bridget who she had seen in here before but they'd never spoken. She had straggly blonde hair and brown eyes, and though a little overweight was pretty. She told Vanessa she worked in Hillary's, a café on Rue Lepic, but was hoping to get a receptionist job in the hotel a couple of doors away. She was surprised Vanessa was only 14 and still at school. She thought she was at least two years older.

Stephan returned with the drinks and sat down. He had a job on the market and had been given a generous Christmas bonus which he intended to blow that night. His friend, Liam, joined them. He had been downstairs watching the women on the stage and suggested they should all go down there later. Stephan had his arm around Bridget and was not being subtle about groping her. He asked Vanessa how her dancing was going, telling his friend that when they were at junior school she was some kind of child superstar. Liam moved closer to Vanessa and wasn't happy when she moved away, avoiding his clumsy advances. Stephan laughed, saying Vanessa was much too discerning for a guy like him.

"Well, her mother isn't," Liam laughed.

Liam's comment disturbed Vanessa. How did he know her mother and what did he mean? She remained calm but resented his remark.

"Yeah, I hear she was some dancer too. Saw her downstairs once. She could certainly move. Probably where you get it from." Liam prodded Nathan and laughed even louder. "Come on Vanessa, give us a dance. Love to see those on stage," he mocked, cupping his hands to his chest and jiggling make believe breasts.

Vanessa felt a tightening in her stomach. She knew her mother came here from time to time. Once, when her mother was more drunk than usual, she told two men that her daughter was not only pretty but a terrific dancer. When they suggested she should get herself downstairs her mother just laughed, frightening Vanessa who ran out of the bar. Yes, it was quite possible her mother had performed downstairs; Vanessa hated her for that. "You're pathetic," she snarled at Liam.

"Pathetic?" Liam laughed.

"I thought it was only those dirty old perverts who had to pay to see a pair of tits. It must be sad to know you repulse girls so much you're already one of them at your age."

She heard the spite in her voice, and it surprised her. Liam looked at her and she saw the resentment in his eyes. For a moment there was a piercing silence, before Stephan laughed heartedly and suggested she had summed up his friend perfectly.

Liam's look at her lingered and she returned it until he looked away, finished his beer and left, muttering under his breath. Stephan suggested another drink, got up and left the two girls in an awkward silence, which after a minute or so was interrupted by Monique. Vanessa made the introductions.

When Stephan reappeared he offered to get Monique a drink, but she said she'd share Vanessa's and get one later. Stephan said he and Bridget were moving on to another bar along the street and invited Vanessa and Monique to join them. Vanessa declined but thanked him for the invitation.

When they were alone Vanessa told Monique about the incident with Liam who was now standing with another boy at the bar and occasionally looked her way.

"That's Nathan Gurson," Monique informed her. "Thinks he's the local drug dealer. Right dickhead. Seen your mum?"

Vanessa said she hadn't seen her mother for weeks and didn't know where she was living. She needed her to sign some papers which would allow her to be discharged from school so she could take part in a ballet for which she would get paid.

"That's fantastic, Vanessa," Monique enthused.

Monique knew Vanessa attended dance school but until now wasn't aware of just how talented she was. She was genuinely interested, and Vanessa told her about the role. Monique said she'd definitely come to see her. It was scheduled to start in the spring.

Monique told her she'd found a much better place to go at night and they should meet there next week. "Rich boys from private schools there, Vanessa, and only too happy to buy a pretty little kitten like you a drink - without feeling it gives them the right to hit on you."

Vanessa would have to put on more makeup and look older, but that wouldn't be a problem.

When they left, Monique gave Vanessa the money for her bus fare home. She didn't want her walking.

"Now, do your coat up. You'll catch your death," Monique said once they had stepped outside. She reached round Vanessa's neck and unfolded the collar of her coat.

Their faces were close and the vapour from their breath mingled in the cold air. They kissed quickly and then again after a few seconds, this time slowly. The soft touch of Monique's lips and feel of her tongue made Vanessa tingle. Monique broke away. "There," she said, "you won't catch cold now. Take care. See you Wednesday."

Vanessa watched until Monique disappeared around the corner. She could still taste her. She smiled to herself and turned into the alley, a short cut to the bus stop. Suddenly she was aware she wasn't alone.

"Ah, it's the dancer with the lovely tits." It was Liam. He'd just stepped out from behind a pile of empty beer crates. She tried to push past him, but he grabbed her.

"You been upsetting my friend?" The voice came from behind and she knew it was the guy Liam had been talking to at the bar. "So, it's girls you prefer? Well, let's see what you've got to say now, you little whore..."

"Yeah, let's show her what she's been missing," Liam snarled into her ear.

Liam manoeuvred her to the darkest part of the alley. She opened her mouth to scream but a hand quickly covered it. She saw Nathan looking round to ensure there were no prying eyes before moving in to help restrain her. Soon she was pinned against the wall, her heart beating fast, her eyes wide open straining to see. She struggled to breathe, she tried to kick, she bit the hand covering her mouth, hearing the cry of 'bitch' when it was pulled away. A second later her head was pushed back against the wall, and a sickening thud started pounding through her brain.

Hands tugged at her coat, bursting the buttons, two of which pinged to the floor and rolled in a fuzzy slow motion into the darkness. She felt the hot trickle of blood on the back of her neck.

Her hips jerked as rough hands tugged underneath her skirt. Through eyes that were starting to blur she saw teeth in a moving mouth but heard no words. The stench of beer and cigarettes filled her nostrils and bile rose in her throat. She felt her legs being spread, a rough hand scratching between them and then the pain as Liam forced himself inside her. She didn't know how she was still standing, the only sensation a rhythmic thump in her belly.

Suddenly, there was no weight on her and she felt herself slipping downwards. Hands pushed and pulled her until she was laying on her back. The dark grey sky was turning white as she looked up, but then there was more weight on her, and the view of the sky was gone.

She needed to sink into the ground to escape the grunts and gasping of another monster that had smothered her. That pain inside returned, pumping, invading, wrong. Pump, pump, pump, pump. She was drifting, slipping somewhere, before louder noises and shouting reminded her she was still alive. The weight suddenly disappeared, and that grey-white sky returned. Then nothing.

The voice was only a whisper, a woman's voice, but it was gradually growing louder. The touch on her cheek was gentle. She didn't smell beer now; it was more like the gin her mother drank. Her head throbbed but otherwise she felt numb.

"Ma chérie , ma chérie," it was a desperate but gentle voice. "Est-ce que ça va? Est-ce que ça va?" She realised the question had been asked several times. Vanessa opened her eyes and as the words became more coherent so did the image of the kind face responsible for them.

"She's okay," the woman said, turning to the man kneeling beside her. "Are you okay?" she repeated.

Life was returning and Vanessa looked around, gradually realising where she was and trying to recall what had just happened. "There's an ambulance on the way. It won't be long," said the kind lady.

# 46

# MARCH 1990, DELAHAY HOUSE

## VANESSA AND MALISSA

*P*regnancy suited Malissa. She glowed, and although she wobbled about moaning she had back pain, she remained the cheerful friend Vanessa had grown so fond of. Lewis was in bed and the two women sat in the living room, snacking and watching TV.

"I know," said Malissa. "It's disgusting but I just can't help it."

Vanessa was willing to try the pilchard, pineapple and gherkin sandwich Malissa had raved on about but was adamant she did not want it with mayonnaise and brown sauce.

"At least I've given up the cat food," Malissa said in her defence.

Vanessa frowned. "You don't even have a cat."

Malissa smiled. "I used to. Now, tell me what else you did in Paris. Oh, and don't forget you're meant to be taking me to the Moulin Rouge."

"Well, I went to the bank and closed my savings account."

"And did some shopping? What did you buy?"

"No Malissa, no time for shopping. Plus, I need all the money for the dance school."

"Yes, I saw the estimate from the builders."

"It's disgusting, Malissa! Does Henry know you eat this?" Vanessa looked for somewhere to spit out the mouthful of sandwich she'd just tried.

"It's just an acquired taste. I wonder if I'll still crave it after the baby's born?"

Vanessa smiled. They had enjoyed a great few days together. "And I paid a visit to Mademoiselle Lauren."

"Your dance teacher? Tell me more. I bet she was surprised to see you."

"Yes, she was. She hasn't changed much."

"Did you tell her you were now opening a dance school?"

"No, we just talked about old times."

"You were her star pupil. She praised you highly."

"You've talked to her?"

"No, the reference she sent. I was very impressed."

That niggling doubt Vanessa had harboured disappeared with Malissa's casual mention of the reference. It was surely just a formality. She didn't tell Malissa she had seen it.

"Oh, I never knew you had asked for one."

"Well, strictly we should. Company policy, but I must admit I didn't ask until after I discovered what a childhood star you were. I was just curious to discover all your awards. There were many my much too modest friend." She made a sad face. "Sorry, I suppose I should have told you, but you never talk that much about your childhood."

Vanessa mentally digested some of the words contained in the letter. *She came from a humble background, to say the least and received no parental or other outside adult support...*

"Well, her school's much the same really. She's doing okay," Vanessa replied, realising she needn't have doubted Malissa after all, but aware she still harboured her own secret.

"But no other star I bet," smiled Malissa. "Hey, you should ask her for advice. I'm sure she'll be only too happy to help. So, when do you think the builders will start?"

Vanessa shook off that pang of guilt that invaded, tilted her head and smiled sarcastically. "They say these things take time. They need a *licencia de obra mayor and obra menor and certificado de conversión comercial.*"

"Sounds complicated. You want me to have a word with Henry? He could pull a few strings."

"I already think they believe it's all part and parcel of the new hotel and they're really keen to get on with that. In fact, the old warehouse was being knocked down when I left."

"I presume the villa's still standing. You know, Ness, when I've had this baby I think I'll come out there for the rest of the summer – maternity leave. I miss not being there. Henry too once he's finished messing about with mobile phones in the States. Talking of which, is there a phone in the villa?"

"Yes, last week. I have the number somewhere."

"And the farmhouse?"

"Soon, they've got to run another line up and I said you wouldn't want a pylon, so they have to do more digging."

"Ooh," Malissa said, suddenly adjusting herself in in the armchair. "It's kicking time."

She invited Vanessa to feel her tummy. "Always kicks at night. Now, Lewis was more of a morning person," she said. "Still is. I wonder if it means this one will be a night bird?"

"Probably kicking because of that sandwich," Vanessa said, moving over to Malissa and placing her hand on her tummy. She was surprised by the wonderful feeling that ran through her as she and Malissa shared those special few moments. "It's a girl, Malissa. Definitely," Vanessa said before suggesting she made tea. She needed something to take away the taste of pilchards.

"Four sugars, please," Malissa said with a grimace.

Vanessa shook her head.

Vanessa continued her discussion with Malissa as she waited for the kettle to boil. Whether due to her voluntary disclosure about the reference, the intimacy they just shared when feeling the baby kicking or something else, Vanessa suddenly wanted to be more open with Malissa about her upbringing. Then that little pang of guilt again when she thought her motive might purely be to soften any surprises that Malissa may discover in the future? No, that was Vanessa in Paris, she convinced herself.

She rejoined Malissa in the sitting room. "My mother took me to Mademoiselle Lauren's when I was only four. I think she thought it would get me out the way. We never got on brilliantly, and to tell the truth she had her own... agenda."

Malissa raised an eyebrow. "Agenda?"

"I never had the relationship with my mother that you did. She left my father quite early on, I was about two, and he brought me up. I didn't see her again for a while, but when she did come back she met Philippe and I lived with them for a while. That's when she enrolled me in the dance school."

"I think that was a good decision. But I thought you lived with you father?"

"Yes, I did later. Mum and Philippe split, and it seemed best to live with him. So, it was school, dance school and staying at my dad's, or sometimes at my stepfather's so I could see Gabrielle." Vanessa had never referred to Philippe as her stepfather before.

"How is Gabrielle? You said her nan was more like a mother to her."

"I think she's okay. It'll take a while, but Marguerite is a good mum to her."

Malissa smiled. "It's good she has a good home. I know things couldn't have been easy for you. Oh, did I tell you Henry's latest?"

Vanessa raised her eyebrows.

"Well, if it *is* a girl he loves the name Millie."

"Sounds good, sort of an abbreviation of Malissa."

"I agree. But he thinks Millie *Estrellas* Ovmeister."

"Stars?"

"And Millie, mil, Spanish for a thousand. It's because of that night at the farmhouse, you know, when we slept on the lawn."

"Night of a thousand stars," sang Vanessa. "Typical Henry?"

"Hmm," responded Malissa.

Vanessa loved talking to Malissa but finding the right time to tell her about the less savoury aspects of her life in France was never going to be easy.

# PART V

*Henry and Emma*

*In the distance a beacon*
*Bright in the night*
*Burning until*
*A flickering light*
*Burning until*
*No longer in sight*
*When flame turns to ember*
*And daytime twilight*

# 47

# APRIL 1990, SÖLLER OLD TOWN

## VANESSA AND LORENA

*L*orena was 21, three years younger than Vanessa. She was born in Palma but had lived in Söller since she was two years old. When her parents retired they returned to the mainland and Lorena, who had been employed by the library since she left school, moved into her own two-bedroomed house in one of the quaint cobbled streets just off the main square.

Despite only ever having left the island a handful of times, and then only to visit her parents, Lorena had told Vanessa she yearned to travel and see more of the world. Quiet and shy when they first met, Lorena was now a much more confident woman.

"That bar gives me the creeps, Vanessa," she said as she opened her front door.

"I guess it's not the best place for a quiet chat. Very lovely," Vanessa said as she stepped inside Lorena's house. "I feel you're a little house proud." She smiled and slipped off her shoes.

"Wine?" Lorena asked.

"Yes, please." Vanessa sat at the kitchen table.

Lorena had been up to the farmhouse on a couple of occasions, but this was the first time Vanessa had visited her here. "*Vin blanc*," Lorena said joining Vanessa. "*J'espère que tu aimes.*"

"*Très bien, mademoiselle*," smiled Vanessa.

Shortly after they met, Lorena asked Vanessa to teach her French. Vanessa was very happy to do so and suggested Lorena could teach her Spanish in return. Their conversations now were invariably a mixture of the two languages. Lorena also spoke English reasonably well.

"I wish I had your confidence, Vanessa. I would never go in there on my own."

The bar they had spent the last hour or so in was one Vanessa had visited a couple of times before. It was frequented by local fisherman and not the most convivial place for a couple of young women to enjoy a drink.

Vanessa smiled. "They're okay really. They just see their industry crumbling around them and don't have the same enthusiasm for tourism."

"But the men make me cringe. I think they come there straight off their boats. And the smell! I'm sure they've still got the lobsters in their pockets."

Vanessa laughed out loud and reached across the table, clasping Lorena's hand. "They might not smell as sweet as you, Lorena, and they certainly wouldn't go to the library, but they have their living to make so we shouldn't be too hard on them."

"But I can smell them on my clothes. I almost think I've brought them back here. And their manners, they are so rude."

Vanessa still had hold of Lorena's hand and was looking into her eyes. She knew Lorena was attracted to her, and although they had never openly discussed their sexuality Vanessa didn't doubt Lorena would have guessed that she too preferred to sleep with women.

If she was in Paris maybe her relationship with Lorena would have already developed beyond friendship, but here in Söller Vanessa was a different woman; a woman who enjoyed her own company and the comparative anonymity that went with it. She missed the intimacy of human contact and was sexually attracted to her friend, but would Lorena expect far more commitment than Vanessa was prepared to give? She let go of her hand. "I take it you don't like rough men."

Lorena looked a little unsure how to respond. She dipped her head a little. "I'm not sure I like men at all," she said quietly.

Vanessa smiled kindly. "I've had relationships with men and women, and I think you know it is a woman I'd prefer to sleep with. Here in Söller however, I have found comfort in just being me and I am far from certain

I'd be the ideal partner for anyone, let alone one who may be vulnerable, or looking for love."

She allowed her words to float in the air and started removing the pins from her hair.

"I've only had one relationship," Lorena said, then laughed a little nervously before carrying on. "If you could call it a relationship. We were only 16 and still at school. It lasted a few months and then she moved away. Since then I've wondered but...".

"Wondered if it is women you prefer?" Vanessa took her hand again and squeezed before letting go. "Wondered what you should do if it is? Or if it isn't, is it just a phase?"

Lorena smiled.

"I guess the main thing," Vanessa continued, "is not to be scared and beat yourself up about it. That is one thing I *have* learned."

"Could you teach me?"

Vanessa smiled again. "My dear, Lorena. I could teach you many things, but the main thing you need to learn is it's okay to be you, that your life belongs only to you, and if you choose to let people impact on your life, well, that's your choice and you just need to learn to live with those choices."

"You have... You have no one special in your life?"

"I have many special people in my life, but no one person too special." She removed the blonde wig.

"You're incredibly beautiful, Vanessa," Lorena said as Vanessa shook her hair into place.

"And you Lorena are a very attractive and kind young woman who one day will find the love you dream of."

"And you don't dream? Of love, I mean."

"I can find love in the moment. I can feel loved and I can make others feel loved too. But I am me, a woman of moments maybe. In that bar I was blonde because it suited the moment. I was in disguise but still me, the blonde me. Now, I'm the me who feels relaxed around people I am fond of."

"So you're saying...?" Lorena's voice wasn't much more than a whisper.

"So, I'm saying, in this moment I could undress you and wash away the smell of the fishermen, make them a memory, like Vanessa the blonde. Tomorrow we may have coffee and even be intimate again. But the day after may dawn a different day and those moments will be but beautiful memories."

"But you'd always be my friend?"

"I will be your friend for as long as you want me to be."

"Teach me, Vanessa."

# 48

## APRIL 1990, SÖLLER OLD TOWN
### BAR SAN PERE

*L*orena had told Vanessa that the rundown house that Henry had rented when he first came to Söller used to be owned by two brothers. Lorena didn't know them personally, but if they were still around she was sure they'd drink in one of the two or three bars the other fisherman patronised. It was a long shot that Vanessa would find one of the brothers, but she had received the distinct impression from Henry that these old bars, in this part of town, were the ones he had drunk in, and they represented her best chance of bumping into someone who remembered him.

This was the third evening this week that Vanessa had visited Bar San Pere. It was busier than previous times she'd been in here, so maybe Friday was the fisherman's traditional drinking day. Another possible bar was less than a minute's walk away, but El Draque, the bar she had visited with Lorena, was quite a bit further.

Vanessa recognised several of the men in here now; a few had tried to chat her up. She hadn't needed to be rude when turning down their advances; she just explained she was there in a professional capacity, writing about the decline in the island's fishing industry. Some had insisted on sharing their knowledge, but most now just smiled and said 'hello' and simply got on with their drinking. They were, despite first impressions, decent people.

The owner of this bar had only been here five years. The other bars as far as she could determine, were still run by the people who would have been around in the late seventies; the time Henry first came out here. The barman at El Draque couldn't remember ever having served an Englishman, but the one at the other bar, in response to her casual enquiry, said the Perez brothers (Jose was the name of one of them), who owned the old house, had moved ten years ago. He had seen them around since but they hadn't been in his bar for many years. They used to favour the San Pere as far as he could remember.

Three men she hadn't seen before were already on their second drinks. She spoke Spanish quite well now and could understand most of what was said around her. She heard one of them enquire after the other's brother and paid closer interest when she heard the name Jose. It seemed to Vanessa that one in three fishermen around here were named Jose, but the combination of Jose and brother was worth investigating. She smiled as she approached the bar. One of the men whistled and asked her if she was looking to catch a fisherman.

"I may well be," she said, taking him a little by surprise. Another man, a regular here, told him she was a journalist writing about fishing in Söller.

"Then I'm definitely your man," smiled the fisherman. "Been fishing these waters since I was six years old."

"And now you're fishing well out of your depth, Mikel," another said, causing several around him to laugh out loud.

Mikel moved away from them and offered to pay for Vanessa's drink. He also ordered one for himself, and they sat down at the table Vanessa had been sitting at when Mikel had first entered the bar.

"You're not from round here then?" Mikel said. "I'm Mikel."

"Monique," she smiled.

"So, what brings you here? I mean, writing about fishing can't be that interesting for such a pretty girl."

"You don't think pretty girls can write, Mikel? Is that what a life spent fishing has taught you?"

It wasn't the response he expected, and he looked around briefly. No one seemed to be listening to them.

"I mean, you don't look like a writer," he said a little sheepishly.

Vanessa doubted he had ever met a writer, let alone a pretty one who seemed quite happy to sit in a bar he probably regarded as out of bounds to someone who didn't own a boat; especially someone with shining platinum hair and a cleavage. She softened her approach; she had made her point. "I'm from England. From a place called Cornwall. My uncle owned a fishing business that fell on hard times some time ago and he came out here, to Söller, to see if he could start a new business. He lived here for a while with some fisherman. So, fishing being in the family and fishing going through so many changes and me being a journalist who is very partial to Söller red lobster, it seemed a good story to write."

It was a statement she had made several times in recent weeks, and for a moment she thought it resonated with Mikel. He took a sip of his beer. "Ah, you English. I speak little. Not just fisherman of Söller." He took another swig and Vanessa complimented him on his English. A moment's silence. He reverted to Spanish. "Your uncle was a fisherman you say?"

"No, he was a businessman."

Again, Vanessa could see him searching his mind. Was there a chance Mikel had known Henry? She smiled at him. "Yes, he came out here, 12 years ago. His name was Henry."

This time, she was sure the mention of the name Henry struck a chord. Mikel's face became more serious. He downed his beer and asked Vanessa if she'd like another drink. If he did remember Henry, he didn't appear too enthusiastic about acknowledging it. Accepting another drink would mean she'd have to maintain a charade of being interested in him. But if he did know Henry, she certainly would be. She accepted and he went to the bar. Vanessa took out the notebook from her bag.

As Mikel ordered a drink, he said something to one of the men he'd came in with causing him to momentarily look her way. Vanessa smiled.

Mikel returned from the bar and Vanessa closed her notebook.

"So, you want to know about fishing in Söller?" Mikel asked.

"Yes, anything you can tell me." She had hoped he'd talk more about Henry but was prepared to see where the discussion led.

Mikel proceeded to give her his career history as a fisherman in Söller. He did mention he lived in the town once but didn't mention Henry. By the time he'd finished his story he'd also finished his beer and asked if she'd like another. She could just ask him if his family name was Perez - she'd done that before - but decided to decline his offer and said she should be going.

"Well, if there's anything more you need to know, I'm often here." Mikel said as she put her notebook away.

"That's kind of you, Mikel, but I think I've all the information I need for now. It's my uncle I need to know about. I was very fond of him." She stood up and was about to say goodbye.

"Henry, you say?" Mikel said.

"Yes, Henry. My uncle. Maybe you met him?"

"I knew a Henry," he said.

Vanessa sat back down making it obvious that if he talked about Henry then she was interested in staying. "You did? How wonderful that would be if the Henry you knew was my uncle. I was very close to him and very sad when he died."

"He's dead?"

Vanessa bowed her head a little before looking back up at Mikel smiling sweetly. "Yes, very sad. So young. I think he never got over Emma."

"The blind girl?"

Vanessa's heart skipped a beat at his sudden and unexpected question. The connection, the confirmation. She was desperate to hide her surprise and searched for an appropriate response. She needed to remain calm. She nodded and smiled. "Yes, Emma was blind, and yes, Mikel another drink would be nice, thank you."

He smiled back and while he went to the bar. Vanessa went to the washroom and was pleased to discover it was a better environment than she'd expected; a lack of female patrons no doubt.

She lit a cigarette and studied herself in the mirror, realising how much the blonde wig diluted her resemblance to the woman playing the violin. The excitement she felt two minutes ago had dissipated and a solemnity suddenly came over her as she considered the last snippets of her conversation with Mikel. Henry, Emma, blindness, death. She pulled herself together; these were surely not new revelations. She extinguished the cigarette, freshened up her lipstick, took several deep breaths and went back into the bar.

Mikel and her drink were waiting for her. She smiled and sat back down.

"Thank you, Mikel," she said picking up her drink. "So, you knew my uncle?"

Mikel looked a little reluctant to engage her and took a sip of his beer. She leaned across the table and touched his hand, inviting his gaze to her cleavage. She wanted him to have little doubt that she was interested in hearing his story. "I thought a lot of him and I miss him. No one knows what happened to him out here."

"Happened?"

"Well, he came back a different man."

Mikel thought for a few seconds. "My brother Jose, knew him better."

Vanessa smiled and pushed aside the pang of disappointment, feeling it would have been a more lucrative meeting if it was his brother sitting there. "Your brother?"

"Yes, we both knew him, but Jose used to visit the house where he lived; to collect rent and make sure he was okay. I saw him only once or twice, in here. He was...," Mikel hesitated. "He was unhappy."

Vanessa's mind silently calculated the various 'Emma and Henry' scenarios she had pondered over the years, filtering them to the ones which would have made Henry 'unhappy'.

"Yes, he loved her very much," she said reflectively. Mikel nodded so obviously her statement had context. "So what did he say to you?"

"Say? About fishing?"

Vanessa laughed and touched his hand again. "No, about the blind girl. I think I know quite a lot about what he said about fishing in Söller."

Mikel frowned a little. Malissa smiled.

"Well, he didn't say much really, he just got drunk. He couldn't even walk home. I helped him. I didn't know he was dead. I'm sorry." He took the lid off his tobacco tin and started rolling a cigarette. He asked if she smoked.

"I have mine," she said.

She took a sip of a wine then lit a cigarette. What had she been hoping to discover? What had Henry said that convinced her that his original 'pilgrimage' to Söller and Emma were connected. Why did she believe Mikel, or more likely his brother, had information she sought, and furthermore what was that information? She watched Mikel roll the cigarette his rough weathered fingers surprisingly nimble. Years of practice, no doubt.

Vanessa spoke Spanish adequately but not well enough to use the language subtly enough to steer Mikel toward volunteering information he may not even know he possessed. She would have to be a little more direct. She could always use the excuse that Spanish was not her native tongue.

"So what did Henry say about Emma?" she repeated. "Would your brother know?"

Mikel lit his cigarette and looked at her. Vanessa was aware this was not the conversation he had envisaged. She smiled at him.

"Jose would know more. He talked to him."

"Does your brother still live here?" She appreciated her questions weren't entirely welcome.

"We live together in Valldemossa," he said.

Valldemossa was 15 kilometres away.

"And is he at home now?"

She finished her wine and replaced the empty glass noisily on the table. She could see his mind ticking over, weighing up the disappointment that she seemed more interested in talking to his brother against the opportunity of taking her back home.

"Yes," he said after several seconds. "I could take you to meet him."

It was of some consolation that Mikel and his brother lived outside Söller as it reduced the chances of Vanessa meeting them again. It was nearly one a.m. when Mikel dropped her off at the Blue Water Hotel, a short walk from The Söller Grand, from where Petri, the night porter, was only too happy to give her a lift home. Mikel was disappointed that it was the 'wrong time of the month' for them to have sex, but she couldn't have stayed anyway because she had a flight to catch tomorrow. If, however, she was ever in Majorca again she'd be sure to call on him, but next week she was going to Australia where she had an assignment she expected to last at least six months. She retrieved the piece of paper with his number on it and put it in the bin before stepping under the shower.

Jose was Mikel's older brother. At first, he was reluctant to add anything to the information Vanessa had learned from his brother but Mikel, obviously sensing Vanessa's disappointment, encouraged him to be more forthcoming. "He's dead, it doesn't matter," Mikel had said, "and she knows about the money."

Apparently, after Henry had left, they discovered an appreciable amount of cash in the house. "We had no way of telling him," Jose had said.

Vanessa laughed. "That's so typical of my uncle, so generous but perhaps a little absent minded. Mind you, he had great empathy for the plight of the fisherman in Söller, so maybe it was a gift. I doubt he would have missed it."

That obstacle out of the way, Jose seemed satisfied that Vanessa had no other motive than curiosity, and he was happy to tell her everything he knew about Henry. It was strange he said, that such a wealthy man would choose to stay there. "That's my Uncle Henry alright," Vanessa had interjected. Henry had rented their cottage for two months, but probably only stayed one. He had paid cash in advance and cash for the old car Jose sold him, though he wasn't sure he drove it more than once.

Jose remembered the night in the bar Mikel had referred to. Henry was drunk and showing photographs of the woman he loved and who had drowned shortly before he came to Majorca. "Funny," Jose had said, "As soon as Lorenzo got out the fiddle, Henry started singing and telling him how his woman could play so much better. I thought they were going to fight so I calmed him down and that's when he said sorry and bought all the drinks."

Jose had carried on speaking but Vanessa couldn't listen. Jose had just confirmed her sister was dead. In her heart she had probably believed that was true for some time, but knowing it for sure impacted more than she had imagined. It took some time before Jose's story could punch through the sadness she felt, and she had to ask him to tell her much of it again, explaining her Spanish was still not as good as she'd like it to be.

When she had taken the newspaper clipping out of her bag, she was careful to conceal the name before showing them. "Was this the woman in Henry's photographs?" she asked. If they'd wondered why she was asking they didn't say. Mikel suggested it could be. His brother though, just stared at it before looking up at Vanessa with a mixture of shock and disbelief in his eyes. "It is her," he said. "I have seen that photograph."

During Henry's stay at their farmhouse, Jose often slept in a caravan 100 metres further down the lane. When he did, he'd check on the property ensuring the generator was working and that the electricity was okay. He also changed the bedding weekly. It wasn't unusual for Henry to leave photographs or papers lying about and he could distinctly remember that photograph because it was one of two fastened to some newspaper clippings that were lying on his bed. It was a couple of days after the episode in the bar and he remembered thinking, "That's why he didn't think much of Lorenzo's music."

Vanessa resisted the temptation to ask Jose whether it was also usual for Henry to leave cash 'lying about' and instead asked if he had any of the photographs or indeed the letters he had seen. He didn't have any, but suggested the letters were more like poems and the newspaper clippings, though he did not read English well, seemed to be reports on Emma's death.

She was quiet when Mikel drove her back to Söller. She told him it had been a tiring day but she was very grateful for the chat they'd had. She realised, as far as Emma was concerned, that she was coming to the end of her search. She had never travelled the road between Valldemossa and Söller but even in the darkness could sense its rugged beauty. She thought about Henry and Emma and then she thought about Malissa, about Henry and Malissa, and about the imminent arrival of their second child. When she travelled to England to welcome their new baby perhaps she'd go to Cornwall. That was surely where her sister had drowned.

# 49

# MAY 1990, THE OFFICE OF THE CORNISH TIMES

*H*enry had first visited Söller in October 1977, and according to Jose Perez this was shortly after Emma had drowned. The staff had been very helpful, asking Vanessa if they could assist in her research, and she was sure that if she had given the precise details of what she was looking for, it would have narrowed her search. Perhaps, some of the staff were here in 1977 and remembered the incident? But this was her search, and it was a necessarily secret one.

She couldn't ask Henry about Emma and she couldn't tell him she was her sister. How could she without destabilising her own life and that of those she had come to love? She couldn't ask Alice or Brad; they must have known about Emma but they too were too close to Malissa who didn't.

Henry's cryptic words when he talked about losing something precious remained with her. "You accept that it has gone forever, and you have to tell yourself it never existed otherwise you will spend your whole life searching to replace that which is irreplaceable." She could only believe that for reasons of his own he never wanted Emma mentioned, and those who were aware of his reasons understood why. Vanessa could only try and guess, but her instinct suggested it was because of love; Henry's perception of love.

Jose was sure Henry had told him Emma drowned in the sea and Vanessa could only believe it was in the sea by the cottage in Cornwall; in the very bay she looked upon from that fence with Alice and Lewis the summer before last.

She commenced her search with newspapers dated 30<sup>th</sup> September 1977 and worked backwards. She was into August now and was beginning to think she should have checked the early October editions. As she had been trailing through she considered the similarity between the settings of the cottage at Feelview Bay and Henry and Malissa's villa in Söller, and wondered if Henry saw the similarities too. She stopped turning the wheel on the microfiche viewer and slowly rewound. There - a headline on one of the inside pages read *Feelview Drowning A Tragic Accident, Says Coroner*. The paper was dated 24<sup>th</sup> August 1977.

Vanessa raised her head from the viewer and sat up in the chair. She breathed in deeply for a few moments, preparing herself for what she may read. A minute later she was bringing the small print into focus. She read slowly, digesting each word and trying not to get ahead of herself. And there it was, in the third paragraph; *Emma Ovmeister, 25, was reported dead on arrival at hospital in the early afternoon of 12<sup>th</sup> August ...*

She sat back up and felt the tears welling in her eyes. Vanessa had often felt sad when she thought about Emma, but this was the first time she'd wept. Perhaps just seeing it there - the absolute proof that her sister was no longer alive - had finally hit her.

The nice woman she had talked to earlier passed by and asked if she was alright. Vanessa smiled and said she was, and fetched a coffee from the machine. When she sat back down, she was thinking about her mother and realised she was comparing this moment to that one when she sat in the hospital corridor on the day her mother died. Emma and her mother were intrinsically linked, and that hope that they had somehow managed to finally meet in another world, brought a little comfort to her.

It was nearly 4pm when Vanessa left. She had found the original front page article reporting on Emma's death, published the day after she died. Alice and Charlie were mentioned as the people who discovered her, but there was no mention of Henry and she wondered why. The articles mentioned her blindness, and the original one said she was scheduled to star in a concert in Truro, playing her own music, later that year. The owner of the concert hall remarked on her talent and said "...she'd be greatly missed..."

The only photograph was of the bay she'd drowned in. The report said Emma was a proficient swimmer who often swam alone in the specially constructed area off the beach that was part of the estate. Vanessa noticed the ropes that stretched from the shore cordoning off a section of the sea almost the size of an Olympic swimming pool.

When she was asked if she wanted copies of anything she'd found, Vanessa declined. After switching off the machine she sat in silence for some minutes before tearing up her own newspaper clipping and the letter from Tommy and putting them in the bin. She returned the microfiche films, thanked the staff and left.

She had discovered what had happened to Emma but still had a million questions. Vanessa had never been part of Emma's life, but Emma had become part of hers. Maybe one day there would come a time when so many of those questions could be answered but, in the meantime, Vanessa would carry her older half-sister's image in her heart.

Tomorrow Vanessa would see the smiling face of the greatest friend she had ever known, her baby daughter and her son, Lewis, who Vanessa had come to love. Malissa's husband would also be there; the man who as a child had been deprived of parents, who as a young man had possibly lost his greatest love, and now with whom she may always share an unspoken secret.

# PART VI

*The Söller Dance Academy*

*The child, the dancer, the woman*
*Danced away the fears*
*Her guise no elegant ballgown*
*The mask just there for her tears*

## 50

## SATURDAY 22ND DECEMBER 1990

### MAJORCA

*G*abrielle's request to spend Christmas with her in Majorca surprised Vanessa, but after discussing the possibility with Philippe there seemed little reason why not. He had flown in with her yesterday and would be leaving tomorrow, but Gabrielle would be staying to see in the New Year.

It was warm for December, not quite warm enough to go swimming, but pleasant enough to have a beer on the little beach at the bottom of the peninsula. Malissa and Henry had considered spending Christmas at their villa but decided to spend it at home. Malissa did come out here for a few days in October when Henry had a couple of weeks off work, but they had another child now and wanted her first Christmas to be at Delahay House.

"Thank you for bringing her." Vanessa said as Philippe sat down next to her at the table.

Philippe smiled. "It's a beautiful place, Vanessa. No wonder you love it here."

He noticed the old-fashioned car horn attached to the rock.

Vanessa laughed. "We put it there last summer. We have a swimming competition we call the Blackpool-Brighton challenge. You dive off that rock we call Blackpool, swim round that one, Brighton, then back and squeeze the hooter when you finish."

"Sounds fun," Philippe said. "Gabby swims though I don't think she packed a costume."

"Possibly a bit cold this time of year. Perhaps in the summer. Hey, maybe you and Marguerite could come out? Bring the family. I'm sure you could stay at the villa."

Vanessa told him about how Malissa and Henry had bought the land to build their dream home and how, after coming out here with Malissa, she fell in love with the place and was only too happy to stay. Philippe already knew about the plans for her dance school and, having witnessed her talent as a child, had no doubt she'd make a success of it. Vanessa told him there were one or two obstacles to overcome before they could get the builders in, but hopefully it would be fully operational by the summer.

"I forgot to tell you," Philippe said. "When we were going through Mémé's things, I found your old trophies. I'll have to dig them out - they'll definitely need displaying in your own academy."

Vanessa smiled. Gabrielle had most of her dancing medals, but those Philippe referred to, were probably from when she was very young - before her sister was born.

"I remember 'The Ballerina'," Philippe said. "Me and Gabby saw that one three times, I think. Fantastic. Your mother loved it too."

His suggestion that her mother came to see her performing when she was fifteen surprised her. "I didn't know she came?"

"You didn't?"

"She never mentioned it."

He laughed. "Typical of her. She asked me for the money. I said she could get in for nothing if she talked to you or Lauren. I thought she was just using it as an excuse to get a bit of dosh – you know what she was like."

"You gave her the money?"

He smiled. "And change for an ice-cream."

"Perhaps she just spent it on something else?"

"No, she went. I'm surprised you didn't know. She took a couple of friends, and when I saw her a while after she was telling me all about it." He paused and smiled. "We went for a celebratory drink, ended up back at my house, Gabby was in bed and well... well you know how persuasive your mother could be when she wanted to. I was seeing a woman called

Agnes, and she called by. I tried to explain but... well, I never saw Agnes again."

Vanessa laughed. Her mother could do and say many unpleasant things, but Vanessa had little doubt she could, if so minded, seduce even the most reluctant of men. A warm feeling flowed through her as she remembered what her mother had said on her death bed: "Dance like you danced when I saw you, when you didn't know I was there..." She had always believed her mother was disinterested in her dance success.

"Philippe. Remember we talked about the other child my mother had?"

He nodded.

"Well, I discovered that she died."

"I'm sorry to hear that."

"It's okay."

"How did she die? Was it in England?"

"Yes, when she was young." Vanessa hesitated. "Her name was Sarah. I wonder whether Brie should know?" Vanessa wasn't comfortable to divulge Emma's true identity.

"You know, Vanessa, it's difficult with Gabby. She has never talked about your mother; her real mother, and I wouldn't know what to say. I don't think it would change her life. She was very young when she left and, for her own reasons, your mother chose not to stay in touch. I think you'll know if it's right to tell her. Anyway," he said bringing the subject back to the here and now, "I think Gabby's fallen in love with this place too."

"Thank you for taking care of her."

"She's my daughter, Vanessa. Some men make reasonable fathers you know."

Vanessa smiled and linked his arm. "What time is your flight tomorrow?"

"11:30am."

"Well, I suggest today we go into town. You'll like it - it's very French. Come on, Brie will wonder where we've gone."

~

Lorena came to lunch on Christmas Day. She stayed the night, sleeping in the spare bedroom. Vanessa was pleased Lorena wasn't overtly affectionate and that they never acted like lovers in public. Gabrielle told them about her boyfriend, a boy in the year above her at school. Gabrielle was growing up and Vanessa was pleased she was doing so well under the care of decent parents.

Because of the unseasonably-warm weather, the three of them spent a couple of afternoons on the beach. Neither Gabrielle nor Lorena was as good a swimmer as Vanessa, but their times for the Blackpool- Brighton challenge were recorded in the record book. Before Gabrielle left, she asked Vanessa if she was a lesbian. Vanessa answered as truthfully as she could.

"I always knew anyway," Gabrielle smiled. She didn't judge.

# 51

# JUNE 1991, MAJORCA

## VANESSA AND MALISSA

"To Ness's Dance School," Malissa said, raising her glass.

"Malissa, we are not calling it that. But 'cheers'. To the Söller Dance Academy."

Malissa and Henry had come over for the Whitsun holiday but decided to stay a little longer. Earlier that afternoon, she and Malissa had met with the builders who confirmed the conversion work on the old schoolhouse would start next week. Hopefully they could be up and running by September.

Malissa had left Henry with the children in the villa and come up to the farmhouse. It was the first time Vanessa and Malissa had had some time together in several months.

"Henry's jealous," Malissa said. "Doesn't understand why he's stuck babysitting when he could be enjoying the company of two beautiful women."

Vanessa smiled. She had spent yesterday afternoon on the beach with them and had supper in the villa last night. Henry no longer looked at her as he had done when they first met, which was helping her to forget about Emma and the life her sister and Henry must have once enjoyed together. She was close to Henry and they talked easily, but never as deeply as they had a couple of summers ago. The sun was still a couple of hours from setting and Vanessa could see him in the garden, playing with the children. "I think he'll cope," she smiled.

"Do you know, Ness? I think he's got a thing for women whose names end in *saa*."

Vanessa laughed. "And Estrell*asss*."

"Yes, Ness. I never thought of that. Can't believe he suggested it was a perfectly legitimate name. He sulked for days. Mind you, it doesn't stop him calling her that."

"Well, in Spanish it's Est-tray-uhs," said Vanessa, "so maybe he's bent the rules a little."

"Ness, he's even made up a song." She sang, "A beautiful night, we lay on the grass, me and Miss Keats 'neath mil estrellas…" I've told him *he* can explain that one to her when she asks."

Vanessa laughed again. She could imagine Henry waltzing around the villa, singing his daughter to sleep. "Maybe this garden will always rekindle fond memories," she said.

Malissa smiled and put an arm around her friend. "This place looks so wonderful now, Ness. Can't believe it was two years ago when we first came out here. Who'd have thought we'd be sitting here now? Who'd have thought you'd end up living here and starting a famous dance school."

They were standing by the open kitchen door and suddenly heard a clank from the shed as the generator kicked in.

"Why does it do that? It seems so random. It's like it's got a mind of its own," Malissa said.

"Probably sulking. Probably heard me talking to the builders last week. Knows he'll be obsolete soon. I think I'll miss him."

"Maybe we can clean him up a bit, bring him out in the sunshine and cover him in suitable foliage. A fitting reward for so many years of service. Now, let's get drunk and toast success and happiness and old generators. Henry can sulk and change nappies and you can tell me all about what you've been doing."

When the sun set, they moved inside. Malissa rang the villa to check on the children who, according to Henry, were both in bed. Malissa, however, suspected Henry and Lewis were still playing Nintendo. "Henry is the world's worst liar," she said.

Vanessa giggled, and even though the secret of Emma flashed through her mind, she told her friend all men were terrible liars but that it didn't stop them trying. She opened another bottle.

"So, Miss Vanessa Cozzette," Malissa said, "when do you think you will have children?"

Vanessa gave her the '*I believe you already know the answer to that question, Malissa*' look.

"Well, you know what I mean," Malissa responded, "you don't necessarily need a husband to have children. I'm not that much of a prude. I was just thinking..."

"I could always use that turkey baster I guess, though I'd have to gather the contents somehow."

"Seriously, Ness. I see you with Lewis and Millie and I'm not saying it's imperative or anything like that, but you'd be a great mother."

"Malissa, first you try to get me married to everyone you think may be even half-suitable and now you think it's time to be a mum."

"Hmm," said Malissa and then added, "Did I just say 'hmm'? I keep bloody saying 'hmm'. It's because Henry's been home so much lately."

"You did, I thought I was talking to him for a minute."

"Well then, I withdraw my previous remarks. Men are too much of an influence on our independence."

"All men?"

"You know what I mean," Malissa said, getting up and looking in the kitchen cupboards.

"Cat food?" Vanessa asked.

"Very funny. Crisps. I really fancy crisps. And some cheese."

Vanessa pointed her in the right direction.

"Anyway, how are you getting on with Loretta?"

"Lorena," Vanessa corrected.

"Lorena. Is she the one?" Malissa suddenly hiccupped which caused her to spill the crisps she was pouring into the bowl, then laughed after she bent down to gather them up.

"The one?" Vanessa said. "I don't think so, but the sex is fantastic."

"Ness!" Malissa said horrified. "I do not need that kind of detail..." But they both fell about laughing as Vanessa told her about all the things you could use instead of a penis. With crisps gathered up, more wine, and cheese on the table, they sat back down.

"I love you, Ness," Malissa said earnestly.

"Do you now?"

"Not like Lorena does, well I don't think so. No, more than that. You and me, Ness, we're like that map, whatshisname had, you know Indian Jones..."

"Indiana?"

"Yeah, him, and that treasure map in two halves, you can have one but need the other, and when you put them together you discover the booty – that's like us."

Malissa was usually one of the most pragmatic people you could meet, but Vanessa loved the philosopher a few glasses of wine brought out in her. Their respective upbringings, experiences and sexualities, were polar opposites yet they were the ingredients that when mixed together seemed to produce a more rounded view of life. They often joked that between them they'd make the perfect woman. "Booty? I guess that's treasure. That's very profound, Malissa."

"I am very profound, Vanessa."

Vanessa took her hand. "I love you too. But me and love are words I could never remember putting together, and perhaps coming out here, seeing you and Henry and your life, helps me to do so now. No, Lorena's not the one, nobody I know is the one. But I'm happy. Very happy."

Malissa smiled as Vanessa let go of her hand. "So, I needn't be jealous then?" she said as if she was six years old, then added, "I suppose I could always give it a try."

"I think that would spoil our friendship."

Malissa raised her glass. "To the most wonderful friend a woman could ever have... Even though she doesn't fancy me."

"To the most beautiful woman I know. And who no woman could ever replace," Vanessa replied.

The kitchen door was still open and they sat saying nothing for a couple of minutes; just listening to the crickets and the distant whisper of the waves. When Malissa crunched on a crisp they laughed, both realising she had shattered the relative silence. They drank the wine and finished the cheese.

"Well, I hope Henry's put Lewis to bed," Malissa said. "Early start tomorrow."

"I think he enjoys that 'daddy time' he has with Lewis," Vanessa replied. "Maybe because he missed out so much on that first year."

Malissa agreed. "Well, work's not such an obstacle for him these days, it's more of one for me. And he's certainly not missing out on his *Estrellas* time. Funny, Ness, when Lewis was born it seemed to, I don't know, scare him a bit, but he's different with Millie. Maybe because he was an orphan. I often think about that."

The image of Emma flashed through Vanessa's mind; it always would whenever Malissa mentioned something that reminded her of the secret she harboured. She would always feel guilty but there was no way she could let Malissa know her secret. It didn't affect their relationship and it was irrelevant. She shrugged it off as she had learned to do so well recently and smiled. "You are both wonderful parents, Malissa. Perhaps subconsciously my own experience of childhood, or of parents, is the reason I've never considered becoming one."

She realised she had returned the subject to one Malissa had seemed keen to discuss earlier. Malissa knew much of her comparatively dysfunctional upbringing, but she was grateful it was something she never pressed her on.

"You'll make a wonderful mother one day Vanessa. You'll have a beautiful daughter, and she will have the greatest aunty in the world. Now, get to bed. I trust you're coming to Palma tomorrow and we're catching that 8am train."

Vanessa smiled.

"You have a wonderful home, Ness," Malissa said as she left.

# 52

# AUGUST 1992, SÖLLER HARBOUR

## VANESSA AND BRAD

$\mathcal{T}$ he structural reparations needed to convert the old schoolhouse into a suitable and safe dance studio were more extensive than anticipated. At one time, Vanessa, bitterly disappointed, suggested to Malissa that they sell the property and search for something that wouldn't need so much redevelopment. They looked at one or two other places, but both eventually agreed that the old schoolhouse was ideally situated, offered the space they needed, and once finished would be amongst the most beautiful buildings in town.

As well as the year delay, there was a significant additional cost. Malissa was aware that Vanessa had received a reasonable sum from an old inheritance, but suggested she keep that for a rainy day. "It is raining, Malissa," she'd replied. "Well an even rainier one then," Malissa responded and persuaded Vanessa to allow her to personally lend the money to their company.

The whole town seemed excited by the prospect of the Söller Dance Academy, and while several parents looked forward to sending their children there, Vanessa had been surprised by the number of them who asked whether there'd be classes for adults too.

Some months ago, Sergio, the hotel manager, suggested she teach Salsa at The Grand. It meant closing the bar for a couple of hours, but with the tables and chairs moved to one side the staff created a perfectly adequate space. Salsa quickly became part of the hotel's weekly itinerary, with locals and guests attending. The sessions dovetailed nicely with Vanessa's existing duties as the hotel's 'unofficial' manager's assistant. More recently Vanessa had been using the room on Saturday mornings to teach young children the rudiments of ballet. They were fun sessions, well attended and Vanessa now had to limit numbers. Many of those who attended her classes at The Grand were sure to sign up to the dance school when it opened.

Malissa stayed at the villa regularly, mostly with the children but often with Henry too. When she came out alone she'd invariably stay with Vanessa in the farmhouse. The villa was Malissa and Henry's second home, and whilst they had no intention of using it as a holiday let, they did allow close friends and family to stay there, and Vanessa was always on hand to welcome them.

Malissa and her family had just been out for a couple of weeks and had returned to England a few days ago. Brad, who had been out here for some of that time too, had stayed on to hold further discussions with the firms tendering to furnish the new hotel and to attend a meeting with the Majorcan Building Control Department. Vanessa had witnessed the development of the hotel over the last couple of years and had sat in on several local meetings. Her knowledge of the building industry was non-existent, but she attended on behalf of Ovmeister-Carmichael, and Malissa had told her Brad really appreciated the feedback she gave him; especially on the local gossip which Brad said was important.

Brad rarely stayed at the villa, preferring the more traditional accommodation The Grand offered. The meetings he'd attended over the last few days had seemingly gone well, and he and Vanessa were discussing them over dinner at one of the restaurants on the harbour before he returned to England tomorrow. About 100 metres away, behind a line of fencing, stood the shell of the Ovmeister Harbour Hotel, climbing a third of the way up the mountain it was built into, like four giant grey steps.

"I think, Mr Carmichael, you are very pleased," Vanessa said after Brad had outlined some of the ideas one of the furnishing companies had come up with during his meeting today.

"Vanessa, you will know I wasn't overly optimistic about a hotel here but, yes, I can see it will be a rather impressive building once it's finished.

How long it will take to repay the construction cost is another matter." Brad smiled.

"I've never understood why Henry doesn't take as much interest as I thought he would?"

"Well, he does really. I think he actually regards this project as one of the best he's ever embarked on, certainly hotel-wise. He knows I wasn't that enthusiastic, and I did suggest his love of Söller overrode his rationality, so I think that's why he's given me complete authority over this one."

"Doesn't sound like Henry," Vanessa smiled. "I thought he'd be telling you all his ideas last Wednesday."

"Wednesday?"

"When you arrived. He seemed pretty keen to bring you up to speed."

Last Wednesday, 12th August, was the anniversary of Emma's death and Vanessa was sure she detected a slump in Henry's mood. She and Malissa stayed at the villa while Henry came into town to meet Brad.

"Oh, we were just catching up on several things. I must admit, I did concede the idea of the hotel may not have been such a bad thing though. It will certainly be something we shall both be proud of. So, tell me about the dance school. Seems daft they can build this in two years and take nearly as long to sort out that old schoolhouse."

"The structural work was completed a couple of months ago. The latest delay's due to the red tape of the island's cultural committee but that, at last, seems to be in hand now. Once we get the go-ahead should only be a matter of weeks. So, fingers crossed."

"So, how are the salsa classes?"

"It's a pity you're going home tomorrow. You could have come to Friday's"

Vanessa got the distinct impression Brad was delighted that he would be back home and behind his desk by the time of the next salsa session at The Grand. He did, however, like the idea of a ballroom in the new hotel - "Because they definitely will not allow a casino."

Vanessa was pleased about that.

"What about your ankle? I take it that's fully mended. Have you given up dancing for good? On the stage I mean. Must have been a difficult decision." Brad said.

"I'm surprised I don't miss it," Vanessa said reflectively. "I'm still dancing of sorts and when the dance school's eventually up and running I should be dancing more, but I'm sure it will be absolutely fine. I actually think I enjoy teaching more than performing now."

"And here?"

"Here?"

"It seems you've built a new life for yourself. I can see the attraction. It's like Söller's your home now."

She smiled. She enjoyed Brad's company. Other than once in his office, and a couple of times at Malissa's, Vanessa had only ever seen Brad here in Söller and then it was in the company of Henry and Malissa. He was certainly a man trusted by many and she had learned to understand why. "I think I have, Brad. In fact, I call this home now and not Paris. Though Söller does have a certain resemblance to France."

"Thank God for the EU." Brad smiled.

"We're all Europeans."

"Well, you French and Spanish probably a little more so than your more reserved English cousins."

Vanessa switched the subject back to the last few days they'd enjoyed up at the villa. "So, have you beaten Henry yet? Malissa said he broke 1:40." Vanessa was talking about the Blackpool-Brighton challenge.

Brad rolled his eyes. "I think, Vanessa, he takes it a little more seriously than I do. Plus, he's a better swimmer. So, no, I'm afraid not."

Vanessa smiled. "Hey, Malissa said you might be coming back out before the end of the summer. For a holiday I mean and not hotel checking."

"Well, it is very convenient to combine the two."

"So, you'll come?"

"We'll see."

Georgio, the owner of the restaurant, appeared with a bottle of their finest wine, compliments of the house. He, like several of the restaurant and bar owners, had at first been concerned about the building of such an expansive hotel on their doorstep but had gradually come to appreciate its construction would bring many more visitors to the area.

"So, how is business?" asked Vanessa when Sergio had gone. "Henry seems excited about the mobile phones, told Malissa the potential is enormous."

Brad retrieved his mobile from his pocket. "This is the latest phone," he said. "Works wherever there is a network it can connect to. Hmm, not here unfortunately. The technology in it is was out of date as soon as I bought it. The challenge is to create networks that take advantage of the technology which is constantly evolving. You've heard of the internet?"

Vanessa nodded.

"Well, pretty soon the internet will revolutionise everything. It will be a whole new way of communicating and a phone will become a mobile office, a sort of personal computer that you'd carry around. The challenges are to bring all the technology together and to make it affordable. One day everyone will have a mobile phone."

"And that's the challenge of the New York company?"

"Well, the States are leading the way when it comes to the technology, but it's LA that seems to be the centre of the universe as far as these things are concerned and we've opened a small office there. Recruiting the right people, that's the challenge."

"How interesting. And is that Henry's or your domain?"

"To develop it? To tell the truth, Vanessa, when we talk to people about it we realise just how little we know. It's an exciting opportunity, something we know we have to invest in, and the people we've employed who know about these things earn fortunes. Keeps me awake at night when I think how much they cost us." He paused. "It even worries me more than hotels in Söller."

Vanessa smiled. "So, Henry has an idea, says how simple it is, gets everyone excited then passes it on to his best friend with a bundle of worry."

"I think he calls it a challenge."

"He seems so laid-back, Brad. I can't believe he'd ever worry about anything." She wondered if she was probing Brad to find out what he knew about Emma. "Then again, I guess he comes to see you the moment you arrive to discuss some pressing business issue, so perhaps I do him an injustice."

He looked at her and surely for a brief moment she saw a question in his eye. Did he, like Henry, see something of Emma in her too? "I've known Henry a long time. He may come across as happy-go-lucky, but he can think deeply, and you'd be surprised how much he cares about... about many things."

"I'm not surprised at all, Brad. I've seen it in his eyes. I imagine when he cares about something he does so really deeply. For many good reasons people can find it hard to share things that are close to their hearts, even with those really close to them. I'm sure he secretly worries about the burdens he puts on you." She took a sip of her wine. "Or others he's so fond of." She paused, wondering if he'd interject. He didn't, but neither did he look away. She smiled. "I imagine him tossing and turning too over just how much you're having to pay your mobile men."

Brad laughed and sat back in his chair.

"You're a very beautiful woman, Vanessa."

The comment surprised her. Brad was not a man who made such statements.

"Thank you. You're not bad looking yourself."

Brad took her hand across the table. "I don't suppose you've changed your mind about men?"

Vanessa laughed. "When I do, you'll be the first to know."

They sat in silence for a minute. One thing that had been on Vanessa's mind was the name of the hotel they were building. Ovmeister was an unusual name and the Ovmeister Harbour Hotel could easily remind locals of Henry's first visit here 15 years ago. That could have dire consequences for Henry, for Henry and Malissa and of course the relationship she enjoyed with them.

Brad interrupted her thoughts. "It's funny, Vanessa," he said. "Me, Henry's best friend, you Malissa's. Gives us a kind of symmetry, don't you think?"

Vanessa smiled. "I think about that too. I also believe they are the greatest couple I know. If you need to know what love is, you need only look at them."

"Yes, love like that doesn't come around too often. Henry has told me he is a very lucky man."

"And Malissa has told me she's a very lucky lady."

"Malissa will tell you things," Brad continued, "and Henry me, and I guess in some ways it's up to us to determine what information is for our ears only. We make judgements. True friendship?"

She wondered if Henry had talked to him about her, a remark maybe, something like, *She just reminds me of Emma, Brad.* Vanessa replied, "I believe it is Brad. Maybe over the years we will accumulate knowledge that would have to remain secret."

"Or maybe already have," Brad replied. "And even though we may advocate otherwise, we need to respect why they'd believe things would need to remain that way."

Again a connection. Or was it that Vanessa was simply reading too much into this conversation? Could she ask Brad about Emma? Right now? Discuss her so Brad knew that she knew? Could she tell Brad she was Emma's sister? Would Brad then feel he needed to tell Henry? And if Henry knew, what would be the consequences? It was all part of the same dilemma. Perhaps Brad and Vanessa could then keep the knowledge secret to themselves. Or would that put them in a position where they would have to lie to people they loved?

"You're thinking deeply, Vanessa," Brad said.

She realised she had been staring at him.

She smiled. "Henry may have told you we talked last year. I think he was talking about his love for you..."

"The old love for a friend chestnut," Brad laughed, "it's embarrassing sometimes."

"But lovely," she smiled. "He was telling me about the first time he came out here. Said he'd lost something precious and was seeking some kind of solace. I know that was a long time ago and," she paused, Brad was looking into her eyes, "... Well, I got the impression he wasn't the same self-assured businessman then and if he was drinking in some of the bars in the old town some of the locals will be thinking, 'I wonder if that new hotel is owned by that same Henry Ovmeister who used to get drunk in here'. You know what these local fishermen can be like."

"Indeed," Brad said thoughtfully, maintaining his gaze at her for several seconds, before picking up the wine bottle and topping up their glasses. "I've talked to Henry about that," he continued, "but I don't think you need to worry. From what I understand, he never checked into any kind of hotel, never used a credit card and I doubt he ever told a soul his real name."

"That could have been wise."

"Business practice maybe, Miss Cozzette. We have several businesses you wouldn't immediately associate with Ovmeister-Carmichael. The Grand Hotel is an obvious example and perhaps that business practice unwittingly spills over into our private lives."

Vanessa reflected. Two years ago, when she was asking questions about Henry, she was sure she never mentioned his surname. Perhaps she would have been good in business. She smiled at Brad. "I guess that's okay then."

"I would have thought so."

"And that information we accumulate stays secret. As friends that's simply part of our responsibility," she said cheerfully, reverting to their earlier exchange.

"Not even to be discussed by the respective best friends."

"For in not discussing them, those friends can remain friends too."

"And there, Vanessa, I'm sure you lost me a little," Brad smiled. "To Malissa and Henry." He raised his glass.

"And to friendship."

"And to hotels and dance schools and mobile phones."

# 53

# NOVEMBER 1992, MAJORCA
## THE OPENING OF THE DANCE SCHOOL

$\mathcal{T}$he room that once served as the dinner hall cum gymnasium would be the main dance hall. A stage which could host performances had been built into one end leaving plenty of space for spectators. One of the classrooms had been turned into an office, and within a couple of months the three other old classrooms would become smaller, more specialist studios. How they could best use the small playground at the rear of the property they'd decide later.

Vanessa already had 47 children of varying ages and abilities signed up and she would initially hold 12 sessions per week. At first, she and Malissa discussed delaying the opening until the whole building was converted, but before they could utilise the whole facility they needed to recruit more staff, and Vanessa had yet to meet even one other qualified dance teacher in Söller.

Lorena was keen to learn to dance and had been happy to take the examination that allowed her to teach the basics of ballet to younger children. Assisting Vanessa would not interfere with her job at the library.

Vanessa was at first a little concerned about introducing Malissa to Lorena, but she needn't have worried. The official opening of the Söller Dance Academy was tomorrow, and all three of them had spent the day making last minute preparations to the hall they'd be using for the launch.

They were having dinner in a small bistro just off the main square.

The photograph in the paper showed Malissa shaking hands with Senora Sarita Martinez, headmistress of the old school for 31 years prior to its closure. Maybe it was a hangover from her time in Paris, but Vanessa hadn't wanted her picture displayed.

"I keep telling her she's much too modest," Malissa said to Lorena.

"But Malissa, you are a partner in the business," retorted Vanessa, "and in charge of all PR. I'll do the teaching and you can do what you're best at."

"Are you saying I can't dance, Ness?"

The three of them laughed.

"Well it's done now and tomorrow we can set about telling everybody how wonderful a dance school this will be," Malissa said, withdrawing a wad of papers from her handbag. "Now, these are the applications we've received so far."

They spent the next hour going through the replies they'd received, from the island's dance teachers, in response to the advert they had placed in the Majorcan Times.

# 54

# SEPTEMBER 1994, PARIS

$\mathcal{T}$he immediate success of the dance school exceeded Vanessa and Malissa's expectations. Within a year of its opening they had recruited two full-time, and several part-time teachers. As well as teaching children, they had a good number of adult members who attended evening classes learning Latin and flamenco dancing. They held regular classes too at the recently opened Ovmeister Harbour Hotel.

Malissa, who was spending more time at the villa these days, had replicated a smaller version of The Fenner Agency in Palma where the staff there managed several performers; acts, who in the holiday season, would be assigned to many of the hotels around the island. She seemed to have enjoyed this new challenge and the business had grown rapidly. When Malissa was in England, Vanessa was quite capable of keeping an eye on things. It had been a busy two years and Vanessa had only managed to go to Paris to see Gabrielle on three occasions. Gabrielle had, however, visited her a few times in Söller.

Some time ago, Mademoiselle Lauren had contacted Philippe asking after Vanessa. When Vanessa visited her earlier in the year, Mademoiselle Lauren seemed overjoyed about Vanessa's success in Majorca, and out of the blue suggested that when she eventually retired Vanessa should take over her school in Paris.

The Paris school was ideally located and, although looking a little tired, Mademoiselle Lauren was keen to modernise it and extend its capacity by purchasing the small garage that stood on the land adjacent. Her academy was well established and enjoyed a good reputation, but with no children Mademoiselle Lauren had no obvious candidates to pass her business onto. Vanessa thought it was in Mademoiselle's best interest to sell her business to the highest bidder, but her old dance teacher was adamant that Vanessa consider her proposal. It was a strange turnaround of events and Vanessa had met with her again yesterday to discuss it further.

But before she returned to Majorca, Vanessa had a score to settle. She was nine when her friend, Katriane, just twelve years old, took her own life to escape the attention of her so-called stepfather, Jean Albern, who sexually abused her. The memory of her friend had always been with Vanessa, tucked away somewhere dark in the back of her mind refusing to surface, and maybe reconnecting with Mademoiselle Lauren had brought it more to light.

Vanessa knew Jean Albern liked to stand naked in his stepdaughters bedroom; Vanessa and Katriane had talked about it when they were at the dance school together, but Katriane never told Vanessa that he physically abused her. About three months before she died, Katriane started missing lessons but on the last few occasions she attended, Vanessa could remember asking her if she was alright. She recalled seeing bruises on Katriane's legs and remembered how she said they hindered her in lessons. And she remembered her saying she hated her parents. Vanessa was nine years old and 'hating your parents' was not an alien expression to her, but she had never forgiven herself for not being able to understand the torment her friend must have been going through.

When Katriane didn't turn up for lessons for three consecutive weeks, Vanessa called on the house where she lived, a house she herself had stayed in several times the year before. The house was empty. She was told by a neighbour that Katriane had died from an overdose of sleeping pills, her mother had gone to stay with her family and that Albern had moved out too. Vanessa could remember the walk home that afternoon, her gut wrenching from vomiting, her eyes stinging from the tears, and her heart aching for the incredible sorrow and sadness she felt. She should have done something.

Nobody, including her father who forbid her to go to the police, gave credence to Vanessa's story about Albern's obsession of going into Katriane's bedroom; or to Vanessa's belief that her stepfather was cruel to her. Mademoiselle Lauren was shocked and saddened by the news of Katriane's death, and on Vanessa's insistence telephoned the police only to be told they were already investigating the case and had been talking to her teachers at school. Vanessa later learnt that Katriane's suicide was reported as just another sad story of an unstable and unhappy child taking her own life and Jean Albern was never brought to justice. Vanessa never found out what happened to Katriane's mother, but a couple of years after Katriane's death she met one of her schoolfriends who told Vanessa what Jean Albern had done to his stepdaughter. Vanessa didn't doubt what she told her.

Vanessa had thought about Katriane much over recent years. About her innocence and her vulnerability; things she knew she couldn't have been expected to be aware of at the time but things that weighed heavily upon her now. In essence, Vanessa was abused by Mademoiselle Lauren. She was 15 and, on the face of it, an adult had touched her. It had troubled Vanessa why she hadn't felt abused, and it took her some time to admit to herself that she actually found it amusing to witness her frigid, prim and proper dance teacher turn into a pathetic, obsequious woman willing to shame herself in front of her.

When she was younger and living with her father, Vanessa had twice been touched inappropriately by their rent collector, Monsieur Paige, who called when her father was out. When she had stayed at Katriane's house, she had seen Katriane's stepfather looking at her in the bathroom. But these events were nothing compared to what she imagined Katriane must have gone through. Vanessa realised, that the anger she felt when she sat in Mademoiselle Lauren's office that day she first went back to see her, wasn't for anything that had happened to her, wasn't against her dance teacher, it was for Katriane, and as she parked the car around the corner from the street where the man responsible for her young friend's death now lived, Vanessa felt that anger surge again.

Albern was an old man now, his house not too far from where Vanessa's father had lived. He was, she had learned, weak and dying from cancer.

For several days Vanessa had considered how she could administer justice on behalf of her friend. Plunging a knife into his heart would not be difficult but how could she do that without being caught? Could she do that anyway? A pillow over his head perhaps? Would him being found dead because he had just stopped breathing raise suspicion?

Health care in this part of Paris was regarded as a burden on the state. Albern never left his house but was visited each afternoon by a middle-aged woman. Vanessa didn't know who she was, but an acquaintance suggested she was a carer because as far as they were concerned any family had long since deserted him.

When the woman left at 3:15pm, as she had done each of the last three days, Vanessa knocked at the door. She looked up and down the street while she waited for him to answer. When he did, she was surprised she could still recognise him. She pushed passed him, closing the door behind her.

"Who are you?" he asked, barely able to draw breath to frame the question.

"Let me help you to sit down," she said, ushering him back to his dingy, dirty sitting room.

He smelt as stale as he looked, and she was grateful for the gloves she wore.

"Can I help you?" he whispered, his voice naturally had a degree of concern. It would have been so easy to squeeze that scraggy neck or push him against the mantlepiece.

"I'm a friend of Katriane's." Vanessa said.

His red eyes clearly didn't see very well but they were fixed on her.

"Katriane?" he whispered.

"I'm Vanessa. You used to play with yourself whilst you watched me shower. I was eight."

He screwed up his eyes but other than that showed little reaction. Perhaps she had been hoping her appearance would have induced a heart attack. Maybe his memory had gone? She hoped not. He just sat there, breathing slowly, a whine accompanying each intake of breath and a rasp each exhalation. She wanted to stop him breathing, to watch him die.

She replayed the vision she'd always hold in her mind; Katriane giggling as Vanessa held her fingertips as she tried to balance on her toes. Her smiling face, her joy, so cruelly extinguished by the pathetic wheezing figure slumped in the chair. She gave herself a minute; gave Albern a minute. She needed him to be cognisant; to understand.

Eventually, he nodded. "Have you come to take revenge? It would not be difficult." His words were devoid of emotion; resigned. He knew he hadn't long to live.

She laughed. "Revenge? Stick a knife in you and end your suffering? I think I'd rather watch you die slowly. You are in pain I trust?"

She picked up a cushion and held it in front of him. His eyes remained expressionless. She pushed it into his face. The whining and rasping stopped for a moment but he didn't struggle. When she removed it, his throat rattled as he drew in a lungful of air. After a minute or two, his breathing returned to its whining, rasping rhythm.

She took the pieces of paper she'd written on and the bottle of pills from her handbag. She read the note to him, his confession to the abuse of his stepdaughter and his understanding it led to her suicide. She found a tea tray. On it she put the note, a pen, a glass of water and the pills. She pushed it heavily onto his lap.

"As much as I would enjoy taking your life, Monsieur Albern, I believe in redemption."

She let go of the tray and he held it on his lap.

"Do you believe in God, Monsieur Albern? Or the Devil? Maybe God is more forgiving than me? Maybe that little girl you so cruelly treated is sitting with Him now, looking down and watching you suffer? Maybe cancer is your punishment?"

She had got his attention. His eyes had widened as they followed her around the room.

"Maybe I'm offering you an easy way out. An overdose of sleeping pills, an eye for an eye as it says in the Bible. Confess your sins to those you leave behind in this world in preparation for the next. Just swallow them and sleep, Monsieur Albern... Or spill them on the floor and I'll just go. You may die later this evening, or tomorrow or the day after. When you do, whoever is caring for you will surely be relieved. Each day she knocks at the door praying there'll be no answer. Is she your daughter, Monsieur Albern, a niece perhaps? Or just a social worker who doesn't give a damn? Some part of me hopes it is someone close to you, for confessing to someone who matters gives weight to it, don't you think? There's nothing for you here, Jean Albern, and I just wonder what awaits you."

She approached him and unscrewed the cap on the jar she had transferred the sleeping pills to. She poured the powdered paracetamol into the glass and stirred it into the water.

She carried on talking, wondering whether she would like to see him swallow the pills now, in front of her. She would, however, like to see him sign the letter.

"Sign the letter, Monsieur Albern. I am not an angel of the Lord, but I understand justice, and remorse invariably warrants an easier route to forgiveness. Your confession will save me the trouble of having another letter read at your funeral and the expense of putting it in the paper... It's your choice. If you answer your door tomorrow, I will know what you have chosen. You can never make up for what you have done but if you do take your own life, just as Katriane did, I guess at least there is some symmetry."

She put the pen in his feeble hand and emptied a dozen pills onto the tray. "Sign Monsieur Albern," she instructed. His hand hovered over the note. "Sign," she said again, and he did.

She put several unsigned copies of the note she had written about the room ensuring they would be difficult for him to reach. She considered whether to do the same with the one he had signed. She looked at it. He just looked down at the tray.

"I doubt you will feel a thing, Monsieur Albern. Just sleep and not wake up to face another day of your miserable existence."

She looked out of the kitchen window. A woman was walking her dog, otherwise the street was empty. She waited for her to turn the corner. "You are scum, Monsieur Albern and responsible for ending a child's life," she said as she left.

Jean Albern may or may not take the pills she had given him. He may choose to tell someone he had been visited by a woman who used to know his stepdaughter. She had considered the consequences of that but doubted he would want to go into the reasons. Either way, she couldn't imagine her visit being of any interest to anyone and he would be dead soon.

She did not feel she had exacted justice, maybe she should have done that many years ago, but Jean Albern knew that what he had done all those years ago hadn't been forgotten.

She returned to her car, and removed her hat, glasses and the blonde wig she was wearing. She took off her gloves. It would take the best part of an hour to drive to Philippe's and she looked forward to spending one last evening with Gabrielle before returning to Majorca. She had sorted out some unfinished business and looked forward to getting back to her life in Söller and the end of term production the Söller Dance Academy was staging over the weekend.

# PART VII

*The Revelation*

*Flickering light, shadow forlorn*
*Opaque in the night, enlightened at dawn*

# 55

## AUGUST 1999, MAJORCA

rian Fenner had announced some time ago that he would be retiring at the end of the year. "A new century is surely a most appropriate time to retire," he'd said. Malissa could buy him out and take sole control of the Agency or they could sell it. The Fenner Agency was part of Malissa's life, but without Brian she wasn't sure it would be the same. She told Vanessa, however, she would definitely keep control of the Majorcan enterprise she'd set up on behalf of Fenner's some years ago.

Like so many recent years, Malissa and her family had spent the summer in the Villa. Henry had returned to England. Vanessa couldn't help but notice that he had done so in order to be at home on the 12th August and she doubted his planned visit to Feelview Bay was purely coincidental. Apart from one year, Henry had always been away from his family on the anniversary of Emma's death, but Malissa had never noticed. Then again, it wasn't unusual for them to be apart so why would she? The memory of Emma was still with Vanessa but it no longer haunted her. Even those pangs of guilt, which sometimes surfaced whenever Malissa casually said something that reminded Vanessa of the secret the harboured, had largely disappeared.

It was ten years since Vanessa had taken up residence on the farm-house at the top of the peninsula, ten years that had flown by and which had seen her create a new and wonderful life. Gabrielle would visit at least once a year and Philippe and his family had been out several times. Gabrielle had met Malissa often, but never Henry. She had arrived two days ago, the same day Henry left for England, but maybe she'd still be here when Henry returned.

Vanessa had walked down the hill to join Malissa who was enjoying a bottle of wine by the pool. Lewis and Millie were indoors. It had been very hot during the day, and even now after the sun had disappeared the evening was still warm. She sat down with Malissa who poured her a glass and they resumed their conversation from earlier when Malissa was deliberating about the future of The Fenner Agency.

"Henry says it's up to me. Of course, it is, but I'm surely too young to retire, Ness. Though living out here permanently wouldn't be that bad. And you could always give me a job in the dance school. I used to dance in the West End before I met Brian," Malissa said.

"Can't you just take more of a back seat? I mean, it's not as if it needs your undivided attention anymore, you know, keep in there in an advisory role or something."

"Yeah, if it's sold any buyer would expect me, or Brian, to stay on in some capacity anyway. At least for a couple of years to convince everyone the sale was in everybody's best interest. But... I don't know. It's just... well, it's like giving up a baby."

An innocent phrase but another that momentarily caused Vanessa to think about her mother and Emma. "Well, I can't imagine it would be as bad as that," she said.

"Anyway, I don't have to make any decisions yet. And Brian knows he could take out a good deal of his money if I decided to keep it going - not that he needs it of course. So, tell me what happened with you and Lorena. I really thought she was the one."

Vanessa smiled. "We're still friends," she said.

"I couldn't imagine you ever falling out with anyone, Ness."

"It was always going to be more difficult once she moved to Madrid. We've hardly seen each other in two years."

"Don't you miss her?"

Vanessa smiled. "I always told her she'd find someone more deserving; someone she could have a proper relationship with. We had some good times. I'm happy for her."

"She's met someone else?"

"She hasn't said, but I imagine so. I *hope* so."

"Sometimes, Ness I don't know if you're the kindest, most understanding person someone could ever wish to meet, or a right bitch."

Vanessa laughed. "Maybe both?"

Lewis had started playing the piano, the soft notes floating out to where the women were sitting. "He's developing into a bit of a musician. Funny, we never suggested piano lessons or the like, but he certainly seems to have a passion for music," Malissa said.

"Were you never musical? You must have studied music at school. Your mother would have insisted surely."

"I'm sure my mother would have loved me to be able to play the piano. I played 'Three Blind Mice' on the recorder once."

"Then it must have come from Henry." Vanessa suddenly wondered if she had mentioned Henry in order to find a route to tell her about Emma. Music was the connection this time. She sometimes realised she'd drop these little hints but hadn't done for some time now. She wouldn't tell her of course; she couldn't.

"Well, apparently Henry can play the piano, Malissa replied. "He denies it, says chop sticks is his limit, but Alice let slip he played quite a bit when he was young."

"When they lived together?"

"I guess so. I think he'd secretly like to be good at it. I've seen him watching Lewis and I see the smile in his eyes. He can hold a tune though but don't ever tell him I said that otherwise he'll be singing all the time he's out here. How did the show go?"

Malissa had changed the subject. The show she referred to was a rehearsal for a performance the Dance School were staging next week at the town hall.

"It was good. Some of these girls can really dance, and Mateo, I told you about him?"

Malissa nodded.

"Well, I think he'll steal the show. I think he could really be something."

"One boy, 60 girls. Do these other boys not know what they're missing?"

From indoors Millie suddenly began shouting at Lewis.

"We have David and Pedro too," Vanessa said.

"Either way, that's still 20 each. Better than football."

Lewis suddenly stopped playing then he and Millie appeared at the door. "Mum, will you please tell Lewis it's nearly ten o'clock and some of us are trying to sleep?" Millie folded her arms as she often did when she thought she really ought to emphasise the importance of the point she was making. It always made Vanessa and Malissa giggle. It was actually 9:05 p.m.

"She's always complaining, Mum," said Lewis.

"Well, I guess not all of us appreciate a little light piano music on such a still evening," Malissa said to Vanessa, before turning her attention to her son. "Now Lewis, it is quite late and if Millie's trying to sleep then I guess she has a point."

"You always take her side."

Malissa got up and ushered her children inside. Vanessa listened, smiling to herself as she heard Malissa refereeing between them. Gabrielle was 25 now but Vanessa liked to think she shared a similar love with her stepsiblings when she was Lewis and Millie's age.

Five minutes later Malissa was sitting back down. "Now, where were we?" she said.

"I think we were talking about Lewis and his gift of music."

"Hmm, I don't think Millie would call it a gift."

"Malissa," Vanessa heard herself say seriously.

Malissa raised her eyebrows and poured more wine.

Vanessa smiled. The memory of Emma had invaded but she let it pass. "Nothing, I was just thinking."

"Too much of a lovely night to think, Ness. So, are you going back with Gabrielle next week?"

"No, I'll probably go in September. Mademoiselle Lauren has invited me to her retirement party."

"Ah, the great Mademoiselle Lauren, teacher of the even greater Mademoiselle Cozzette. Funny, your mentor and mine, both retiring at the same time. What will become of her school? From what you say it's quite a thriving business."

Vanessa smiled. "She's talked to me about taking it over?"

"What, and moving out of here. But you love it here. I won't allow it."

Malissa's words were said in jest, but Vanessa appreciated how much Malissa would hate the thought of her moving away from the farmhouse.

"But it's Paris, Malissa, dance capital of the world," Vanessa teased. She had mentioned Mademoiselle's proposal before but hadn't told Malissa she was seriously considering it.

"Rubbish, Söller is."

Vanessa arched an eyebrow.

"Well, it soon will be," Malissa conceded. "Anyway, enough of that. How are Gabrielle and Pascal getting on now they're living together?"

Vanessa smiled. "I've never seen her so happy. Young love I guess."

A couple of years ago, Vanessa had used her savings and the remainder of the money from Lord Felix, to put down the deposit on an apartment in Paris. Gabrielle and one of her friends moved in, paying Vanessa a peppercorn rent but shortly after her engagement to Pascal, her friend moved out and since then Gabrielle and Pascal had lived there together.

"Ness, you have still not taken me to the Moulin Rouge."

"But that's Paris. The greatest cabaret shows are surely here in Söller?"

When they finished their wine, Vanessa strolled back up the hill to the farmhouse. Mademoiselle Lauren had extended and refurbished the dance school and Vanessa had taught there several times over the last couple of years. She was sure if she accepted Mademoiselle Lauren's proposal she could make the school even more successful. It would, however, mean spending considerably more time in Paris and Malissa was right; she loved it here. Söller and the farmhouse were her home.

Gabrielle was in bed. They still had four days together. Seeing Gabrielle grown up and happy and witnessing the way she and Malissa got on gave Vanessa a great sense of joy. It had been some time since Vanessa had thought about her other sister as much as she had this evening, but every so often Malissa would say something that triggered her memory.

# 56

## OCTOBER 1999, PARIS

### VANESSA AND GABRIELLE

"So, you'll be living here for good?" Gabrielle asked.

Vanessa couldn't tell whether her sister was thrilled or horrified at the prospect of Vanessa living with her and her boyfriend. "Would that suit you and Pascal?" she smiled.

Gabrielle thought for a moment. "There's plenty of room and I could always chuck him out anyway."

Vanessa reached across the table. "He's a good man, Brie, and something tells me you'd hate to throw him out – like the fact you're engaged! No, I love my little farmhouse by the sea. I think I'll only live here when I'm in Paris. And I'll try not to get in the way."

"I remember when we used to talk about living together, Ness. It hasn't worked out too bad has it?"

They were sitting in the same café they used to visit when their mother was alive; when Vanessa would meet her sister after school. They hadn't been here for several years but it felt familiar. Gabrielle was right, 'it hadn't worked out too bad' and taking over the running of Mademoiselle Lauren's academy next year would mean she and Gabrielle would see one another so much more.

"Anyway," Gabrielle continued, "if all goes to plan, we should have our own place within a couple of years. You never know, we might even buy yours. So, when do you start?"

Vanessa smiled. "I can take over whenever it's convenient really, but Mademoiselle Lauren is only planning to work until Christmas so if I haven't found another teacher to cover for her by then I could be here full-time in January."

"And I always thought she was an old bag?"

Gabrielle had met Mademoiselle Lauren several times when they were younger and Vanessa understood why she would have formed such an opinion.

Vanessa laughed. "She was a bit of a taskmaster, but she did teach me to dance."

"And looked after you when Mum wasn't there."

Vanessa had never told Gabrielle the more sordid details of her young dancing career, but Gabrielle had certainly witnessed the strained relations between her and their mother. "Mum did not have an easy life, Brie, and many of the things she did were a product of what happened to her."

"I hardly remember her as a mother. Is that bad?"

It wasn't the first time Gabrielle had asked Vanessa that question. One day she would tell her more, so she might understand. "No, Brie, it's not bad. I believe she loved us very much. It was just the times and, as you say, look how everything has worked out."

"Me and Pascal getting married and you, shortly to be the most famous dance teacher in Europe. What more could we want? And, of course, I've got used to the fact I'll never be an aunty, well, on your side I mean."

"But one day a mother?"

Gabrielle smiled and fell silent for a minute. Just when Vanessa thought she might tell her she was pregnant she lowered her voice and said something that left Vanessa struggling for a response. "Dad said he thought Mum had another child."

"Another child?" What had Philippe told her?

"Yes, when she was young. Way before you even."

Vanessa took a sip of her coffee. She didn't want to lie, but neither could she tell her the whole truth. Gabrielle's remark was casual, she didn't seem overly concerned.

"My father told me the same story and when Mum died, she mentioned it too." She tried to sound casual.

"So, it's true?"

It still just sounded like curiosity. "From what I understand Brie, she did. Probably when she was only 14 or 15. It was a girl and she was taken away from her."

"So, you know?"

"I know some."

"And you didn't tell me because I was too young to know?"

"I guess I was unsure. I guess I thought one day I should tell you but..."

"It's okay Ness. I know you always looked out for me and would have thought it for the best. It doesn't matter." She paused. "Is that bad? That I said it doesn't matter?"

Vanessa considered whether Gabrielle's seemingly casual reaction to the news was genuine. She had just discovered, like Vanessa had, that she had a half-sister. She could also be hurt that Vanessa had not seen fit to tell her. Gabrielle had never regarded their biological mother as her 'Mum' but Vanessa was sure Gabrielle had always valued *her* as her greatest confidant and as a sister who she could trust implicitly.

"No, of course not Brie, it's not bad at all. It may be bad I never told you."

"I think I can remember the arguments when Mum used to come round and see Dad, and I can remember you arguing with her, but I never knew her as my mum. It was Mémé and then Marguerite who were my mum. I didn't even cry when she died."

"You were young."

"But you loved our mum."

Her words resonated with Vanessa. Yes, she had loved her mother, but possibly had only realised that since her death. She was satisfied Gabrielle did not seem too disturbed by the revelation of Emma. "Mum left me when I was two. She came back, and for some years, when she first married your dad, I can remember being very happy. Yes, I loved her and knew she loved me. She left again when you were very young. I think sometimes it may be because of what happened to her. Maybe she thought she could never be a good mother."

"But you could have still lived with me and Dad."

"It was different then, Brie. It wouldn't have seemed right at the time. Anyway, I had my own dad, remember."

Gabrielle looked at her. She was a woman now and not so easily convinced as she used to be.

"He wasn't the best father in the world, I must admit," Vanessa conceded, "but as we've said, all's well that ends well."

"I used to wonder who looked after you. You know when we used to meet up. I often wondered why you couldn't come back to our house and live."

"I know you did Brie. You'd often asked. Now, drink up so we can get home and get changed."

"Sometimes, Ness, you're very secretive. But I couldn't wish for a better sister." She reached across the table and squeezed Vanessa's hand.

Vanessa paid the bill.

"Is she still alive?" Gabrielle asked when she'd finished her coffee.

"Alive?"

"The daughter Mum had. Dad never told me what happened to her."

Vanessa smiled. "No, Brie, she's not alive. She died many years ago. Now, come on, I think you should wear that lilac dress I bought you for Christmas."

# DECEMBER 28TH, 1999, MAJORCA

$\mathcal{G}$abrielle was in Portugal with Pascal. It had been the first Christmas since Gabrielle's birth that Vanessa hadn't spent time with her. Malissa's family were here, and so were Brad and his wife, Julie. In three days' time the villa would be hosting a New Year's Eve party to see in the new millennium and many of Malissa and Henry's friends would also be attending.

Lewis and Millie were staying at the farmhouse with Vanessa. It seemed to Vanessa that Lewis always preferred to stay in the farmhouse whenever he came out here and that was fine by her. She had watched Malissa's children grow and had a great affinity with both.

Christmas had been wonderful but tonight they were having a small family gathering at The Söller Grand. Over the next couple of days, she and Malissa would be making sure everything was in place for the party they'd planned to see in the New Year and that would be a good time to tell her she was taking over Mademoiselle Lauren's dance school.

Henry had been in a reflective mood over Christmas. "Because he's never liked New Year, Ness, something to do with the most obvious evidence of the passing of time, and a new millennium, well that gives him serious cause for concern," Malissa had informed her.

Over the years, Vanessa had grown very fond of Henry. They had become close friends, which perhaps wouldn't have been possible if her sexuality was different. They discussed many things, but rarely their lives before they met. She empathised with the feeling of abandonment he surely felt, and maybe he felt that too; maybe that was their great connection.

Lewis called up the stairs. "Mum said they're leaving in five minutes."

"Ok," Vanessa called from the bedroom.

"You not coming?" she said to Lewis as she passed him in the kitchen.

"Nope. Got out of that one, Vanessa."

"Well, have a good time. See you later."

She made her way down the slope towards the villa. In the distance the blue and mauve lights of the Ovmeister Harbour Hotel cascaded down the hillside merging with those of the little bars and cafés around the harbour and the trail of illuminations that fringed Söller Bay. It was a view she would sorely miss.

Malissa and Henry came out of the villa, hand in hand. She smiled as she greeted them. This would be a wonderful evening; as would the next few days spent celebrating the turn of the century with people she'd come to regard as family.

# FEBRUARY 2000, PARIS

*V*anessa wasn't surprised when Madam Martin told her she'd be leaving the dance school at the end of term. She had been Mademoiselle Lauren's bookkeeper for 15 years, was well into her sixties and could not conjure up any enthusiasm for the new computerised system recently installed in the office. Vanessa wondered if Gabrielle would consider the position. She was a qualified accountant, good with people and someone she could trust to look after the business when she was away. Vanessa knew she would miss Majorca but had underestimated just how much, and once the dance school was truly up and running here hoped she could split her time at least equally between the two schools.

She opened the door to the apartment. Pascal was dressed up and standing in the hallway.

"You off out?" she asked.

"To the cinema, as soon as your sister's ready," Pascal replied looking at his watch.

"I heard that," shouted Gabrielle from the bedroom and 30 seconds later she appeared. She kissed Vanessa and told her Malissa had phoned. Vanessa had noticed two missed calls from Malissa on her mobile too. Within two minutes Gabrielle and Pascal had left; she'd talk to her about the bookkeeping job tomorrow.

Vanessa kicked off her shoes and ran a bath. She was flying over to see

Malissa the day after tomorrow and assumed Malissa was double checking that she was still coming. She'd ring her while the bath was running.

Malissa answered straight away but said she couldn't speak right now as she was talking to Brad. She sounded troubled and Vanessa asked her what was wrong. There was a pause. "I wouldn't know where to start, Vanessa," she said. She checked to see if Vanessa was still coming as they'd planned, said something about a fire and that if she couldn't call back tonight she'd tell her all about it when they met. Immediately she put the phone down, Vanessa knew the cause of Malissa's distress was Emma.

It was ten p.m. when she decided to phone Brad.

"Hi, Brad."

"Vanessa, you okay?"

"I'm fine, but I fear Malissa's not. I was thinking she'd phone me. I've tried to ring her but she's not answering."

Brad paused. Some years ago, when his company was building the hotel in Söller, they talked weekly. Since then much of their relationship centred around the fact that they were the respective best friends of Malissa and Henry. His pause suggested something was wrong and Vanessa sensed he was calculating how much he could share. "Brad?" she prompted.

"Yes, sorry Vanessa. I was with her when you rang. Malissa and Henry have a problem." he said. "You are seeing her on Friday aren't you?"

"Yes, I am."

"Good, she's going to need you."

"What's happened, Brad?"

Half an hour later she hung up. Gabrielle and Pascal returned at 11 p.m. and she was grateful they went straight to bed. Vanessa sat in the lounge. In less than 48 hours she would be trying to comfort the greatest friend she had ever known. She would be trying to help her come to terms with something that had just rocked her world; something Vanessa had known for ten years, and the feeling of guilt ate into her. She was desperate to comfort Malissa, to be there for her, to be her strength, but had little idea how she would be able to do that.

The house Henry had lived in as a child, and which had been turned into a boarding school for blind children, had burned down. Among the debris of that tragic event was the revelation of Emma; a woman Henry had loved deeply and had kept secret from his wife for so many years.

Vanessa's heart ached for her friend and the love she shared with Henry. Had the revelation, as Malissa had suggested to Brad, really shattered the love she and Henry shared? A love shattered because he never told her about Emma? Surely, the love Malissa and Henry shared would overcome the fact that Henry had loved someone else?

Someone else. That someone else was Vanessa's half-sister. That someone else was a secret she had kept from both Malissa and Henry. Emma the gentle blind girl who played the violin and who had grown up with her best friend's husband. Emma who died so tragically. Emma the precious something Henry had lost; so precious he could never bring himself to talk about her.

# DELAHAY HOUSE

## VANESSA AND MALISSA 3 DAYS AFTER THE FIRE

*V*anessa had no idea how she could comfort Malissa, no idea how to tell her what she knew about Emma and no idea if their own friendship would survive if she did. She had spoken to Malissa yesterday on the phone but did little more than listen.

As soon as she answered the door Malissa threw her arms around her. Malissa's eyes were sad, or angry, Vanessa couldn't quite tell, but she was certainly not the same woman she had celebrated Christmas with. They sat down in the living room, a room where they had sat so many times before and a room where Malissa once nonchalantly mentioned the name Emma.

Most of Malissa's information had come from Brad. Henry, who since the fire had been living in his flat in Kensington, refused to talk about Emma. Malissa told her what she knew, so much of it just confirmation of what Vanessa had discovered, and the secret Vanessa harboured tore her apart as she listened. Sometimes Malissa spoke with an anger Vanessa had rarely seen but mostly she talked with sadness and disbelief.

As Malissa relayed what had happened, Vanessa tried to force from her mind all those images she had already conjured up of the life that Emma had led; of the life Emma and Henry had led. For many years, Vanessa had wanted to know more about the relationship they shared but not under these circumstances. Not like this. She desperately fought to push the fact that Emma was her sister to one side so she could concentrate in offering whatever support she could to Malissa. She hated seeing Malissa like this and hated the possibility the love between her and Henry could be destroyed. And all the time her secret about Emma gnawed at her, eating her from somewhere deep inside.

Henry and Emma had been adopted from the same orphanage before they had reached their first birthdays. They grew up together and later fell in love. They never married. "Some fuckin' teenage crush, eh Ness?" Malissa said during one of her more volatile moments. When Emma was 25 she drowned whilst swimming off the beach at Feelview Bay. "Fuckin' Feelview. 'Cos you can feel the view. For fucks sake, Alice knew, everyone knew."

It took Malissa some time to tell Vanessa that Emma was blind, and when she did Vanessa saw a great sadness come over her friend. It was not necessarily because of her blindness, Vanessa thought, but more because it reinforced Malissa's belief that Henry really loved Emma.

Vanessa did not interrupt. She listened intently, desperately searching for the right thing to say, but hoped that her mere presence there was, at that moment, comfort enough. They had been talking for over an hour before Malissa was able to calm down and Vanessa held her as she tried to regain some composure.

When she finally managed a smile Malissa apologised; she hadn't offered Vanessa a cup of tea. While she put the kettle on Vanessa asked if she could freshen up; it had been a long journey.

Vanessa felt physically sick by the time she got to the bathroom. A great conflict splintered her mind and pulled at her heart strings. She closed her eyes and tried to think. Malissa believed in love. She trusted people and had not experienced the things Vanessa had. Malissa didn't have her strength, not in that way. By the time she came back down, Vanessa had convinced herself that revealing she was Emma's sister would in no way assist the situation and, as difficult as it was to keep her secret, decided she would not be telling Malissa today.

Lewis and Millie were at school but Veronica would be bringing them home soon. Malissa had calmed down and Vanessa had somehow managed to cast aside her own secret and felt, at last, that she was there purely for Malissa and could be the friend Malissa so desperately needed.

"But how didn't I know, Ness?" she said. It was just sadness in her voice now.

Vanessa realised Malissa didn't know because nobody who did know, including her, thought it necessary to tell her. What could she answer?

Malissa continued. "Brad said I didn't know because Henry didn't want anyone to know. He said it was too painful for him, for Henry I mean. Too painful to tell his wife about a woman he used to live with. How can I be expected to understand that?"

"Is Henry expecting you to understand?" Vanessa asked softly.

"That's what I find so hard, Ness. When I saw him at the cottage, he just looked so... so different. It was like he didn't expect me to understand. He didn't try to justify it or defend himself or anything like that. He just... he just stood there like someone I didn't know. It was almost as if I was intruding into something. His wife – intruding?"

The cottage Malissa referred to was their place near Newbury. They had met there the day after the fire and that was the last time Malissa had seen him.

Vanessa was impressed how Malissa could hide her distress from her children, and after they were in bed Vanessa and Malissa's conversation continued into the night. Malissa was almost in a state of shock and Vanessa could understand why. She was deeply hurt and found the situation impossible to understand. Vanessa was sure it wasn't solely because she had been kept in the dark; it was her perception of the love Henry and Emma must have shared, that also, so clearly played on her mind.

They slept in the same bed that night and Malissa even managed a smile, joking that she must be the first woman Vanessa had ever slept with who could resist the temptation to make love to her.

Vanessa got up before the children woke, made breakfast and took them to school. They knew something was wrong and seemed to appreciate the distraction Vanessa brought by simply being there. She would stay with them as long as Malissa wanted, but right now there was little else she could do to ease Malissa's pain.

# 60

# MAY 2000, MAJORCA

## VANESSA AND MALISSA

*V*anessa and Malissa had arranged to meet up at the villa over the Easter break. It had been some time since they'd last got together there.

She had visited Malissa three times in England since the fire and they had spoken regularly on the phone. The secret of Emma had driven a wedge between Malissa and Henry which was proving impossible to shift, not helped, it seemed, because Henry simply refused to talk about her.

Vanessa had great sympathy for Malissa's plight, but also for Henry. Somehow she understood why Henry felt unable to deal with the situation; somehow, she felt his pain too. Was it because she had, for the last ten years, imagined the great love Henry had shared with her sister?

Several times, Vanessa had wanted to tell Malissa that she was Emma's sister. She had even contemplated telling Henry or Brad, but what would it achieve besides easing her own conscience? *Sometimes, Miss Cozzette, withholding information requires a greater strength; is a greater responsibility, for its revelation may only cause pain to those you'd least like to hurt.* She remembered Henry's words, though of course, withholding his love affair with Emma from his wife did seem to counter that philosophy.

When Vanessa suggested to Malissa that keeping Emma a secret was the only way Henry had felt able to deal with her loss, their relationship came under a degree of pressure; Malissa felt she was defending Henry.

Their underlying bond, however, was solid and Malissa appreciated Vanessa was just trying to help her understand.

Back in Söller, though, and together there for the first time since last Christmas, Malissa smiled, something she hadn't done much over the last few months. Vanessa also detected a subtle change in her attitude towards Henry. It seemed she wanted to know more about Emma, about Henry and Emma, and Brad had agreed to tell her all he knew; no holds barred.

Brad had recently taken Malissa to the house in Notting Hill that Henry and Emma once shared, showing her photographs and even the collection of violins that were stored there. Malissa had brought some of the photographs with her and Vanessa tried to shut out the fact that Malissa was showing her images of her teenage sister.

Strangely though, Vanessa had started to feel more comfortable. Yes, she was Emma's sister, yes, she knew that Emma and Henry were once lovers and, yes, she continued to keep that knowledge to herself. But as Malissa tried to understand why Henry had kept Emma such a secret, Vanessa realised she herself also needed to appreciate why, and that seemed to give her and Malissa some kind of empathy; a strange sense of purpose. Emma had impacted on them both and, although from completely different perspectives, Vanessa was in the perfect position to help Malissa understand the life Henry and Emma once lived. And this Malissa had said, was what she needed to do.

"She was a truly beautiful woman, Ness, and I don't mean just to look at. Poor Brad, I do put him through it and he's been really truthful, even when he thinks the truth might hurt."

"The truth?"

"The truth that they were so very much in love."

Malissa couldn't hold back the tears and Vanessa held her. They were sitting at the patio table outside the farmhouse, as they had done on so many occasions over the years. It was late afternoon and Lewis and Millie were on the beach.

"It's strange, Ness," Malissa said when she'd stopped crying, "but when I was looking through the photographs, I didn't see Henry, I saw another man. Still Henry but a younger version. Looking at him and Emma was like looking at a..." she paused, "a fairytale. I mean, they were so young. Sometimes I thought I was prying."

When Vanessa was looking at some of the photographs with Malissa earlier, she was, once or twice, surprised Malissa hadn't remarked on Vanessa's likeness to Emma. Maybe because she was now 15 years older than most of the images of her sister the likeness that Vanessa perceived was more part of her memory.

"You've still not seen Henry?"

"No, Ness. Well, only once when I collected the children. We've spoken and he's talked to the children. I don't know what's going through his mind."

"And he's still in New York?"

"Yes. Brad phones him, but Henry doesn't seem to want to talk to him either. I don't know if he's coming home. The children miss him and I'm running out of things I can tell them."

"They seem okay."

"Well, I guess they've got used to Henry being away and I think Henry manages to hide whatever he feels from them." She laughed sarcastically. "And we know he's pretty good at that."

Vanessa smiled and thought the same remark could apply to her, but it was good Malissa could still inject some humour. "So, what now?"

"I don't know. It still feels like Henry's a stranger. I miss him terribly but since the fire he's not the man I knew."

Vanessa took her hands. "He's still Henry, Malissa. And he's a good man."

"I thought so."

"You know so."

Vanessa was careful not to defend him too much. "It was a love in another time. I can't say exactly why he didn't tell you but I've no doubt *he* thought it was for the best."

Malissa looked at her. It wasn't the first time Vanessa had tried to justify her husband's actions but at least Malissa no longer dismissed her comments out of hand. A honk from the old hooter interrupted their thoughts.

"I wonder if that's Millie finally beating him," Vanessa smiled.

"Well, if Lewis comes running up the hill complaining, I'd be sure you're right. Come on, enough of me and my woes, how's the dance school in Paris? And we must pop into town tomorrow. I need to check up on Ness's Dance School."

"It's called the Söller Dance Academy."
"Whatever."

# 61

# APRIL 2002 NOTTING HILL, LONDON

*T*he year following the revelation of Emma had impacted hard on Malissa. When she also discovered that the book which helped launched her career with Fenner's when she and Henry first met was actually written by her husband, Malissa regarded it as another betrayal by him and she filed for divorce.

"But surely he was just helping you?" Vanessa had suggested, desperately trying to convince her to change her mind, but Malissa was in no position to consider it anything other than another deception.

Vanessa had no doubt that Malissa and Henry still loved each other, but Henry was also facing his own demons. Malissa and Brad told her that Henry had always believed he was responsible for Emma's death, something Vanessa remembered the Söller fisherman, Jose Perez, had alluded to. According to Brad, Henry was also struggling with the guilt of keeping Emma a secret from Malissa. They were miles away from a reconciliation but Vanessa understood when Malissa told her she was not divorcing Henry, not the Henry she knew, she was "divorcing someone else...".

Other than the filing of the papers and making the divorce legal, the services of solicitors were not called upon. Malissa asked for no settlement nor, as far as Vanessa could determine, did either of them change any ownership of the property or shares they owned.

Strangely, following the divorce Henry and Malissa had started talking, and now, a year later, Malissa had even suggested that divorcing Henry was the best thing she could have done; it had helped him, freed him to finally face the issues he had suppressed for years. Vanessa understood what Malissa meant.

Henry still spent most of his time in New York but talked regularly to the children, and they stayed with him in his house in Kensington whenever he came home. Somehow Vanessa couldn't help but regard the situation as more akin to a temporary separation. She wondered if, deep in her heart, Malissa did too.

Vanessa had known for many years that Emma was an accomplished violinist, but Malissa had told her that she was so much more than that. Earlier today, Lewis had been playing some of the music that Emma had once written, music Malissa had discovered at the house Henry and Emma once lived at in London. It was strange to hear Malissa enthusing about Emma's talent and further evidence, Vanessa thought, that her friend was trying to understand the relationship her ex-husband once shared with the beautiful blind girl.

The London property where Emma and Henry once lived was still owned by Henry and, used these days, to accommodate visitors to their company. Much memorabilia of Henry's past was locked up in one of the bedrooms. In visiting the house and sifting through the evidence of their relationship, Malissa had peeked into the love Emma and Henry had shared.

Vanessa had come with Malissa to the house today to collect the remaining physical memories of Emma that were stored there. Henry had instructed Brad to sell the house and find a suitable home for the violins and any other articles that linked him to Emma. "Trying to come to terms with the loss," Malissa had said, but for reasons of her own, Malissa was not prepared to let them go.

"Voila," Malissa said as they entered the bedroom.

Vanessa looked around the room. A photograph of Emma was on the mantlepiece and no doubt many more were in the cardboard boxes on the floor. Four violin cases leaned against the wall.

Vanessa wasn't sure what she felt. She was, for the first time, undeniably standing in her sister's bedroom. There had been many occasions over the last year or so, when Vanessa had wanted to tell Malissa that Emma was her sister; wanted to tell her for reasons other than clearing her own conscience. She wanted Malissa to know, so Malissa too, could appreciate the sadness she also felt; so they could share some kind of yearning to discover the truth. But how could she tell her? There was a moment when they were having lunch earlier when it seemed opportune, but it was scuppered when Malissa suddenly suggested she was beginning to understand why Henry felt unable to talk about Emma.

"So, as strange as it seems, Ness, I cannot let Henry destroy the memory of Emma. Mad or what?"

"No, Malissa, not mad. I think it's love and your appreciation of something few people would understand."

Malissa opened her mouth to answer but didn't. Instead she opened one of the violin boxes and drew out the instrument. She scraped the bow across the strings. "It's difficult to imagine how you can make such a beautiful sound on one of these," she said.

Vanessa smiled. "So, what will you do with them?"

"I don't know, store them I guess."

"For what?"

"I wish I knew the answer to that."

"Do you believe she took her own life?" asked Vanessa. Malissa had told her that the official verdict into Emma's death was a tragic accident, but Brad had told Malissa that Henry certainly considered it could have been suicide.

"I think about that a lot. Brad seems to think it was possible. I like to think not, but as I've got to know more about her all I've discovered is kindness and I wonder if she... never mind."

Malissa was putting the violin back in the case and folding the tops down on the cardboard boxes that had been opened. Vanessa sensed a serenity about her, so different to how she was a year ago.

"I try and put myself in her shoes," Malissa continued. "I know Henry, and I can imagine the gentleness of the love they shared. I wonder what went through her mind when she was told she'd never have children. I can imagine how Henry would have talked about children and about the new lives they'd create out of their love for one another and... Well, you know what Henry's like, Ness, when he's enthused about something. Brad said he hated himself for not knowing she couldn't have children. If he did know, he wouldn't have gone on about it, he would have just reassured her. She was so kind, Ness, like an angel."

Malissa paused. She was kneeling on the floor and looked up at Vanessa, her eyes moist. "I wonder if her kindness..." She was unable to finish the sentence and Vanessa sat down and held her as she burst into tears.

"Anyway," Malissa said when she'd recovered and they'd stood up, "whatever it is, whatever it was, it doesn't feel right to destroy her memory."

"And will you tell Henry you have them?"

"No. Not yet anyway. Henry still won't talk to me about her and I've learned not to press him. Brad said he's starting to make peace with himself though."

Malissa used to talk about Henry's struggle in harsh tones, but not these days.

"It's that quaint suburban upbringing of mine you always talk about," Malissa smiled. "Fantastic to live, but it does tend to make you believe everything in the world is rosy. Come on let's go. Told Lewis and Millie that Aunty Ness was buying them pizza tonight."

"You're allowing them pizza on a school night? God, you're getting soft Malissa."

# 62

# SEPTEMBER 2004, MAJORCA

## A BALLET IN PALMA

*S*ince Vanessa had taken over the dance school in Paris four years ago, the number of pupils had doubled. Mademoiselle Lauren retained a share of the business, which included the freehold of the building, but when she moved to the South of France confirmed to Vanessa that she had bequeathed her remaining interest in the enterprise to her in her will. She had no dependants.

Vanessa spent her time between Söller and Paris. Gabrielle was based at the Paris school but looked after the financial and administrative affairs of both establishments. Several of Vanessa's pupils had found placements with celebrated dance companies, and the youngsters in the Paris school were often called upon to take part in events staged at the city's theatres.

The Söller school had only a third of the number of pupils, but yesterday several of them had made their stage debut at the Auditorium de Palma de Mallorca, the island's second most important theatre. The ballet was to run for four days. Malissa had joined Vanessa for today's performance, and before catching the train back to Söller thought a celebratory drink was in order.

"We should have champagne, Ness. My treat," Malissa said as they walked through the door of the club she'd always been curious to visit and which was only 400 metres from the theatre.

"In here?" Vanessa was surprised at Malissa's choice of venue.

It was more of a night club and not the kind of establishment they'd usually choose to have a drink together. It was, however, early evening and it was only background music that greeted them as they entered. Malissa ordered champagne. "This is the bar Brad rescued Henry from in 1977. Just wanted a look."

They sat down. Only a dozen or so of the tables that arced their way around the dance floor were occupied. They wouldn't fill up for several hours yet.

"I wonder how much it's changed?" Malissa said. "Apparently Brad found him hunched over a table amongst the locals. He paid the bill, took Henry back to his hotel and then brought him home."

"Typical Brad." Vanessa smiled.

"Typical Henry?" Malissa questioned.

"Henry then? Who knows? He would have been a young man."

"Well, 25." Malissa confirmed.

They talked about the ballet they'd just watched their pupils perform in and drank their champagne. Malissa, who had long since been repaid the money she lent to the business, didn't take any money from the profits of the dance school, but was adamant she wouldn't sell her stake in it. "It's my connection to you. And to the theatre. When you're famous then I'll be famous too."

Vanessa smiled. Malissa spent half of her time at the villa these days. She kept in touch with the business she'd set up in Palma but had little to do with its day-to-day running. Fenner's had been sold some time ago, but Malissa still held a non-executive post which seemed to comprise her attending the odd board meeting and any corporate events. It was at one of these functions, last year, that Malissa met Robert, a member of the French civil service. "So, what do you think of Robert?" she asked.

Vanessa frowned. "Well, he's educated, presentable and French. And he travels a lot which I imagine suits you."

"He's asked me to go on holiday with him. To the Seychelles where he's hoping his next secondment will be."

"A tropical paradise. Are you going?"

"Of course. Why shouldn't I?"

"Just wondered?"

"Just wondered why I shouldn't spend two weeks in a tropical paradise?"

"Was just wondering Henry?"

Vanessa sensed that Malissa was trying to steer the subject towards her ex-husband.

Henry and Malissa had become great friends. They talked regularly and still spent holidays together with their children in Söller. They didn't sleep together, and the ghost of Emma still seemed to come between them, but Vanessa saw the look in their eyes when they were there.

"Henry and I are divorced but we're best friends."

"Hmm," said Vanessa, giving her friend one of those looks.

"You sound like Henry."

"Seriously, Malissa, I see the way you still look at each other. You sure there's no chance?"

"I love Henry, Ness. Always have, always will. I'll never love anyone how I loved him. Maybe he could never have loved anyone like he loved Emma. Anyway, he's never shown he's jealous of Robert."

"Would you want him to?"

Malissa ignored the question and ordered more olives.

"I've been thinking, Ness. Why don't we make a ballet using Emma's music?"

"Emma's?"

"Why not. Everyone I've shown it to says it's being wasted just lying about in the villa, hidden from the world. It'll make a great ballet. Maybe we could stage it at the Palma Theatre itself."

"Why would you do that? Apart from it making a great ballet, I mean."

Malissa popped an olive into her mouth. "I feel it would be a good thing to do."

Vanessa smiled at Malissa's almost nonchalant statement. "Well I guess it wouldn't be impossible. Using her music, I mean. Getting a place on the stage at the Palma Theatre might be another thing..."

"You could use your influence, get the big knobs in Paris to have a word. Even bring in some of those dancers. Or what's her name who went to Moscow?"

Malissa had changed over the years. She was more understanding and open to suggestions that would have never sat easily with her in the past, but Vanessa loved it when she reverted to the woman she first met; the woman who believed anything was possible if you put your mind to it. She continued to outline her ideas and by the time they got back home both were enthused by Malissa's unexpected idea.

In bed that night Vanessa contemplated the real reason Malissa thought it so important to breathe life into Emma's music. She also wondered how much of her own enthusiasm for the project was to honour her dead sister, and how much was to help fulfil a sense of purpose Malissa obviously held.

## NOVEMBER 2004, NEW YORK

### VANESSA AND HENRY

*H*enry spent every school holiday in Söller with Malissa and the children, sleeping in the spare room of the farmhouse. Brad would sometimes visit too, and when Vanessa was there the days they spent at the villa were not so far removed from those wonderful holidays they all enjoyed in the nineties.

Vanessa and Henry's relationship had developed too and they would, from time to time, talk by telephone updating one another on their respective life's in New York and Paris. Henry would sometimes subtly ask about Malissa but they never discussed Emma. Vanessa understood why Henry would allude to the special connection he thought they shared and whilst their relationship was completely convivial, it was perhaps necessarily guarded. "Like two people on the fringe who observe and wonder, but never judge" Henry had said.

Vanessa had never been to New York. Last year, Malissa had said she was most welcome to join them when she and the children visited Henry, but work commitments prevented her from doing so. Henry had often invited her too, and she was pleased she had finally managed to find a suitable window in her busy schedule to accept. Henry had arranged several outings for her over the last couple of days so she could appreciate the city, but suggested they meet tonight for dinner in the bar he owned in Maddison Avenue, where Lewis would be playing the piano as they ate.

Lewis often visited his father, loved the city and had been Vanessa's tour guide for the day. She was unable to make his eighteenth birthday party last month, so by way of a belated present they had taken lunch on one of the tourist boats that cruised the Hudson River.

Henry owned two bars in the city in partnership with a guy called Mike who he met four years ago. Both bars hosted various talent competitions at weekends, but during the week the main bar at this venue was closed and the furniture rearranged in a style more akin to an upmarket restaurant.

Henry had seen her as soon as she walked in, and after a drink at the bar, they sat down for dinner. Lewis was playing the piano and the music added to the intimate atmosphere of the restaurant.

"Have you met Anna?" Vanessa asked as they were looking through the menu.

"Anna?"

"Lewis's girlfriend."

"Ah, that Anna. Well, yes and no. She sings here, but Lewis has told me their relationship is merely one of two professional musicians. Not boyfriend girlfriend."

"He's growing up fast, Henry."

Henry looked over at the piano, pride in his son so clearly evident in his smile.

"He's a good lad," he said. "Now, how was your boat trip? I hope you didn't eat too much; I've told Maurice he needs to impress you." Maurice was the chef here.

Vanessa thought she may have eaten more at lunchtime than she intended. "So, the bars are a success I take it?"

"Well, it's a different type of business. You'd never make a million but both cover their costs. You'll like Mike. Perhaps if you've time tomorrow we'll pop downtown and see him."

"And the writing for the New York Times? You never told me you had a *weekly* column. I'm impressed."

Henry smiled. "Sometimes, Vanessa, we forget to count our blessings. I don't seem to be much use to the office out here these days, save the odd lunch or two, and the Times columns were a bit of a surprise. Wanted me to write about business, about the ethical approach. All the rage apparently, but to be honest I don't understand the big deal really."

Henry had always had a flare for business. It was difficult to say exactly what had motivated him, but it certainly wasn't money. He had offices here in New York, in Los Angeles, in London and Dubai and Vanessa didn't doubt there were others around the globe. Underpinning the success of his companies was the ethos that stemmed from the way he so naturally cared for people and their aspirations, and she doubted he knew just how much he was respected.

The waiter appeared. "Mr Ovmeister, it's good to see you again" he said.

Henry smiled. "And you, Carlos. This is Miss Cozzette. Not only one of the most beautiful women in this world who you cannot help but fall in love with, but the most talented of dancers too. And very particular about her food."

Carlos smiled and recommended one or two dishes.

"Henry, I do believe you enjoy embarrassing people," Vanessa said when Carlos had departed with their order.

"Miss Cozzette, I was purely stating the obvious. And the truth."

"But you have never seen me dance."

"Hmm. But I have information as to your ability from the most reliable of sources. And as for your beauty, well, that is surely not open to any kind of debate."

He would often unashamedly compliment her, and she had always thought it was her sexuality which allowed him to be so open. Perhaps that was the reason they had become such good friends? Malissa and Brad were great friends too. Maybe everybody should have a good friend of the opposite sex? Sometimes, however, she'd catch him look at her the way he did when they first met, and she wondered if he still saw Emma. "Henry, if only you were a woman," she smiled.

"But then, my beautiful friend... if I were, maybe I would become insanely jealous and possessive." He reached across the table and squeezed her hand. Polite applause broke out as Lewis finished his rendition of Für Elise and Henry looked at him and smiled.

Henry was a handsome man. He had told her of one or two relationships he'd had since the divorce but there was nothing serious as far as Vanessa could tell. If they talked about Malissa, moreover about Robert and Malissa, she sensed the pain in his eyes no matter how much he tried to disguise it, and it was at these times Vanessa really wished she could see into his heart.

"Did Malissa tell you my mother may have lived in a street not far from your dance school? "Henry asked.

"Rue de Valmy. Yes, she told me. Said you were trying to trace your father too."

"Her real name was Francesca De Hay."

"Do you have a racehorse named after her?"

Henry laughed. "She'll always be Delores to me."

"So, you must have known of her some time ago?"

"I knew her name. Well, her assumed name. I guess Malissa told you she was a bit of a war hero?"

Vanessa nodded.

"When Emma died, I collected all the letters Aunt Rose had left me, one or two of which told me about my mother. I did a bit of research then but... well, I abandoned it I guess. Probably shouldn't have done, I think it's been haunting me ever since. But, this time round, well after the fire and everything, it did seem important to try and find out some more. Lay ghosts to rest as it were."

"And now it's giving you comfort?"

"Yes. I should have faced the past a long time ago... I'm sure you know that."

Henry had learned over the years that it was safe to talk a little more openly to Malissa about his early life. Malissa said he still seemed to hold back when it came to Emma, but he talked enthusiastically about the discoveries he had made about his parents. "In a way," Malissa had said, "I think that when he opens up about his mother he's feeling his way towards talking about Emma more."

Henry talked to Vanessa more openly now too, but whenever Malissa or Henry talked about Emma she was aware they were talking about her sister. She had grown used to the secret she still harboured and on several occasions had tried to tell both of them who she was but the time never seemed quite right.

Much that Henry then told her about his parents, Vanessa had already heard from Malissa. His mother, the woman he knew as Delores Delahay, left France following the death of her parents at the outbreak of the war. She joined the French Resistance and lived undercover in Germany. She fell in love with a German officer and gave birth to Henry in March 1952. Henry was sent to England when he was six months old and later that year his mother and father were murdered in a revenge attack in Berlin.

He finished his account. Vanessa smiled but wished she could be so open about *her* mother; about *Emma's* mother. Surely she would be able to... one day.

"I've promised myself to visit there one day, the place my mother grew up," Henry said. "Perhaps you'll be my guide?"

"I'd love to be, Henry."

Lewis resumed playing and their starters arrived. Vanessa realised she had eaten too much earlier. Henry read her thoughts. He lowered his voice. "I haven't eaten since breakfast, I'm starving. Try some, and if it's okay, when Carlos isn't looking I'll steal some from your plate."

No wonder her sister had loved Henry. Who wouldn't?

## 64

JULY 2005, THE VILLA IN MAJORCA

MALISSA AND VANESSA

*V*anessa had spent the last month or so in Söller, covering for one of her staff who had suffered an injury. She'd been listening to the tapes of Emma's music and had taken the first tentative steps in choreographing a suitable ballet for her students. While she relished the challenge, the music reminded her of the secret she still kept from Malissa.

With her children away and Henry still in New York, Malissa had decided to come out to the villa a few weeks earlier than usual. Malissa had recently accepted Robert's proposal of marriage, and though no firm arrangements had been made in respect of a date her decision to marry again seemed to have given her much cause for deliberation. They were sitting at the patio table outside the villa, watching the sun go down and talking, and though Vanessa was trying to engage in the conversation the secret of Emma weighed very heavily on her.

"Have you told Henry yet?" Vanessa asked.

"Not yet but I think he'll understand."

"Would you want him too?"

Malissa frowned and changed the subject which was her usual response whenever she was compelled to consider her relationship with Henry and any notions of a possible reconciliation. "Do you think I should tell him about Emma's music?"

"I think sometimes, Malissa, you'd like to tell Henry many things. And then I ask myself why. I see the way you look at him and how he looks at you. Perhaps you are trying to tell him something else?"

Malissa smiled, got up and went into the kitchen. She returned with another bottle of wine, which she opened and poured before sitting back down. It had been a particularly hot day. It would be a warm evening. She lit the lantern on the table and brought the subject back to Emma's music and the choreography Vanessa had recently been working on.

"So, how's it going?" she asked.

"I think it has every possibility of working. We'd use the three individual pieces we discussed and use the one she called 'The Butterfly and the Sage' as the main theme for the story. I spoke to Alejandro, you know, Alejandro Sanchez at the theatre in Palma? – and he seems very open to the idea. Just need to get a suitable story."

Malissa smiled. "Jenny, she's the children's writer I told you about, has this idea about a forest where the happy butterflies meet the sad and lonely bear and help him find the family he lost after some catastrophic event. She's going to email it over."

"A bear, that's interesting. And butterflies. Yeah, I think that would work."

"You okay, Ness?"

"Yes fine, just a bit... no, I'm fine." It was the second time Malissa had asked her if she was okay.

Maybe it was because they had talked so much about her since working on the ballet, but Vanessa couldn't stop thinking about Emma. Malissa talked about her in glowing terms, she even talked affectionately about the love Henry and Emma shared and Vanessa's compulsion to tell Malissa the truth was beginning to overwhelm her.

"Maybe I should tell him," said Malissa thoughtfully. "About the music I mean. He must think it's been destroyed. I never would have imagined he could have let it go so easy."

Vanessa desperately wanted to say, "*Maybe I should tell you Emma was my sister.*" Instead she said she doubted it was easy for Henry to let go of Emma's memory.

"So, I shouldn't tell him?"

"Well, if we used the music and staged a ballet for everyone to see, I guess you'd have to."

"Quite. And then there's the question of who actually owns the music."

"Malissa..." Vanessa said deliberately.

Malissa looked at her and raised her eyebrows as if expecting Vanessa to say something serious.

"Malissa. We all have secrets. Sometimes we keep secrets because we believe it is for the best."

Malissa looked at her for a couple of seconds, a question in her eyes perhaps. She poured more wine and Vanessa wondered what she was thinking.

"Henry has really tried to put the memory of Emma aside," Malissa said deliberately. "He's talked about his past with me, about his mother and about his father, and whilst I can't say he can talk so openly about Emma, I think I can understand why. Sometimes, like you say, we believe we keep secrets for the overall good."

Vanessa felt a welling inside; a build up of emotion that threatened to erupt at any minute. This woman opposite, her best friend, a person who had shown her nothing but love deserved to know the truth. What did she mean 'secrets'? Emma's music? Henry's secret? Or something else. Vanessa had to tell her.

"Let's have a smoke," Malissa said suddenly.

Malissa always had a packet of Vogue Menthols in the drawer. When she returned, they lit up and Malissa switched the subject back to Robert and where they could live once they were married. Not many options seemed to appeal to Malissa. Before she agreed to marry Robert, she had embraced the idea of living in the villa on a more permanent basis.

" I love this place so much, Ness, I'd hate to give it up. But it wouldn't be right for us to live here."

"Because of Henry?"

"Yes, because of Henry. It is our place. And yours of course, but not just because of that."

"Perhaps you think giving up the villa would be like giving up Henry?"

"It would be giving up so many things. No. Robert's idea is we live in France. Closer to you, of course, when you're there so that's not so bad."

"About 250 miles."

"You know what I mean. Anyway, we could meet up here every

month. Robert's bound to be travelling and the Söller school needs much more attention than the Paris one."

"Are you thinking about selling your shareholding to me?" Vanessa joked.

"I'm thinking about what a wonderful friend you are."

That last comment refocused Vanessa's thoughts to the guilt she held. She could feel her heart quicken. Her body was telling her now was the time. But how? How could she relieve herself of the secret she held without shattering the most wonderful friendship she had ever known? Malissa's kind and pretty face glowed in the light of the lantern. Her eyes looked at her. She wondered what they saw. Vanessa brought the subject back to secrets.

"Sometimes we keep things to ourselves and have to live with them," she said.

"Like Emma's music?"

"Yes like that... Or Brad."

"Vanessa that was so wrong. Me and Brad both know that and it's in the past. End of. That's a secret that could do nothing but harm innocent people. It was a mistake and something both Brad and I will have to live with."

"But you told me."

"Because we're friends, Ness. God, I had to tell someone."

Earlier that year, Malissa and Brad had sex. It wasn't planned and was over in a matter of minutes. Both said it should never have happened.

Vanessa smiled at her protestations, but hoped the mention of Brad and that secret, might help steer the conversation back to her own.

"You're friends with Henry," Malissa was continuing her protest, "and I don't doubt you love him, Ness. Maybe like I love Brad. Maybe me and Brad was inevitable, like getting something out of the way. I don't know. And I doubt he knows either. Why it happened I mean. I just thank God we both know it will never happen again."

Malissa folded her arms and sat back in the chair as if emphasising her point. They looked at one another for a moment before Malissa sighed lent forward and took a sip of her wine. It was a beautiful serene evening.

"And I have secrets too," Vanessa said seriously. "Something I've been wanting to share for a long time," She reached across the table taking hold of Malissa's hand.

"Ness," Malissa interrupted, almost whining, "as much as I love you, and believe me I do, I don't think I could show you love in that way. You are beautiful and..."

Vanessa laughed out loud. "Sweet, lovely Malissa. I love you dearly too, but no, Malissa, a desire to sleep with you is not the secret I'm referring to."

Malissa smiled and squeezed her hand. "Well, it nearly happened once."

Vanessa smiled back and gently drew away her hand. She drank her wine and looked into Malissa's eyes. "You are a very special woman, Malissa. You have shown me nothing but kindness. You are the best friend a woman could ever had."

She reached for Malissa's hand again and squeezed tightly before letting go. She felt the beat of her heart and the pressure of tears behind her eyes. She knew she was going to tell her. "I have something to tell you that you will find difficult to understand. I have tried so many times to tell you but could never find the right moment, and on balance always believed keeping it secret was the best thing."

"You've slept with Henry?"

"No, Malissa, I have not slept with Henry. Wrong gender, remember?"

"Funny, Ness. If you said you had it would have made me feel better about Brad. And in a funny way I wouldn't have regarded that as deceit. How strange is that? I don't think I'd have been jealous either; that may be the wrong word. Maybe I was jealous of Emma once, of Emma and Henry, but really, I was in awe of them. I could never replace or compete with that love and I think now I see it for the wonderful story it was. I used to believe I was used, but not once did I ever *feel* used, and if I helped repair Henry's heart and brought some happiness back then that's something I'm very proud of. That's love."

Malissa had distracted her but somehow her interruption seemed fitting. "And very profound," Vanessa said softly.

Vanessa took a deep breath and refocused her attention. Malissa sat up straighter in her chair – perhaps she saw the seriousness in Vanessa's eyes.

"I have had relationships with men." Vanessa said. "I was raped when I was 14, two men, boys really. In order to get by, even look after my father ..." She paused. She saw the concern in Malissa's eyes.

Malissa reached over again and took her hand. "I'm sorry, Ness. I didn't know. I think I know so little about your past sometimes but I know it wasn't easy."

Vanessa smiled softly but continued. "When something like that happens, you lose your sense of self-worth. You certainly lose your childhood, your innocence. I had no mother, not really, and as much as I wanted to believe my father loved me, there were times I thought I was simply just his best asset... Those men thought they could use me. They did use me, but I used them too. I could steal money when they slept or threaten to tell their wives..."

"I'm so sorry Ness."

"Mademoiselle Lauren wasn't much better than those bastards, but at least she was gentle and things didn't turn out too badly. And she taught me to dance. I hit the jackpot with Etienne, the son of a man who wanted to be President. The money I got from his father meant I could choose who I slept with. Fuck me, it even gave me the money to get to England and without that..."

Vanessa paused and swallowed to dispel the lump in her throat. She tried to fight the tears that were stinging her eyes. "Without that, without that pay off I would never have met you, never have had the wonderful friend I have, never have had the dance schools and never have had the chance to be sitting here."

Vanessa drew away her hand and poured more wine. She could feel herself shaking, felt cold despite the heat of the night, but tried to maintain some sort of composure as the tears began to roll down her cheeks.

"Just before my father died, I came to England. I was searching for someone; someone my mother had told me about..."

Her voice was cracking now, the words she wanted to say seemed to choke her. "I didn't know what I would find, but the person I sought was no longer there."

She drank her wine, desperate for the liquid to undo the tangle she felt in her throat so that her words could find formation. "What I did discover led me inevitably to you. To us and to the friendship I have always cherished so deeply. When you took me in, you showed me love, love I had never known. It was the first time I thought somebody cared, really cared. I felt love. It led me to you." She paused and, through watery eyes, saw Malissa's concern in the flickering light of the lantern. "It led me to you, Malissa..."

"I love you, Ness, and whatever it is I will understand."

"It led me to you because I was looking for Henry." Vanessa was sobbing now. "I had found what I was looking for and I realised it was gone, it wasn't there, and I wanted to go back. Sharing my discovery couldn't change things, not for the good. Telling anyone why I came to England wouldn't have made it better. But I didn't go back to France and we became friends. And then you asked me to come out here with you and I felt comfort and love, and that I belonged, and everything else just seemed irrelevant. I wanted to forget and so thought my secret was best to remain that, a secret, and I'm so, so sorry if I got it wrong, so sorry I couldn't tell you before. I am so sorry, Malissa."

Tears streamed down her face but she made no attempt to wipe them away. She could hear herself sobbing, tasted the saltiness of her tears and felt the ache in the back of her throat as it tried to hold on to those last words that once out, would have so much impact. She found Malissa's hand and held it tightly, fearing Malissa would pull it away. "No, Malissa, I have never slept with Henry." She took a deep breath. "But my sister has."

"Gabrielle?" Malissa whispered.

"No, Malissa, not Gabrielle. I never met the sister who slept with Henry. She was blind, Malissa, blind... and she died so very, very young."

Vanessa was terrified of the impact her revelation may have had, but Malissa stood up, rounded the table and cradled Vanessa in her arms as both of them cried for many minutes. Through her sobbing, Vanessa was aware of the gentleness of Malissa's embrace and her reassuring, soft whispers of, "It's okay, Ness, shhh. It's okay."

Malissa's reaction to her revelation was not one Vanessa was expecting. In truth, she hadn't known what to expect. Vanessa sat there crying, apologising profusely, overwhelmed by the release of a burden that had weighed so heavily on her and for so long

When Vanessa eventually stopped crying, she felt like a child. Like a child who had been consoled by a loving mother. For the first time in her life she had experienced the flood of empathy and love that can only be provided by someone who genuinely cares. Sometime past before they felt able to speak. Malissa did first.

"You know, Ness, now you've told me... it's all falling into place. I can't believe I didn't see it sooner."

Vanessa could not let go of her hand.

"Maybe I didn't want to see," Malissa continued. "Maybe it's always been some deep connection we've always shared."

It was nearly midnight. The crickets were chirping, and the air was still and warm, comforting. Bright stars studded a deep blue sky and beyond the orange groves the waves broke gently on the beach. It was as though their thoughts and feelings were circling gently around them, cushioned by the gentleness of the night and falling onto them softly like a blanket of love and understanding.

When Vanessa stopped crying, she felt exposed and vulnerable, but so safe as long as Malissa was there. When she spoke, the words came from her heart. Vanessa was, for the first time, sharing feelings she thought she could never share, and the gentleness of her story barely disturbed the serenity of the evening. "My grandmother's name was Edith Broudier," she whispered. "She married in France and gave birth to a daughter. Edith's husband was killed at the outset of the war, and during the liberation of Paris Edith met an English soldier and they planned to marry. When Edith moved to London to meet up with him, he wasn't there, and Edith and her nine-year-old daughter - Anna - my mother, had to fend for themselves..."

They didn't go to bed that night. Vanessa's fears that her revelation would shatter their wonderful friendship were totally unfounded. They cuddled up on one of the bed chairs by the pool and talked. It was as though they had found the missing pieces of some bizarre puzzle and were gradually putting them together.

Vanessa told Malissa about her life, about her mother and father, about Mademoiselle Lauren and Monique. About the clubs she had to dance in in order to survive and how she had extorted money from men. She told her the sad story of Katriane, and whenever Malissa sought clarification Vanessa was happy to tell her the truth.

It was the first time Vanessa had ever opened her heart to anybody, and she was surprised when she talked about Emma how she herself found her own closure regarding her death; Emma, a woman who had impacted so much upon their lives and had brought them together.

She told Malissa how meeting her had changed her life, and throughout their conversations Malissa had to reassure her she needn't feel the guilt that had enveloped her for so many years.

They talked about Henry and the new and wonderful relationship that continued to develop between him and Malissa. They talked about Lewis and Millie and family, and the children Emma could never have. Lewis and Millie. Malissa and Henry's children. "Children," Malissa said, "who would never have been born had Emma not died."

And they talked about Emma, and Malissa told her how she had come to love Emma's memory, how she had discovered the depth of the love Emma and Henry must have shared, and how she could never have competed with that. And Malissa talked about her love for Henry and how it would never die, and as the sun rose bringing another new day, Malissa said "...it lit up the ocean like embracing everything good can light up your understanding of love."

They spent the next three days at the villa. They slept together at night, comforted by a love only they understood. By the time Millie arrived they were even closer, friends who shared something deeper than either of them could ever have imagined.

Henry should, of course, know the truth about Vanessa, but how to tell him, neither were entirely sure. He would be arriving with Lewis in a week or so for their summer holiday, but maybe there'd be a better time to tell him, and maybe it would be better to hear the story from Vanessa herself.

On the flight back to Paris, Vanessa had a peace in her heart she had never known. Tomorrow she'd be going to Gabrielle's to celebrate hers and Pascal's third wedding anniversary, and at the weekend she'd call on her old friend Bernard at the Moulin Rouge to arrange the night out she had always promised to the greatest friend a woman could ever have.

# PART VIII

*Fifi*

*Is love measured by love's perception*
*Perceived and so bound by its rules*
*Or is it love without preconception*
*That's love which is immeasurable?*

# 65

## EARLY DECEMBER 2005

## VANESSA'S APARTMENT PARIS

"*H*e's here," said Malissa, peeping out of the window. "Or should I say *mon futur mari est arrive?*"

Vanessa smiled. "Your French is fine."

"Well, it's about time I understood what all those influential friends of his are saying. And those women, I wonder what they say sometimes too. I'll miss you, Ness."

Vanessa hugged her until the doorbell rang. When they broke their embrace the two women looked at one another for a moment.

"Remember, you'll make a wonderful mother," Malissa said softly as she turned to answer the door.

She let Robert in. He greeted them and, picking up Malissa's suitcases to put in the car, confirmed that their flight was on schedule.

"And I'll miss you too," Vanessa said, taking Malissa's hand. "Now, go. You'll have a wonderful time."

They kissed and Malissa headed out of the door. "Oh, by the way," she said. "I've left you a present. It's in your bedroom. Take care," and she was gone.

Vanessa watched them drive away. As she did, she was aware of the smile on her face. Malissa was spending the next three weeks in the Seychelles with Robert, but for the last six days she and Malissa had enjoyed each other's company in Paris, culminating last night with a visit to the Moulin Rouge.

During the last few months, they had grown even closer and discussed so much; discussed feelings and thoughts that seemed so tangible and so right when they were together, but bordered on the ridiculous when Vanessa was alone with them.

Henry was coming to Paris next week. Vanessa had promised to show him the neighbourhood in which his mother was born and Malissa had agreed with her that it could be the right time to tell him the truth.

Vanessa didn't doubt Malissa still loved Henry. She didn't doubt that he loved her, and she struggled to understand exactly why neither of them would yield to their true feelings. What was the obstacle that still stood between them?

She found it almost impossible to believe that Malissa's love for Henry was so profound, so utterly selfless that she believed the greatest gift he could receive was a child of the same bloodline as Emma; the child Emma could never have. When Malissa first mentioned it, Vanessa had laughed – was her friend really saying that *she* should have a baby with her ex-husband? But as they talked, and as Malissa became more and more philosophical, Vanessa saw something in her eyes that drew her in, making her also believe it was simply the most natural and wonderful attestation of a love so few people would ever understand.

She smiled recalling the wonderful week they had just had together. The next time she'd see Malissa would be Christmas and she wondered what they might be discussing then. Vanessa went into the bedroom. On the bed was a parcel, addressed simply 'For Ness x'.

She opened it. There was an envelope addressed to Henry and a framed photograph. Taken on the beach at the villa it was the photograph she had always loved; Malissa and her laughing with their arms around each other. It was taken the day they first introduced Henry and Brad to the Blackpool-Brighton Challenge more than 15 years ago.

On the reverse and in French, the words Vanessa had said to her that night four months ago when Malissa asked why she never told her about Emma. *"Because I know what it's like to be hurt and I could never knowingly do or say something that could ever hurt someone I love."*

And below that, in English

*Thank you for never having hurt me.*

Clipped to the envelope for Henry was a note. *Give this to Henry when you tell him.x*

She studied it, contemplating its contents but knew she wouldn't open it. Butterflies suddenly fluttered through her and she had to shake them off. She looked at the photo again and smiled, then wandered back into the kitchen wondering just what would represent the greatest gift she could give to Malissa at Christmas.

# 66

# DECEMBER 2005, PARIS

## VANESSA AND HENRY

*A*lthough Gabrielle had been to Majorca several times and met Malissa on many occasions, she had never met Henry. When they did meet, this afternoon at the dance school, Vanessa saw that flash of a question in Henry's eyes when he said 'hello'; that momentary look, the same one she herself had received when they first met when Vanessa was even younger than her sister. Did Gabrielle stir a distant memory of Emma too?

Earlier, Vanessa had shown Henry the neighbourhood where his mother was raised. Discovering the fate of his mother had obviously been important to him and he enthused about her on several occasions, relaying many tales of her heroism he had learned from his research. Vanessa was not an orphan but her own upbringing, where her mother was so often absent, seemed to encourage Henry to confide in her. She'd always suspected he thought they had that in common.

Of course, what they did have in common was a connection to Emma, and while Henry had yet to be told that Emma was her half-sister, Vanessa had always felt that somewhere deep in his soul, somewhere irretrievable, he may already have considered it. A feeling that now slept peacefully perhaps. A dormant memory, unsure whether it needed to be disturbed.

Henry had gone back to his hotel and, after Vanessa finished at the dance school, she went back home to change. She had arranged for them to meet for dinner in a little restaurant by the Palais Garnier, in an avenue she knew would be bejewelled with festive fairy lights. As she expected, Henry loved the venue and he wasn't surprised she and Malissa regarded it as their favourite.

Since they'd arrived at the restaurant, they'd talked much about the dance school here and the success Vanessa had made of it. They talked about the Söller dance school too, and the achievements of some of the pupils. Henry had asked about any plans she had afoot, but she didn't tell him about the ballet using Emma's music she and Malissa had been devising.

Vanessa wanted to tell Henry that she was Emma's sister. Unlike her feeling towards Malissa, Vanessa had never considered she had deceived Henry. She always remembered a conversation in the early days at Söller; the day he first saw the old schoolhouse, when Vanessa felt he had deliberately steered the subject away from the revelation of their respective secrets. She had agonised about how to tell Malissa, terrified of the impact it would have on her and their relationship, but with Henry she was only concerned for the effect it may have on him.

Perhaps she could have told him this morning when they toured the streets in which his mother was born. In hindsight it may have been an appropriate time.

It was strange, but Vanessa somehow felt Henry would be more shocked by the fact she had chosen to tell him than by the revelation itself. She even believed telling him would give him comfort, provide an opportunity for him to say to her so much he may have wanted to say to her sister, and even help bring an end to the anguish and confusion she instinctively knew he still held in his heart. Choosing the right time to tell him was her dilemma.

Their coffees were on the table when Vanessa returned from the bathroom. She sat down.

"Malissa tells me you and Gabrielle are coming for Christmas," he said.

"Yes, and her husband. They're looking forward to it. Pascal's never been to England before."

"Yeah, Majorca would be warmer. Bit of a shock to her system when she gets back. Malissa I mean."

Malissa was away with Robert, and although Henry appeared casual about it Vanessa knew it did pull on his heart strings.

"Strange that she always chooses to spend Christmas with you, Henry."

"I think, Vanessa, you'll find she regards Christmas as family time. I am, after all, the father of her children, there by default maybe."

Apart from the year of the fire, Malissa and Henry had spent every Christmas as a family.

Vanessa smiled, thinking how she could switch the subject to Emma. "So, that's the end of your search?"

"I think so," replied Henry. "It was good to see that she led at least some of her life in a kinder environment."

"I imagine she was a wonderful woman."

"I think she was. My father didn't turn out too bad either."

"And I know you are a good man, Henry."

Henry raised an eyebrow. She rarely put 'good' and 'man' together in the same sentence.

"And Emma?" she ventured

"Emma?"

"You must have thought about tracing her parents."

"I've thought about that many times over the years. Did you know *her* mother was French too? Or so I believe. I found that out after she died. That's probably why you used to remind me of her, the French connection I mean. I loved it when Emma spoke French. She had learned several languages actually, and I didn't always understand what she said, but maybe French was in her genes. Who knows? And of course, *my* mother was French. And the hair, when you wore it shorter, sort of reminded me."

It was the first time in all the years she had known him that Henry had alluded so directly to the resemblance.

"That's interesting," she said, smiling and lifting her hair above her shoulders.

Henry smiled. "But other than that, I never dug further, though a couple of years ago I thought about using the same people who tracked down my mother to look into it. But, Vanessa, some things are perhaps best left alone. Emma was Emma and that's it I guess."

"So, she was born in France?"

"Emma? No, I'm sure she was born in London. Well, I assume she was. I imagine it's a strange story and maybe a sad one. I don't know. Who knows - one day, perhaps?"

"Rescued from St Mary's?"

She could see him searching his mind. Malissa must have told her the name of the orphanage.

He smiled. "My aunt often told me about the time she first saw us in a cot together. Cuddling under a blanket, two peas in a pod she said."

Vanessa was touched by the vision of the two babies lying side by side. She remembered reading one of Henry's poems when he referred to them as twin souls. Vanessa saw she had evoked memories, but they seemed to be fond ones and that he was okay to continue talking.

"What happened to her mother? Is she still alive?"

"I doubt it. I don't know exactly why I say that, but something tells me not. The orphanage wouldn't disclose any details. Once, not long after Emma died, I burst in there. It had already closed but was still some kind of refuge and I thought they'd be someone there who could tell me something. I was drunk and demanded to know about Emma. They called the police and I ended up in a cell overnight. But I did meet someone who knew someone who had worked there and had apparently met her mother. Said she was very young. Anyway, it seemed she just disappeared. Maybe I could have asked him more, but back then I wasn't really in a fit state to do anything. I was just... I was just angry, heartbroken, I guess. No, one day I might try and find out more but to tell the truth, I'd be pretty scared."

"And your Aunt. Did she ever say anything else?"

"Aunt Rose? No, she didn't. And maybe I regret not asking her more. She left quite a lot of letters for me after she died, remember the ones I showed you in New York...?"

Vanessa nodded.

"But none for Emma," he concluded.

Henry paused and finished his coffee. "I was surprised none made a mention of her. Sometimes I worry she felt she never existed. And sometimes I think I didn't help that by forbidding people talking about her after she died."

Vanessa reached across the table and took his hand. "She existed, Henry. She had love."

Henry smiled but his eyes displayed a moment of sadness. He shook it off and ordered another coffee.

"Tell me about her," Vanessa said softly. "About you and her. I don't mean to pry but it does sound like a fairytale."

"No, it's fine. I should have talked about her long before now. To Malissa, to other people. She should never have been a secret."

She squeezed his hand and gently let go.

He continued; his mood suddenly lighter. "We were young. They say love is for the young and if that's the case I had love in spades. She was the most wonderful human being I had ever known, and pretty. God she was beautiful. And clever, and you should have heard her play the violin. Or the piano, or any other instrument for that matter."

Vanessa was always aware that Henry could feel he was being too effusive when he talked about Emma in this way; that what he was saying might make its way back to Malissa, but she reassured him. "Malissa knows you adored her."

"I loved Malissa too. I still love Malissa. I always will. They are not that dissimilar, both sort of... innocent, believers in love. Or something like that."

"I think Emma believed she was truly loved."

"Yes, I loved her. We were happy. If I had died with her, I could easily have said I had as much happiness as a man could ever expect." His coffee arrived. He thanked the waitress and then looked at Vanessa his face momentarily more reflective. "And I'm sure she was happy too." It was almost a question.

Through his eyes she saw the goodness in his heart, saw his love, saw why Malissa and Emma would have loved him. She thought about Malissa's absurd suggestion that she should have his child, the child Emma could never have had, and in that moment Malissa's suggestion suddenly seemed so right. Her heart skipped a beat.

"But you didn't die with her. You found happiness again with Malissa."

"Yes, I did."

"Malissa is a wonderful woman, Henry."

He smiled broadly.

"I've talked to her so much these last couple of years," Vanessa continued, "and shared so many...." She paused. "So many wonderful moments."

Henry raised his eyebrows and smiled. She wondered what he was thinking. Remembering her sexuality, she laughed in case his thoughts were heading that way. "I'm talking about talking to her Henry, exchanging feelings and stories of our past lives. About secrets." She smiled and leant forward. "And I don't just mean about Brad."

Henry looked surprised, but surely he knew Malissa wouldn't have been able to keep the secret of Brad from her. Vanessa knew Brad would have also confessed to Henry. Before he could reply, she decided it was time to change the subject. She didn't feel it right to tell him about Emma just yet and they'd surely discuss the Brad episode later. "By the way. I'm taking you to the ballet tonight," she added.

"Ballet?"

"Henry, I will show you a ballet that I'm sure you will appreciate. We've half an hour until its starts. And tomorrow I will show you *my* Paris."

Henry planned to be in Paris for three days, but with his children away there was no reason his journey to London couldn't be delayed. She would have plenty of time to tell him.

It was gone midnight by the time they arrived at the bar at Henry's hotel. Both were feeling the effects of a long day and several bottles of wine. Vanessa suggested maybe it was time to go home. She lived on the other side of the city and while she was sure she could easily summon a taxi she sensed that Henry, like her, did not want the evening to end.

"Well, I've a rather palatial couch in my room, Miss Cozzette, so you are most welcome to my bed."

"I'm surprised Henry, considering your remarks earlier, that you are not suggesting I share *your* bed. Or your rather palatial couch," Vanessa replied.

The ballet they saw had featured several scantily-clad dancers. Henry had asked if she had chosen that particular show for his benefit or hers, after which he apologised, defending himself by reminding her she was an extremely attractive woman and he a red-blooded male.

"Hmm. My remarks were totally unforgiveable, out of order, and I apologise."

She took his hand. "Henry, if only you were a woman."

The barman who was within earshot raised an eyebrow which sent her and Henry into a fit of giggles. The mood between them was light, the more serious discussions they had held over dinner seemingly discarded, but Vanessa remained determined to tell him about Emma.

Henry's phone ring. He apologised and answered. It was Lewis.

Vanessa watched as Henry, sharing in the excitement that was being relayed to him, talked so lovingly to his son. Vanessa half guessed the news Lewis was telling him, but when he hung up Henry confirmed that Lewis's girlfriend had been offered a recording contract - singing Lewis's songs.

"He has a gift, Henry," she said.

Henry smiled and asked the barman to top up their glasses.

"Children are wonderful," she continued. "You must be very proud. It seems music is in his heart, part of his soul. A gift from heaven perhaps."

His brow furrowed slightly. In his eyes that question, that tinge of sadness she had seen so many times but shouldn't be there. What did his eyes see in hers?

"Yes, they are," he said slowly. "And with Lewis I've no idea where that talent comes from. It certainly wasn't me."

Vanessa smiled. "But you play the piano well."

"Not as well as some."

"Like those who play at the Albert Hall."

She didn't phrase it as a question. His eyes studied her intently and she was hoping he saw Emma.

"Royal," he whispered after a moment.

Vanessa raised her eyebrows.

"Royal Albert Hall, Vanessa. She'd always remind me of its proper status."

He had picked on the connection to Emma. "Yes, I can imagine she would have."

She let her comment hang and focused on his eyes. He looked briefly away, then back. She could see him struggling to decide whether to follow where she was trying to lead him or keep the subject light.

"We have discussed it. Malissa and I," she said after several seconds.

"My ability to play the piano?"

She laughed. "We have discussed that Henry, but more so, we've talked about mysterious forces, about how something of Emma lives on through you, in Lewis."

She half expected a 'hmm' and then a remark designed to change the subject, but no; he took a sip of brandy. "Emma couldn't have children," he said gently.

"I know, Henry. Me and Malissa have talked about that too. And how wonderful it would be if something of Emma lived in another human being."

"Malissa talks about Emma like that?"

"You'd be surprised."

Henry's mouth opened, seemingly trying to form the next question, but the moment was broken when a party of residents came noisily into the room and approached the bar.

She took his hand and smiled. "Tomorrow, Henry, I shall show you where I lived. I shall tell you all about my mother and my upbringing and why I came to England. But it's been a long day and if you're serious about that bed I think it's time we slept."

"Well, Miss Cozzette," he said, returning to the Henry he most liked to display as he placed his empty glass on the bar, "it's been quite a day."

In the lift they said little. She had no doubt Henry was mulling over the conversations they'd just had. She detected he wanted to ask more but seemed so unsure whether to do so.

They entered his room. He tried to make light conversation as he poured himself a drink and retrieved a blanket and a pillow from the wardrobe. Vanessa grabbed one of the dressing gowns and went into the bathroom.

She undressed and slipped into the gown and studied herself in the mirror, trying to see the sister she had never known. She thought about Malissa, and she thought about Henry. She had never contemplated having sex with either of them, yet with both she felt she understood the meaning of love.

She felt her heart pounding as she slipped the envelope Malissa had given her into the pocket of her dressing gown. She was going to tell Henry the truth. She had little idea of the consequences, but she was sure he was ready; sure that deep down he already knew. She just had to wake up that memory.

Henry was lying on the couch when Vanessa emerged from the bathroom. The room was dimly lit, and they looked at one another for several seconds. She smiled, walked over and sat down beside him.

"Malissa is a very special woman, Henry," she said, and handed him the envelope.

He looked at it. And then at her. "From Malissa?"

He would have recognised the handwriting.

She touched his arm and looked into his eyes. "She wrote it shortly after I told her about my sister. The orphaned sister I never knew. Malissa said I should give it to you when I thought the time was right to tell you."

It was as though she had handed him a key. A key to unlock a door he had been too afraid to open. He looked into her eyes, into her heart, gradually opening that door and letting in the light. His moist eyes furrowed as the realisation set in.

"Your..." He paused and swallowed, desperate to form his words. "Your..." He clasped her hand. "Your older sister."

It wasn't a question.

"Yes," she whispered, and as the tears began to seep from his eyes, she cradled his head to her chest.

## 67

## SEPTEMBER 2006, VANESSA'S APARTMENT PARIS

### FIFI

*V*anessa giggled to herself as she listened to Malissa who, in a combination of English and 'Malissa French', a language only Vanessa understood, chatted in the hallway explaining the situation to the midwife. "No, Emma was Vanessa's *sister,* but she *couldn't* have a baby." And, "Yes, Henry - *Fifi's father,* is my husband who I told you about." And then, "No, because Vanessa *doesn't* like men."

Then she heard Malissa thanking the midwife for stopping by, the front door close and a few seconds later an exasperated Malissa appeared at the bedroom door. "You know, Ness, for all the faults with our health service, I do believe our midwives at home are a little more 'with it' than yours."

Vanessa laughed.

"I explained," Malissa continued, "that I was not your same-sex partner. That I am marrying *les tres important* secrétaire des affaires étrangères next year, and it is the equally *très* important Monsieur Ovmeister who is Fifi's father. I think next time she comes, Ness, you should take time to explain the situation, so she understands."

"Perhaps her knowledge of the French governmental system isn't as it should be," Vanessa laughed, "but as for explaining, I'm not sure whether I could get her to understand that either." She checked on her tiny baby daughter who was still sleeping in the cot beside the bed.

"Hmm, maybe you're right. Anyway, I was thinking, Ness. By the time we get this ballet to the theatre Fifi will be old enough to be a butterfly. You want tea?"

"I'd prefer a glass of wine."

"Herbal tea," Malissa said firmly and headed back out to the kitchen.

Vanessa smiled to herself. Poor midwife. She didn't doubt the conversation she'd been having with Malissa was a little different to those she'd usually have with a friend who had assigned herself to look after a new mother and her baby.

Was it strange Henry wasn't here? Was it stranger that Vanessa didn't think so? What exactly would Malissa or Vanessa consider strange after the journey they'd been on?

For the past few years Vanessa had yearned to be a mother. But she was single, approaching 40 and preferred to sleep with women; hardly ideal foundations from which to launch such a campaign. A year ago, Malissa suggested she have Henry's child. As ridiculous as the suggestion was, it happened, and it happened because of love; a love so few people would easily understand.

Vanessa knew Malissa still loved Henry, and knew Henry still loved Malissa. Maybe the arrival of Fifi would somehow help to unravel the knots on the ropes that kept them that little distance apart. Robert had asked Vanessa earlier this year whether she thought Malissa still loved Henry. She would certainly be more truthful with him next time they met.

Vanessa had discovered love; love she once thought could never exist and a love in which she would shroud her daughter. Love from two people who had impacted so positively on her life. Two people who loved so naturally that it was only right that they be together; and surely she could help them realise that.

In the kitchen, Malissa was on the phone to Henry. He'd just landed at the airport. She came back into the bedroom with two glasses and a bottle of wine.

"Well, the odd one during recovery won't do any harm," she said, her face as alive and as beautiful as the day Vanessa walked into her office seeking Emma, the sister she had never known.


THE END

Join my mailing list to receive a free book of poems, written by Henry Ovmeister himself.

You'll also get the chance to be part of my Advanced Reader Team and receive freebies, exclusives, and lots more.

**www.littlebearpublications.co.uk**

**To the outside world, their romance belonged in a fairy tale.**

Beautiful people living a wonderful life. A life he thought he'd never find.

Henry Ovmeister came to terms with his past a long time ago. He buried it deep in his soul – a place where it needn't be disturbed – and moved on.

When Henry meets Malissa, he builds a whole new life. He never tells her about his former life, and he never needs to. They are the perfect match. They are happy.

But when a place sacred to Henry catches fire, everything goes up in flames. Secrets are revealed. Memories tumble out. And Henry must confront the ghosts that have haunted him.

Will Henry and Malissa find their happy ending? Or will Henry's complex family history tear them apart?

∿

Discover the story behind Henry and Malissa's fairy-tale romance in *Vanessa*'s breath taking companion novel *The Butterfly and the Bear*.
### Now available on Amazon.

# ACKNOWLEDGMENTS

I'd like to thank Cara Thurlbourn for her ideas about book covers and assistance in the promotion of this novel. I am also indebted to those who read *The Butterfly And The Bear* for their kind words and encouragement to write this sequel.

Printed in Great Britain
by Amazon